LOUELLA BRYANT

SHELTERING ANGEL
OF BELLEAU WOOD

A NOVEL OF ONE WOMAN'S LIFE AFTER TITANIC

Black Rose Writing | Texas

ISBN: 978-1-68513-706-9
LIBRARY OF CONGRESS CONTROL NUMBER: 2025944915
PUBLISHED BY BLACK ROSE WRITING
www.blackrosewriting.com

Printed in the United States of America
Suggested Retail Price (SRP) $21.95

Sheltering Angel of Belleau Wood is printed in Book Antiqua

Dedicated to the memory of Florence Thayer Cumings Swain
1876-1949

Praise for
Sheltering Angel of Belleau Wood

"In this meticulously researched WWII novel, an aging woman vividly relives the major events of the Twentieth Century from the sinking of the Titanic (which she survived) to the Great War (which took her son) by sharing a fragile and treasured box of letters with her granddaughter. *Sheltering Angel of Belleau Wood* is as quiet as a funeral, as thunderous as a battlefield."
–Jim DeFilippi author of *Duck Alley* and *The Mules of Monte Cassino*

"*In Sheltering Angel of Belleau Wood,* Louella Bryant shows how Florence Cumings Swain's emotional memories of surviving the sinking of the Titanic influenced the rest of her life. Readers who have experienced the death of a loved one will identify with Florence's grief as she ponders her losses, especially the passing of her soldier son Wells at the battle of Belleau Wood. Bryant writes with deep compassion for Florence, who asks difficult questions about war and how it disrupts people's lives. As a Gold Star mother, I recommend *Sheltering Angel of Belleau Wood* that shows one woman's journey through grief and into hope and healing."
–Joan Donaldson, author of *Ae Fonde Kiss*

"In Bryant's historical novel, as World War II rages, a box of 25-year-old letters turns the thoughts of a twice-widowed Titanic survivor back to World War I.... An addictive, well-composed, and historically engaging read."
–*Kirkus Review*

"A well-researched and engaging story of one resilient, independent woman's enduring loves, tragic losses, and haunting memories."
-Liza Nash Taylor, author of *Etiquette for Runaways* and *In All Good Faith*

"*Sheltering Angel of Belleau Wood* is a deeply moving and beautifully written novel bridging two world wars through the lens of one woman's heartbreaking losses and enduring strength. Bryant shares Florence's journey, from surviving the Titanic to mentoring her granddaughter on the home front as WWII unfolds, weaving a powerful narrative of generational resilience and the haunting costs of war. The author's use of letters to transport readers to WWI adds a poignant depth, and the subtle hints of ghosts and angels provide a spiritual dimension. A 5-star story of courage, loss, love, and the profound questions surrounding war that never go away."
-Cam Torrens, award-winning author of the *Tyler Zahn mystery series*

SHELTERING ANGEL
OF BELLEAU WOOD

"It must be told, the story of
our country's part in the World War. . . .
We have such a wealth of tomorrows on our mind that we
forget our yesterdays, their glory and bitter cost."
~ **Adeline Adams, on American artists in WWI, 1921**

"What passing-bells for these who die as cattle?
— Only the monstrous anger of the guns.
Only the stuttering rifles' rapid rattle
Can patter out their hasty orisons.
No mockeries now for them; no prayers nor bells;
Nor any voice of mourning save the choirs —
The shrill, demented choirs of wailing shells;
And bugles calling for them from sad shires...."
~Wilfred Owen (1893-1918), from *Anthem for Doomed Youth*

1

York Harbor, Maine, June 1943

Thayer sits across from me in the parlor, his fingers laced together, head down showing the bald spot atop his head. Bradley agreed to give him my maiden name at birth and I'm fond of it, but Thayer prefers Tax, his childhood nickname. He is so much like his father, full of vitality and good cheer. He surveys the room, the cool blue walls and high ceiling lending an airy feel. I had the cushions of the wicker sofa and chairs covered with washable fabric, everything designed for summer ease and ocean breezes. At the back, tall windows big as doors look out to a patio surrounded by a stone wall, low and wide for sitting. The Cumings clan toasted each other with cocktails out there on many an evening.

"What will you do with this behemoth?" Thayer lifts his head and swipes one hand, palm up, around the room.

"The York Harbor house has been in the family for two generations, but I'm ready to let go of it," I tell him.

"You mean sell it?"

I take a sip of the tumbler of chilled wine Thayer has brought me. The cold of the glass and the slippery beads of condensation please me. I prefer the bitter taste of white wine to a fruity red, the color of blood. And since the Second World War began, all we've been able to buy are American wines, not nearly the quality of the French vintages German officers are enjoying in occupied Paris with dinners of foie gras and buttery sauces.

"For the little time I spend here, the house requires too much upkeep—property taxes, caretaker's fees, membership in the club, repairs for the old structure." I lift my gaze to the ceiling. Here on the coast of Maine with the ocean just yards from the summer house, there is nothing left of my family except my youngest son, now a middle-aged man. All York Harbor holds for me are memories.

He looks at me as if he has just had the most wonderful idea.

"Then I'll buy the place from you," he says. "You won't even have to put it on the market."

I read hurt on his face. If his brothers were alive, the house would have come to all three of them. They could have shared the expenses.

"With your family and the apartment in New York, can you afford upkeep?"

He dips his head again, his cheeks holding his mouth tight. "I can manage it."

I know he loves Maine, but for years after the *Titanic* disaster, I couldn't bring myself to be near the ocean. That night plagues me still—the permeating cold, the snap of a fissure in the iceberg, the massive ship creaking and cracking in two. Bradley and I were married for sixteen years before the ghostly ship carried him to the sea bottom. Bradley—my first and truest love.

"I didn't think you'd want to be burdened with it alone."

Thayer looks at the worn cotton rug and shakes his head. "It's not a burden."

My chest expands with a breath of surrender. "Then I'll have Bert make the change in the trust." After Bradley died, his business partner Bert Marckwald dissolved their brokerage on

Wall Street and became a banker. Bert was Bradley's best friend—and became mine.

Thayer grins. I don't need thanks. The York Harbor house is his inheritance, the most precious gift I can offer him. I know it's an emotional moment for him, so he changes the subject.

"Uncle Bert was always in love with you."

When our boys were young, Bert had dinner with us so often he asked them to call him Uncle Bert. They seemed to like the idea.

"I loved Bert like a younger brother. Still do."

A moment follows when neither of us speaks. What is there to say? Bradley and two of my three sons—all gone. An odd rush of gratitude washes over me. I still have a son, and God willing, he will live on to old age.

Thayer presses his lips together. He's back to the subject of the house.

"You never learned to drive, did you?"

"Drive? When I can hail a cab to anywhere in Manhattan?"

"You know I'd bring you up here anytime you like."

"That would be fine." I doubt after this visit I'll come to Maine again. I will never see Bradley at the tiller of his sailboat, the boys jumping off the side for a swim, the squeals of delight, my husband in his element experiencing pure joy. I have come only now at Thayer's suggestion to clear out a few things.

"I don't like leaving you alone for a week, but I've got to get back to the office," he says.

I cock my head. "Your business is important—and the new baby." I lift my glass to him. "I promise I won't get into trouble here."

His eyebrows lift as he stands from the chair. "I've forgotten—there's something I want you to look at."

He leaves the room and I hear him rummaging in a bedroom closet. When he returns, he's carrying a box I recognize. It held a pair of kid leather pumps I bought back in the 1920s. Tan with a strap across the top. My favorite shoes I wore until the leather cracked. The pumps are long gone, but I kept the box thinking it might be useful. The name Simpson is printed in fading red ink on the end. Size seven.

"What's this?" I know the contents without lifting the top. I put the letters there myself. All the letters. Tossed in random order.

"This'll keep you busy for most of the week." He sets the box on the floor beside the divan.

"I want to throw them out—the whole lot of them."

"Muz—" He uses the endearment all my sons called me. "I won't hear of tossing them, but something ought to be done before they disintegrate—donate them to Harvard or have them typed into a book for Jack's kids and grandchildren."

"You take them, then."

"All right, but I insist you go through them this week and we'll make a decision about what to do with them when I come back on Friday."

I don't want to read letters written two and a half decades ago, even if they are from my sons. The Great War was supposed to be our last. It's challenging enough living through this Second World War.

When Thayer bends to kiss my cheek, I catch the scent of his sweet aftershave. Citrus and cinnamon.

"I'll see you in a week, Muz." He points across the room. "You know where the telephone is. Call me if you need anything and I'll spring right up from Manhattan."

"I will, darling," I say, and I let my only living son slip quietly out the door.

2

The Box

Once I'm alone, I stare at the box holding the letters. It reminds me of an infant's coffin.

I'm not ready. Food first.

On a kitchen shelf I find a package of rice, but cooking it would take too much effort. I open the icebox and see something wrapped in butcher's paper. Thayer must have put it there, but meat doesn't appeal to me. Hunger hasn't found me yet. I spot a jar of fresh cream for the morning coffee—so considerate of him. And he thought to buy cheese—bleu and a hunk of cheddar. Next to the cheeses is a small carton of fresh blueberries. Wild Maine blueberries don't ripen until sometime in July. Thayer must have brought these from New York. I take out the carton and put it on the counter, along with the cheeses, and get a plate from the cupboard. Cheese sliced, I sprinkle blueberries atop. That and a few limp crackers will suffice for dinner. Another evening I might go out if I feel up for a walk—to work up an appetite.

The wine rack above the icebox holds several bottles. Summers in Maine are for white wine. Dust films the red bottles that might have sat for several summers. Luckily there's still half the bottle of chardonnay Thayer opened. From the freezer, I muscle ice cubes from the metal tray, drop three cubes into my glass, then pour the wine almost to the tumbler's brim.

Back in my chair, I nibble the cheese and sip the wine while I watch the box as if it might spring to life. The cardboard is still intact. Thayer must have stored it on an upper shelf in the closet.

Usually boxes deteriorate from moisture and wear. But then, this one probably hasn't been touched in over a decade.

It's not the box but the contents that concern me. Is death different if you see it coming? Sudden death is more tragic — no opportunity to say goodbye. It took my second husband Chess weeks to die. I had long chats with him during his illness. He said he had no regrets about his life except wishing he had met me sooner. I held his hand until he seemed to drift off to sleep, and I knew he was gone.

How can any good exist in the world when death is always near?

Carrying the cheese plate in one hand and tumbler in the other, I go out to the terrace. The two metal chairs look as if they've been newly painted — Thayer's doing, probably because he knew I was coming. He has always tried to please me.

I sit and perch the tumbler on the flat arm, the plate on my lap. From color photos I've seen in magazines, sunsets over the Atlantic are less flamboyant than on the west coast where the ball of fire glows red as it sinks into the water. Here on an evening with wisps of clouds, the expanse of sky pinks over the horizon as the light bends across the continent. At times like this, Bradley might reach over from the other chair and take my hand, the thin gold band on his ring finger reflecting the waning light. I gave him the ring on our first anniversary. A symbol of our eternal union, he had said.

Chess preferred not to wear a ring, claiming the jewelry made it harder to grip a golf club. He came to the Maine house a few times but seemed like an awkward visitor, tapping his foot until we could leave. On our first trip to York Harbor together, we had just married and he drove his new Crane-Simplex, a wedding gift from Standard Oil where he was general counsel. Even with the fancy car, the trip took half a day and we stopped for early lunch in New Haven. I was eager to get to Maine and show him the lighthouse on Boon Island, but Chess dawdled over coffee at the café and talked about automobiles, golf, and the future of the oil industry. I had been working in the Midtown Manhattan shelter houses with women who had never held a golf club and would never own an automobile, but I respected the work Chess did. When finally we reached York, he spent the week reading a book or walking alone—as if he felt Bradley watching him.

For what must be most of an hour I watch the sea, an ocean of calm that soothes me. The wine helps. I have less tolerance for alcohol than in my younger days when Bradley and I thought nothing of finishing a first and then a second bottle, often with Bert. How long ago was that? Lately I find myself asking what day it is, what month, what year. But not what moment. There is but this moment with this tumbler of cold wine, this salty breeze, this sunset. That's how I've gotten through.

When I piece it together with my heart, I find no fear of death. Fear left me years ago. When we love someone long enough, sooner or later one or the other will die, a feeling at once menacing and precious. If only I had spoken to the ship's captain. If only I had approached the chairman of the White Star Line about the ice warnings, about slowing down.

But, then, nothing is permanent. Each wave washing the shore is different from the one before it, different from the one that follows. To think we will not die is foolish—and yet essential for living, at least for the young. For many reasons, death has befriended me. I look forward to shaking Death's hand.

When the gloaming settles in, I go back inside and turn on a light. The bulb is glaring and breaks whatever spell the sunset cast. A candle would be better. Wasn't there a thick candle somewhere? Scented with pine, I think. It may have burned low and been thrown out since I was last in Maine.

On the way to the kitchen I stumble over a corner of the box as if it wants my attention.

The box of ghosts.

"You'll have to wait," I tell the ghosts. "I'd like another glass of wine first."

I've forgotten to fill the ice cube tray and what ice is left has melted. After I fill the tray under the faucet, I slip it back into the little freezer compartment. Why didn't I put the wine bottle in the icebox to chill?

The neighbors next door might have ice, but when I check out the window, the house is dark. Probably they have not yet opened the place for the summer. Drinking warm chardonnay is out of the question.

I put the wine bottle in the icebox, and in a kitchen drawer I find the pine candle and a box of wood matches. I set the candle on a saucer, strike a match on the rough side of the box, and light the wick. At first the wick sputters and sparks and then the flame settles into a quiet flicker.

I take the candle to the parlor and turn off the lamp. For a full minute I stare at the blue and yellow light, an inanimate thing brought to life. The parlor looks different in candlelight. The bookcase shelves hold volumes whose spines have lost their color except for the soft glitter of gold titles. On the fireplace mantel, silver frames gleam, a dozen of them. I know each photograph—Thayer, Jack, Wells as laughing children, the water behind them turned sepia with age. In the boat so far out on the water, Bradley is a dark outline, one hand on the tiller, the other cleating the mainsail line. One of the boys—the oldest, Jack—adjusts the jib, both of them looking into the wind, facing a future neither of them knew would come too soon.

The wine has made my thoughts too random to focus on a novel, and it's too early to go to bed. Instead, I look at the box. If I don't open the lid tonight, I might never.

The box is heavier than I expected. As heavy as corpses—two of them. I set it beside me on the divan. The cardboard smells of an old bookstore and has a faint green tinge near the bottom, a hint of mold from the salt air.

"We'd best get to it," I say to the lid, thinking I will just organize the letters tonight, the way I received them. That just makes good sense.

I flip up the lid, afraid mice might have gotten inside. Or bugs of some kind.

There are no bugs, no mice. Where I expect a rubble of envelopes and sheets of paper tossed in thoughtlessly, I find envelopes lined up one behind the other like a troop of soldiers. Atop the soldiers, a small note:

Muz, I've arranged the letters in order for you. And I found this under them. I'll see you next weekend. Love, Tax.

I lay the note aside and behind it, a waxy sheet bordered with lace. Inside the border, an image of a gilded boat drawn over a lake by two swans. The caption reads, "The Barque of Love." I'd forgotten the valentine. There had been so much packing, so many final preparations for the sail to Europe. Valentine's Day was just weeks before we were to board the ship *Oceanic,* bound for Europe.

When I turn the card over, I recognize the familiar handwriting: "My dearest Florrie, my love for you is deeper than the ocean. Your devoted Bradley."

"I still feel that way," a voice says — more of an echo, a spoken memory. A cool hand covers my own. He is a slow, sun-warmed breeze that takes my breath away. I turn my face toward him, toward those brown eyes, that handsome face I recognize.

"Read me a letter," he breathes.

"Must I?"

"They bring our sons back to me — to us."

I know nothing can bring them back, but I want the fantasy.

"I might be able to do this," I murmur, "as long as you're here."

"I am here." A faint uttering that could be mistaken for waves kissing the shore.

His hand drops away when I reach for the first envelope and slide out the letter. "October 12, 1914," I read, my lips forming the words but hardly a sound coming from them.

Dear Muz,

When I entered St. George's School as a fourth former, we were told England has sent troops to France to hold off the German army. The students voted to form an infantry battalion because the U.S. is sure to get involved and 70 of us are sharpening our mettle, preparing for the great conflict.

Our instructor is a West Point graduate who requisitioned khaki uniforms to help us take our practice seriously. Here are my first training exercises:

1. Honor the colors by standing at attention and saluting.

2. Military posture: Stand straight, stomach in, chest out, heels close.

3. Hold the rifle on the left shoulder, forefinger and thumb to the side of the stock, the other three supporting the butt.

The government sent us 100 Springfield-built Krag rifles. We are required to learn the Manual of Arms before we can practice shooting at targets.

"We took Wells to Rhode Island for his first year at St. George's. Do you remember that, Bradley?"

"I was with you, yes. It was the fall of 1911."

"He was twelve."

"First form, they called it."

"I didn't want to send him away at such a young age."

"I was sent away, Florrie. It's how things worked. Still do."

"It was a beautiful landscape, the school buildings on a cliff overlooking Second Beach. Jack was already there, and I thought they'd be protected, safe from all harm."

Bradley doesn't answer.

I bring my eyes back to the paper.

Jack is quick at learning the rules. I probably shouldn't tell you this, but he says he plans to join the Army as soon as the U.S. enters the conflict. That may be sooner than we expect. But don't worry, Muz. He'll be a swell soldier.

Bradley's voice is low, sorrowful. "You couldn't stop war from coming, Florrie."

"You knew?"

"I was watching, yes."

"They wanted to be men, but how were they to know the risks they were taking? We didn't raise our boys to be soldiers. And we certainly didn't raise them to be sacrificed."

"Finish our boy's letter," Bradley says, an exhale of air.

I read again.

When I am not training, I practice piano and attend classes, but military readiness is always on my mind. I dearly hope you are comfortable and safe there in Manhattan. I look forward to coming home for the holidays. In the meantime, all my love, your own Wells

I turn toward where Bradley sits. "I told you we should have sent the boys to a local school in Manhattan. They wouldn't have drilled with rifles at ages fifteen and seventeen."

A soft grumble comes from him. We argued about schools many times.

By the time Wells was in fourth form, he confronted the decision to follow his brother and turn away from all advantages and opportunities the school offered him and consider joining the military. War was the polar opposite of anything he had experienced before.

I sigh and lay the letter aside.

Whenever Thayer and I walked in Central Park, he picked up a stick and pretended to shoot at "Krauts," as he called them. He was just ten in 1914 and I could hold onto him for a couple more years before he, too, went off to boarding school as Bradley had insisted. But he hadn't wanted to be sent away. "You need a man in the house," he said. How was a child so young so wise? Too wise to think about fighting and killing. Isn't that what soldiers are about? Killing the enemy? Kill or be killed? Is that what it takes to protect a country's borders? Is there no diplomacy, sitting at table and talking out their differences?

Every time Thayer held a stick to his shoulder and made gunfire noises, I had asked him to stop or distracted him with a sweet. Warring, I suppose, is innate in human nature. Even in ancient times the gods fought each other, especially belligerent Aries. Athena was the goddess of war but she also ruled over reason, wisdom, and justice. Men might have good reason to fight, but in my opinion violence should be a last resort— especially if it involves my sons.

By now ice cubes must have formed in the freezer and the wine should be chilled. I leave the box and in the kitchen check the ice tray. The water is cold but far from solid. How long does it take ice to freeze? The water that April night was twenty-eight degrees. The iceberg must have broken off from Greenland and floated into the shipping route. One would think after that bitter night I would never look at ice again. Habits are habits, of course, even if some find it gauche to water down the wine. Ever since my last goodbye to Bradley as I boarded the lifeboat, I have not cared a whit what people think.

The cheese plate needs rinsing. I dry it with a dishtowel and put it away to delay getting to the next letter. There are things that need tending to, anyway. The silver pitcher Bradley won playing tennis at Harvard wants polishing. I lift it from the shelf and run a finger over the engraved initials—JBC 1893. In the morning I'll check the cupboards for silver polish. Afterward, I'll clip flowers from the garden to bring some life into the house, and I reach to a top shelf for the crystal vase that has been there since before Bradley's parents died.

I open the icebox and touch the wine bottle. Chilled enough to drink even without ice, and I dribble some into the glass and take it back to the divan, back to the box. If Bradley is still there, I don't sense him. As I've learned, he comes and goes and I know it's impossible to hold onto him for very long.

Taking a sip of the chardonnay for courage, I open the next letter dated November 12, 1915. I regretted getting the letter then, regret it even now.

Dear Muz,

This is a hard letter for me to write, but I know you'll understand. First, you must know I am progressing in my music studies. Chopin's etudes are now like child's play, and I've nearly accomplished Mozart's Rondo alla turca, sonata number 11, at least the third movement, the Turkish March. I can't wait to play it for you on the baby grand at the brownstone.

I am on the football team here. I play receiver, and coach allows me to wear gloves to protect my hands. He says I need to bulk up, but with classes, piano practice, chapel, sports, and military drills, I haven't time for lifting weights in the gym. At least I can outrun most of the defensemen.

Now I steel myself once again for the unhappy news that starts the boulder rolling down the hill.

Muz, I hope you won't be dismayed, but I have decided to leave school at the end of this year. My grades have been outstanding and if you are willing to hire a tutor to help me with lessons I will miss in my final year, Princeton has agreed to accept me next fall into the class of 1921. If the war intensifies, the school will give me leave for military duty with the understanding I may return to complete my degree after my time in service. And I shall not be alone. Did you meet Dickie Fairfield on your visits here? He is on the football team with me, not very good at it though. Tennis is his game. After graduation Dickie intends to put off entering college and enlist. Quincy Howe, as well, and Julian Little. Philip Herrick in 6th form is signing up, too. So I'll have good company.

I know this information may upset you, but please believe I am capable of making my own decisions. Jack has written me that his work is with Division Headquarters and not terribly dangerous. With my older brother keeping an eye on me, you may rest easy.

Let me know about the tutor. Difficult times call for difficult decisions, Muz, but to be a man, I must pull Excalibur from the stone. Your own Wells

I don't want to think about Wells joining the military. Instead, I think about his love of music.

"I always found Mozart challenging. I never even attempted Sonata 11."

"I enjoyed hearing you play Chopin." Bradley is back.

"You forgave my mistakes."

"I never heard a mistake."

I look again at the faded blue ink. "We hired that tutor, didn't we?"

"It was cheaper than another year's tuition at boarding school."

I don't turn toward him, afraid looking at him will make him evaporate.

"You always measured things by money."

"That was my profession, darling."

"I wish I had talked him into finishing secondary school before going off to college."

"There was war, Florrie. When a young man wants to show his bravery, there is no talking him out of it."

Bradley and I disagreed about many things during our years of marriage and usually I conceded. But on this issue, he was right. If I had discouraged Wells from joining the war effort, his desire to be part of something larger than himself would have grown stronger.

"It doesn't make any sense," I say. "Why is war idealized?"

"That's a simple answer, my dearest. War is embedded in human history from King Arthur's Knights of the Round Table and Shakespeare's MacBeth to modern history."

I banter with him like old times. "Wells was an artist, a musician, not a warrior."

"Warriors have guarded civilization for thousands of years, as far back as Gilgamesh. Combatants are a cog in every nation's machinery. All men are soldiers of some kind."

All men—even the men on the *Titanic* who weren't allowed into lifeboats. "You showed the greatest courage that April night. I always thought you would come back to me."

"I did come back, Florrie. Did I not tell you that afternoon in Paris when we were at Père Lachaise Cemetery that my soul would seek you out?"

"You did, yes." I take another sip of wine. "Nine years before I wed Chess, I waited. Have you read about Rome's Vestal Virgins, how they were buried alive if they violated their vows of chastity? When I met Chess, I felt I would be thrown into an underground tomb to suffocate for my betrayal to you."

"I was the one buried alive, Florrie. Buried by the unforgiving and uncaring sea."

"And I had to keep living—for you and for our sons. Someone said life must be reaffirmed because of its tragedies, not in spite of them."

"Life itself is tragic."

I smile at the word "life," as if Bradley's heart is beating, his lungs are drawing breath. Even after a third glass of wine, I know better.

I fold the letter, put it back into its envelope, and file it at the other end of the box. After I blow out the candle, I sit in darkness except for moonlight coming through the window. Then I wander again to the terrace and sit on the stone wall. The moon is nearly full, and I watch the waves froth and lap the shore.

"The terrace was what sold my parents on the house." Bradley has followed me.

The front of the house faces York Street. Luckily, the homes across the road are below our vantage and allow a view of the water. But it's better to cross the street and take the trail to the beach where to the north one can catch the glow from Nubble Lighthouse.

"Our boys used to hike up to the keeper's residence." I tilt my head. "I haven't been there in years. It had gingerbread trim and miniature lighthouses atop the railing."

"Yes." His voice is a soft breeze. He's leaving again.

Directly across the water, the Boon Island Light casts its beacon's glow. After *Titanic,* I never felt alone in York Harbor with the lighthouses standing guard. Even now I sense I'm surrounded by loved ones. On nights when the moon was just right, we could see the Milky Way. Somewhere in that vast galaxy, there must be another mother who has lost sons and husbands and who at this very moment is watching, arms around me in mutual sorrow.

A light wind picks up and brings me to shiver, but I linger rather than go back inside.

Wells was right about difficult times, starting in spring of 1915 when a German submarine torpedoed the British liner *Lusitania* on its way from New York to Liverpool. Seven hundred of the nearly two thousand aboard survived, the rest lost, many of them Americans. I know about sinking ships. For *Titanic*, the torpedo was an iceberg.

The scents of coastal Maine have always rid me of any thought but the here and now. I suck in a lungful of sea air, and in that moment I can forget the past. The future is anyone's guess.

3

The Ghost

Losing Bradley was as much as I thought my heart could endure, and even then I wasn't convinced I'd survive. It was because of the boys that I lifted my head and stumbled forward. A few years later I fell to my knees and prayed for French and English soldiers to repel the Huns before America entered the war and my sons joined the fight. But my prayers weren't answered. The Higher Power had different ideas, but how a loving God could condone such savagery escapes me.

For two cents, I'd burn the entire box of letters rather than go back to another heartache. But that would be another kind of killing.

It's odd, though, how I'm like a visitor from the future who has time traveled back twenty years with full awareness of how things will turn out for people living then. If I could reach them through the paper, I would warn my sons. But it was an era when even a mother's warning wouldn't slow the momentum of war nor the desire of young men to be heroes.

Now here we are in another war, and I have not an inkling how this one will end.

Inside, I turn on a sconce above the mantel and scan the framed photos. I reach for one—the one I always reach for—and hold it under the light. Wells is standing straight, not at attention but wearing the uniform of the Marines, so thick I can make out tiny threads of the wool on the jacket. Two large pockets, one on each side. Pewter buttons march up the middle to where the high collar covers most of his neck. The fourth button from the top, at his stomach, looks to strain against the material, and I'm glad to see he must have been eating well. Epaulets decorate the jacket shoulders. In spite of my always advising him to stand straight, his shoulders droop as if he's leaning over the piano keys or bending to follow the puck down the ice as he did at school. A brimmed hat sits flat atop his head. He has small ears. His eyes — the Cumings eyes, slant ever so slightly downward at the outer corners so he seems pensive, even sad. But the mouth, the full lips, although not turned up in a smile, give his face a pleasant expression as if he wants his mother to know he is proud to be in uniform. The camera is chest-height looking up into the face of an angel, a handsome boy who might be years younger than his eighteen birthdays. Where I saw my middle son as artistic, even delicate, he accepted the command to be noble, put on the mantle of warrior, and serve as protector with his country's allies.

I take the photo of Wells back to the divan and switch on the lamp, blinking in the brightness. My weak eyes require more light for reading than they used to, and it's now pitch dark without the lamp. I reach for one more letter, this one dated September 1, 1917.

Dear Muz, as I settle into my room at Princeton, the campus feels strangely empty. More than half the upperclassmen have enlisted in the military, and those left behind either have some malady or plan to enlist later. Since the fighting began, Princeton students have traveled to Europe to help with relief and humanitarian missions. I feel as if we are all in this together.

There is an old slogan here, "Princeton in the Nation's Service." Since America declared war on Germany, alumni have been returning to campus for Reserve Officers Corps training. Some of the grounds have even been plowed for farming to feed troops. Many of the faculty, too, have left to enlist, and we will not have a varsity football team this fall because there are not enough players. So much for defeating old Harvard.

One of my classmates, August Rubel, registered for classes, paid his tuition, and then took a train to New York to sign up for ambulance service. He was on a ship to France later that very day. President Roosevelt even came to campus and gave a speech about national strength and international duty.

Muz, I intend to complete the semester and return to New York for Christmas. But who knows how things will develop? No matter what happens, know that you are in my thoughts and in my heart. Your very own, Wells

"Oh, Wells, if you had known you would be one of more than a hundred Princeton students to die in the fighting —."

"Harvard lost more," Bradley murmurs. "Four hundred."

"You didn't know about the war. You were busy trying not to drown."

"I didn't drown, my love. My blood froze in my veins."

"I can't talk about that. Not now."

"Then tell me about this fellow Chester, my successor."

"Must I?" I press the letter into the back of the box.

"It might help take your mind off the letters."

"Can you stand to know?"

"Of course, my darling Florrie. I will always be your most treasured."

I lace my fingers together in my lap. I must be getting sleepy to think I'm talking to Bradley's ghost. But he's right — I need a distraction.

"Chess and I met through mutual friends."

"Madeleine Astor?"

"Oh, no. Mrs. Astor remarried four years after her husband —"

"The ship. I know. But go on."

"We met in 1919, just after the war ended. Chess was a year younger, and I didn't think he'd be interested in a widow with three—no, at that time two—grown sons. He was divorced but had no children. I'd never met anyone from Iowa." I can't help smiling at the memory. "He was nice. Isn't that what they say about Iowans? We courted, if that's the word, and said our vows in 1921, a year before Jack's wedding to Margaret."

I glance toward my first husband, a cloud of evening fog. "It was a quiet ceremony. I didn't want a fuss."

"Florrie, I've never known you to fuss."

"He worked too hard—at least, when he wasn't on the golf course." I didn't begrudge him playing golf and, anyway, most of those games were with clients or business partners. "I traveled with him on business trips abroad. Can you believe I got back on an ocean liner? Having lost you and Wells, I suppose I didn't care if the ship went down." I bring two fingers to my lips. How much can he bear to hear?

"I can bear more."

"Well, then, we spent time in Britain, Italy, Belgium, and—"

"France."

"Yes, France."

"How did he die?"

"Wells?"

"I know how Wells died. I mean Chester."

"In a cold December he caught an influenza, a bad one that migrated to his lungs and caused pneumonia. His passing was peaceful. Not like—"

"Not like April 1912."

"Not like April 1912, no. And not like Belleau Wood."

"You had better read another letter." His voice is growing faint.

"I read them all twenty years ago, Bradley."

"Then read them again — to me."

A sigh escapes me. "All right." I pinch the next envelope in the row. "This one is from Jack. It's dated September 10, 1917."

"I had been dead five and a half years then."

"Don't remind me, darling."

"Sorry, my love. Please do go on."

Dearest Mother, here I am in Cambridge near the church where Grandfather preached and where you were a girl. I feel close to you here and close to Father, too. I hope to be the man he was, but every day we hear of America entering the war. I am told if I finish the first semester at Harvard, I might achieve the rank of officer and after we win the war against Germany, I can return to my studies with a military pension. There is no "if" but a matter of "when" I shall don the uniform.

Bradley asks me a question I've asked myself. "How did you feel about Jack going into the army?"

"I didn't discourage him. Our boys were strong-willed. All I could do was pray for their survival."

"I've watched them from afar," he says. "Strong-willed indeed. What more does he say?"

"He asks me not to be concerned. He'll have training in France. 'This war is necessary,' he says, 'and I am confident I have the ability to do my part.'"

"You raised our boys to be good men, Florrie."

A bitter sadness squeezes my chest. "Good men who die before their mother."

"There was nothing you could have done to prevent it."

"That's kind of you, my love."

I bring my myself back to the letter. "He asks me to give Bardie a kiss for him and sends one to me." I don't recall how the nickname Bardie came about. She never wanted to be addressed as "Grandma" or even "Nana." Her given name was Ella. They had a special bond, those two. Every summer he spent a week with her roaming Boston's museums and historic sites, and she spoiled him horribly. When she died in her eighties, he wept for days.

Bradley's voice is low, as if he's speaking from a great depth. "And so the world turns. And turns. And turns."

4

Margaret

A chill catches me, and I get up to close the terrace door. But as I reach for the knob, the screech of an owl pierces the quiet, an ominous sound that causes me to scan the parlor. When I'm convinced no one is hiding behind a chair or a curtain, I listen a moment to the slow pulse of waves rolling onto the sand.

I'm about to shut the door when the brrr-ing of the telephone startles me. Probably Thayer checking in, although he's been gone only a few hours. Maybe a wrong number.

When I answer with "Hello," I hear a familiar voice.

"Mrs. Swain, is that you?"

It's Margaret, Jack's wife—Jack's widow. Of course she would use the name Swain. Funny that sometimes I still think of myself as Mrs. Cumings. She was Margaret Cumings when she met her second husband, but they've been married three years and she is now Mrs. Smithson. She didn't invite me to the Bermuda wedding and in good taste Margaret had only her sister in attendance. I wish she would call me Danny as her three children do, but she keeps a pleasant formality between us.

"Yes, I'm here in Maine, Margaret." As the older woman, it's perfectly fine to address my daughter-in-law—if that's what I can still call her—by her first name. She rarely calls, and I push away the thought of some bad news.

"I tried you in New York and then called Tax." She and Thayer have always been close enough for her to be familiar with him. "He told me you're there for the week. Are you alone?"

"Yes, quite alone." I look at the divan to see if Bradley is there, my specter of a first husband, but he has made himself scarce.

"May we come to see you tomorrow? We'll drive up from Bedford Hills. Eva and I have a favor to ask of you."

I think of saying I'm busy, but that would be dishonest. Besides, I'm always glad to see my oldest granddaughter.

"It's a long way," I say. "Is Oliver driving you?"

"No, Oliver's on a diplomatic trip. I'll take his car and we'll stop in Worcester. There are some good shops there. May we bring you something?"

Young women these days can take on anything.

"If you're here by early afternoon, I'll have lunch ready." More likely it will be dinner and an overnight. I like Margaret. She is a striking woman and it's not her fault Jack left her. But "left" is not the right word. Leaving was never what he wanted.

"Don't worry yourself about lunch," Margaret says. "We'll eat something along the way. Eva is looking forward to the trip—and to seeing you."

Whatever the favor is, it must require asking in person. Although, I can't imagine what benefit I might be to Margaret and Eva.

After we hang up, I close the terrace door and turn the bolt lock. Since the Great War, I haven't taken safety for granted. Three years ago German armies took France, and the following year the U.S. entered the war. Today's *Times* reported the Allies have launched a bombing offensive against Germany. The Air Force dropped four hundred tons of bombs and lost a number of planes. This is not a war in the trenches—mostly this is a war of the air, except British Prime Minister Winston Churchill and President Roosevelt are plotting an attack across the English Channel. They're calling it D-day.

It looks like twenty years after the first war ended, Germany is still determined to occupy most of Europe, and the Allies are just as determined to stop them.

What did my sons fight for?

When Bradley and I were planning our fateful trip, we didn't need a crystal ball to see trouble on the horizon. Jack was fourteen then and Wells twelve. What I didn't foresee was that five years later when America entered the war, both boys would be old enough to serve. Jack was assigned to the 26th Division, a section of educated men from New England. The Yankee Division, it was called, the first organized under the American flag. After ten days of training in France, he was sent into enemy territory for full combat. Wells, as always, would follow his brother as soon as he turned eighteen.

Traveling up to Maine and reading the yellowed letters have taken my energy, but I feel compelled to open one more envelope tonight. When I pick up the next in line, I see it is from Wells.

February 14, 1918

Dear Muz,

I have arrived at Parris Island in South Carolina. From the train, a boat ferried us along the Beaufort River. As soon as we landed, we lined up to be processed and evaluated for being sound of body and mind before taking the oath of enlistment. Our barracks is a bunkhouse with cots, each covered with a thin mattress. We sleep close together, 16 lined up along two walls. In between are heaters, for which I am grateful as it is a chilly February even here.

I was fortunate to undergo ROTC training at Princeton, which got me ready for enlisting in the Marines. We are told most of the 80 acres at Parris Island is solid ground, but a portion is wetlands. I expect we will undergo training on both land and sea.

I'm glad he was warm. Glad also he was with other men. As little boys, my three sometimes played war games, as if they knew about war. They must have studied the Civil War in school, so of course they shot imaginary guns at imaginary enemies. For the men at Parris Island, war was still a concept, an ideal of heroism. That's why men fight, isn't it—believing they can make themselves into heroes?

But let me get back to the letter.

The recruiting officer has told us our training will last eight weeks. The first three weeks are devoted to instruction, drills, physical exercise, bayonet fighting, personal combat, wall scaling, and rope climbing. The final weeks will be for marksmanship practice, slow fire at 600 yards, three times as far as I shot at targets at school.

It is not to be all drill and work, though. After our initial training, we will keep fit with baseball games, boxing, and wrestling matches. There are several thousand of us here and although I am one of the youngest recruits, I am getting so strong you may not recognize me when I return.

Thank you for sending the journal with the leather cover. When I can't get a letter to you, I will write on the pages of the journal so you can read them at a later time. For now, you may write me here for the next few weeks, and I hope to receive a letter from you (and perhaps a bit of candy).

With love, your own Wells

I wish Parris Island had kept him longer. Kept him at least until July when the tide turned and the American forces drove back the German army. But as my mother used to say, if wishes were horses, beggars would ride. I would gladly be a beggar if wishing would bring Wells back. I miss his gentleness, his beauty. He had not yet used a razor and his cheeks were soft, as if he had been kissed by seraphim. When he went into service, it seemed just weeks since his voice had the high pitch of innocence, a soprano in the school choir, singing feathery notes. So much promise, so many aspirations. He was determined to compose, perform, teach. Music was all he cared about, my artistic son, the one most like me. The one I worried about. Worried that he was overshadowed by his older brother whose marks were high and who was bound for success in life. Overshadowed, too, by young Thayer's rambunctiousness and demands for attention. I was afraid Wells felt neglected and retreated into his world of music and the inner chamber of his thoughts. He might have thought being a soldier would give him a chance to prove himself against his brothers. But he didn't have to punish himself with drills and long hikes to show his mother he was worthy. Oh Wells, you were always worthy, my love.

One more letter tonight. This one is to my mother. She wrote Jack weekly while he was in France and cherished every letter from him, all of which she saved. I imagine he was cautious, writing in generalities rather than giving her gruesome details of the war.

This one is dated March 29, 1918. He tells Bardie he spent two months at the front where active fighting took place. In eastern France near the German border, I imagine. The day after his division reached a new location, "the grand bataille began" with shelling and bombing precisely where his battalion had trained. He doesn't say anything about casualties, but he may not have been given that information. He told his grandmother he was not in the line of fire.

He mentions a small town between Paris and Strasbourg— Rimaucourt, I think he later told me. In the town is a large chateau built in 400 A.D and restored in the 18th century by its newest owner, a Paris merchant. Jack always had a fascination with antiquity and although he would have been delighted to stay and explore the ruins and churches, there was a war on and his job was to transport a division of soldiers and officers to safety. His duties as lieutenant required him to be in close contact with the staff officers, have telephones installed, get the motorcycle courier service running, and "a thousand and one odd jobs" to see headquarters ran smoothly. Jack was solid and reliable, and I have no doubt he did his job well. He was eighteen when he left Harvard and enlisted in the army as a private in the Massachusetts Cavalry. That was 1916, the year before President Wilson declared the country at war. At least Jack was close to home then. Within months, my brilliant son was given a promotion to corporal and the next year to sergeant while he was in France. It must have been his proficiency in the French language that got him the rank of lieutenant. As an officer, he wouldn't be fighting on the front lines. I could not have endured losing two sons to the war.

My thoughts drift to the mothers and wives who waited those agonizing days in April 1912 to hear if their loved ones had survived the sinking of the *Titanic*. I waited, too, listening for the telephone to ring, for the front door to open. Listening for the voice I knew so well and loved so dearly.

I pat the divan next to me. "Where are you now, my darling Bradley?"

When there is no answer, I bring myself back to Jack's letter.

One of the chauffeurs transporting officers received the Croix de Guerre for driving a car under shellfire. No one was out of danger. Jack visited the front to inspect the trenches and artillery, dodging shellfire each time. While in the field, he met French families and spoke with them in their language. "My French is getting along quite well," he writes.

He mentions receiving Bardie's card with Edward Hale's poem, "The Man Without a Country." "The last stanza stopped my breath," he writes. "The 'dying shall go down / to the vile dust from whence he sprung, / Unwept, unhonour'd, and unsung.' I'm afraid those words may predict the demise of many men in my brigade. I wanted to put the poem on the bulletin board, but it is used strictly for military purposes."

I've read Hale's story about the American Army lieutenant accused of treason. During his trial, he renounced his country and was sentenced to spend the rest of his days at sea and, I can guess, without a single letter from his mother. Nor she from him. Of course, the story could well have stood for the death of a son. At least I have these communications from my own sons.

Jack finishes:

I served on a General Court Martial at the front. It was tedious but interesting, but I am forbidden to tell what it was about.

After we left the front, we went to a quiet little town way behind the lines, the cleanest town I have seen in France. I was billeted in the house of an old widow, and her guest room had a large, warm bed. We were there about three days, and I had some time to talk with her. She is very worried about the war but has a brave spirit.

Jack must have given the woman a sense that all would be well. I know what it's like to be a widow alone. With Thayer in boarding school, I had only kind friends and hired help, none of whom understood the depth of my sadness. At least the enemy wasn't closing in on my home—unless I consider death the enemy.

Jack writes his grandmother about getting sunburned during a four-day hike. He was on horseback as the infantrymen walked alongside. I imagine even at the end of March the weather was warm, especially atop a burdened horse, and he might have shed his uniform jacket. The Army offered him no defense against the sun.

He writes that each night he and the other officers were billeted in houses, the enlisted men on straw in barns. I'm sure they were all tired at the end of a day of hiking and went to bed after an evening meal. Jack always ate with his men. I never knew my son to show arrogance.

  SHELTERING ANGEL OF BELLEAU WOOD

Now we are settled in another small town where we expect to stay for a month, but with another big battle on, we shall probably move to the front in two or three days.

Well, I am called now for a conference with one of the General's aides about reorganizing the Division Headquarters, so must go.

Heaps of love to you, Jack

My mother didn't mention the sunburn to me at the time. She knew I would worry. I already fretted about my boy dodging bullets. But I hear Jack's voice through the pages of his letter, full of confidence in the face of a horrid situation. As a youth, Jack had a maturity beyond his years. He was soft-spoken but held sway over his younger brothers. Where Wells and Thayer kept the housekeeper busy picking up their toys and clothes from the floor or hung over doorknobs, Jack's room was spotless. Socks and underwear in the bureau top drawer, polo shirts in the middle, trousers at the bottom. Even books on his shelf arranged alphabetically by author. And yet, he was friendly, and I never saw him quarrel with anyone—unless it was with Thayer when he came into Jack's room and left a mess. My youngest had trouble pronouncing his own name, and it was Jack who took to calling him "Tax" because, he said, it was much easier for everyone.

In 1912 when Bradley and I spent weeks in France, no one talked of war except for rumblings which we hoped were rumors. We enjoyed a pleasant six-day cruise on the liner *Oceanic* and toured galleries and museums, ate sumptuous meals, laughed, and luxuriated in the finery of the Edwardian age. My dress hems brushed the polished floors. By the time my two sons were soldiers, hems had risen well above the ankles. With men at war, women had to join the workforce, and shorter skirts were less likely to catch in machinery. I was glad for more practical wartime hemlines—one small thing to be grateful for during those harrowing years.

My blurry vision makes it hard to read the faded ink, even under bright light. I suppose I ought to see what I have to serve Margaret and Eva tomorrow, but that can wait until morning. Now I'll take myself to bed and wonder what favor they have to ask of me.

5

Jack

A horrid dream wakes me with a start. Out the window, morning light pinks the eastern horizon. I must have awakened three times during the black of night, each time from a vision of urgency, struggling to rescue a child in danger. There were other helpless children, too, and I knew I couldn't save them all.

I sit up and rub my temples. With any luck, I'll catch a nap before my visitors arrive today. In the meantime—coffee.

At the Maine house, a well pump draws from an aquifer with million-year-old water that makes for excellent coffee. To relieve the pipes of water that has sat over the winter, I let the faucet run. When the stream feels cool, I fill the percolator three-quarters full, scoop coffee grounds into the metal basket, and strike a match to the burner.

While the water heats, I take a cup and ready it on its saucer. I don't want to sit in the dining room alone and prefer to plant myself by the window. Margaret and Eva won't arrive until late afternoon. It's an hours-long drive and I want Margaret to take her time, especially driving with my granddaughter. Precious cargo.

When the coffee perks, I get the cream from the icebox and pour some into a small pitcher. I like the ceremony of making and serving coffee, even if just for myself.

My stomach gurgles, and I realize I must be hungry. Thayer gave the house the gift of an electric toaster. I've never used it, but the contraption looks simple—a slot in the top wide enough for a thick slice of bread. The bread box is empty, though, so I get out the blueberries from last night, drop a handful into a bowl, and pour cream over them. That should hold me until I walk to the market for supplies.

The sun is low in the sky and too bright to face this morning. Instead, I wander to the parlor. The box is still there. Did I expect it to hide itself away while I slept? I don't want to look at the tomblike thing, but I pluck the next letter and push it into my skirt pocket, then go back to the kitchen and pour the coffee, swirl in some cream. Settled onto the stool, I pull the letter out and unfold the paper. It's another from Jack, my eldest son who became a man the moment his father died. Instead of mourning the loss, he turned to care for his mother. How fortunate I have been for such kind and brave sons.

April 8, 1918

Dearest Muz,

Both the outgoing and incoming mail has been terribly mixed this last three weeks on account of moving. My last letter was written in our rest sector behind the lines, but here we are at the front again, holding our own and everybody knee-deep in the mud after eight days of rain.

Incidentally, this is the ninth town where we have spent one night or more since our previous trip to the front. On the last hike up with the horses, I was sent on ahead as billeting officer. It is my duty to arrange with French mayors of small towns, called Mayor des Cantonments in larger towns, for billets for officers, men, horses, wagons, kitchens, arrange for drinking water and water for the horses, etc. So you see, I must be able to speak some French to do all this.

The terrifically rotten weather has kept action down in our sector, so everyone is waiting to see something big when it clears up. Even now the windows are shaking from artillery fire. I can see the guns, but they haven't picked on us yet.

He meant the Big Guns, the long-barreled cannons on wheels soldiers pulled across the fields of France, scarring the earth beneath them. Scarring—and killing—men, too. Jack was always sponge-like about learning, from world events and economics to the workings of the large artillery he taught infantry soldiers how to operate. I've since read that more than half of battlefield casualties were caused by artillery shells exploding and buffeting the bodies of American men with shrapnel, small lead balls inside the larger shell. When the shell discharges, the lead balls shoot out like bullets across the battlefield.

I know these facts well. I wish I hadn't needed to know about shrapnel.

Did you meet a fellow named Sachs who lived on East 64th Street? He stays in my room with me now. I have known him a couple of months but we did not realize until last night that we used to live so near each other. He is awfully nice.

I sip my coffee and recollect Jack's way of relieving my worry by changing the subject. I love him for that.

I haven't received any mail since I last wrote, but I am terrifically busy. My letters can be addressed to A.P.O. 709. Got a letter from Wells not long ago. He is somewhere in France now but I have no way of locating him.

I think of you very often these days, Muz, as I always do and shall around April 15th. Know your boys' love is always with you.

Your own, Jack

"Jack," I speak aloud, "I'm glad lead did not find you and that the enemy was not concerned about a billeting officer. Thank goodness you were warm and safe in some kind person's home and able to rest. I wish your brother had had a similar opportunity—or any opportunity."

This is no time for tears. Margaret and Eva are on their way, a good excuse to put away the box—fold the flaps and slide it back into the closet for someone else to find. I've lived through so much—ocean liners sinking, war, now embroiled in a second major war, and so much loss. Let someone else discover the heartache. And yet these letters are from my cherished sons, and every word brings them to me warm and alive and bravely answering a call to duty.

As the daughter of a Unitarian minister, I rely on Bible verses for consolation, and I recall in Corinthians Paul wrote as children of God we experience "dying, and yet we live on; beaten, and yet not killed; sorrowful, yet always rejoicing." Why I continue to live on is a mystery when so many times I wanted to die when those I love died. A verse in Psalms says joy is found on the other side of suffering. I found pleasant moments with Chess, although I don't know if I can call those years joyful. But perhaps I think about myself too much. It's time to think about today. There is much to be done before Eva and Margaret arrive.

I finish my coffee and the blueberries and put the cream back in the icebox. The clippers have always been in a drawer of the entryway cabinet, and I find them there. A pair of old garden gloves is with them, and I slip them on. I'm the appointed gardener, and the glove fingers are curved to my fingers. Margaret was always busy with the children, and Thayer's wife Virginia claims she has no green thumb and is bound to put a hex on anything growing in soil. So the gardens, such as they are, depend on me. I don't mind. Working with living things, nurturing the bushes and perennials, lifts my mood.

Outside, high clouds unfurl like gauze across the sky. Most of the lilacs have gone by, but the peonies are just coming into bloom. Their scent is exquisite. White blossoms as big as my hand show a thin strip of red at the center. It must be the fertilizer I spread around them late last summer. My heart rejoices to know nature is coming back to life, proof that death is not permanent. I clip several peony blossoms, spikes of rhododendron, and several false indigo that are about to bloom. Some of the lower boughs on the evergreen bushes are brown and brittle, and I snip those and pile them aside. Clematis is growing on the arbor, but I don't touch those delicate vines and let them put on their white and purple show.

While I work, I think about the letter from my sweet Jack around the anniversary of the *Titanic* disaster. When you lose a father, the date of that loss is a black square on a calendar. Thirty-one years ago, I fell into a waking sleep. My senses were so dulled that at a restaurant I couldn't hear the waiter ask what I wanted to order. Words on the menu had no meaning. I walked the streets of Manhattan not knowing or caring where I was or where I was going. Or why. The clop-clop of horse hooves, whir of trolley wheels on metal tracks, and stutter of car engines all merged into a grating racket. Time was frozen in a single moment of icy horror I tried with every cell in my body to undo. A horror that would be forever part of me.

A line from the Gilgamesh Epic comes back to me. After the death of a loved one, it said, "You will be left alone, unable to understand / In a world where nothing lives anymore / As you thought it did." The world changed for me in April 1912, changed again in June 1918 and twice more when Jack and Chess died. What is the line in Ecclesiastes? *There is a time to be born and a time to die, a time to kill and a time to heal.* My memory is woeful. Something about breaking down, weeping and mourning but also a time to laugh and to dance. I have not laughed much in the past years and no dancing since the last night aboard *Titanic.* What a glorious night that was. An absolutely glorious night.

Am I smiling? Yes, smiling at the sunrise, at the fragrance of these flowers, at the memory of the hours before everything turned to darkness.

Some familiar music interrupts my thoughts. A Chopin etude wafting from a house across the road, one I played on the piano in the Manhattan brownstone, Wells next to me on the bench, watching my hands. Within days he was playing the etude from memory. And another, and another after that. He played by ear until he started reading music, played for the delight of his fingertips moving as if by magic over the keys.

With an armload of flowers and greens, I mosey back to the house. My granddaughter is coming, and I have much to be thankful for.

The old vase awaits the flowers and I arrange them, saving some for another vase from a flower delivery years ago. One arrangement sits on the entry cabinet as a welcome and the other brings the dining table to life. I'm fond of the antique oak table, its lyre-shaped legs carved with leaf designs that look like ancient stone carvings. It's French, I think, although I don't know the provenance. Probably owned at one time by a sea captain and purchased from a shop here in York Harbor, or so I'd like to imagine.

With a few flowers left, I stick them into two glasses for the room where Margaret and Eva will stay. If I had time, I might fill the house with flowers. But, then, I don't want the rooms to look funereal. I've had enough of funerals.

I check the clock — almost ten. Still plenty of time to get to the market and back before they arrive.

6

Eva

While I await my guests, I think about Margaret. Where sometimes I am awkward and flounder for words, she seems always to know the right thing to say even in the most trying of circumstances. When Chess was ill, she sent a bouquet of asters and a card with a Bible verse from the chapter of Peter that went something like, "The God of Grace, after you have suffered a little while, will Himself restore you and make you strong, firm, and straight." This even after her own husband, my son Jack, suffered a deadly stroke while Chess barely clung to life. Within a month, both Margaret and I were widows, she for the first time, I for the second. Jack was not yet forty years old when he died suddenly, as if slamming a door behind him, while Chess lingered for months. I admit Margaret bore her loss better than I did mine.

Where does a woman turn when she is left alone? After Bradley died, I reached for my boys. For many years, our *Titanic* steward Andrew Cunningham visited me when his liner sailed into New York Harbor. I was always glad to see him. He reminded me of bittersweet days when he and Bradley made a connection through their Scottish roots. In the years immediately after the disaster, Andrew brought gifts for the boys—a book his own son Sandy liked, a wind-up toy, and candies. After Wells died, he brought flowers. Dear Andrew, how he helped me in those awful days on the *Carpathia*, helped us to the captain's quarters, helped me to Bert's car the rainy night we finally docked in New York. Bert peppered Andrew with questions as he stood in a stranger's shoes with rain pelting him. How lucky he was to survive, to swim from the sinking ship to our woeful and overburdened lifeboat. By 1930, after decades of stewarding for passengers who had more wealth than he could imagine, he spoke of giving up the work. He had not gotten rich, but sometimes wealth is measured in a cup of hot tea on a cold evening when heartache is so great it is inexpressible and nearly unsurvivable.

Andrew is gone now, another loss. He once told me we have only to do our best in life, to follow the ball on the soggy part of the field as well as on the ground that is firm underfoot. But sometimes, Andrew, it's better to wait for the sun to come out and dry up the field. The sun always comes out eventually, does it not?

After Chess died, I went inward, to the memory of school days, my sister going off to college. I have no regrets about Papa using the college fund for Elena. I wouldn't have met Bradley if I'd gone. How we sparred, joking, me letting him have the upper hand. Then our wedding, our home in Boston, Bradley's friend Bert Marckwald, Jack's birth, then Wells and the move to Manhattan, Thayer coming along a few years later. Then the ship, the liner, its opulence — its storied foundering.

Margaret, with three young children, cast her eyes toward Oliver. Or as a widower himself, he sought her out and they made a connection through their mutual grief.

These thoughts fly through my mind between the time Margaret stops the car in front of the house and the moment Eva tears out and up the walk to the front door where I meet her with open arms.

"Danny!" she blurts, "We're finally here!"

As a toddler, her older brother Bradley, who pronounced his own name as Bally, had trouble with "Granny" and called me Danny. Since then, I've been Danny to all three of my grandchildren. I prefer Danny anyway. The name makes me feel younger.

"Finally," I echo. I avoid saying "at last" as the word has a dismal note of finality. I want beginnings every time I see my granddaughter.

"There's so much to tell you," she says.

Behind her, Margaret struggles to get a suitcase from the trunk of the car.

"Shall we help your mother before you tell me?"

"Oh, posh—poor Mum."

Margaret always looks put together, even after a long drive, not an extra ounce to her slender frame. Who would know she has given birth to a trio of children? As usual, her dress is of the latest fashion, but she could wear a flour sack and make it look good. Hair perfectly coifed, she looks years younger than her early forties and wears just enough makeup to bring a blush to her cheeks and lips, though I've seen her here on Maine mornings when she was beguiling without any makeup at all.

Together we extract the suitcase from the car. Such a cumbersome bag for one overnight. How long do they plan to stay, I wonder?

"I'm sorry about the weight," Margaret says as we drag the luggage into the house. "Eva is a fashion maven these days. It may be her calling."

I'm confused. "It's a warm spring. She shouldn't need more than a bathing costume and a robe for the beach—although the water is still quite chilly." Or maybe they have put their clothes together into a single bag—still too much for one overnight. And what is the favor to be asked of me?

Margaret ignores my comment. "You've opened the house nicely." She looks around the parlor then bends to catch the scent of peonies in the glass vase. "It's just as I remember."

I smile at what she's probably forgotten. "Except for the houseful of children dashing in and out, laughter, chatter, drinks being poured, talk of tides and sails, brightwork and wind directions, the possibility of rain."

"That was all part of the fun." She opens the door to the terrace and takes a deep breath. "Oh, I do love the fresh smell of the ocean."

"You have the ocean at your house in Bermuda, don't you?" I can't help myself.

"It's not the same. Bermuda scents are saccharine—honeysuckle, pineapple, and guava. Then there are the horrid whiffs of rotting seaweed." She gives me a stiff smile. "One must take the bad with the good, I suppose."

"I like Bermuda," Eva says, "except for that smell." She wrinkles her nose.

"Maine has seaweed, too, but usually the tide washes it out to sea," I say.

It's getting on to late afternoon, and I rub my arms to warm them.

Margaret notices. "We should go back inside."

She wanders to the mantel and picks up a silver frame with a photograph of Jack in his uniform and Thayer wearing a suit. I'm between them. I don't recall the occasion, but Jack must have been home from France and Thayer had not yet entered military duty.

"This was taken before I met Jack," Margaret says. "While he was in France, he was writing to some girl—Sue, I think her name was." I note the change in her voice—a hint of sadness. "Things happened so fast in those days. Somehow he lost touch with her." She gave a hint of a nod to the photo before replacing it on the mantel. "Lucky for me."

"That's my father?" Eva puts her nose close to the photo. "I like the way he looks in a uniform. But I've read the Great War was beastly."

Beastly is a mild word for what happened in France. Now those years have been reduced to numbers—ten million dead, tens of thousands succumbed to the Spanish flu, a contagion that gripped the trenches. When a soldier came down with the fever, he was pulled out and replaced with a fresh recruit. Sixty thousand Americans killed in action, one of them my middle son. My Wells Bradley Cumings. How many mothers wept with me?

Eva changes the subject. "What shall we do now, Danny?"

I've asked myself that question so many times. What shall a woman do who has lost sons and husbands? Eva pulls me away from anything to do with war.

"Maybe you could help me with supper," I say.

"Oh, we needn't bother with that, need we, Mum?"

Margaret says, "I've made a reservation for us at the Reading Room. I haven't been there in years."

The Reading Room, a deceptively understated name for a private club, perches on a bluff overlooking the rocky coastline and harbor below. I believe the architecture is called English picturesque, a curving mansion that looks out to a serene and breathtaking landscape. Bradley and I attended lectures and parties there, and at least once or twice when we were in Maine we had dinner in the dining room. Chess and I dined there several years ago.

"I'm not sure I have the right dress for the Reading Room," I say.

"Oh, I have dozens of dresses," Eva blurts. "You may borrow one of mine."

I can't hold myself back from asking, "Why have you so many clothes at the seashore, my darling?"

Eva looks at her mother. Margaret clears her throat.

"Oliver is being reassigned to Guatemala City, and I've got to set up the house there. Joanie will come with us, but Bally is doing his basic training in Virginia, and Eva refuses to go. She says she'd rather stay with you for a few weeks." She turns toward Eva then back to me. "We hope you'll agree."

My mind is twirling. What do I do with a precocious teenager? And how many weeks are "a few"? Eva would have to occupy herself here in Maine before we return to New York. It will be easier to keep her busy there. Certainly the arrangement could work out—even be rather fun. And some youthful exuberance may be just what I need.

But before I can speak, Eva says, "I'll be going away for my last year of school at the end of summer, so I'll only be a bother for a little while."

"Young lady—you a bother? I can't imagine you ever being a bother." I pull back my shoulders and take a breath. "Of course you'll stay with me. I'd enjoy your company."

Margaret pats her hair as if a strand is out of place. A strand is never out of place. "Good. Get dressed for dinner, then. It will be my treat and absolutely no arguing about it."

When we arrive at the Reading Room, I realize I'm quite hungry. Margaret orders a bottle of chardonnay.

"Half a glass for the young lady," she tells the server. In Europe children as young as twelve have a smidgen of wine with dinner. The French believe wine is healthy. When I ask for ice, the server doesn't blink. At the menu prices, he knows not to act shocked.

Our table is by the wide windows opening to the gentle whisper of surf creeping onto a slice of beach. When I pull a shawl around my shoulders, our server notices and begins to close the windows. Ever since the night in the lifeboat, a chill has been with me. I had taken off my coat to cover my steward, wet from swimming in the frigid water. Yet I felt no cold then. It wasn't until the next day aboard Carpathia when there was no sign of Bradley—that's when the cold clutched me. Clutches me still.

I ask the server to leave the windows open. I want to breathe in as much of Maine as I can during my short time in York Harbor.

He brings the wine and a glass of ice. After he pours, I spoon ice cubes into my goblet, and we lift our glasses to each other. Being with these two women, both of whom I hold dear, is reason for good cheer.

When the server inquires if we're ready to order, I haven't looked at the menu, but I don't need to. I ask for my usual starter, a cup of the lobster bisque and the farmer's greens. Eva doesn't hesitate to request the scallop entrée, and Margaret chooses the cod. Hearty appetites for these young women.

While we wait for our dinners, I pose a question to Eva. "Let's see—how old are you now, young lady?"

"I'll be seventeen next month." She scrunches her nose. "Doesn't that sound old?"

I'm not in the least offended. Half a century ago when I was her age seems like only months.

"In some ways, yes, seventeen is a millennium. But tell me—what adventures have you had in so many years?"

"You knew Daddy took us to live in Paris, didn't you?" Eva says.

"Yes, I received a few letters from your father."

"I'm sorry we didn't write more," Margaret says. "The children kept us busy. Eva was nine then, and Joanie just a toddler."

"Daddy loved Paris so much," Eva says. "I studied at College des Abeilles while we were there. We raised bees and collected their honey. Did you know they are the most important insect in the world?"

"I suppose they are. Our farms rely on them for pollination." I add, "What other exciting things have you been up to?" I'm hoping she won't mention her father's death.

She taps a finger on her chin and raises her face toward the ceiling. Then she lands on an idea.

"Have I told you I went to the birthday party of a movie star?"

"A real movie star?"

Margaret interjects. "A child star. Oliver set it up shortly after we married. The Temple family have a house in Bermuda and Oliver thought Eva would enjoy meeting their daughter Shirley."

"Shirley is two years younger than I am," Eva says. "That's an eternity, you know."

I hold in a laugh. "An eternity, no doubt."

"Her gifts were dolls and dresses—as if she didn't have enough of them already."

"I can imagine." I'm enjoying the conversation even though I can't at all imagine. "Have you seen any of her movies?"

Margaret again. "We've been preoccupied."

"Her latest was *The Little Princess* about the Boer war." Eva looks at her mother. "I haven't told Mum, but we watched the movie at the party. The Boers were South African farmers who wanted independence from England, so the English had to fight them. It was all about gold in South Africa, you know."

I have a memory of the Boer war, although I didn't know much about it at the time. As Bradley would say, there are many reasons for war, gold being simply one of them. But I'm impressed with all Eva knows about the Boer situation.

"Did you like the movie?"

"It was all right." She lifts her brows. "Overly dramatic, if you ask me."

"Of course." I raise my napkin to my mouth to hide a smile. My granddaughter is mature for her age. Time is an irreversible sequence of events and experiences. It seems for every moment of pleasure there have been hours, days, even years of conflict. I'm glad not to relive those desperately unhappy times. I don't wish Eva heartbreak, but life has its balance. There will always be adversity, and adversity will make her strong, as it has done for me. The key is to stay tender and not build a hard shell of protection. We're not rid of challenging times, but with Eva I can look toward the future.

7

House Full of Rooms

I'm up and making coffee the next morning when Margaret comes from the bedroom.

"I have to get back to New York," she says.

"Coffee first?"

"Yes, thank you. I'd like to say goodbye to Eva, but she'll probably sleep a while longer."

I pour her a cup. She declines cream and drinks her coffee black. Probably one reason for her trim figure. We sit in the kitchen so as not to wake Eva.

She turns her cup around on the saucer as if she's deep in thought. "Did I ever tell you how Jack died?"

"An aneurism, I think the doctor said." I set down my cup. "Bleeding around the brain, but I don't know what might have caused it."

"You may have noticed," Margaret says, "he had sores on his neck and arms."

"I wondered about the sores but didn't mention it. I thought he was taking care of them."

"It was a type of cancer. That's what caused the aneurism."

"Cancer? From what?"

"Although he didn't talk about it, I know he was on the front lines much of the time. There was mustard gas. That could have caused the cancer, the slow-growing kind."

The war, then, took both my sons.

I have to turn away, wash my coffee cup in the sink. "I hope he didn't suffer."

"The sores were irritating but in the end, no, he didn't suffer." Margaret takes a handkerchief from her purse and dabs at her nose. "Mrs. Swain, I loved him. I want you to know that." Our eyes find each other. "I loved him deeply in a way I could never love another."

I know what she's saying. There is love and there is gratitude. Gratitude and companionship. They go hand in hand.

"Margaret, a writer wisely wrote there is no need for love but to love more. I know you adored Jack. You adore your three children, too. Give yourself permission to love Oliver. No one, especially not I, will fault you for that."

In an uncharacteristic gesture, she stands and puts her arms around me. I feel her tremble and embrace her back.

"I've left a note by Eva's bed," she says. "I'll call and write. Enjoy each other. She's really an exceptional girl."

"I have no doubt about that."

After Margaret leaves, I have another cup of coffee while I wait for Eva to wake up and think about my conversation with her mother. Years ago—I believe I was not yet eighteen, I read a story in *Scribner's Magazine* by the writer Edith Wharton. As I recall, the title was "The Fulness of Life" in which she says a woman's nature is like a house full of rooms. In the outer room, we host friends for tea and talk in pleasantries. In a more intimate room we encounter family and our closest friends. I believe Chess was content in my most exterior rooms, but I was content, too, with his understated brilliance, his boyish sincerity. He had no ambition to see me for anything other than what I offered to him—an amicable companion, a welcoming bedmate, an independent woman who made no demands on him.

Love is different when we are in our twenties as opposed to our forties. In our early years, we are impulsive, passionate, in a rush to find ourselves. By forty, we have learned patience, maturity, acceptance. We know who we are and, if we're lucky, we have found a sort of contentment—not settling for less than we deserve, but more likely to make our own way in a sure and well-marked direction. More slowly than in our youth, perhaps, but also more cognizant, more observant. And more grateful for each sunrise, each glistening of dew on a grassy field, and grateful even for the skin and bone and muscle that hold us upright and walk us forward.

Wharton writes about other rooms, too, rooms whose doors are shut and no one bothers to turn the knob—if they can even find their way to these closed-up rooms. The innermost room is where the soul sits alone, waiting for a footstep that never comes. When Bradley promised his soul would seek me out, I waited nearly three decades for him to find me. He knew the way to my interior chambers, but he may not have dared enter. Lately, though, I sense his phantom knock, and I wait to hear his footstep. Maybe the letters are the footsteps of my sons coming through the ink.

I wash Margaret's cup and set it in the rack before I go to the parlor. Eva startles me.

"I didn't hear you get up," I say. She is sitting on the floor in front of the box, her fingers combing through the envelopes.

"These are from my father." She doesn't look up.

"Yes. A long time ago. I meant to put them away."

"I'm glad you didn't. Are these from when he was a soldier in the Great War?"

"Yes—a very good soldier."

She frowns, thinking. "Why didn't he ever speak of it—the war, I mean?"

"I'm afraid it was too appalling to speak of."

She picks up a few other letters. "And who wrote these?"

Where Jack's penmanship slants to the right, Wells' writing leans the other direction since he was lefthanded. Eva must take after him. Jack used to call her Lefty Lou after the lefthanded baseball player.

"Those are from your Uncle Wells."

"Have I met Wells?"

How do I tell her about Wells?

She looks at me with a question on her face. "Is anything the matter?"

I take a breath. "You can meet Wells through his writing."

"My father mentioned another brother—besides Uncle Tax. But all he said was that he had died." She lifts a thin notebook from the box. "What is this?"

I know well what it is—the journal I sent to Wells when he was at Parris Island. I haven't had the courage to read it. Maybe Eva will give me courage.

She walks her fingers over the letters. "Would you mind if I read these?"

I try to brighten. "How about breakfast first?"

After dinner last night, Margaret stopped at the market and let Eva pick out foods she likes for the week. The kitchen is now fully stocked—even two more bottles of chardonnay. Milk and orange juice for Eva. I fry several strips of bacon, and the house suddenly smells like it did years ago on a summer morning with children chattering and men readying the dinghy to row out to the boat. Thayer's newfangled toaster comes in handy for toasting bread, and I scramble eggs for us. Margaret even thought to purchase a jar of strawberry jam. With a meal in the making and spatula scraping the cast-iron frypan, I feel a lightness I haven't felt in a very long time.

We eat at the dining table, Eva with a letter under her elbow.

"This one is written April 12, 1918. It's addressed to someone named Bardie," she says. "Do I know this person?"

"You might have a vague memory of her. Your great-grandmother died when you were five."

"I recall being afraid of her. She was tall, I think—or I was very small. And she was wearing white. I thought she was an angel."

"Yes," I say. "She was an angel."

Eva goes back to Jack's letter addressed to Bardie and reads to herself. In a minute she says, "Listen to this: 'At last, after continuous rain and terrible mud for ten days, the sun is out, bringing with it flowers and buds on the trees, and also increased activity in the air and on the front.' What is the front, Danny?"

I want to tell her I have no idea, but I make a pledge to myself right then and there to be honest with her. If she wants to know about her father, I have to tell her.

"The front is where the fighting is happening. The worst of the fighting."

"Oh," is all she says. Then she reads aloud again. "Tonight I am on duty in the General's office. Have to stay awake all night at his telephone to answer calls. At present it is 2:15 A.M. I am reclining in a cozy chair before a blazing fire in a sumptuous room the General is using as an office. Outside, the guns are roaring and shaking the old chateau like a heavy person jumping up and down on weak flooring in an old rattling house."

She stops and looks across the table at me. "Doesn't he write well?"

"Yes," I agree. "Very well." Jack was my scholar. He never asked me to edit his compositions and always received exemplary marks for them.

"He mentions gas masks. They had to be able to get them on in six seconds in case gas was upon them. What sort of gas?"

Eva asks hard questions. I'm not eager to give answers, but she has a right to know.

"The German soldiers launched mustard gas at the Americans. What I've read of mustard gas is that its sulfur blisters skin and damages eyes. If inhaled, it causes choking that could cause death."

"Hence, the masks?"

"Yes. A soldier may not feel the effects immediately, but they might develop later." I don't say a soldier like her father.

I can see her thinking. "And the masks allowed soldiers to breathe through a screen that filtered out the gas?"

"That was the hope."

"My father wore one of those masks," she says.

"I trust he did."

"But his death could have had something to do with the mustard gas exposure." She looks at me, her face almost pleading.

"Effects from the gas can show up years later, yes. But no one knows for sure, my darling."

As if speaking to herself, she mumbles, "Gassing is a cowardly way to fight a war."

She folds the letter and lays it on the table. Then she takes her plate and mine to the kitchen. We don't speak for a while, and I hear her washing up in the sink. It feels important to give her time to think about what she has read.

When she returns, she says, "Would you mind if I read one more?"

"Of course. Take the next letter so they stay in order."

I wait while she goes to the box and returns to the table.

"This one doesn't have a date," she says. "It's written to 'My dear Dr. Townsend.' Who is he?"

"He was the rector of the church we attended."

"Hmmm," she hums. "My father compliments the rector's sermons and says he appreciates the rector's thoughtfulness in sending him the *Atlantic Monthly*." She cocks her head. "How in the world did the magazine get through to him?"

"I don't know how those things worked." Is it awful of me to say I'm enjoying going through the letters with Eva? At least, much more than reading them alone. Her interest in the details of her father's war business shows a high intelligence — so like him.

Her quizzical expression turns to a frown. "He says, 'At the time of writing everyone is astir about the Grande Bataille.' I know some French, but I'm not sure what that means."

"It translates to big battle. I think it means just that." I'm afraid I tempered that definition. Jack meant the bloodiest battle, the battle that caused the most deaths. The battle of Belleau Wood—where Wells was killed—was a Grande Bataille.

"'The poor old widow with whom I am billeted nearly weeps to think the Germans might reach here,'" Eva continues from the letter. "'In fact, the French people I have spoken with have sacrificed about all that is possible and are barely standing the current strain.'" She puts the letter down. "He doesn't talk about his own sacrifice in just being there to defend French territory."

I heave a sigh. "That was just like your father. He had a selfless quality—even in supporting American allies."

Eva doesn't ask to read another letter. She sniffs. "Maybe we could go for a walk on the beach now."

My heart swells for this girl—this young woman. "A walk on the beach would be delightful."

8

Wells

Directly across York Road, a wooden stairway with a railing on both sides takes us over rocks and reeds down to York Harbor beach. Under the noonday sun, the water is azure and the sand so fine it packs almost as tight as pavement, easy walking in shoes. Eva takes off her plimsolls and lets them dangle from her fingers as we meander. Huge dormered houses—all painted white—stand above a rocky ledge, their chimneys suggesting multiple fireplaces. The slender beach, even narrower at high tide, curves along a bay where the water breaks gently.

"I used to swim here every morning," I tell Eva.

"Isn't the water cold?"

"This time of year, yes, it's quite chilly."

She pads to the water, lets a wave wash over her feet, backs up, pads forward again.

"I'm going in," she says.

"Did you wear your bathing costume?"

"Oh, Danny, they're called swim suits now. And yes, I'm wearing mine."

She takes off her kimono and drops it on the sand along with her shoes. My daring granddaughter wades in as if the water is tepid. Years ago, before I had children, I would run toward the water during this very time of year and dive under without a second thought. Now I get chilblains on my skin just thinking about it. When she raises her arms above her head and arcs her lithe little body into the frosty water, I have no choice but to join her.

Under my robe, my swim suit, as she calls it, is more of a dress with a swing skirt. We women of a certain age practice modesty to hide our old skin, mine as wrinkled as crepe paper. I put on the costume after breakfast in case, like old times, I decide to go in.

We both gasp in water that must not be more than fifty degrees. I taste salt on my lips and suddenly think of Bradley wearing his tuxedo as the ship sank. The water was less than thirty degrees, a crew member had told us earlier, and the salt kept it from freezing. Andrew swam the length of a football field to my lifeboat with no complaint of the cold. Compared to that night, fifty degrees is entirely tolerable. I turn onto my back and float, the sun warming my face as my body temperature drops.

When I look toward shore, Eva is standing on the sand shivering, her kimono wrapped around her. One arm folded over her chest, the other signals to me and I hear her yelling, "Danny, come out! Danny! You'll catch your death!"

The very words I said to Bradley the night he walked home from the office in a Boston snowstorm. He didn't catch his death—Death caught him.

When I reach her, she holds my robe for me.

"I thought you'd never come out," she says. "You frightened me, Danny."

I ignore her concern. "Let's go make tea, shall we?" I say. "We need to warm up."

While we have tea at the dining table, I see Eva has taken another letter from the box.

"Shall I read you one from Wells?" she asks. "I'm eager to see what he was like."

I want Eva to know Wells, his gentle nature, not what he went through in the last weeks of his life. But Bradley said there will always be war, and she may as well understand its agonizing necessity.

"He begins his letter 'Dear Muz.' I heard Daddy call you that. It's precious."

I have one son left to address me that way and hope with all my soul Thayer outlives me.

"Wells writes it's April — the 12th or 13th, I can't tell."

Whenever I hear the April date, I shudder. It was days after the rescue before I could feel my feet again. Sometimes when I think about those hours in the lifeboat, they become numb again.

"His regiment, the 6th Marines, is about to sail for France," Eva says. "I've wanted to go to Paris again. I don't recall much from the year we lived there. I was so young. Have you been, Danny?"

I'm thinking, you wouldn't want to go to France under the circumstances Jack first went. And certainly not now with the Germans occupying Paris. But I say, "Yes, I've been a few times."

"Was it lovely when you were there?" she asks.

"It was, yes." I don't want to dwell on the details of her father's and uncle's experiences. There was nothing lovely about the war.

"He says he has learned hand-to-hand combat skills and martial arts and completes five-K and eight-K hikes at the end of each day." She looks up from the letter. "What is a K?"

"It's a metric measurement. Less than a mile, I think."

She tilts her head, questioning. "I wonder if that's before supper."

"I imagine so," I offer. "They wouldn't want to hike on full stomachs."

Eva agrees. "He also says the recruits had their photos taken in their uniforms. He writes, 'We were not permitted to smile, but I'm sending you a smile from my heart.'" She looks around the sitting room. "Did you get the photo, Danny?"

I nod toward the mantel. "You'll find it there."

She goes to the mantel and brings the frame back with the photo of Wells.

"Oh, he's so handsome," she says. "So distinguished."

"Is that the end of the letter?" I want to hear more. This business of war is easier to absorb through Eva's voice.

"No. He adds that he passed the swimming drills. Goodness—they had to swim in the ocean wearing all their gear and practice taking it off underwater."

I think of our morning dip. "Even in South Carolina, I imagine the water was cold in April."

"Oh, but he had all that equipment on. And struggling with it, he probably didn't get cold." She gives me a sympathetic look. "Don't worry, Danny. I'm sure he performed the task well."

It is too late for worrying. But I did worry then. Every minute of the day.

"He writes there will be more training once he gets to France." Her eyes skim the paper. "And you may not hear from him but he will write to you in his little leather journal." She glances at me. "You must have given him the journal."

The journal I haven't had the courage to read. Maybe Eva will help me through it—if she can bear it.

"He ends by saying 'When the time comes, I will be ready.'" She cocks her head at me. "Danny, I know he died, but he feels so alive in his letters."

She is remarkably beautiful—blonde hair curling around her high cheeks still pink from our dip in the ocean. I suppose all almost-seventeen-year-old girls are beautiful, but Eva has an essence that radiates within her. If I know anything, she has a brilliant life ahead of her.

After she folds the letter, she sits quietly studying the picture of my middle son. What I wouldn't give to hear a Chopin etude at this very moment.

9

The Cliff Walk

After lunch Eva wants to read Wells' journal, but I'm not yet up to it. Instead, I suggest we hike along the cliff walk.

"What's the cliff walk?" she asks.

"Just as it sounds," I say, "a high walk above the shore. Native Americans walked there twelve thousand years ago. You'll be hiking through history."

"Is it a long walk?"

"A mile to the end and back. A few stairs, but not steep."

"I imagine there are spectacular views," she says. "I'd love to go."

"Do you have long trousers and walking shoes? There might be wild rose thorns and poison ivy."

Her face lights up. "Oh, Danny, I brought everything."

From the size of her suitcase, I don't doubt it.

We change and cross the road to the path leading to the cliff walk. The trail is narrow, forcing us into single file. Eva hesitates, probably tentative about the terrain, and I take the lead.

We pass wild rose bushes with small pink flowers Eva stops to sniff.

"Be careful of the thorns," I tell her. "They're lethal."

She laughs. "Danny, you exaggerate."

Purple bleeding heart stems reach out to us with their dangling pink blossoms, and violas and trillium raise their white and violet heads. From below, the susurration of waves climbing onto the pebbly beach reaches us, a sound that always relaxes me. The afternoon is unusually warm for the Maine coast and when warm air settles above cold water, fog forms. The tide is coming in and I can feel mist dampening my face.

Behind me, I hear Eva's lyrical voice singing. It's a song I know well.

"'In Dublin's fair city where the girls are so pretty, I first set my eyes on sweet Molly Malone.'"

My breath catches. Bradley used to sing the song to our sons. They always joined in, their voices echoing off the rafters.

"'As she wheeled her wheelbarrow through streets broad and narrow crying, Cockles and mussels, alive, alive, oh!'"

The boys liked the chorus the best, and I join Eva now.

"'Alive alive, oh-oh, alive alive, oh-oh.'"

Suddenly I hear another voice, a masculine one. It's coming from behind us.

"'Crying, Cockles and mussels, alive, alive, oh.'"

It's Jack's voice.

Eva stops singing. When I turn around, I can see her through the fog that has rolled in, her face white with fright. I can't make out who's behind her, but his singing starts again.

"'She was a fishmonger and sure 'twas no wonder for so were her father and mother before.'"

Then the man has caught up to her, standing over her. He's Jack's height, Jack's build.

"'And they both wheeled their barrows through streets broad and narrow crying.'" He stops and says, "Come on. Sing it with me."

I can see him now—a complete stranger.

Eva hesitates, then joins him.

"'Cockles and mussels, alive, alive, oh.'"

"I've always loved that song," he says.

Eva turns sideways and allows him to pass so he's standing between us.

He has a nice face, probably the age Jack was when he died. But he isn't Jack.

"I sing this song to my daughter and she joins me on the chorus," he says. "Will you sing the chorus with me?"

And standing on the cliff walk above the beach where my boys swam, the three of us finish the chorus.

Then the man says, "Mind if I pass you? My wife and daughter are way ahead."

Both Eva and I stand stark still while he disappears into the fog.

"That was odd," she says quietly. "Daddy—"

I finish her thought. "Sang that song to you?" I want to tell her it wasn't odd at all. It was Jack coming through to her—to both of us—as Bradley came through last night. I'm old enough to believe there are no coincidences.

When we start again, I let Eva walk in front. My vision is blurry and the fog doesn't help. Neither of us speaks and we march forward in silence. I thought she might like to see the fancy houses above the cliff walk, but they're hidden in the haze.

By the end of the trail the fog has thinned and nearly dissipated as it tends to do on the coast. I suggest we take the stairs down to the beach and wait for the fog to clear. She agrees and we find a driftwood log to perch on side by side. We sit listening to the sea for a minute or two in an easy silence. I think of Margaret, Oliver, and her sister Joannie moving to Guatemala and how she may miss them.

"Eva," I say, "what do you call your stepfather?"

"That is the question of the year." She laughs. "My sister calls him Papa, but I can't bring myself to speak as if he's my father. When Mum asked him what he wanted us to call him, he said it didn't matter—whatever we wanted."

"Did you land on something?"

"At first I tried Mr. Smithson but he said anything but that— he has so much formality in his life already."

"I suppose he does." I admire Oliver's diplomatic work, but it requires a bit too much decorum for my taste.

"It seems disrespectful to call him Oliver," Eva says. "Lately I've been calling him Uncle O."

"Is he all right with that?"

"I think he cringed the first time I used it, but he didn't object." She picks up a stick and uses it to turn over a stone. An insect skitters out and darts over the beach. "He has a son, you know."

"I didn't know that."

"His name is Oliver Junior. He's twenty, I think. He's in the military—I forget which branch."

I feel my shoulders tremble. The country is in another major war, another life at stake.

After a minute of thoughtful quiet, Eva says, "It was strange, wasn't it? I mean the fellow whose voice sounded like Daddy's."

"A coincidence indeed." I let her think the meeting was accidental, but I'm convinced it was no accident.

"Daddy used to sing us lots of songs," she says.

I like talking about Jack. "What's another one?"

"Hmm." She looks out at the water, thinking. "One Christmas he surprised us with a box of clementines and presented them singing 'Oh My Darling Clementine.' A tragic song, but Daddy had a way of making fun of even the most dire situations."

"Poor Clementine, lost and gone forever," I say, even though I don't see the humor in being forever gone.

"And her shoes were size nine," Eva adds with a giggle.

"Darling Clementine had very big feet," I say. Our laughter echoes from the water.

"That was a jolly Christmas." The moment passes and Eva's face drops.

I try to get her glee back. "Do you have another song?"

She pulls her lips between her teeth. I know she's trying to be cheerful for me.

"I especially like one about Lake Pontchartrain. I don't know if I can recall it, but it goes something like—"

She starts to sing, her voice clear and bright.

"'It was on one bright March morning I bid New Orleans adieu. And I took the road to—' somewhere, 'My fortune to renew.' Sorry I don't remember all the words, but the last lines of the first stanza are about longing for the lakes of Pontchartrain."

I wish I knew the song so I could help her, but I say, "I don't recall your father going to New Orleans."

"He said the song reminded him of Paris."

I nod. "The French settled New Orleans."

"No doubt, but when he was in France, he saw a chateau. Château de Pontchartrain, he called it. Somewhere west of Versailles." She pokes at more rocks. "A noble French family had it built centuries ago."

Jack must have seen the chateau during the war. Knowing Jack, he would want to balance the dreariness of fighting by seeking out anything pleasant. In one of his letters he mentioned attending the opera in Paris when he was on leave. My dear, dear Jack.

"The first few times he sang the song, I cried at the last verse," Eva says.

"Can you sing it for me?"

"I'm not sure of the exact lyrics. Something about the man asking the Creole girl to marry him, but she's in love with someone far at sea. So he tells her fare thee well and he'll never see his bonny girl again. Although he's heartbroken, he promises to lift a glass to her health." She pauses. "That's what Daddy would do, turn his back on his heartache and get on with his life."

There was a young New York woman Jack wrote to when he was in the army. She came to visit me a few times while he was away, but I don't know if he ever saw her after the war or whether he drank to her health.

I give Eva a sympathetic look. "I suppose every person has one who got away, as they say."

"Did you? I mean, did you love someone before my grandfather?"

I want to laugh. Bradley was my first love, and he convinced me I was his—and his last.

"No. Your grandfather was the one who got away, I'm afraid."

When Eva realizes what I've said, she puts her arm around my shoulders.

"I'm so sorry," she says. "I didn't mean—"

"It was a long time ago, darling girl. No need to apologize."

Another quiet moment passes, and Eva twitches as if she wants to say something.

Finally, "Danny, you haven't spoken about the *Titanic* disaster. Will you tell me about it?"

A sigh escapes me. I've vowed never to speak of that night—and the nights that followed waiting for word of my husband. But I owe her an answer.

"When you're in the moment of a catastrophe, the mind shuts down so every cell of your body can focus on surviving. I didn't retain many details."

She looks at me, probably wanting to know how the historical event relates to her. "There must be something."

"It was cold," I start. "And dark. No moon and a billion stars so close I felt I could touch them. But they had no warmth."

"And my grandfather?"

"He was—" I don't know if I can continue. "He was brave."

When the fog lifts, we both gasp at an osprey winging directly in front of us. I'm always stunned at what large birds they are. Once, I saw an osprey and an eagle attack each other in midair above the ocean. To me, they're both majestic birds well deserving of harmony with nature. If they were at war about something as trivial as a fish, well, there are fish aplenty in this vast ocean.

10

Titanic

Eva and I finish a simple dinner and do a quick washing up.

"After supper seems as good a time as any to read more letters from my father," she says.

"Then we ought to."

I'm fatigued from the day's activities, but Eva's energy buoys me. We settle in the parlor, and I look for the next in the lineup and check the postmark.

"This is another one in April."

"You should read this one, Danny. There might be something urgent in it."

"Very well." I unfold the letter. "It's dated—"

Eva is impatient. "Dated when?"

"April 15." How could I ever forget the date? The frigid early morning when the *Titanic* went down. And with it, my true love.

"Oh." She must understand the significance of that anniversary. "But he's writing in 1918, a very different time."

Six years. Six years that felt like an eternity.

When I don't respond, she reaches out her hand. "Would you like me to read it?"

I pass her the paper, and she begins.

Dear Mother, I am thinking of you today and have said a little prayer for you and Father. I have been sent back to the rest area with five men to arrange for the storing of the General's baggage but return to the front tomorrow. I am sleeping in the General's bedroom in a chateau, a very large room with a high ceiling. It is built out from the side of a valley, very high up, and looks down the valley on three little lakes bordered with high trees with lush green leaves. The front is of white stone and four stories in height. One side has terraces going down hundreds of feet to the valley. The other side has walled gardens and big trees. I am living in such style it is hard to believe there is war here.

Eva pauses. "His description of the chateau is like being there with him. He's so, so—"

"Perceptive?"

"Yes. I wish he'd say where the chateau is. I'd love to see it someday."

I consider for a moment. "That might be possible."

"Do you think it could be Château Pontchartrain?"

"I think it very well could be. I don't suppose his letter tells the name of the chateau, though. That wouldn't have made it past the censors."

Eva continues reading.

The chateau has twenty-five bedrooms, and the salon is as large and high as Dodsworth's Ballroom with heavy pink silk drapes, comfortable chairs and lounges and huge mirrors. There is also a pool room which we have used.

"What is Dodsworth?" Eva asks.

"The Dodsworths were a prominent and wealthy English family in the early 1900s. During the Great War, the two daughters cleaned barracks and worked in a munitions factory. A film aired in theaters several years ago titled *Dodsworth*, but Jack wouldn't have seen it in 1918."

"I see," Eva says, but I can tell she's not interested in the Dodsworth daughters.

"He says, 'I am in fine health, getting good food and sleep but would like to see a little more action.' Fighting, I guess he means. It sounds as if he's bored. Imagine wanting more action in the middle of a war."

"From a mother's point of view, I'd rather he be bored."

"Listen to how he ends the letter," she says. "'I love you many, many more times than I can tell in a letter. Your own, Jack.'" She gives me a sympathetic look. "It was sweet of him to think of you on the occasion of—"

I finish her sentence. "His father's death."

For the second time today, Eva's eyes brim with tears. "I know how he felt." Her voice trembles. "But he wanted me to be strong for Mum. And I'll be strong for you, Danny."

"I know you're strong, Eva. But you should realize when one we love dies, that person is so much a part of us that we die a sort of death, too. You have a responsibility to live for them, just as I do."

She wipes her cheeks with her fingertips. "Danny, where do you think Wells is at the time of this letter?"

A good question. But I don't want to alarm Eva. "Jack heard from him in April, so Wells would have landed in France and spent a few more weeks in training." I think for a second. "I don't recall getting any other letters from him."

"Then we should read his journal," Eva suggests.

I try to sound sunny. "It's getting late. What about one more from Jack tonight?" I want Jack's optimism, his good cheer. Wells' experience in the infantry would be a very different view of war.

Eva takes out the next letter, dated April 21.

"He calls you Mother in this one. Darling Mother, in fact."

I bob my head with a familiar pleasure, and she reads.

We are back at the front. I spent the night on the way up with the Colonel commanding the Advance Zone of the American Service. He treated me graciously, gave me supper, and at 9:30 P.M., his pajamas, making me very much at home. We had an interesting talk about aviation, and I learned the true status of air affairs but am not at liberty to disclose.

Eva stops and giggles. "I can picture my father wearing the Colonel's pajamas. Didn't he have pajamas of his own?"

"I suspect with as little sleep as they were getting, your father went to bed half dressed."

"Oh, that wouldn't do at all sharing a room with a superior officer." She scans his letter. "He's at the front now, Danny."

When I arrived at the front, I found ten of our men had been sent to the trenches as runners, liaison agents between various posts. The next day the Colonel sent me with ten more runners and we found ourselves in the middle of an attack. Our truck was nearly hit by shells. The truck was too big a target, so we left it and walked the rest of the way. Twice we were under gas and had to put on our masks in a half-mile field where artillery fire was underway. That is where the fun started.

Eva stops. "Fun? My father had quite a sense of humor for such a perilous situation. It's a wonder a bullet didn't hit him or that awful mustard gas didn't choke him to death."

I can't answer. My heart is in my throat, blocking my voice. I don't want her to go on, but I'm not able to stop her.

As we sprinted across the field, shells burst all around us and we fell on our bellies every five yards to avoid shrapnel. It is quite an experience listening to the scream of an approaching shell and not knowing where it is going to land.

Eva's hand goes to her neck. "Danny, he was in the middle of a battle and could have been killed, but he still makes jokes. Quite an experience? Indeed."

I want her to finish the letter—finish the letter so I can again be assured Jack made it through this awful day.

On the way back, I stopped the truck at a broken down ambulance, transferred two wounded men to our truck and rushed them to a hospital. So you see, once in a while we get away from headquarters, experience a bit of the front and take our chances.

"'Once in a while' being shot at is far too often," I say.
Eva promises, "I'm near the end of the letter."
"Thank goodness," I breathe.

I have received another batch of Literary Digests, Times, Vanity Fair, and a welcome box with stick candy. Thanks a thousand times. I got a letter from Uncle Bert Marckwald sending me encouragement. How kind of him to show such great affection for me. I am very well, surviving the end of a month of intense, cold rain and heavy clouds which finally let up a bit. Give my love to everyone, but most of all for you, dear Muz. Affectionately, Jack.

I hadn't realized the tension I was holding in my shoulders until she finished the letter. It's been decades since I read it, but even now I shudder to think what Jack went through.
"Are you sure you want to continue learning about the war, Eva?"
"Danny," she says, "of course I do."
"It might get worse. I don't know if you can stand it."
"I can stand it. This is my father. I want to learn everything."

11

Floating

After Eva and I say goodnight, I find my room chilly and recall opening a window earlier in the day to let in fresh air. I close the window and bend to the hearth. Thayer has laid kindling and paper next to a small stack of logs, anticipating I'd want a fire. Each of the bedrooms upstairs has a fireplace, the only source of heat in the 1800s when the house was built. The two maids' bedrooms are on the first floor and get heat from the enormous fireplace in the parlor. Twentieth-century humans aren't as robust as the early English and Scottish ancestors who first settled here. They were rugged farmers and fishermen whose wives kept the kitchen fires burning for making breads and stews. Coming into the house with its fragrant aromas must have been greatly welcoming.

Once the logs catch, I climb into bed under a quilt and watch light from the flickering flames dance on the walls. In summers Bradley and I used to pack the children's things and take the train to York. Then we all hopped onto a trolley that ran down York Street and let us off directly in front of the house. Getting here was part of the adventure. Bradley had wanted an automobile, but I thought that would take the fun away from the all-day journey. I wish now I had allowed him that indulgence even though we had no more space to keep a car in Manhattan than we had stable for a horse.

As I am drifting to sleep, I sense someone beside me. I put out my hand and feel nothing but cool air, as if I'm reaching into vapor.

"Bradley?"

"Yes, my love."

I'm glad to find him here. Being with Bradley was always easy, as if I belonged beside him.

"I've wanted to ask you—are you in contact with Wells?"

"Wells is at peace. Don't call to him. Don't disturb him. He has won eternal rest."

"Did he suffer horribly? I mean, at the end?"

His voice is consoling. He understands a mother's torment. "You do not need to know about that."

"Then tell me—why did you never come to me when I was with Chess?"

He's evasive. "I was there. Watching you."

"Watching me with Chess?"

"It gave me pleasure when he made love to you."

The ghost of my husband embarrasses me, yet if I were honest, whenever Chess and I made love, I had a sense Bradley was there like a voyeur in the closet.

"Chess was a good husband," I say.

"For a Midwesterner," Bradley says.

"Don't be jealous, darling."

"You know, underneath our proper Boston polish, we Brahmins are quite passionate."

"As I recall." I feel my cheeks pink again.

"You remember?"

Through the thin fabric of my nightgown I feel his cool hands on my skin, and warmth fans over me.

"I touched you here," he says, "and here."

"Our granddaughter is sleeping in the next room," I say, my breath deepening.

His voice is a whisper now. "And especially here."

Pleasure overwhelms me. Am I dreaming or is Bradley really here, loving me? When I reach my arms around him, I feel as if I'm hugging water, a barely discernable resistance.

Then, faint as a sleepy child, he says, "When you are in the ocean, I feel closest to you. Swim to me."

"Tomorrow, my love," I say. "Tomorrow."

"How did you sleep, Danny?" Eva asks in the morning.

"You must have worn me out yesterday, Eva. I slept like I was floating on a silk cloud."

"I heard you talking in your sleep."

"I sometimes do that." I feel the corners of my lips turn up.

She pours herself a glass of milk. "Shall we have a quick swim before breakfast?"

"Good idea, but after coffee." I set the percolator on the burner.

"I don't understand the affinity for coffee," Eva says. "It has such a bitter taste."

"It's ritual. Make the coffee, smell the coffee, pour the coffee into a cherished cup, swirl in cream and sip while contemplating the day ahead."

Eva laughs. "I'll allow you your coffee, but I want to read another of my father's letters while you perform your ritual."

She takes the next letter from the box and gives me the report.

"It's written April 28, 1918, and addressed to 'Darling Mother.' It's so sweet that he calls you darling."

I enjoy hearing Eva tell me about her father, her voice tinged with melancholy.

"He writes that it's quiet where he is except for an occasional rumble or shaking of the house. He must be fairly far from the fighting. The weather is pleasant and he's sleeping well but says he worries about Wells being among the Marines in the muck. Daddy never liked getting dirty. That was Daddy—always well dressed."

"I'm glad he's thinking about Wells," I say.

"And listen to this—he went to a dance at the Hospital for Refugees. An actual dance."

"The one run by the American Fund for the French Wounded, I think. It was important to support wounded soldiers." I understand the irony, though. Bradley and I were dancing the very night the ship hit the iceberg. I wouldn't wish an iceberg—or any kind of catastrophe—on anyone.

"He says he didn't dance much, but I'm surprised he danced at all. I don't recall Mum and him ever going to a dance. He says he enjoyed the music, though, and seeing and talking to American girls." Eva looks up from the letter. "Did he really admit that to his mother?"

"It was just innocent talk. He was probably in uniform and on his best behavior."

Eva raises her eyebrows. "How interesting—he says he has been riding a horse the General bought for his daughter. A vet nearly blinded the horse, and it was put in the care of the stable sergeant. The sergeant was a hunt whip at Norfolk and helped the poor animal." Eva gives me a frown. "What's a hunt whip?"

"I believe it's the member of the hunting team who keeps the dogs from straying during a chase. Don't ask me how I know that. There aren't many fields to chase foxes in Manhattan."

"Anyway, he says the horse hasn't much of a gait." She reads from the letter, 'so I guess I shall go back to my polo pony, though he is rather light for my weight. We have had some enjoyable rides through the woods here. It used to be a hunting forest and is full of paths and roads good for a long gallop.' Daddy must have been an excellent rider."

"He was with the cavalry much of the time. He and your grandfather rented horses and rode the trails of Central Park, and he played polo a few times at the country club."

"I've never ridden. Never cared about it, really."

"I'm sure during the war, horses were more useful than vehicles for reaching the battlefields. In today's war, the generals prefer aircraft bombers to horses."

Eva goes back to the page. "Daddy says his Uncle Bert sent him five hundred of his favorite cigarettes." Eva looks up at me. "I never heard him talk about Uncle Bert."

I let a few seconds go by before I say, "Bert met me at the dock after—" I can't finish.

"After you were rescued?"

I nod. "I'm indebted to Bert for so much."

"Will I have a chance to meet him?"

"When we get to New York, I'd like that. I'm sure Bert would, too."

Eva goes back to the letter. "He adds, 'I have plenty of money and am trying to save what I don't spend on my equipment.'" She flicks a quick smile at me. "He was always frugal."

"Even with his family?"

"Oh, we had nice clothes and all, but Daddy was like the giant counting his golden eggs atop Jack's beanstalk."

"So like his father," I say.

I put my cup and Eva's milk glass in the sink and turn to her. "Now, how about that swim?"

Eva goes in first, takes a quick dip and wades back to the shore. She is lissome with the grace of her mother.

"Your turn, Danny," she says.

"Has the water warmed up since yesterday?"

Eva lets go a gurgling laugh. "Not a bit."

The shore slopes off slowly, and I run through soft surf creeping its way over the sand, first up to my ankles, then my knees. When I reach waist-deep water, I fall forward. Immediately I feel myself being pulled in deeper until I can no longer touch bottom. Is it an undertow? A riptide?

I start to flail and splash but make no progress.

Bradley—I can't go. Not just yet. Eva is on the beach watching.

I am not a strong swimmer, but I was taught to stroke parallel to the shore when I'm in a riptide. Eva walks along the sand waving her arms. She's calling me to come in from the cold water but I drop below the surface. Eons ago during swimming lessons the instructor said if you find yourself underwater and lose your sense of what's up and what's down, blow a bubble and follow it. Bubbles always seek the surface.

Just as my head bobs up and I gasp for air, I see Eva run into the water, knees high. I swim a few yards until my feet find the bottom.

She reaches me and in a panicked voice asks, "What happened?"

"I don't know." I wipe seawater from my cheeks.

"Are you crying?"

"I—don't know."

"Goodness," she says. "What a fright. Let's go to the house and change. I'd like to walk to the drugstore. Mum says there's a soda fountain that will serve us bacon and eggs. I'm starving."

It's nearly a mile to the drugstore, and we take the road along the river.

"In days past," I tell Eva, "schooners anchored in York River. You might still see one while you're here. The old wooden ships are mostly for tourists now."

"That would be nice." She sounds distracted and I wonder if she has something on her mind.

I try again. "John Hancock operated a wharf and business here. He was the first signer of the Declaration of Independence, you know."

"I know." Again, Eva is not her usual enthusiastic self.

When we come to a bench overlooking the river, I declare my age insists we stop for a rest. She agrees and I notice she has a canvas bag under her arm, a small one used for the jib of the Herreshoff sailboat we used to have. She must have found the bag in a closet.

After a minute, I ask, "Eva, is something bothering you? Are you homesick?"

"Homesick? No—I got over that years ago. I don't really have a home now with Mum and Uncle O in Guatemala."

"Then—"

"I have to tell you," she says, "after you went to bed last evening, I started reading the journal Wells wrote. I stayed up late into the night."

I have never opened the leather journal. The little book was sent to me the year after he died, along with a few of his other possessions, a sharp-shooter pin, a paybook with a few entries of monies received, a small knife. I was afraid of what I might find in those pages. Afraid, too, the book would fall apart like dry autumn leaves. Even if the journal held together, the pencil writing would probably be too faded to read.

When I can't think of what to say, Eva takes the book from the sail bag. I gasp at seeing the leather dried and cracked, the corners broken off, the edges of the pages crinkled from moisture and yellowed with age.

"Were you able to read it?" I say.

"Some of it. Much of the writing is faint or murky."

Again, I can't find words. I am glad, though, that Eva read the journal. She's braver than I am.

"Would you like to hear some of it?" she asks.

"I might be able to bear it coming from you."

"All right." She pulls out a thin sheet of paper from inside the front cover. "This is a letter he must have meant to send you."

May 1, 1918

Dearest Muz,

My 6th Marine Division is one battalion of 30,000 Marines in the Expeditionary Forces. We landed at the port of Saint-Nazaire on the east coast of France and were greeted by crowds of French people cheering as if we were heroes before we fired a single shot. For them the war has been going on for four years. Imagine four years of fearing for your country, for your homes, for your very lives. If the tables were turned and the U.S. came under attack, I hope the French would do the same for us. I can imagine the dread of these poor people, and I intend to do everything I can to help them. The week aboard ship with so many men was tiring, but I didn't get much sleep. I would like to have stayed on the coast for a while to recover from the voyage, but we came to perform our duty, and duty calls.

She turns the paper over with delicate fingers, as if she's reading an ancient text, something from *The Book of Kells*.

Immediately upon landing we were loaded into trucks forming a convoy for the long trip west. We are able to sit, which is where I am beginning this letter to you. The bed of the truck is open to the sky with tall sides so all I can see are the tops of trees and the clouds overhead. "Bed" is not the correct word because we are crowded in and able to sit but our shoulders bump against each other. I'm sorry if my writing is sloppy. I hope you can decipher it.

I stop her. "My poor Wells. He had no idea what he was getting into."

"I'm afraid it gets worse," she says. "Shall I go on?"

I hesitate for the length of a breath. "I suppose you ought to."

"All right."

We have been wearing our uniforms for a week, and under the high sun the wool itches, but no one complains. There are worse conditions to come, I fear. Tonight if we are lucky, a friendly farmer will allow us to sleep in his barn in case of rain. I do love the smell of horses and silage. If we are unlucky, we will bed down in an open field and pray for clear, starry skies.

I hope when we arrive at our destination east of Paris the captain will take this letter and post it to you. If not, I will tuck it into the journal you sent me. From then on, my messages to you will be on the pages of the little book. All my love, Wells

"He never mailed the letter." Eva looks at me for a reaction. I bite the inside of my cheek and tell myself the war—that war, at least—is over.

"The odd thing is," Eva says, "in Daddy's previous letter he writes of receiving a handsome new uniform that fits him so perfectly he had his picture taken in it. And Wells says, 'We were restricted in what we could load into our packs, but I did stuff in an extra pair of drawers. Clean braies is a pleasure I took for granted back in boarding school days. I took a lot for granted then. Muz, I swear to you I will never take any comfort or privilege for granted again.'"

She wrinkles her brow, thinking. "Danny, how can two brothers have such different experiences?"

I lower my eyes to my hands, left hand squeezing the fingers of the right.

"I wish I knew," I say. I gaze at the river, sun sparkling on the surface. Low tide uncovers a small island where cormorants and gulls sun themselves. Farther upriver salt marshes host waterfowl, crabs, mussels, and small mammals. During wars — in spite of wars — life goes on.

"What do you say we go have something to eat?" I get up and offer her my hand. Slowly Eva closes the journal and slips it into the bag.

12

Thayer

When we return to the house, Thayer calls to see how I'm getting on.

"York Harbor is not quite as exciting as New York," he says. "If you want to come back to the city before the weekend, I'll come fetch you tomorrow."

My granddaughter is curled up on the divan with the box of letters.

"Eva is here, Thayer. We'll have most of the summer to spend in the city. Besides, tomorrow is Wednesday. Come Saturday as planned."

Thayer agrees, and Eva bobs her head yes and goes back to a letter.

After I hang up, I ask her if she would like to visit a nearby art gallery this afternoon.

"I'd rather read, if you don't mind." She swings her arm over the box.

My heart aches for what she must be experiencing. Her father has come back to her through his letters and she's getting to know his younger brother.

"I can read them to myself if it disturbs you," she says.

I don't want Eva to enter the Great War alone. I'm going to have to tramp there with her, a past I barely lived through myself. But we carry bygone pains within us, and I suppose we must go back in order to find relief. Maybe we need to bring Jack and Wells to life so we can say a proper goodbye. Then, as Bradley says, let them rest.

LOUELLA BRYANT

"No," I tell her. "You must read them to me—at least the highlights." I recall some of Jack's letters are full of mundane news, his way of letting me know he's all right, even if he isn't. Jack never wanted me to worry. I wonder what he'd think about his daughter reading his thoughts so many years later.

"Good, then." She lifts a page to the light coming through the window behind her. "Here it's May 8, and Jack writes about a general he respects, someone I never heard of. Soldiers cheered him by waving their hats. Then he writes he received another letter from Wells. Only that. And Wells is somewhere in France." She looks at me with a puzzled expression. "Why doesn't he say more about what Wells told him?"

When I don't answer because I have no answer, she continues, "He hopes to keep in close touch with Wells from now on."

I try to smile, but my face is frozen. Instead I say, "Big brother is always looking out for his younger sibling." On one of his visits after the *Titanic* sank, my steward Andrew told me about the sheltering angel in a Celtic blessing. The protective angel looks over the person assigned to her, "so nothing can harm you," Andrew said. He believed he had an angel beside him the night the ship sank. I must have had one, too. If he could have reached Wells, Jack might have been the angel for his brother.

"Jack seems like someone I've never met," Eva says. "In fact, I hadn't met him in 1918 and so I feel as if I'm reading a stranger's words. That's why I'll hereafter refer to him as Jack rather than Daddy or my father."

"You will meet him six years from then, darling girl, and he will be enthralled with you." My face relaxes to recall Jack's joy at having a daughter. Eva was his forgiveness, he used to say, for every bad deed he had ever done.

"He makes it seem like the war was not so bad. In fact, he wants you to believe he's actually enjoying himself. He writes, 'Aix-les-Bains and Paris are the only cities allowed to be

     SHELTERING ANGEL OF BELLEAU WOOD

mentioned. Aix has long been a vacation destination for nobility and the wealthy. It is on Lake Bourget in eastern France with a Roman ruin, the Temple of Diana, and a château. It is also a leave camp on the way south. I must repeat that for over a month there have been no horrors of war for us, so get that out of people's heads and tear up the lying newspapers.'"

Eva crinkles her eyes. "I don't understand, Danny," she says. "Jack gives the impression they're all on vacation. He says, 'If my letters have come regularly to you, we are still where we were on April 7, a rather long time for a division to be at the front. There is very little to tell, as you can see from the American communiques. I get a lot of exercise now, ride twice a day, walk, play baseball, etc., and am feeling great. I have played and umpired several games of baseball in our leisure hours, and the weather has been exceedingly hot until today when after a spell of perfect weather, it is cold and rainy.'"

"He may not be telling the whole story," I say. "But he is an officer with the duty of seeing after generals. If he says the front is safe and even pleasant when he's tending the officers, let's be thankful."

"I think he's lying to you, Danny," Eva says. "I've read about the Great War. It was horrifying. Why would he lie? It seems so—" I see her searching for the words. "So dishonest."

I pull my lips between my teeth. "I think I know why. Do you recall his letter about being under attack at the front when he was delivering supplies? Shells exploding around him?"

"Yes—he was lucky not to be shot."

"I wrote him to please not tell me about fighting. It upset me." I feel cowardly telling Eva what I wrote in my letter, but the war came so soon after the trauma of 1912, the shrieks and moans of people in the water, our attempts to save the dying, my unbearable fright for Bradley's safety. Eva has no way of knowing what it means to hang between life and death. I hope she never does.

"So he made up a fantasy for you about baseball games and charming horseback rides and advises you not to read lies the newspapers made up?"

"I suppose he was protecting me," I say.

"Or protecting himself by imagining things more pleasant than what he was living."

She could be right on both counts.

"In spite of what Jack advised," I tell her, "of course I read the papers. I had two sons at risk, after all. Jack and I both preferred to believe the fantasy.

"It was Wells who was living the most gruesome reality." Then in a soft voice she adds, "But if you'd rather not hear his thoughts—"

"No. It's time I hear from my sons directly." I could face anything with the determination of this young woman.

"Then listen to what Wells says in the journal on the very same day as Jack's letter."

My division is now in the small town of Chateau-Thierry (I could not write you the location in a letter, but I can here, knowing you will not read it until the war is over). It is "the Front," which is where fighting is expected to happen. Our trench is three feet wide and five feet deep to protect us from enemy fire but not deep enough to stand up straight without getting our heads blown off. I have not straightened my back in what feels like days and must always duck to avoid shrapnel or a grenade. Rain has made everything muddy and my uniform is damp most of the time until rare instances when the sun comes out. If we sleep, it is on the earth itself. I think of my cot in a Parris Island tent and wish I had been more grateful for such luxury.

Some men in my company have caught a flu and have been removed to a makeshift infirmary. The rest of us are heavily fraught with the worst fears we have ever known. All the allied armies are waiting to receive the onslaught of the German troops, and the two questions in the minds of everyone are — can allied troops hold and are the American troops ready? When the American Expeditionary Forces were gathering, everything was in confusion. Our battalion has had to endure privations. By that I mean very little drinking water and even less food. We expect when things get organized, supplies will arrive more regularly.

Thinking of Wells suffering without food or water is as difficult as fretting about an enemy attack. There's a chance he could have dodged shellfire, but how would he have the strength to defend himself when he was weak with hunger? I know these are a mother's worries—even after her son is dead.

"Shall I go on?" Eva asks.

With my hand against my cheek, I force a subtle nod.

I have had several cigarettes. I coughed through the first one and thought I would throw up. But oddly, a cigarette can calm the nerves, just holding it and having a whiff of the burning tobacco. It's much more pleasant than the other odors, human, animal, gunpowder, and metal. When the order comes to put out cigarettes, we know combat is about to begin. Worse is the noise, the boom-boom-boom of the big guns that makes our trench feel as if an earthquake is shaking it or the ping of a bullet hitting a helmet or another piece of metal. A bullet entering a chest makes no noise at all unless it is the tear of fabric. But that sound is so slight it is lost in the uproar.

My own chest heaves with a sob. My heart is beating for Wells, but I don't stop Eva from reading on.

Muz, do not worry about me being afraid. I was at first excited on the march toward Chateau-Thierry the way a boy thinks fighting with toy guns in pretend wars is exciting. But when we arrived here and the rain began to fall and I could hear the big guns firing, I felt panic, like an actor waiting backstage for his cue to make his appearance. He is at first shaking with fright. But if he has practiced his lines, once he gets onstage, he knows what he has to do and his fright turns to doing the job he is trained for. In that way, once we approached the front, I remembered what I had to do and fear left me. We have good men directing us, so don't worry about me. I am doing the job I need to do for my country.

Eva stops. In a trembling voice she says, "Jack had no way of knowing what Wells was experiencing. If he had any way of communicating with him, he might have found a way reach him and pull him away from the danger"

"He couldn't have done that," I say. "He'd have been court-martialed. Wells was a private, an infantryman, a Marine. Keep reading and you might understand."

"Wells is such a dear fellow," Eva says. "Listen to what he writes next."

Muz, I think back to my days running carefree through Central Park, to mornings at the St. George's chapel, to learning Latin and geometry, neither of which do me any good here on the battlefield. I would dearly like to see my brother. Surely Jack can look me up and see where I am. But whether he can get to me is the question. I imagine he is far from the front and in a clean uniform. Jack has always been a hero to me, correcting my faults in all things except the piano. I excel him there. It would do me a world of good to have him by my side.

"Just two years apart in age, they were always together," I say. "Grade school, summer camps, boarding school, and here in York Harbor. Wells laughed at Jack's silly antics, even when they weren't funny. Whatever Jack was up to, Wells wanted to be involved. They played tennis against each other and skied together on winter breaks, Jack always winning." I take a breath. What I don't say is that when it came to war, Jack was again the winner.

"I think the journal gives a truer sense of what the war was like," Eva says. "Especially what it was like to have been barely a man and fighting for his life." She turns a page of the journal and begins to read.

"This entry is dated May 25."

Muz, we aren't always shooting and dodging shellfire. Sometimes we must brave what we call metal rain to hammer posts into the soft ground and roll out barbed wire to protect our position. The worst is the mustard gas when we have to pull masks over our heads and peer through glass eyeholes. The mask must be tight so no gas seeps in that might burn the lungs and suffocate us. Even then I feel dizzy and near suffocation. The gas lies heavy on the ground and sometimes takes an hour to dissipate. One brave man will risk taking off the mask when he thinks the air has cleared. But so far I am unscathed and have not had to fire a single shot.

"So far," Eva says. "I read in my history book about a soldier who wrote home to his mother that he had not yet been killed, but it was only a matter of time." She bores into me. "Why did you let Wells go to war, Danny?"

Her question unsettles me. "Eva, please don't blame me. I was the sole parent at that point. Wells and Jack were old enough to make their own decisions without consulting me." How many times have I asked myself what Bradley would have said, what he might have done to stop them—Wells, at least. But it's futile to rethink what has passed.

Eva is back at the journal. "Wells says he often thinks if he had stayed at Princeton, he'd be studying philosophy and the classics. He'd be sweating over papers about the ancients, like the siege of Athens and the Visigoth invasion of Rome, writing them from the safety of his desk. All the fighting would be done on the pages of books, not on the rain-soaked fields of northern France. He would be coming home for holidays and thinking about music and attending symphonies instead of squatting in a bunker, praying to all that is holy not to be hit by enemy fire."

Eva raises her head toward the window where rain drips down the glass. "Danny," she says, "he's almost nineteen and hasn't begun to live in the world other than being a student."

I swallow the lump in my throat. "A good student. A promising scholar."

"What kind of student would he have been after Belleau Wood?"

"Why don't you read another of Jack's letters," I say. "You can tell it to me after I make us a cup of tea." I need tea to settle my nerves, and I need her father's optimism.

13

Over the Top

Eva cradles a cup of tea, her blonde hair parted on the right and held back on the left with one of the many barrettes she brought. Today's clip is tortoiseshell. Her wavy locks fall to the shoulders. She has chosen a short-sleeve blouse, open at the neck, and a pair of cuffed shorts that show off her shapely legs. Inquisitive blue eyes shine with an intensity that demands honest answers. I never had such self-confidence when I was sixteen.

Now she unfolds the June 5 letter from her father. As she reads to me, I can see Jack clearly. A mother knows a son's every gesture, his tone of voice, the way he walks with a long stride or sits listening with hands resting palm-to-palm on his lap. He is a man sure of himself yet not arrogant—well, a tad arrogant perhaps because of how he rushed into maturity after his father died, a burden he bore well.

Jack types his letters on onionskin, sometimes hitting keys so hard they break through the paper. A lowercase O might be missing its middle or a period might be a tiny hole rather than an ink mark. His sentences show a composure so characteristic of him. He was my solid son, my reliable one.

Eva begins reading: "Darling Muz, there is not much news and we are not in the big drive, as the newspapers are probably saying."

"Of course," I break in. "He is not in the infantry. A lieutenant's responsibility is to serve behind the lines, and Jack was good at what he did. Thank heaven he wasn't part of the big drive."

"But," Eva says, "he mentions a raid 'over the top for prisoners.' What does that mean?"

"I believe the Germans were trying to capture enemy soldiers to use as bargaining collateral. I can't recall whether they were successful, but it must have meant the American soldiers were advancing." I know they didn't capture Wells. He might have lived if he'd been in a prison camp.

"Jack says he and some others were on the terrace overlooking the battlefield," Eva reads:

Then suddenly there were a great many flashes over the line as the artillery barrage started. It took nearly half a minute for the sound to reach us, as the wind was blowing the other way, but when it did come, it sure was some noise. This continuous flashing and steady banging – just as steady as I am pounding this machine, and I can go pretty fast now – kept up for a solid hour. It certainly was perfection in artillery barrage. At this time I cannot know the outcome of the infantry side of it.

She pauses. "He makes it sound as if he was watching Independence Day fireworks."

"I wish he could say where he is or let us know where Wells might be."

Eva frowns at the letter. "He seems to be saying observation airplanes fly over the field and then drop messages or signals to the men on the ground."

"That would be the De Havilland DH-4 aircraft, as I recall. They were British biplanes used for observation and artillery spotting. Jack said he was grateful for them."

She looks up for a moment. "I guess Jack telephoned the superior officers when he got a message. They stayed clear of most of the actual fighting."

I agree with her and add, "Majors and generals were older men with more experience in warfare. They were the brains of the military strategy and couldn't risk being wounded."

"After the attack," Eva says, "Jack is offered a staff officer's Ford vehicle and drives to a small town nearby for a concert. He says, 'There were twenty drummers, twenty blarious (large bugles), and the regular band of thirty pieces. It is perfectly melodious music.'"

Eva wrinkles her nose. "Sounds dreadfully loud, if you ask me."

Her reaction makes me laugh. "Military music," I say. "It probably sounded like a Sousa march with drums. Appropriate for the time."

"How is it that one minute he's watching men killing other men in war and the next minute he's driving a car to a concert?"

"We can't know what the circumstances were like," I tell her. "And we don't know what his orders were. I'm sure the superior officers were concerned about keeping morale up."

"Anyway," Eva says, "he advises that you not think for a minute he is being subjected to the 'terrific onslaught of the *sale Bouches*.' Doesn't *sale* mean dirty in French?"

I know it's a derogatory term for the German army, but I tell her, "It's an expression the French had for the Germans. There was a lot of name-calling during the war. The Germans called the American soldiers *teufel hunden* — devil dogs because of their highly trained fighting ability."

"*Teufel hunden*?" Eva asks.

"They were vicious wild dogs in Bavarian folklore."

For a minute Eva studies the photographs on the mantel. "I suppose thinking of the enemy as dirty, vicious animals takes away their humanity and makes it easier to kill them."

I hate the word "kill" coming from her lips. When men wage war, do they think about how the violence affects children, the psychological impact on them? I think not. But for both of us, I need to change the subject.

"Would you like more tea?"

Eva shakes her head no. "I haven't told you how Jack's letter ends."

I sigh. She is so persistent. "All right."

"Before he signs off, he says 'We are resigned to a long war.' But, Danny, wasn't the war nearly over by autumn of 1918?"

"Nearly, yes." There is more to say, but I want to protect her from the appalling details of those last battles. If she keeps reading Wells' journal, she may find out for herself.

"There is a poem," I tell her, "a famous one by Alfred, Lord Tennyson—I'm sure you know the one I mean. If I recall, one stanza goes, 'Theirs not to make reply, Theirs not to reason why, Theirs but to do and die.' Unfortunately, such is the way of war, the way war has always been since the beginning of time."

She uncurls her legs from the divan and goes to the mantel. "I know the poem," she says. "But here we are in another war just two decades later."

She picks up the photograph of Jack and Thayer with me, the same one her mother studied. The three of us are perched on a railing, a bay behind us. It was taken here in York. Missing is my middle son, my sweet Wells who will remain forever in French soil. At least for him the fighting is over.

"The U.S. and Britain are planning to bomb German submarine yards and aircraft factories any day," Eva says. "Imagine the mess. The Germans could well bomb the U.S. in revenge."

"Who told you that, Eva?"

"Oliver. As a diplomat, he has to know everything going on in the world. At least he hasn't been assigned to a country in Europe. All the consulates there must have been shut down by now." She replaces the photograph on the mantel. "I wouldn't want Mum in harm's way."

More violence. More young men dying. "I wouldn't want any of you in harm's way," I say.

Eva turns to me. I'm thinking she has another unanswerable question that delves to the heart of human motivation, but she says, "I'm rather hungry. Do you think we could have something to eat?"

14

Spanish Influenza

"Jack is in the hospital," Eva says.

I feel my brow furrow. "What do you mean?" It's Thursday morning and she is slurping a bowl of cereal. She says she prefers cereal over scrambled eggs and bacon, which make her feel f-a-t. She spells the word as if it's too vile to speak. Slim as she is at sixteen, she's already watching her waistline.

"His letter of June 23 says he has Spanish Influenza. It's not serious, he says, and lots of other fellows are in the hospital with him." Another spoonful of cereal. "He must have gotten the flu at the Corps School where he's studying—" The letter is at her elbow and she hesitates, checking the exact terms. "Stokes Trench Mortars and 37-guns. He says he likes learning about the artillery."

I bring my coffee and a slice of toast to the table and sit with her. I see now she has several unfolded letters beside her bowl.

"What's today's date?" I ask.

"I'm not sure."

I get up and open the front door. On the step outside is *The York Weekly*, which arrives every Wednesday. The masthead reads June 23.

When I show the paper to Eva, she says, "How odd."

If Jack was down with the Spanish flu, he must have been having aches, a sore throat, chest pains, a cough. If he hadn't been treated, the flu could have led to shortness of breath, pneumonia, and death. It was probably remnants of Spanish flu that took Chess. I waited too long to get him to a hospital but as an officer, Jack would have been hospitalized immediately. It wasn't the flu that killed Jack.

Today's date marks the beginning of the final battle of Belleau Wood—the last battle for my dear Wells.

"Oh," Eva says, "Jack gives the address for Wells and says he has heard from him and Wells is all right and still in training."

I don't contradict, but I know Jack is telling another lie. Either that or the mail was woefully slow. Wells had been fighting in the trenches since the first of June—three weeks by the time of Jack's letter.

"Jack was in the Corps school for an entire month," Eva says, "which he considers a privilege."

"There weren't many privileges during the war," I offer.

"Here's his schedule: Up at 6:15, breakfast at 7:00, then physical games, which he says are 'very amusing.' From 9:00 to 11:00 they drill with rifles. At noon they have lunch and from 1:30 to 5:00 they drill again and sit for lectures. Supper is at 6:00 and a study period from 7:00 to 9:00. Later the YMCA officers' club shows movies and vaudeville acts. Different officers play piano during the movies and the men sing and whistle." Eva snorts a little laugh. "He says, 'They have volleyball courts, a Victrola, magazines, and some cushioned Morris chairs.' The food is good and plenty of it, but rather plain. He sleeps lined up with other men on cots in big barracks but says he's snug and cozy. Goodness," she says, "even the weather is nice." She glances up from the page. "It certainly doesn't sound like wartime."

"Jack is my sunny son." I use present tense because as Bradley once said, the dead surround us and live in us. We are who we are, we live where we live, we speak the way we speak because of them. We are their hopes, their dreams, and their desires. And surely Jack is alive in this vivacious and clever young woman sitting across from me.

She has finished her cereal and pushes her bowl aside. "He mentions Sue again," she says. "Was she his sweetheart?"

A tricky question. Sue was a bright girl with, as my mother would say, a good head on her shoulders. A pretty head, too, I might add. I never heard Jack laugh as much as he did with Sue on those rare holidays when they were both in New York. Romances are difficult with both people off at boarding schools during the year and summer houses over the long break. Add a war into the mix, and there wasn't much time for romance. Love was transmitted through ink on a page, and that ink meant everything to a soldier. He lived for those perfumed envelopes sealed with a kiss. For Sue, though, the war went on too long. She met a medical student with a promising future, and that was that. We lost touch after their marriage. Jack never said whether his heart was broken. I imagine it was.

"Sue was a faithful pen pal while Jack was in France," I tell her, hoping she believes Sue was nothing more than that to him.

She slides the top page aside and reads the one under it. "Jack says he is 'destined'—what a dramatic word—to spend many months behind the lines. His commanding officer assigned him to be instructor to a new division that just arrived. He mentions 'behind the lines' again in case you might be worried." She looks at me again. Of course I was worried.

"After the Stokes Mortar class, he'll be teaching soldiers in four regiments for eight weeks," Eva reports. "He's also interpreter for French soldiers, oversees billets for officers, and is commanding officer of three-hundred men." She glances up. "He's certainly busy, isn't he?"

"I'd say so." I nibble my toast, and Eva continues.

"Major General Edwards is a particularly kind and agreeable superior, he says. Gosh—Jack is hobnobbing with generals. He's rather important, isn't he?"

"Does he say anything else about Wells?" I ask.

Eva skims the page. "Not since the last letter."

His letters are dated in July now. I know tragically well why he hasn't heard more from his younger brother.

For a moment I am unable to speak. For all his good fortune, Jack must have intercepted the angel I sent for his protection. Unfortunately, the winged seraph was not able to find her way through the fog and mustard gas to Wells.

Eva studies another letter. "This one is to Bar. That must be your mother."

"Yes. Bardie, he called her. If he wrote 'Bar,' he must be in a rush."

"He tells her he's instructing the 29th Division but they had to keep moving." She scowls at the page. "I wish he could say where he is. I'd like to follow him on a map. Anyway, he had a twenty-three-hour auto ride with just an hour of sleep. I didn't know France was so vast."

I think of traveling in France with Bradley, mostly taking the train or taxis. We didn't get very far outside Paris then. Chess had a car when he took me there on a business trip, but that was ten years later when there were more roads. Still, with an auto it wouldn't have taken so long even to travel from Calais to Marseille—unless one had to avoid artillery fire.

"He probably stayed a night somewhere, which added to the travel time," I say.

"I think you're right," Eva says. "Imagine a caravan of thirty cars to transport so many troops. He calls it a 'mixed up and tiring week.' Finally, he found himself in a rest resort for the French troops." She smiles at me, her eyebrows arched in surprise. "A rest resort? In the middle of a war?"

Her voice is thick with skepticism.

"He doesn't say where the resort is, but he mentions having a new friend he met there," Eva says, "His name is Lieutenant Charles Monnier of the French army. Jack says he has an angelic face and was born on Jersey Island off the northern coast of France. His parents are French aristocrats with a house in

Versailles. And the lieutenant has invited Jack to visit." She puts the letter down. "Oh, I'd love to see Versailles someday."

"Of course you will," I say. "Is that the end of the letter?"

"No, it goes on." She hesitates. "He tells you not to worry and that the sector is the most quiet he has seen, but Danny, isn't it strange that he speaks of walking between guns through heavy rain and mud to oversee the infantry in the awful trenches? If they're shooting these mortars and 37-guns—" She glances toward me. "What's a 37-gun?"

"I think he means 37 millimeter machine guns."

"But what are they aiming at? Certainly Jack hasn't set up targets for them."

"That is interesting." I can't say more than that because the papers said fighting had intensified. In July the allied powers were very close to defeating the German armies, but they dare not let up in showing military strength. If Jack was the single officer overseeing so many men in the trenches, I know his life was in danger. But I also know he came home without a scratch—at least not a physical one.

Eva is still pondering. "He had his picture taken with Lieutenant Monnier in front of a trench with German territory showing in the background. Wouldn't it be dangerous to be so close to the enemy?"

"If I recall, there were protests in Germany against the war and their military was weakening. Kaiser Wilhelm was growing frustrated."

"But the American military needs to keep up a strong appearance," she says. "And Jack is still writing you." She's living the experience as if it is happening now, living it with Jack. "At the end of July he goes to Paris and is staying with someone named Frank. Who is that, Danny?

"Frank Moses. He was living in Paris at the time as a military liaison. He was a good friend of your grandfather."

"How sweet."

Eva goes back to Jack's letter. "He ran into Harry Robbins in Paris."

I answer, anticipating she'd want more information on Robbins. "Harry was a Marine. He and Jack were in boarding school together."

"Jack says Harry told him Wells is most likely back from the front after some heavy fighting." Eva puts a hand to her forehead. "Oh, if that were only true." She goes back to the letter. "He finishes by saying 'I wish I were at the Maine house to enjoy the ocean.'" Eva drops her head and says, "I wish he were here, too."

I know what's coming next and even after all this time, I'm not sure I can stand it.

15

Mozart

It's Friday, our last day in Maine before Thayer arrives. After I have my coffee, Eva wants an early morning swim and suggests I watch from the shore. She's probably afraid her old grandmother will drown.

Afterward, while she changes, I wind the Victrola and put on the recording of Mozart's Sonata 11, the one Wells learned. When Eva comes down from her room, she looks at the record player.

"What is that music?" she asks.

"Mozart."

"I've heard it before." She looks positively puzzled. "Why is it so familiar?"

"It's the Turkish March, one of the most well-known pieces in classical music." I pause to let her listen. "At the time Mozart wrote it, he lived in Vienna on the cusp of the Ottoman empire. When the Ottomans failed in their attack on Vienna, they left their influence through music."

"How ironic, then," Eva says, "to play this music as we're reading about Germany invading France in 1918 and invading again today."

"The Ottomans didn't succeed and neither did the Germans in the Great War. I doubt they'll succeed this time, either."

Eva's face still shows puzzlement. "But it's more than that." She shakes her head. "Oh, well, wherever I heard the music will come to me eventually."

I take the needle from the record. "I'd like to show you a bit of York Harbor today."

Eva gazes at the box of letters and presses her lips together. I hope she won't insist on reading more of them. They positively wear me out.

"You should see Stage Neck up close. It's a short walk and a good history lesson."

Eva rolls her eyes. To please me, she says, "Of course" and dutifully slips on her plimsolls.

"Okay to wear one of these hats?" She's studying three sunhats on hooks by the front door. "I don't want to get sunburned."

"Any one you'd like." I'm trying to sound cheerful.

She chooses a wide-brimmed straw hat with a blue ribbon headband. I've never thought that one very attractive until I see it on Eva, her golden hair tucked behind her little ears.

"It's low tide," I say. "Let's go along the beach. It runs right to the point."

"All right." I hear a tiny inflection when I mention the beach and wonder if she's homesick for Bermuda and her mother.

When we fall into pace with each other, she narrows her eyes ahead and asks, "Was Stage Neck always such a pretty spot?"

"Not like it is now," I answer. "In colonial times Stage Neck was an island that got its name when fishermen built long tables—stages, they called them—to dry and salt fish for preserving. The stages were first set up in the village but people complained about the smell, so they relocated the operation to the island." I sound like a schoolteacher, but when she doesn't comment, I keep going. "Eventually someone had the idea of building a causeway across a shallow part of the river to make access easier."

"And the beach formed when the tide deposited sand against the causeway?" At least she's mildly interested.

"Precisely."

She sniffs the air. "All I smell now is the ocean."

"A fort was here during the Revolutionary War." I point to the right where a pond lies between the causeway and the river. "If we had a rowboat, we could see parts of the foundation below the water."

Eva turns toward the water and speaks as if talking to herself. "More wars. It seems the entire world measures time from war to war."

I'd like a few hours without talk of war, and I pretend not to hear her.

"In the late eighteen hundreds a developer saw income potential here. He cleared away the fishing shanties and built a posh hotel."

"That hotel on the point?" She looks toward the building, her hand shading her eyes under the brim of the hat.

"No, the first hotel was made of local wood, all four stories of it. It was here on my first visit to York Harbor. That was the late eighteen-hundreds when your grandfather and I were first married." I remember when he brought me here to spend a weekend with his parents. They were warm and welcoming people.

"What happened to the original hotel?" she asks.

"It burned completely to the ground. Fortunately, it was winter — 1916, I think — and there weren't many visitors."

Eva squints at the building. "This one is red brick."

"It was built to withstand fires and gales. The builder was like the smartest of the three pigs."

She snorts a soft laugh.

We climb out onto the rocks and watch the waves roll. I fill my lungs with the sweet air and feel my chest expand. High clouds sweep across the periwinkle sky. In June the sun is less aggressive than in mid-summer and pleasantly warming.

I glance at Eva who looks to be lost in her thoughts. Posing the typical grandmotherly question, I say, "What would you like to be in a few years—a stockbroker like your father?"

"I'm useless at math," she says.

"What do you enjoy, then?"

She thinks a moment. "I might make a good diplomat. You know, entertaining people, having parties and such, making sure everyone is happy. Like my stepfather."

"Yes—I do think you'd be good at that."

She twirls a lock of hair around a finger. "I'll be sorry to leave here."

"You can come here anytime you like."

"Could we take the letters back to New York?"

I don't want the letters in my apartment. Maine is a place for memories and nostalgia. I prefer to keep the past here where I can visit it if I feel called.

"I'll be selling my apartment soon and moving to a smaller place. I'll want as little to pack up as possible."

"Then could we finish them tonight and tomorrow morning before Uncle Tax arrives?"

Although I hate to disappoint my granddaughter, I must be firm about this.

"Let's compromise," I say. "We'll read as many letters as we care to, and we'll take Wells' journal. You can have as much time as you like reading it in New York."

She hesitates as if she's considering my offer. Finally she says, "All right," her reluctant concession.

I push myself to my feet. "The tide's coming in. We should start back."

16

Croque Monsieurs

"Eva, since it's our last evening in York Harbor, would you like to have dinner at the Reading Room? There's dancing afterward."

"Dancing?" She's sitting on the divan, the box on the coffee table in front of her. I can tell by her tone she's suspicious about any old-fashioned dancing I might suggest.

I'm at the dining table folding clothes I've just laundered so we can pack them. "It's usually the summer residents. Probably not many teenagers, but you might enjoy the music."

She considers a moment then says, "No thank you."

"Then we'll have to pull together what the English call an ice-box supper." It's a courtesy to clean out the icebox since I don't know when Thayer will stay here next. I wouldn't want anything to spoil. "Maybe just *croque monsieurs*?"

She grins. "You mean grilled ham and cheese? That sounds delicious."

Maybe she's not so dour as I thought. I suppose it's natural for teenage girls to be moody. Eva has every right to be. She misses her father and is facing major changes in her life—her final year of boarding school and her family moving across the continent.

"I hope this week hasn't been too awfully dismal for you," I say.

"*Au contraire*," she says, exercising her French lessons. "I wish we could stay longer."

"Because of the letters?" I ask.

"Not only that," she says. "I can feel my father here."

"Then you should read another of his letters."

She has one on her lap. "This one doesn't have a date." She reads ahead before she reports the contents to me. "I think Jack is placating you—again. He's at the front and in charge of all the Stokes Mortar and 37-guns in the trenches. He's doing the work of three in addition to handling new soldiers with no experience. He adds that the sector is quiet—the most quiet one he has seen. Do you believe that?"

"I wanted to believe it then, yes."

Eva continues. "Listen to this: 'The last few days have been terrifically muddy because of heavy rains and the trenches are no fun.' Yet he sleeps in a room with a bed and is not staying in a dugout. Would he leave his troops in the trenches and sleep inside somewhere? Is it possible there's no fighting after dark?"

"I don't know, darling," I say. "I have no way of knowing."

"It seems he's moving around a lot from one division to another. And he spent several days in Paris with Frank. He must have cherished his time there, which is why he had us live in Paris for an entire year." Another sigh. "I'd like to go back—that is, unless it's now to become a German city."

Eva has returned us to today's concern—the Second World War. I want to show her some optimism in these dire times. "It will take more than occupation by German troops to turn Paris into another Munich. Now, why don't you read us a page from Wells' book?"

"I'll try to find a cheerful part." She turns two pages ahead. "Here," she says.

We are moving soon to Belleau Wood near the town of Bouresches. My battalion, the 6th Marine, will be on the front lines. I don't know how much I'll be able to write you from there as the action will be fierce. You will be in my thoughts, Muz, and I trust you'll keep me in yours.

"We should think of Belleau Wood for what it was before the war and what it might be again after all these years," I tell Eva. I've finished the folding and pull out a chair to sit while I tell her what I know about how pleasant a place Belleau Wood once was. "A Parisian businessman owned the land east of Paris — several hundred acres, I think. He used the preserve for hunting with clients and friends. There was a chateau and stone shelters nestled in the woods for resting from hunting deer and game birds. Except for hunters' gunfire, it was tranquil. The Marne River flows not far away."

"Woods and a tranquil river," Eva says, "where horrible battles of the war occurred." She looks again at the journal. "I'll read you just a little more," she says.

I have been training to be a soldier since Princeton and before that at boarding school, and although I have been practicing for several years, it feels as if I was born a soldier and will die a soldier. How can there be anything else for me if more than 20% of my life has been in military drilling? I imagined becoming a concert pianist, but what if my hands are injured? What if rather than hearing music in my head all I hear are explosions of munitions, screams of pain from the wounded, death cries of horses in the line of fire, shouts of orders from sergeants and lieutenants, and curses from my fellows who regret joining this damned militia? What will become of me then? Muz, I know it hurts you to read these words, and I am sorry for that. It may well be you will never read them, never have your hands on this little notebook, and so I write the truth as I know it.

I don't want Eva to see the pain in my heart through the tears running down my cheeks. Quietly I stand and excuse myself. I go into the bathroom and hold onto the sink to keep my knees from buckling. Somehow I found strength in April 1912 during the worst disaster in maritime history, fifteen hundred dying around our lifeboat and my dear Bradley lost amidst the chaos of the greatest ship afloat slowly disappearing into the depths of the sea. If I could survive that, I can stand learning what my son endured. For his sake, I can stand it.

I wash and dry my face, and after a few minutes I go back to the parlor room and sit next to Eva on the divan. I take a deep breath and say, "Read me more."

"You're sure?" she asks.

"I'm sure."

"All right," she says and begins, "June 10, 1918."

The 6th Marine Division has arrived in Belleau Wood, and we are camped in a bunker, a roughed-out dwelling. Even in the open air we bend our backs so we don't become a target for the enemy.

Although we are being hurled into the maelstrom of war, I am well trained and ready to fight. I must admit, though, it is hard feeling as cut off as I do now from friends, my brothers, and you, Muz. It would ease me considerably to hear from you, but receiving mail here is impossible.

Muz, I'm very glad you're not here to witness what I am seeing, wounded men, men with fever, men in such fear that they have soiled their uniforms. I am holding up and being brave, but I would appreciate it if you will say a prayer for me.

When Eva puts down the paper, I take her hand. Hers is warm. Mine is ice cold.

"Wells was with the thousands of others who did the work they were bidden to do — without rest — while all I could do was wait on the other side of the world. Wait and hope."

For a moment we sit listening to the ocean whisper through an open window, her sorrow and mine between us. We women persevere through adversity and raise our heads above it in order to do what needs to be done.

I pat her hand. "Now, darling Eva, let's start packing. Your Uncle Tax will be here tomorrow, and he's never late."

"All right," she says. We both know we'll each say a prayer tonight.

17

The Second Ghost

That night I am too fatigued to make a fire, and I slip into bed and pull the covers up. Even so, sleep eludes me. I try to push from my mind the fighting at Belleau Wood. When Jack came home, he gave me details he thought I could stand—the thunder of heavy artillery, metal rubble falling like rain, shouts of anger, cries of wounded men. The ground itself shuddering from the weight of the battle.

I did stand it, but barely.

Moonlight comes through the window, casting the room in an eerie glow. In the doorway, a figure appears standing, flickering like a bulb about to burn out.

An electric charge goes through me.

"It's you, Jack, isn't it?"

No answer. He has never appeared to me before. Is it his daughter or the letters that have brought him?

"It's too soon to visit," I tell him. "I need time to stop looking for you on Cliff Walks, expecting your footfall on the front step."

His mouth opens.

"Don't speak. Speaking will keep you locked between the past and eternity."

A wail escapes his ghostly lips. The wind?

I read his heart without a word spoken. You think you failed your brother, that you should have been his protector. You might have made him wait, stay in school another year, told him the fight would be too abhorrent even for the strongest of men. Maybe, Jack. But you weren't his father. You had your own struggles. And how were you or I to know what he would face—the filth of the trenches, the terror of the assault? Wells was in a hurry to become a man, and neither of us could have stopped him. You are not to blame, and there is no shame in his death. He was victorious, and the victory set him free. For that, we must be glad.

In all Jack's years growing up, I never saw him shed a tear. Now water shines on his cheeks and his face contorts with agony.

I whisper, "It was his time, as you had yours and I will have mine. Now go, my love, and let me sleep."

That was the last I remember until morning.

When I come from the bedroom in the morning, Eva is in the kitchen pouring herself what's left of the milk.

"I had the strangest dream," she says.

"Do you want to talk about it?"

"My father was in my bedroom. He had a sweet expression on his face and stood, just looking at me. I was so touched at seeing him. I said 'Hello,' but he didn't answer." Eva looks at me with a longing I haven't seen before. "I desperately wanted to get up and hug him, but it was as if I was paralyzed. My legs and arms had turned to cement."

I don't tell her I had a similar dream—if it was a dream at all.

"What did he look like?" I ask.

"Younger than he did in the last years." She stares out the window and narrows her eyes. "And he was wearing a uniform."

A shiver shakes me. "I imagine the dream was from reading his letters."

"But it seemed so real, as if he was really there, standing in front of me. I could almost reach out and touch him. And his eyes were glistening as if he had tears in them."

I don't want to frighten her. Instead, I say, "Sometimes it's hard to tell dreams from reality. Perhaps they are our fondest wish coming to us while we're sleeping."

"But—why would he be crying?"

I can tell Eva wants to argue that her father appeared in the flesh, which even at almost seventeen she should understand is impossible. To redirect her attention, I start making coffee as I normally do. When there is a paranormal event, it's important to follow regular routines. The ghosts—if that's what they are—have no intention of harming us.

"The moon was nearly full last night, Eva. Everything looks different in moonlight."

"I suppose." She sounds disappointed.

"Are you packed?" I ask.

"Almost," she says.

"Then finish up. We still have things to do before we leave the house."

"All right." She moves slowly, taking a moment to look out at the water.

While Eva finishes packing, I take a last look around the old house. York Harbor doesn't have the magical quality for me it once did. I miss children running through the house. I miss sweeping up tracked-in sand from the floor and making piles of sandwiches for a quick lunch so they could get back to the beach. Every task had joyfulness in it. No wonder older people always look sad. So much more is behind me rather than ahead of me. At my age, every moment is fleeting.

"Anybody home?" It's Thayer, arriving earlier than expected.

"Hello, dear." I greet him at the door. "You must have left Manhattan in the middle of the night."

"Practically." He gives me a kiss on the cheek. "And where's my lovely niece?"

"She's right here." Eva is dragging her suitcase down the stairs. It's almost as large as one of the trunks I took on the first cruise to Europe, the trunks that are now at the bottom of the sea.

"Uncle Tax, it's wonderful to see you!" It's the bounciest I've seen my granddaughter since she arrived.

"You've grown." He meets her in the sitting room with a hug.

"I'll be seventeen next month."

"Impossible." He gives her a toothy smile. "We shall have to have a celebration in New York."

"Something to eat, Thayer?" I offer.

"Maybe just coffee. We can stop along the way."

While I heat coffee, I hear Eva quizzing her uncle in the other room.

"How are Aunt Ginny and the baby?"

"They're fine," he says. "Little Gay is a sweetheart. Ginny is having the apartment redecorated. Workmen come in and out all day." He grins. "I can escape to the office, at least."

"My father says you wrote him a letter in French. Is that true?" she asks.

"I can't recall. If he said so, it must be accurate. But I doubt my French was very good."

I bring the cup to where Thayer sits on the divan, Eva across from him. Luckily he takes his coffee black since we've finished both the cream and the milk.

Eva asks him a perfectly grownup question. "And how is your work at the advertising company?"

Thayer sits back on the divan, cup on his knee. "As Calvin Coolidge so smartly said, 'The business of America is business.' And advertising is what keeps business going."

"Better business than war," I offer.

"After the Great War, advertising became as American as cherry pie," Thayer says. "I'm not saying we sell snake oil, but fifty years ago when Lydia Pinkham's Vegetable Compound was supposed to cure all female ailments, it was discovered her compound was mostly just booze. We have more integrity than that now."

"What do you mean?" Eva asks.

Thayer pulls his mouth to the side. "We advertise good products and snag buyers' attention with catchy jingles."

"Like what?" She is so inquisitive—a sign of intelligence.

Thayer puts his cup on the coffee table. "Just a minute." He holds up an index finger and goes out to the car. When he returns, he has two bottles of Pepsi Cola and hands one to Eva and one to me. Then he starts singing: "Pepsi Cola hits the spot. Twelve full ounces, that's a lot. Twice as much for a nickel, too. Pepsi Cola is the drink for you." He winks at Eva and adds, "Refreshing without filling."

Eva laughs and covers her mouth with her hand. "Uncle Tax, you are so funny," she says.

"You'll have to drink those over ice," he says. "It's better that way."

It's nice to hear laughter ringing through the old house, especially after days of reading about war.

"Why don't you both enjoy your Pepsi while I load your bags into the car." He raises an eyebrow at Eva's luggage—a good word for a bag that must be lugged. "I'd better start with this one," he says. "It looks like Eva is moving in."

As we drive away, I turn for a last look at the York Harbor house. The sun is out and light reflects on the window glass. It must be my imagination, but I can make out two figures—and a wavering outline of a third—watching from a front room window.

"Wait." The word erupts from me.

Thayer steps on the brake. "Did you forget something?"

My head clears. There are no such things as ghosts—are there? It's just my desire to see three people I have loved deeply, three people who walked the earth with me for a brief time.

"No" I glance at Thayer. "Sorry, darling. Keep going."

He's a good driver, both hands on the wheel, eyes on the road. After an hour Eva folds herself on the back seat and appears to fall asleep.

"Will you be able to keep up with a teenager for an entire summer?" Thayer asks.

"Keep up?"

"I mean, think of things to occupy her. If you need help, you can send her to us for a few nights. Ginny would like the company."

"Thayer, Eva makes me feel young. I have great plans for us."

"Such as?"

I glance behind at Eva. She may be just resting her eyes and listening.

"I want her to enjoy herself. The Junior League's debutante ball is the middle of December. She'll be the perfect age. There's so much to do to get ready."

"My niece a debutante?"

"If you had been a daughter instead of a son, I'd have had you in a ball gown."

Thayer gives me a quick grimace before he brings his eyes back to the road. "Sorry to disappoint you, Muz. If you'd like me to try on a ballgown, just say the word."

I put my hand on his shoulder. "You're perfect as you are, and I couldn't love you more." When I see the corners of his lips turn up, I know all is well between us.

"Did you read the letters?" he asks.

"Some of them. Up until—"

"Until Jack learns about Wells?"

"Almost. Eva wanted to take the box to New York, but I told her we should leave it."

Thayer clears his throat but doesn't say anything.

I let a few seconds pass before I say, "Eva misses her father."

"It was a great loss for her," he says. "I miss him, too, but it gets easier, Muz."

Out the window, a Massachusetts forest stands thick and green.

"Unfortunately," I say, "his death was a great loss for all of us."

18

Chess

My apartment—or I should say Chess' apartment—is in a thirteen-story cooperative built in 1914 near East 72nd Street and the park. With mahogany floors, woodwork, and fireplace with a marble mantelpiece, the place feels like Chess—distinguished, tasteful, sturdy. Family photos—mine and Chess'—sit in silver frames on the mantel. I had my baby grand piano settled in a corner, its shiny black surface reflecting light. I rarely play it now, but I couldn't bear to let it go. Of the three bedrooms, Chess used one as an office, which I have now claimed as a den. One is for guests, and the largest is—was—ours. Without Chess, the formal dining room is rarely used, although we could seat twelve around the table. The kitchen is Rosa's domain, large enough for her to work her meal magic while Eva and I poke around for snacks. In nice weather Eva can read in the private courtyard, shaded by the surrounding buildings.

Thayer puts Eva's heavy bag down and goes back for mine. When he returns, he's holding my suitcase in one hand and his other arm is wrapped around the box. The dreaded box.

"We were meant to leave that," I tell him. "It's like inviting ghosts into the apartment."

"I thought you'd want it." He glances at Eva. "At least, my niece will want it."

"Yes," she says, "I'd love to finish reading the letters."

"And then we'll throw them into the incinerator in the basement."

Thayer frowns at me. "You'll do no such thing. They're history, Muz. They're our family history."

I want to tell him they're a history I don't care to live through again, but I concede with a roll of my eyes. "Then at least put them in the den, out of the way."

When we say goodbye, he promises to stop by and check on us. While Eva looks around the apartment, I scan the newspaper for the latest news. The Allies have launched a bombing offensive against Germany, the Air Force lost sixteen planes in the fighting, and race riots have broken out in Detroit. A trolley crashed, Toscanini is scheduled to direct a concert for women in the Armed Forces, and a postal worker stabbed his estranged wife to death. And there are a number of engagement notices and wedding announcements. I can always count on the *Times* for both good news and bad.

Within an hour of arriving, Eva says she wants to see downtown Manhattan. I've spent years exploring downtown and midtown, but it would be pleasurable to see the city through her blue eyes.

"Then let's take a taxi."

"The subway would be more of an adventure," she says.

"I've lived in New York City for more than forty years, but I still get turned around. Without taxi drivers, I might never get where I need to go."

"Then a taxi is fine," she says. "When I learn my way around the city, I'll lead you."

I have the driver take us to Washington Square. As he barrels down 5th Avenue, Eva stares out the window at people hurrying along sidewalks and buildings towering on either side of us. I hear her intake of breath when the driver swerves around other cars, in a hurry to get us where we're going so he can pick up another fare.

He lets us out in front of the Washington arch honoring the first President and the War of Independence. The sky is azure, and even on a weekday it seems everyone is out. In the square a woman pushes a baby carriage, a small band plays jazz music — saxophone, tall bass, some sort of African-looking drum. Men in fedoras and women in rayon or cotton dresses sit lined up on park benches reading newspapers.

"In the seventeen hundreds this area was called Potter's Field," I tell Eva, "where public executions were held."

"Goodness," she says, her usual response. "Why was there so much fascination with executing people? I hope there were no beheadings. So much blood to clean up."

She's wearing a dress that falls just below the knee and cinched at her narrow waist with a belt. Her blonde hair shines golden under the late June sun. I wish I had worn a sunhat to shield my old face and cover my silver hair. At Eva's age I was finished with schooling and living with my parents in Cambridge, a minister's daughter whose greatest hope was that a beau would find me at my father's Sunday homily. Luckily, one special young man bumped my elbow after the service while we chose cookies from the fellowship table. Where are you now, Bradley, my fellowship fellow?

At the Seventh Street end of the park, a crowd has gathered around an airplane. It looks to be a bomber, silver glinting in the sun.

"How in the world?" Eva says.

"Nothing in New York will surprise you," I say. "There's so much ingenuity here."

"They probably took the wings off and brought it up the river on a barge," she suggests.

"That would make sense," I offer. "You are a clever girl."

A sign by the airplane promotes buying war bonds to finance military operations in Europe, and women and men are lined up to make purchases. Eva stands transfixed by the hordes of people, voices merging with the music, the noise of traffic. She has been transported from the protective calm of Bermuda and

Maine to busyness brought by war. We each were born after one devastating war—mine the Civil War—and plunged into another. I pray she comes through this one without heartache.

After a time, Eva says, "I'd like to see Times Square."

"We should take another taxi. It's a very long walk."

Eva looks concerned about me. "If you're up to it, I'd rather have a bit of exercise after such a long drive."

I give in to my energetic granddaughter. "All right—as long as we stop for dinner along the way."

"Yes—I'm a bit hungry," she agrees.

"Let's take Sixth Avenue. You'll get a sense of the different neighborhoods. We're in Greenwich Village now. Just to the north is Chelsea which is mostly residences and art galleries."

"And shops?" she asks.

My granddaughter is predictable. "Some shops, yes." I caution her about carrying bags when we have so far to walk.

"Danny," she says, "the Cliff Walk at York Harbor was a mile each way and we managed that handily. I'll carry any bags we accumulate."

At a shoe shop she tries on a pair of Mary Janes with a peep-hole toe and likes them so much I buy them, the first bag she must carry. At another shop she finds a red beret which she says was all the rage in Paris when she was there. When she adds they remind her of her father, I insist on buying it and am glad she decides to wear it, slanted on one side the way she says Parisians wear them.

In New York one can either saunter along or be swept up with the tide of the crowd. Sixth Avenue foot traffic is somewhere in between. We follow the elevated track as a train roars overhead, and fruit vendors sell berries, oranges, bananas, and mangoes imported from the tropics. A potpourri of smells assaults us—sweet fruit scents, the metallic pong from the rails, greasy fried foods wafting from luncheonettes, exotic perfume from a gaudily dressed woman passing by us. Shops shaded with red and orange awnings entice buyers with window displays of mannequins wearing pastel outfits, and dogs strain forward pulling on leashes. All is hustle and bustle.

"I've never seen anything like Manhattan," Eva says.

When finally we near Times Square, I tell her I must have something to eat and turn two blocks west to Sardi's. Inside, I approach the maitre d' and apologize for not having a reservation. It's the dinner hour, and we'll be lucky to be seated.

"Do you have a table for two?" I ask, fingers crossed behind me.

"I'm afraid not," he says. Then he looks at Eva, entrancing in her red beret, and his face lights up. "Oh—I may have something if you don't mind eating in the bar area."

As he leads us through the dining room to a table, Eva scans the walls papered with caricatures of patrons, each in a black frame.

Once we're seated, she asks, "Who are all these sketches of?"

"Famous people. You might recognize some of them," I say. "The features are grossly exaggerated, and some stars have been a bit offended by them."

"I can see why." She studies a picture near where we're seated. "The one of Maureen O'Sullivan isn't too bad."

"She was Jane in the Tarzan movie. Did you see it?" I ask.

"No. I haven't much time for movies."

"I see. You must know of Laurence Olivier, though. Gloria Swanson is just there." I point over my shoulder. "With Ethel Barrymore."

"I've heard of them." Eva twists her head to look at more of the sketches. "I'd like to be an artist."

"No longer a diplomat?"

"A diplomat who paints," she says.

"That is entirely possible, my dear."

The server comes and takes our order. Eva asks for Sardi's signature cannelloni dish and a Pepsi Cola. Apparently she enjoyed her uncle's gift enough to have another. I'm famished after the walk and choose steak medallions and a glass of white wine—and ice. Fortunately, we're not far from Times Square where it should be easy to catch a taxi.

By evening Times Square is alive with lights, people, traffic, and music filtering out from clubs, a sensory carnival. A huge billboard advertising Camel cigarettes depicts a man smoking, actual smoke billowing from his mouth into the New York air. A Palace Theatre marquee announces a movie starring Alan Ladd.

"I'd like to see a play or even a movie," Eva says. "Would that be possible?"

"If you like." I haven't seen a show in years and hardly ever come to the theater district, but I wouldn't dream of letting Eva go without me.

There are nearly two million people on the island of Manhattan, and the streets are crowded this evening. On every corner sailors in blue or white and soldiers in field-gray mingle in groups of two or three watching the lighted billboards. They appear jovial and relaxed, not at all fearful of a future that will send them into combat. Unlike the Great War, this one is fought mostly in the sky or behind the protection of heavy equipment.

A sailor eyes Eva, then grabs her by the arm and says, "How about a kiss for a fella about to ship out to war, pretty miss?" From the wide flap of the collar at his back and the cap tilted on his head, I'm guessing he's an enlisted man.

Eva leans from him, turning her face away.

"Just one little kiss."

I step in front of her to break his clasp. "Let go of my granddaughter, sailor," I tell him. "And may heaven protect you in battle." He apologizes and moves on to have better luck with the next ingenue.

"Thank you," Eva breathes.

I had thought of showing Eva the shelter houses where for years I did charity work, but everything has changed. I might not be able to protect her from war-struck madness.

"We need to catch a taxi before the dim-out," I tell Eva. "All these lights will be turned off in case enemy planes fly over."

"How sad," Eva says. "How very tragic."

"Yes, war is tragic," I agree.

The sky, what I can see of it between skyscrapers, is heavy with clouds. When a drizzle begins to fall, I lift my arm to signal a cab.

19

Rosa

My housekeeper Rosa worked the week I was gone, and the apartment is spotless. When I called ahead to tell her I would have a guest for the summer, she supplied the kitchen with dishes from the deli we need only heat up to enjoy. She made up the guestroom where Eva will stay and placed a bouquet of flowers beside the neat bed. It's been so long since I've had guests that Rosa must be as thrilled as I am for the company.

I help Eva drag the monster suitcase into the bedroom and oversee the unpacking. Sweaters and lingerie go in drawers of the bureau. Eva hands dresses to Rosa who puts them on hangers and lines them up in the closet and arranges shoes in neat rows underneath the dresses. The wardrobe looks like a spring garden of colors.

While Eva puts her toiletries in the bathroom, Rosa goes to check the suitcase for more contents. She reaches in and lifts the old leather journal just as Eva comes back in.

"Please don't touch that," she says. "It's very delicate." She takes the book from Rosa's hand. "But thank you for your help," she adds.

After Rosa leaves for the night, I offer Eva a cup of tea. "We've had a long day. Would you rather turn in?"

"No," she says, "tea would be nice."

While I brew a pot of tea, Eva explores the apartment. I didn't have much to do with the decorating—Chess said I should leave that to the professionals. The professionals must have been men. Navy blue sofa and chairs. The rug has a gray design and the draperies are a matching gray. The den is smaller than the living area, and I find it cozier even though it, too, is done in dark blue upholstery. At least the dining room is papered in a subtle design on a white background. The apartment felt confining to me at first—almost like a cloister—but I've grown used to it. I suppose as an aging woman twice widowed, a convent is the order of the day. Eventually I bought some throw pillows in pastel colors to brighten up the sofa and chairs. Chess either didn't object or didn't notice.

I bring the tea and cups to the coffee table where Eva is reading the journal.

"Would you like to hear some of this?" She looks at me and I read concern in her face. "It's not so awful," she says.

Maybe from fatigue, I relent. "Then, yes. Please do read."

"There is no date on many of these." She takes a breath and begins.

I am eighteen years of age and have shaved my face a total of three times. After the first and second shaves, I had to wait for the nicks to heal. The sight of my own blood dripping down my chin was distressing, but the fellows said I ought to try again. By the third time, I got the hang of shaving. But now we can't waste water for such a luxury and without mirrors, I dare not bring a razor close to my skin.

"It gets better from here," Eva says with a half smile.

Muz, if you must know, I've hardly ever kissed a girl. I say hardly because there was one night at a boarding school dance with girls from the Wheeler School when a young lady agreed to accompany me up the steps of the chapel tower to the very top where we could see the lights of Newport. She let me put my hand over hers, and when I felt her cold skin, I put my arm around her. And, yes, she let me kiss her. But just once, Muz. She tasted of the fruit punch we had drunk. When the wind came up, she asked to return to the dance. I was reluctant to agree but being a gentleman, I helped her down the steps in case she tripped over the hem of her long dress. I'd have liked to kiss more girls and even marry one (if you approved). Maybe when this damned war is over I'll meet someone like my own mother, a girl with intelligence and sweetness. Maybe she will play the flute or the violin and I'll accompany her on the piano.

Eva's voice trembles as she reads the last two sentences. "Your boys all love you very much," she says.

"I believe they did." Eva doesn't mention my use of past tense.

I pour tea for us and add a dot of cream to Eva's.

"Shall I read more?" she asks.

"If it's not too disturbing. I don't need nightmares tonight."

"This one is harmless, I think." She begins again.

It's hard to believe these hands that now are calloused and blistered once held a china cup and a silver fork and pressed piano keys to make lilting melodies. Now mud cakes under my nails and when I bite them because I have no scissors, I taste grit. But here in the trenches, earth is my dearest friend. Mounds of earth shield me from rifle fire and from grenades that explode so close they leave my ears ringing.

If I make it through to July 11, I'll be nineteen. Even though that sounds young, I feel old. I don't mean as old as Jack or as old as you, but as ancient as the warriors of all the wars that came before this one. As old as the Romans who fought off the Visigoths in the 4th century. See, Muz? I retained something from that ancient history class.

Eva looks up from the journal. "His birthday is four days before mine." She sips her tea. "Danny, I'm afraid the entry gets more difficult."

"Then let's put the book aside for tonight," I tell her. "Tomorrow we'll explore more of New York. And later, if you like, you can continue reading me my son's thoughts."

In the middle of the night, I have a vision. It may be a dream but often, as Eva says, dreams and reality are indistinguishable. In the vision Wells is in his uniform, drenched with rain and bent from exhaustion. It is evening, but in the little light I see him lying in a rubble of still bodies. A Hun rises from a trench and launches a single grenade. There is an explosion. Rock, mud, and shrapnel scatter and strike my boy in his stomach. He squirms in the mud, gulping for air.

I know I'm awake now. It was a dream, the same dream I've had for the past twenty years. I tell myself I'm in New York, safe in my own home, my granddaughter in the next room. Even so, a weight bears down on me. I want to go out, breathe fresh air, but I can't rise from my bed.

In the morning I go to the kitchen expecting Eva to be up before me. When she isn't, I start to panic. Could she have gone out to look around? Not knowing the area, she might get lost—or worse.

When I peek into her room, I see she is still sleeping and relief washes over me. I may not have been able to protect Wells from war or Bradley from a sinking ship, but I will guard my granddaughter with my very life.

Rosa readied the coffee before she left last night, and I light the burner and wait for the pot to perk. In the meantime, I try to erase the dream from my mind. The odds of that battle—the battle of Belleau Wood—were overwhelmingly in Germany's favor. In school we learned that about 480 BC three hundred Spartans held back half a million Persians. At Belleau Wood, an area half the size of Central Park, the ratio of German troops to Marines was not much better. The fact that the Marines drove back the Germans was nothing short of a miracle.

When the coffee is ready, I pour myself a cup. Rosa should be here soon. How fortunate I am to have a faithful housekeeper—I detest the term maid. She was a teenager when she lived in one of the shelter houses where I volunteered. Now she supports herself and takes care of her aging employer. I'm not fond of being alone, and Rosa is more like a kind and helpful friend than a servant, another word I detest.

Rosa arrives and starts breakfast. The aroma of frying bacon must reach Eva's bedroom because she comes padding out in slippers and bathrobe. How is it the young look so appealing when they haven't yet rubbed sleep from their eyes?

"Good morning, darling," I say. "Breakfast, then what do you say about a walk through Central Park?"

Eva nods. Apparently her voice hasn't shifted into gear yet. Her first words are, "Good morning, Rosa."

It must have been the sizzling bacon.

"Breakfast in five minutes," Rosa says. "Better get dressed, Miss Eva."

Eva shuffles to her room and emerges ten minutes later wide awake and sparkling. Rosa has set the table and is bringing out the food—bacon, fried eggs, toast, and a bowl of orange sections. When I'm alone, I have just toast with butter. I can't fathom how after last night's dinner my granddaughter can be hungry, but she eats with relish. I've forgotten how teenagers have such huge appetites.

"Tell me about Central Park," she says between bites. "I want to know everything about New York."

"I admit I don't know too much," I tell her. "Before the Civil War it was swampy and rocky land with small farms and ramshackle shacks. When New Yorkers decided they needed some public greenspace, eight hundred acres of the land was cleared."

"Goodness," Eva says, a slice of crispy bacon between thumb and forefinger.

"The park was designed by a Connecticut landscape architect named Olmsted. Growing up, your father and his brothers thought it was their playground. With plenty of space to run and get dirty, they believed the park belonged to them. I suppose, in a way, it did."

"Will we have time to read more of the journal?" Eva asks.

I was hoping she had had enough of dismal war details. But it sounds like my dear Wells—and her father—have captured her heart.

"Of course," I say. "We'll make some time."

20

Central Park

I haven't strolled through the park in years. Chess and I split our time between Manhattan and our weekend house in Bedford Hills. He was too busy to take a walk that didn't lead to a golf course or a business office. Now I'm seeing the park through Eva's fresh eyes.

In fact, everything is new in these war-torn days. Open spaces on the park's grounds have been tilled for growing vegetables as part of a war-effort campaign. One sign says, "Dig for Victory." Other signs mark air-raid shelters and the air-raid precautions headquarters. I suppose there is every chance German bombers loaded with explosives will fly across the ocean, and New York will likely be a target. I take note of these shelters. And everywhere, as Dylan Thomas wrote in a poem, "the groves are blue with sailors." It was a recent poem where Thomas reflected on his childhood during the Great War decades earlier. When we live through a war, it never leaves us.

Eva and I follow a wide walking path until we near Columbus Circle. A tall and weighty memorial honors soldiers who served in the Spanish-American War in 1898, just fourteen years before the *Titanic* sank.

"Why is there a woman atop the monument?" Eva points to the gilded statue riding a clamshell chariot drawn by seahorses.

"I believe that's the goddess Columbia symbolizing America's triumph in the war."

She walks around the colossal memorial that takes up an entire corner of the park.

"How awful," she says reading the inscription. "More than two hundred fifty American sailors died when the battleship Maine exploded in Havana harbor." She shakes her head. "And then we were at war with Spain."

I want to distract her from war, but war is all around us. How can I protect my granddaughter from the horrors?

"Danny," she says, "I want to be a volunteer while I'm here. Everyone is involved in aiding the soldiers, and it doesn't seem right that I just fritter away my time."

I was afraid things would come to this. We should have stayed in York Harbor. But for a girl as bright and energetic as Eva, living with her old grandmother is a bit of a fritter.

"Do you have any idea how you might get involved?" I want to suggest something like office work where she'll be away from crowds. Maybe something here in the park.

"Yesterday in Times Square I saw a sign asking for volunteers at a soda shop for servicemen. How hard could it be to serve colas at a counter?"

I should blame Thayer for this idea but truth be told, I suppose with signs about war at every turn, it's inevitable Eva would want to be involved. It seems too soon to let her go out on her own, but I certainly don't have the energy to stand behind a counter for hours with her. How many times have I had to let someone go? All I can do is pray for her safety.

"If you'll allow it, Danny, I can take the subway to Midtown."

"You certainly will not take the subway," I say. "I'll put you in a taxi myself."

Eva leans in and kisses my cheek. "Oh, you are a dear," she says.

Before supper, Eva gets out the journal.

"I'd like you to hear this section," she says.

I'm not sure I want to hear it, and I feel my guard go up. I know my son died a horrible death, but I suppose I should learn about it from his own words. When I don't answer, she begins.

We are infested with lice, of all things. As if being shot at is not enough, we have these tiny vermin in our scalps and under our clothes. And no place to bathe. We ignore them except to use our bayonets to pick them from the seams of our uniforms. The rats here are like pets, little dogs always begging for treats. If the rats would eat lice, I would happily give them as many as they would like.

I am desperate to find some beauty to write you about. Horses drawing munitions wagons are crossing behind us along a poor excuse for a road. In the mist, they look surreal and mystical, like four-legged phantoms. Fog drifts over the field this morning. It is early and quiet and the sun has not broken through the clouds.

I cling to the soil the way a child clings to his mother. Mother Earth is aptly named for a soldier at war. I think of the poem we were asked to memorize in grammar school. That feels so far behind me that I have trouble believing those days were real. Now I recall just the last stanza of Emerson's poem "Earth Song":

> *They called me theirs,*
> *Who so controlled me;*
> *Yet every one*
> *Wished to stay, and is gone,*
> *How am I theirs,*
> *If they cannot hold me,*
> *But I hold them?*

I always liked that riddle, but now it has a deeper meaning for me.

The shelling will start again in a few hours. I hope in the quiet time enemy troops have not moved so close we can see their faces. Forgive me for saying it, but I could not bear to see the face of a man I must kill.

"That's enough." I have to stop her. Rosa is making our supper before she leaves for the night, and if the main course is meat, I won't be able to touch a bite with lice and rats and the word "kill" still ringing in my ears.

"It's such eloquent writing, Danny," Eva says. "So many poets have written about death. Keats, for example. And Emily Dickinson—Death kindly stopped for her. Even Shakespeare's "No longer mourn for me when I am dead.""

"True," I say, "but that doesn't mean I want to dwell on death."

"It's called the final resting place to which we all shall go."

How poetic my granddaughter is. But I'd rather give my attention to living than to dying.

I can hear Rosa in the kitchen plating food. Before she serves, I bring up the subject of the debut.

"Eva, I'd like to take you shopping. That is, when you're not serving colas to soldiers."

"More shopping?"

"This shopping is special. We'll be looking for a long white gown."

Eva squints one eye. "Danny, you know I was christened as a baby."

"The Junior League has scheduled a debutante ball for late December. You'll be on holiday break from school. I can arrange for an invitation."

"I've heard girls at school talking about their debut, but I don't know much about it."

I'm glad she didn't say no. Eva needs something to look forward to, some joy.

"It won't hurt to look, maybe try on some dresses. You'll have fittings, of course, but they shouldn't interfere with your volunteer work."

Rosa brings the plates to the table—chicken Marsala, one of her best dishes. She uses American sherry since we can't get French wines. Even so, it smells delicious.

Eva thanks Rosa while she butters a roll. "Then we should consider the dress my birthday gift. That's more than extravagant," she says.

"I take that as a yes? You'll come to New York and attend the ball?"

"Danny, yes, and of course yes. I'd come to New York to be with you at Christmas with or without a debutante ball."

It must have been the idea of Eva spending Christmas in New York that allowed me a good night's sleep. In fact, I have slept so late that Eva is in the kitchen with Rosa when I wander in.

"Coffee ready, Mrs. Swain." Rosa hands me a cup and saucer, coffee with light cream, no sugar, the way I like it.

"Thank you, Rosa." I take the cup and have that first revitalizing sip. "Why are you up so early, Eva?" I ask.

"I'm going downtown to sign up for that volunteer position. I want them to see how eager I am to help."

"I should go with you just to make sure—"

"Nonsense," Eva says. "Rosa will hail me a taxi. I must be wearing you out. Why don't you relax today and I'll be back this afternoon."

"Then let me give you the fare. I'll just get my—"

"Danny, I have the fare. You haven't let me spend a nickel since I've been with you."

"What about breakfast?" I'm clutching, I know, but I'm responsible for this young woman and not ready to let her fly alone.

"I had cereal." She looks at Rosa for confirmation. Rosa nods. "And I'll get something at the soda fountain. Drinks and food are free for volunteers."

I emit a sigh. I'm used to Eva's company and not sure what I'll do all day. But I say, "All right—good luck, darling." And I give her a cheek kiss before she heads out the door with Rosa.

Alone, I wander through the rooms. Should I start packing for the move? No—Bert hasn't brought the papers for the new place yet, and the realtor hasn't put this one on the market. No hurry on packing. Shop for Eva's gown? No—I really must take her with me. Then I see Eva has left the journal on the dining table. The tattered old thing.

I turn toward the kitchen and pour myself more coffee. Rosa should be back in a few minutes and will busy herself with making beds. She'll tidy up, help with laundry. I needn't do any of that, and she'd rather I didn't. She makes sure my place is neater and cleaner than I could ever do.

The journal pulls at me. I sit down with the coffee and run my hand over the aged leather cover. When I bought it, the leather was pebble-grained and tan. Now the cover is worn smooth and darkened by age and muddy fingers. It's as soft as calfskin. As soft as a young man's skin—Wells' skin.

I don't want to open the cover, but my fingers don't obey. Eva has left a marker, a slip of paper where she stopped reading. I pick up where she left off. If it gets to be too much, I'll stop.

We were told the American forces would be fighting behind the French Army, but the French soldiers are exhausted, many of them sick. They retreated to recover, requiring the Marines to take the front. We are beyond tired, but we are fit and well trained even if we must act on empty stomachs. Our impulses are honed for survival, for victory.

If I am honest and admit it, I am frightened. Only this dugout protects me from death, such protection as it is. I wish this war to be a bad dream—a movie in a bad dream. I keep waiting for the lights to go on, for the movie to be over. For a normal morning in a normal life. A life I'll never take for granted again.

The war is not what he imagined, but maybe it never is. I suppose there can be no bravery unless there is also fear. In storybooks, a dragon is a fearsome animal, but the knight confronts it even as the creature breathes fire at him. The Germans were hundreds, thousands of fire-breathing dragons, except the fire came from their metal mouths.

My brave boy, what else have you to say?

Yesterday I saw a man die. He was shot standing beside me. I'm lucky. The bullet barely missed me. His name was Sam Kelly. He was in my battalion and we had become friends. The bullet went into his temple. I don't mean to shock you, Muz, but you should know how hard this war is. Kelly's lips curled back to show his teeth. He had brushed them just this morning even though we had no toothpaste. Kelly was like that, complaining of needing a bath and clean socks. No one has mentioned the odor of dirty socks. The smell of gunpowder and the stink of blood and death overwhelm any other scent.

I am told if I am shot, I will not feel pain. At least not until later. A few wounded men said they didn't know they had been shot until they found a hole in a sleeve or a shoulder of the uniform. They were taken behind the lines where there is a makeshift hospital. And I'm sorry to say rudely made coffins are stacked for the poor fellows who don't make it. The coffins are loaded onto a flatbed wagon and carted off for burial. The enemy doesn't bother with coffins. Dead men are no threat to them.

Rosa returns, and I have an excuse to stop reading. She brings me toast with butter and jam. I must look a fright because she says, "Are you all right, Mrs. Swain?" I can't answer. The night the *Titanic* sank, the first mate threatened to shoot men who tried to board lifeboats before women and children. From my own lifeboat I heard gunshots—the captain shooting flares, gunshot to alert a ship five miles away, engines off because of the iceberg danger. Around our lifeboat, dead bodies floated in life vests and looked much like I imagine the battlefield of Belleau Wood.

I have no hunger for breakfast. Despite the hour, despite myself, what I need right now is a whiskey. Chess kept the cabinet stocked with spirits and liqueurs for entertaining.

Rosa has gone to Eva's room to make up the bed and straighten. She'll attend to my room next. I go to the kitchen to get a glass. Chess would choose a cut-glass tumbler for whiskey he drank neat, as he called it — without ice. But of course I require ice. The freezer compartment is too small to hold anything but the ice tray. I take it out and put it on the counter with one hand, the other still holding the glass. I don't know why it doesn't occur to me to put down the glass. I'm not thinking straight. When I try to release a cube from the tray, the glass slips from my hand and hits the counter. Glass slivers pierce the pad below my thumb. Blood oozes out and drips onto the floor.

Rosa must have heard the glass and my clumsiness with the ice tray. She appears as I stand dumbly staring at the crimson droplets.

"Oh, Mrs. Swain," she says. "Let me help." She examines my hand then presses a dish towel to the wound. Oddly, I feel no pain. As Wells said.

"No need for stitches, I think," Rosa says. "But you sit and I get a bandage."

She leads me back to the table and helps me into a chair. I know the cut is not deadly. I also know it is ill-advised to try to make myself a whiskey before breakfast.

While I wait for Rosa, my fingers curled to hold the dishcloth to the cut, I read another paragraph of the journal.

I have seen things I don't want to tell you about, but I must write them down as a record of history. When I leave this place, I will hand the diary off to someone who doesn't know me, maybe a journalist who will print a record of what this war is really like. I want to be anonymous, invisible, a no-man, so when I return I can begin anew as if I was never here in these pools of rainwater turned purple with the blood of men, Germans and mine both red, both of us following orders to fight to the death.

Wells, you did fight to the death, my darling, the unkind death. And you will never be anonymous, not if I can help it. You are, and forever will be, a hero.

When Rosa comes with the bandage, the bleeding has almost stopped. The cut is not bad, and she wipes it with alcohol. The sting is pleasant. I bite my lips between my teeth and enjoy the pain. She applies an adhesive and says, "Next time you call me." Then she goes to the kitchen to clean up the mess.

21

Will

In late afternoon Eva comes in glowing, and I get up from the sofa to greet her.

"Danny! What happened to your hand?" she asks.

I glance at the bandage. "A small cut. Not important."

Rosa harrumphs from the kitchen.

I roll my eyes at Rosa's intrusion. "How was your first day at the soda shop?"

"Glorious!" she says. "I've met so many people." She plops into a cushioned chair.

"All soldiers?"

"Sailors and Waves, too."

"Waves? Women in the Navy?" I sit across from her, trying to hide my concern. "Eva, please don't think about joining the military."

"Oh, Danny, no," she says. "I have another year of school. And lots of plans after that."

"I'd like to hear about those plans."

She's still enamored with her day. "I had a nice conversation with a fellow. He's a Marine and says he knows my brother. They were in school together."

"Really? What's his name?"

"Will." She's positively beaming. "Will Robbins."

"Harry Robbins' son?" Harry came to visit me when he returned from the war. Jack must have told him about Wells, and he wanted to give me his condolences. The Robbinses are a respected Boston family.

"Harry Robbins could be his father, yes," Eva says.

"And he went to school with Bally?"

"Both in boarding school and college, but Bally joined the Army after his first semester at Harvard. Will stayed until the end of his freshman year. And Danny, Will asked to see me before he deploys to Europe. Could we have him for tea on Sunday?"

Rosa doesn't work on Sunday, and I now have this bandage to deal with. But I'm eager to meet Harry's boy.

"What is today?" I look at my watch as if it will tell me today is Friday. By Sunday the cut should be well enough for me to handle tea.

Eva looks at my hand. "I'll do everything. You won't have to lift a finger."

I can't bear to disappoint my granddaughter. "All right, then. I'll get cookies from the bakery. I hope your friend likes tea." If Eva notices the touch of emphasis on the word friend, she doesn't react.

"Oh, Danny, you are so sweet! He'll love tea." She thinks for a second and then adds, "And you should know he's very shy."

Saturday morning Eva is due back at the soda shop. Over breakfast, she stutters, "I — I wonder if — "

"If what?" Is she nervous about Will's visit tomorrow?

"Maybe I should get something done with my hair."

In my opinion, her hair is perfect, but I offer to call my salon to see if they can fit her in.

She insists on getting downtown by herself, and I force myself to unclench my fingers and let the pretty bird fly. I don't ask whether she takes a taxi or the subway. I know she won't walk because the young are always in a hurry.

My salon has an opening, and when Eva returns from the soda shop in the afternoon, I go with her to have her hair done. My own silvery hair is coarse and curly, and I keep it short. Eva likes her hair longer, and she asks for just a trim of her blonde locks.

On the way home, we stop at a bakery and I buy pastries and cookies for Sunday's tea with a few more for her soldier to take with him on his trip across the ocean.

To calm her nerves, I suggest Eva go to church with me Sunday morning. All Souls on Lexington Avenue was the first Unitarian church in Manhattan, attended by such luminaries as Herman Melville and William Cullen Bryant. Like the services of our church in Cambridge, the prayers are simple and everyone is welcome. The minister's homily is about the exodus of the Israelites to the desert and their conquering and occupation of Canaan.

After the service Eva says, "Aren't Unitarians pacifists?"

"Not exactly," I say. "We've always held universal acceptance as one of our values. And we believe conflict should be settled by nonviolent means."

"But we're in the middle of a war."

I want to answer her as honestly as I can, as honestly as I know how. Opposing a war while a war is raging has to be handled delicately.

"As the mother of three men who put on uniforms, I have to believe in supporting our troops," I tell her. "That doesn't mean I agree with shooting and bombing to resolve a dispute. I wish there were no wars. But since there are, we should do everything we can to bring our soldiers home safe."

Eva gives a slow nod. She's a bright young woman and I know she wants to do what's right. Now I'm eager to meet her new friend and find out if he's Mr. Right for her.

"Good afternoon, Mrs. Swain." The young man holds out his hand. "Private First Class Robbins. I'm very happy to meet you."

I take his hand and he gives a warm but gentle squeeze. He's handsome in his blue uniform and glows with innocence. His face is boyish, not chiseled like Montgomery Clift's. I saw Clift in a few Broadway shows before he tried to join the Army. No one could believe he failed the physical because of dysentery. Private Robbins, on the other hand, is the picture of health.

Eva motions toward the living room and invites us to sit down.

"Danny, I'll bring out the tea and cookies," she says. "Will, you sit on the sofa."

Already she's giving the orders. Will may be a private, but Eva will surely be the superior officer. He watches her disappear into the kitchen then glances at me before lowering his gaze to the coffee table. Her beau, if that's what he is, seems nervous around me, and I try to think how to put him at ease.

"Eva tells me you were at Harvard."

He brightens. "Yes. My father went there. He joined up after graduating and still serves with the Air Corps."

"And your father went to school with Eva's father?"

"I believe he was a year behind Mr. Cumings. Now he's a trustee at the school."

It sounds like he'd rather talk about his father than about himself. Eva was right about his shyness.

"You and your father are very close, I take it?"

"We are," he says. "We both love sailing."

Eva brings the cookies and pastries arranged on a tray, then goes back to the kitchen for the teapot and cups. I want to ask Will about sailing, what kind of boat his father had, where he sailed, but I don't want to pepper him with questions. Besides, he's probably preoccupied with where he'll be stationed when he deploys. Preoccupied also with my granddaughter.

After Eva pours tea, she sits beside Will on the sofa.

"Did Will tell you his father is a Provost Marshal?" She glances at him.

"He didn't." More about his father when what I really want to know about is his father's son. But I'll follow the discussion.

"He's in charge of the Army Military Police Corps," Will says.

"What about you, Will?" I ask. "What are your aspirations? Do you plan to stay in the military after the war ends?" I assume, of course, the war will end. Don't all wars end? And then begin again and end again?

"I'm not sure," he says. I can tell he wants to look at Eva, as if she'll tell him what to do after he's discharged. Instead, he takes a napkin and puts a cookie on it, bites into the cookie while holding the napkin under his chin. When a crumb rolls onto the knee of his trousers, he brushes it off with the backs of his fingers.

I change the subject. "Where do you live in the Boston area, Will?"

"Beverly Farms," he says, "close to West Beach."

I notice Will takes his tea with lots of cream. Eva should have brought sugar. He seems the type who likes sweets.

"Eva's father was born in Boston."

Will looks at Eva as if he's pleased they have more in common that he thought.

As we talk more about Boston and New York, about the war effort and Eva's volunteer job at the soda fountain, Will appears to relax. He laughs at some little joke Eva makes. Their elbows touch. I try to imagine what Jack would say about this lad. In my opinion, he seems almost too good to be true, and I wait for the other shoe to drop. But maybe there is no other shoe. In that case, I think Jack would give Will his approval.

The teacups are empty and Will has had a second cookie while Eva still nibbles her first. I glance at the pendulum clock and see an hour has gone by. Finally Will poses what he has come to ask.

"Mrs. Swain, I have a few more days in New York before I ship out. Would it be all right if I call on Eva? Maybe take her to see a movie or a play?"

Eva speaks up on Will's behalf. "You remember, Danny, on our first day in New York I said I'd like to see a show."

"I do recall." Should I require they take me along as chaperone? Of course, that would be silly. There's a war on, and young people feel they haven't much time. They fall in love, run off to be married, and wives have children with absent fathers. Maybe they don't have much time at all.

22

My Brother Jack

When Will comes to call on Eva, I expect him to be in uniform again, but he's wearing a white shirt under a sport coat. The shirt has a spread collar open at the neck, trousers pleated below the belt. He seems more comfortable with the casual look and greets me with a smile.

Eva is still in her room, last minute grooming.

"She'll be out any second," I say and think how to engage him in conversation. "What will you see tonight?"

"I'm taking Eva to the film *The Song of Bernadette*."

I can't worry about the movie with a teenager who has visions of the Virgin Mary. I've had visions of my own.

"I read the review in the *Times*. It stars Jennifer Jones, doesn't it?"

"I'm not sure." He tilts his head to look around me, expecting Eva. I'm not the one he wants to chat with.

"Can I get you anything?" I'm thinking the timid man might like a belt of something from Chess' liquor cabinet.

"No, thank you. I'll—"

Fortunately, Eva appears in the nick of time.

"Will," she says. "You look positively dashing." Without taking her eyes off Will, she says, "We won't be late, Danny."

"Good. Get the doorman to escort you up the elevator." But they're gone, leaving my words hanging in the air.

When I turn around, Rosa is peeking around the corner from the kitchen.

"Don't worry, Mrs. Swain," she says. "He a nice fellow."

"Rosa," I say, "I certainly hope you're right."

I excuse Rosa early that night.

"Soup on the stove for your dinner," she says before she leaves.

The soup is really a hearty stew, and a small portion is all I want. Rosa scolds me if I clean up after myself, so when I finish I set the dish in the sink and turn in early. The boudoir lamp on the nightstand gives just enough light to read a few entries of the journal. Wells was a year older than Eva is now. She tells me Will is nineteen, the age Wells would have been if he had lived two weeks longer. Wells never had the chance for a first date, so tonight I want to feel close to him through his words. I open the book where I've left the marker.

It is a beautiful, cloudless day. The field across from us is abloom with blood-red poppies. I'm amazed how with so much destruction nature still perseveres. I have not been here long in what once must have been pristine forest, and this is not the way I wanted to see France, the country of Debussy and Chopin. But even here in such dismal circumstances I often hear the music of my own compositions which I have no way of writing down unless in this journal. Music was my escape from the world. But I've exchanged the sweet piano etudes running through my head for Wagner's opera music and Tchaikovsky's 1812 Overture, full orchestra, moaning tubas, and booming drums. My music now is the stutter of machine-gun fire, the bark of a rifle, the splatter of rock and earth. When I return, my taste in music will be different. The whole world will be different, I have no doubt.

Wells probably heard Wagner's "Ride of the Valkyries," martial music with churning strings and brazen brass. Chess enjoyed taking me to the symphony, and he taught me to listen for melody and rhythm. Bradley preferred modern music like "Let Me Call You Sweetheart" and "By the Light of the Silvery

Moon." There was no moon the night the *Titanic* went down, my darling.

One day Mendelssohn's "Wedding March" will play as Eva walks down the aisle in her wedding gown. The groom might be Will waiting for her at the altar, a thrill my middle son will never experience. If Eva's beau ever finds himself in such a brutal battle, I hope he will empty his heart to his mother the way Wells has.

I doubt Eva will have time or inclination to finish the journal, so I can abide one more entry tonight.

I am not dead, Muz, but I feel as if I am. My body is numb. My fingers have gripped my rifle so hard I fear they will never uncurl. Will I ever play Chopin or Mozart again? And how could I concentrate on Plato, Sophocles and Hamlet after the savage fighting at Belleau Wood?

I often think of the German soldiers, how they are probably just like us, terrified nearly to death to face the U.S. Marines. They must know our strength and our commitment to overthrow our enemies. I haven't killed a man yet and do not look forward to the time I must shoot someone who may be just like me. He might listen to Brahms or Bach. He might have been to a concert of Handel's Messiah. How could I shoot such a man? The answer is because I am a Marine. I must pretend I am having target practice, but in this case the target will be running toward me. The Germans call us Devil Dogs, a name that gives me shivers.

Slowly I replace the marker and reach to turn off the light, but sleep eludes me. Wagner pounds through my head and I toss and turn as if dodging bullets. It's much later when I hear Eva come in and tiptoe to her room. The last I hear from her is a sigh. Finally, I can sleep.

Sleep is not always friendly. I am underground trapped alone in cold mud, clawing my way toward the surface. When I try to cry out, dirt fills my mouth, suffocating me. I cough and try to breathe, but I can manage only a groan.

Then Eva is at my bedside.

"Danny," she says, "you're having a nightmare."

I jolt awake, groggy, confused. When I realize where I am, I say, "Oh—sorry. Go back to bed."

After she leaves, I get up and open the window just a crack. Fresh night air pours in. A chill is better than suffocation. When I crawl back into bed, I give myself to Morpheus.

23

Black Market Steaks

I find Eva in the kitchen with Rosa the following morning. Rosa is mixing biscuit dough and has grated cheese for omelets while Eva waits for the kettle to heat water for tea, her cup on the island next to her.

"Danny, have you been reading the journal?" Eva asks. "I saw it on your nightstand and expect that's what gave you the nightmare last night."

I dodge her question with one of my own. "How was your evening with Will?"

She waits so long I regret asking. Did my mother ever pose such a question about an evening with Bradley?

"Nice," she says at last. "But it's hard to get to know someone at a movie theater."

I notice Rosa nodding, listening in.

"I imagine it is." Bradley and I did most of our courting at my parents' parsonage. We took afternoon walks around Cambridge and sometimes went into Boston to stroll through a museum. If I saw him in the evening, he was a guest at our dinner table, my father evaluating him with a battery of questions. But Eva's father isn't here to deliver his battery.

"Will has asked me to go with him to a museum this afternoon and have dinner afterward. It's his last night, and he wants to make it special."

Rosa turns her head and gives me a sly smile, her wise eyes signaling approval.

"I told him I didn't think you'd object,"' Eva says.

My objection is another evening of being alone, of fretting. But I say, "Of course you may go."

"Thank you, Danny." Her face is alight.

"You like him, don't you?"

She raises her hand to her cheek. "I like him very much."

"Then you'll get good at writing letters."

Rosa slides a cup of coffee across the island toward me.

"I'm sure the mail is much better than it was in the Great War," Eva says.

I have every hope this war won't be fought in muddy trenches. Even so, some American men like Will — good-hearted, ingenuous boys — will walk off troop ships and go straight to their butchering. Six months earlier, they were playing football and going to school dances. They had never seen a gun. Yet they are about to face the toughest fighters in the world — hard, professional killers.

No matter how you cast it, there is nothing pleasant about war — unless you read my son Jack's letters, that is.

While Eva is getting ready for her date, a knock comes at the door. Is Will so early? And who would our doorman Henry permit upstairs without calling me? Thayer, probably.

I open to find Bert Marckwald standing in his business suit, hair beginning to gray. Still alarmingly handsome with his sky-blue eyes, twinkling even behind wire-rimmed glasses.

"Hello, Florrie," he says and steps in to kiss me on both cheeks. Very European of him.

"Lovely to see you, Bert."

"I was in the neighborhood," he says. "Thought I'd welcome you back from dreary old Maine."

"Maine is anything but dreary." I turn toward the kitchen. "Rosa, would you make a fresh pot of coffee?"

"I'd stay for coffee, but maybe you can make me a better offer," Bert says. "How about a whiskey to thank me for this gift." He raises a bag that looks to weigh a pound or more.

"What's this?"

"Steaks. Three good size T-bones. Tax told me you had company."

"How in the world have you gotten steaks?" I ask. "Did you save up your ration tickets?"

He puts a finger to his lips as if he's about to reveal a secret. "Bankers know how to navigate the black market. Thought you might need some protein."

Rosa must be listening. She comes in and says, "Maybe I set another place for supper?"

I grin at Bert. "I suppose you've just been invited, Mr. Marckwald."

"Oh, for heaven's sake," he says. "Absolutely not. The steaks are for you, my darling Florrie. Tonight you will have dinner out with me."

Bert still exudes charisma. He was six years younger than Bradley, making him sixty-four, three years younger than I am. He carries his age well.

"With Isabelle gone and the children grown, I don't know what to do with myself most evenings," he says. "Usually I dine at the club alone. If I'm lucky, some poor sucker will join me because he feels sorry for me."

"The last three years since she passed away have been difficult, haven't they?"

He gives a sad shake of his head. "Miss her like crazy."

Bert jerks his chin toward the kitchen. "Rosa, cancel the coffee." He wanders to the liquor cabinet. "There's something about you, Florrie, that brings out the devil in me." He reaches for a bottle of whiskey and a glass tumbler.

"Bert, it's three o'clock in the afternoon."

"I work bankers' hours. Besides, speaking of dreary, I don't want to go back to that empty house in Bedford Hills with nothing but servants, none of them as nice as Rosa."

Rosa enters with an ice bucket and a tray of her homemade ginger cookies, puts the bucket on the cabinet and the cookies on the coffee table. Bert hands her the bag of steaks.

"Join me, Florrie," Bert says. He has poured a finger of whiskey into another tumbler, uses the silver tongs to drop in two cubes of ice, then offers the whiskey to me.

"You are a rascal, Bert Marckwald," I tease.

He sinks into a chair. "I consider that a compliment."

I sit on the sofa and wait to see what he has on his mind. He scans the living room. "I should think about moving back to Manhattan."

"I thought you liked Bedford Hills."

"True. I like being away from the madding crowds." He looks at something over my shoulder, a landscape painting Chess bought on one of his business trips. "'O thou cruel of heart, thou madding worker of anguish.'"

"I don't know that quote. Who wrote it? Or did you make it up?"

"I don't recall the author. Things I learned at Yale are in a mental repository I dip into now and then. Anyway, I have to be downtown during the day. That's plenty of madness for me."

The ice cubes have watered down my whiskey and I take a sip. Bert has nearly finished his.

"What madness?" Eva comes from her bedroom, looking scrubbed and smelling of lavender.

Bert jumps to his feet. "Who have we here?" he says.

She is wearing a pink flowered dress with padded shoulders and a matching belt and has her hair pulled away from her face with barrettes. I believe she has rouged her cheeks and lips for her beau. I introduce her as my granddaughter, and she holds out her hand.

"Eva Cumings?" Bert asks, taking her hand. "Are you Jack's daughter?"

"I am indeed," she says.

"I've known your father since he was a kid."

When Eva drops her head, Bert says, "I'm very sorry for your loss. Jack and I were close."

She looks up again. "I'm pleased to meet you, Mr. Marckwald. Danny has spoken about you."

"I hope your grandmother hasn't given you all the sordid details."

"Nothing sordid at all." Eva is poised for her age, her mother's influence, no doubt. Joanie, the youngest, is more like Jack—full of zest and good humor.

Another knock at the door, and Eva rushes to greet Will. He's dressed much as he was yesterday, but today he's wearing a tie. His hair is slicked tight to his head. When he looks at Eva, it's as if no one else is in the room.

Eva introduces Will as a soldier about to deploy.

"Are you from a military family?" Bert asks.

"Yes, sir." Will stands up straighter. "My father served in the infantry during the first war and is deployed in France at the moment. He holds the rank of colonel."

"You must be very proud," Bert says.

"I am, sir." I expect Will to salute. Instead, he addresses Eva. "We really must rush. The museum closes at five."

"Which museum?" Bert asks.

"The Metropolitan, sir."

"Good choice. Be sure to see the Artists for Victory exhibit. I like Curry's landscape. Rather forceful but well done."

"We'll look for it, sir," Will says.

"I'm ready," Eva tells him. She looks at Bert, "Please come visit again, Mr. Marckwald."

Bert pretends a frown. "Your father always called me Uncle Bert, young lady, and I expect you to do likewise."

"All right, Uncle Bert." And to me, "I won't be late, Danny."

After they leave, Bert says, "Your granddaughter is quite a looker."

"She comes by it naturally. I mean her mother." I point to Bert's empty tumbler on the coffee table. He hasn't touched the ginger cookies. "Another drink?"

"Not unless you take me up on that dinner offer."

"Bert—this is a difficult time of year for me. I'd rather not go out."

"We ought to celebrate birthdays instead of tragedies, Florrie. But I understand." He presses his lips together and thinks a minute. "All right, then. If your Rosa can fix up dinner for two, I'll join you." He sits again and holds up his empty tumbler. "But first, let's both have another whiskey."

I tell Rosa to cook two steaks and take the third home for herself. She refuses at first, but it doesn't take much to convince her. She probably hasn't had red meat since the war started.

While she prepares dinner, Bert excuses himself to run out and buy a bottle of wine. He comes back with two bottles—a white for me and a red for himself. Both California wines.

"The Sine Qua Non is this year's vintage," he says. "It's chilled, so you'd better drink it right away." He goes to the kitchen and gets two wine glasses, one with ice for me. Rosa set the dining table to put us across from each other.

"This will never do," Bert says. He moves his setting to the end, closer to me. When Rosa brings out our plates with the steaks, mashed potatoes, and greens from a victory garden, he reaches out and squeezes my hand as a sort of grace.

I give Rosa a smile and thank her.

"I leave you now," she says. "In the morning I will clean up."

"Good night, Rosa," Bert says as she leaves.

"Rosa is a fine cook. I know you'll enjoy this dinner."

"I've never had a disappointing meal with you, Florrie." He holds up his goblet. "A toast to—"

"To those no longer with us." I finish his toast.

"And to forty years of friendship," Bert adds.

We click our glasses, white against red. Already I'm feeling the whiskey, and if Bert has anything to say about it, I'll drink most of a bottle of his wine. I haven't had much alcohol since Eva has been with me, but seeing Bert is always a special occasion.

"You're right," he says after a bite of his steak. "Your housekeeper has some magic in her. The steak is done perfectly."

Bert is a good-natured fellow, and we talk of Maine, his fondness for Cape Cod, his grandchildren.

"When do you expect we'll close on the apartment at 755 Park? I'm eager to move in." I skim my eyes around the wood and dark colors of what I will always consider Chess' quarters.

"It's still in probate, but I'm trying to move things along. Hold on just a couple more months." Bert raises his head and looks toward the ceiling. "You should put this place on the market in early September. I'll have the realtor get in touch."

I let a sigh escape me. Eva will be back at school then. At least she won't have to go through the upheaval of moving.

We're finishing dinner when he says, "I saw Jack several times while I was in Paris, but I didn't get anywhere near the front. Tell me what you know about the situation in Belleau Wood."

"I've never wanted to speak about it."

"Florrie, if you don't get it off your chest, it will bore a hole in you."

"The hole is already there."

"We all have those empty places. As bad as it was for me to learn about Wells, it was worse for Jack."

"Why have you never told me before? You were there, Bert."

"You weren't ready. Now you have Eva as a buffer." He pushes his plate to the side. "Florrie, the more you know, the closer you'll feel to Wells." He lights a cigarette. Rosa has left an ashtray on the table for him.

I surrender with a sigh. Bert is the only one I trust to tell me the details of the battle. Eva has been reading the letters and the journal with a desire to know everything about her father and her uncle. I have to channel her bravery.

"All right," I say.

He pours more wine into my glass and says, "You'll need this."

I take a sip before he begins.

"In early June, a French lieutenant advised the major commanding the Marine brigade to withdraw to the hills overlooking the south bank of the Marne River. They'd have a good observation post to plan their offensive. The major refused. His men would hold the line, he said. The lieutenant insisted the troops cross the Marne because he intended to blow up the bridge, the only escape from the battle. Again the major rebuffed him." He draws on the cigarette. "Mistake number one."

He pauses to drink more wine. I look at the bottle of white wine. Half remains. His bottle is nearly empty.

"In the following days," he continues, "the Marines repositioned their units, expecting an imminent attack. The troops were tense, and their fatigue added to their anxiety. Some of them hadn't eaten or slept for days."

When they were growing up, my boys were always hungry. If Wells had had a good meal, he might have run faster. He might have dodged the gunfire.

"The Huns attacked from machine-gun nests hidden in the thick woods. The firing seemed to come from everywhere." Bert hesitates and taps his cigarette on the ashtray. "Wells was in the 6th regiment and his commander, Colonel Catlin, was wounded in the chest with a bullet through a lung. A soldier dragged him out of the fire and a surgeon drove him to a hospital in Paris. Another colonel took his place and the fighting went on.

I imagine the Grim Reaper mowing down men with his scythe, my son obeying orders to offer his life to the Reaper.

"It gets worse, doesn't it?" I twist my wine goblet and watch the wine swirl around. Bert ignores my question.

"That evening the roar of shelling continued through the night." He doesn't look at me. Instead, he regards his cigarette as if he's fascinated by tobacco burning. "In the morning the Huns threw mustard gas, forcing the troops to put on their masks. Impossible to see with those things, much less shoot. At least the enemy steered clear for a while."

"What was the purpose of the gas?" I'm asking my wine glass. Looking at Bert makes his description of the battlefield too real.

"It was meant to disable the troops, not kill them. It caused panic because the gas had to be washed or beaten out of their uniforms so it didn't seep through and blister their skin." He shakes his head. "Horrible. stuff. It took out half the brigade. But there was a chance the German troops were weakened as well."

"There was still hope at that point?" How foolish of me to think for a single second Wells might have survived. He might have survived, come home to New York, and started his life over.

"The Boches were desperate."

I stop him. "A funny word Boches. The *Times* used it, and Jack wrote about the Boches in his letters."

"The French word for Germans. Some of them who spoke English took uniforms from Americans dead in the fields and infiltrated the Marines' ranks. Wells' brigade was green and made some errors."

I stop him. "There must have been confusion, but what sort of errors do you mean?"

He shrugs. "Ripping off a mask too soon, standing to look over the trench wall. Trying too hard to be heroes."

"They were heroes — all of them."

"Yes, they were. And when the order came to attack, the men ran toward the machine-gun fire, not away from it."

I know where Bert is going, and I swallow the last of the wine in my glass. He pours me more. The ice cubes have melted and the wine has warmed, but I don't care. I can hardly taste it anyway.

"Are you still with me?" he asks.

"I'm cruelly aware of how the story ends."

"But now how it unfolded. Shall I go on?"

Again I reach into myself for a hard place that can withstand this agony. My son's agony.

"Yes. Go on."

Bert reaches for my hand. "For twelve days, the fighting was incessant in muddy and rutted terrain, but the Americans advanced forward on their bellies through the muck, crawling over their dead and wounded comrades, their uniforms soaking up the blood from those fallen."

He squeezes my hand as if he's in pain himself.

"Those still alive in the mud had to be left. Anyone who stopped to help them risked losing his own life and disobeying commands."

He bites his lips between his teeth as if he can't believe the situation. Neither can I.

"In mid-June, the Allies took more than five hundred Germans prisoner," he says.

"But the fighting wasn't over." I know it wasn't over — fighting is never over. And in mid-June my son was still alive.

"Here's how it ended, Florrie." He taps his cigarette again. "Around June 25th the situation looked hopeless. The commander ordered large artillery to be brought in, and the big guns launched round after round of shells into the woods from early morning until late afternoon that day."

He puffs on his cigarette and blows the smoke away from me. Then he presses the butt into the ashtray. "I've got to give it to the Boches. They continued fighting as the Americans moved in closer. Late in June as gunners kept firing, the Marines kept advancing, Wells among them."

My breath catches and I feel a sharp pain in my stomach.

"The official report said Wells probably fell on June 26, the worst day of fighting at Belleau Wood."

"What difference does the date make? My son was killed. That's the bottom line." I can hear resentment in my own voice, but I don't want to be resentful—not with Bert.

He lets go of my hand. The worst is over.

"Ironically—and tragically for Wells—the Germans surrendered later that day. Belleau Wood has been called the Gettysburg of the Great War because the battle ultimately rescued American troops and allies from almost certain defeat." His sky blue eyes bore into me. "Florrie, Wells was so close to the finish line. So close."

He sniffs and swipes a thumb across his cheek. "By June 30th, Belleau Wood was renamed Bois de Brigade de Marine."

"June 30th is the day Wells died."

"Yes." He hesitates a few seconds. He must know I've said the word "died" too many times. What else can I say? Passed away? Crossed over? Disappeared?

"After that," he says, "a Marine couldn't walk down the sidewalks of Paris without being kissed by grateful Parisians." Bert's face has a wispy half smile. "I'm sorry Wells missed that."

I see my son rocking in the mud, gulping for air. The rain is on his face and his father is in his eyes.

Bert is patient with me, comfortable in our silence. The sign of a true friend. "Florrie," he says finally, "we don't get to write the script in this life. We're just actors on the stage."

"Tell me about the hospital," I say. "I want to feel close to Wells, as if I'm at his bedside."

"I don't know that, Florrie. I wish I could have gotten to him, but I didn't find out until after the fact."

I start to feel dizzy and try to stand up, but I fall back into the chair.

"You'd better let me put you to bed," he says.

"No, Mr. Marckwald. That would not be at all proper."

"I'm not worried about propriety. Besides, I feel responsible for your condition."

"Just give me a minute." I push myself again from my chair and find my way to the bathroom where I retch, emptying myself of the best steak I've tasted in a long time, the potatoes, the wine, and the whiskey. When I'm finished, I fall onto the bed.

Sometime in the night I wake and come from the bedroom to check on Bert, but he's gone.

24

Worst Fears

I have no idea what time it is when the rattle of pans and plates reaches me. Rosa must be cleaning the kitchen. I didn't hear Eva come in last night, but the voices in the kitchen must be hers with Rosa. Probably talking about me and why I'm still in bed so late. Sitting up, I lean against the pillows, my head swimming. Somehow I got into my nightgown and tossed my clothes on the chair across the room. Next to the bed is the journal and to delay facing the day, I open to read the last entry in the left-handed slant I know well.

The sounds of war are indistinguishable one from another, all noise combined into one loud roar. A few minutes ago a German shell flew not more than three feet over my head. The field beyond our dugout is littered with too many dead to count, some American, some German. Death does not discriminate. It seems odd that I am no longer afraid. This war is a job and only that — a job for which I applied, and for which I have been trained. We, my comrades and I, await the command "Over the top," which means we must run directly into the line of machine-gun fire. We must snuff out the few gunners left. The Colonel has ordered us to fix bayonets. We are going into the woods to pick them off or take them prisoner. Afterward, I hope to join Jack in Paris for a good long rest. But now we go on the attack. May the Almighty protect me.

The rest of the pages are blank, but for some reason I open the back cover. Two papers fall out. One is from the French curé, the chief priest of a parish. It's a letter addressed just to "Sir."

The French considering my son Wells a hero doesn't bring him back. I have a bitter taste in my mouth, the bitterness of regret, of guilt, of living when he no longer lives. My stomach lurches, and I barely reach the bathroom before I throw up again.

Eva comes in and finds me washing my face.

"Danny, are you ill?" Her own face is strained with concern.

"I'm fine," I answer. "Be out in a few minutes." After a deep breath and an adjustment to my hair, I dress and go to the kitchen.

Rosa glances at me. "Look like you need coffee, Mrs. Swain." She has a cup ready for me.

I take my coffee to the den where Eva shuffles through letters and sit on the sofa next to her. "Tell me about your evening with Will."

She has the look of someone trying to make the best of a sad situation. "He kissed me," she says.

"He must be taken with you."

"Danny, he told me he loves me."

I sip my coffee before I respond. "Of course he loves you, Eva. You are absolutely lovable. Will is going away for who knows how long. He'll be lonely and homesick, and he wants to believe you'll be thinking of him."

"Of course I will. I can hardly think of anything else." She swings her head as if to loosen Will from her thoughts. "But what about you? Did Uncle Bert stay awhile?"

I tell her about dinner but not about the two bottles of wine Bert brought. "He gave me details of Wells' last battle," I say.

"Was it upsetting to you?"

"Yes, but nothing I didn't know."

Eva looks at the paper open on her lap. "I was just reading the letter where Jack finds out about Wells. It's dated at the beginning of August, two months after the battle of Belleau Wood."

"Do you want to read it to me?"

"I'd like to — if I can get through it." She takes a breath.

Darling, Muz, how can I write you this letter; it is so hard! I thought you had sacrificed enough in letting Wells and myself come into this war without having to undergo the greatest sacrifice of all, the loss of one of your own boys. I wish I were with you to comfort you. I myself have not recovered from the suddenness of it all.

She stops and stares at me. "You already knew, didn't you?"

I look into my coffee cup. "Yes. But finish reading."

She begins again.

As you know, I was in Paris going from the 29th to the 79th Division. I met Van Duzer Burton at the Crillon and he asked me how Wells was.

I explain to Eva that the Crillon is a palace near the Champs-Elysées turned into a fancy hotel and restaurant. "Jack was probably there having dinner. What a horrible way to hear such upsetting news and so long after the fact."

Eva studies the letter. "That was the first time he had heard Wells had been wounded. He immediately went to a Red Cross hospital where his friend Dick Dilworth was confined, having nearly lost his arm from a wound about ten days earlier. Dick told him Wells was wounded through the stomach by shrapnel in heavy fighting. Dick and some others carried him off the field."

She turns to me. "He stayed at his post even after he was wounded, Danny."

"I don't think he was able to get himself off the battlefield."

She pulls the paper closer to her face. "He says the next morning Col. Harvey Gibson, head of the Red Cross, gave Jack his car and he and a major went to the hospitals near the front to look for Wells. That night when he got back, Frank told him Wells had died in a field hospital. He says, 'It was unbelievable that my dear brother could have been taken away so suddenly.'"

Eva stops and puts down the letter. "How did you learn about Wells?"

"His commanding officer cabled me after Wells died to confirm my worst fears." Actually, I knew the minute it happened. I sensed his passing, but Eva probably won't believe that. I had thought about going to Europe to find Jack and tell him in person, but that would have taken days by boat and who knows whether I would have found him at all. It's odd how I couldn't grieve then. I held only bitterness in my heart. I wanted my son back and I wanted an apology, a knee scraping, honest apology for my two other sons and their loss of a brother, an apology for their unbearable pain and mine. I didn't care whether God placed judgment on my soul. If God threw crushing stones of heartache at me, I would catch them and roll them up a mountain until the hollow in the core of my body was filled and my heart healed beyond any empty promise of eternal life.

Wells was killed six years after Bradley died, Bradley and fifteen hundred other passengers and crew of *Titanic.* There was no room inside me for more anguish. My veins were still full of ice from those hours sitting in a lifeboat two miles above the ocean floor, the night dark and cold—so cold. Now, with Eva, I feel the ice melting, the heat of anguish dissolving the frost. At last I sense a warmth coming over me.

"You know, Danny," Eva says, "I believe the death of his brother gave Jack a different perspective. He says, 'In this war I have seen men wounded and dead at the front but never realized what it meant until now. The best families of England and France have been experiencing these losses for far too many years, but the seriousness is just beginning to dawn on us. Mother darling, I know you must be terribly broken up, but try to think what a noble thing it is to die for one's country and for those we are defending.'" She raises her damp eyes to me before she continues. "He ends with 'Muz, dear, all my love, thoughts, and prayers are with you if they will comfort you just a little.'"

Rosa comes to the doorway. "Would you like breakfast now?"

It's nearly the noon hour, but by now I believe my stomach is settled enough to have a bite of something.

"Will you join me, Eva?"

"Yes." She presses a finger beneath her nose and sniffs. "Breakfast is just what we both need."

25

Bridal Shop

I have an idea for a distraction. "Eva, take the day off from your work and let's go shopping."

She looks surprised. "Shopping for what?"

"You're going to need a dress. And shoes."

"All right." Her brows draw together with suspicion.

"And it wouldn't hurt to put on something nice," I add.

We cross to Madison Avenue and start walking toward downtown.

"Your birthday is coming soon, Eva. Any idea what you'd like to do?"

She looks up at one of the tall buildings. "I still haven't seen a Broadway show."

"Ah." I nod. "I'll talk to your Uncle Tax."

When I stop at a bridal shop, she frowns. "Danny, a bridal shop? That's a little premature, isn't it?"

"Never mind," I say. "Let's just go in."

When Eva and I step into the shop, we're greeted by cool, perfumed air, a welcome on this hot July afternoon. Puffy white gowns hang along the walls as if standing in line. A sales attendant approaches us, a slender man in a pinstriped suit with a vest, his dark hair combed close to his scalp. Expensive lace-up shoes. These employees are paid to dress well.

"Welcome, ladies. My name is Stephen." His voice is pinched an octave higher than I expect. "Let me guess — debutante ball?"

"That's right," I tell him.

The man takes a step back and appraises Eva feet to head. "You have natural beauty and good bones. I can see you in an off-the-shoulder style." He signals with his left hand as he turns to the right. "Come along with me."

We follow him to a rack deeper in the shop. Eva leans toward me, hand cupping her mouth. She puts her hand on my arm. "Danny, are you sure about this?"

"We discussed this, darling," I tell her. "Besides, the ball is a benefit for the war effort."

"Oh," she says. "In that case—"

"The party isn't until December," Stephen announces. "Plenty of time for fittings."

"See if your fellow can get leave for Christmas." I wink at her. "You'll need an escort."

Stephen clears his throat to get our attention. "There are rules for the dress," he says. "It must be white or a very pale pastel. Maximum 144-inch flair in the skirt." He squints at Eva. "I suggest modesty for you. A dress should not detract from your beauty."

She blushes but says nothing.

"Now—tulle? Or silk faille?"

"Nothing too extravagant, please," she says. "Rayon maybe."

"Oh, heavens." One of Stephen's hands goes to the knot at the neck of his tie. "Anything but rayon."

I break in. "Let her try on several." I grin at Eva. "As many as you like. And don't worry about the price."

"Oh, Danny." When she hugs me, I can feel her excitement.

For an hour I sit on a hardback chair by the dressing room as Eva parades out in dress after dress to assess herself in a tall mirror. I didn't have the opportunity to be presented to society. My pastor father counted every penny. We lived close to the bone, as Thoreau wrote. I wore my sister's hand-me-downs or mended and remade my mother's old skirts. Even after I married Bradley and he became a successful stockbroker, we never lived beyond our means, especially with three children. Chess left me well off enough to be generous with my grandchildren, and I don't want to deny Eva anything.

When she goes to try on another dress, Stephen calls to her in the changing chamber. "Let me know if you need help."

"I'm fine," she says, and I don't doubt it.

After the third time she comes out to evaluate herself in the mirrors, Stephen says, "She's stunning in every one of them."

I give him a nod. "I'm afraid this is going to be a difficult decision."

Finally, Eva settles on a simple dress in a cream color with wide straps that tie atop her shoulders. It's sophisticated and understated with a silky border around the hem. She shines in it.

Stephen sets up a fitting for next week. I'm famished and tell Eva we must have lunch somewhere nearby. I don't have the strength for a long walk this afternoon.

Back on Madison, I suggest we shop for shoes before we eat. Low heels so she doesn't totter.

"I have those Mary Janes you bought me when we first got to New York," she says.

"Those are brown, darling. You need shoes to match the dress."

"But what if—" she starts.

"What if the war doesn't go as planned?" I shake my head. "During war nothing is predictable, and it's foolish to lay stock in what might happen six months from now. Better to think about today but be prepared for tomorrow, whatever may come. Besides, getting ready for a formal ball is the best antidote to horrible war news."

We find a perfect pair of shoes in a shop, and back outside I lead her to a restaurant on 55th Street.

"Let's celebrate," I say. "I'm taking my granddaughter to Le Pavillion."

"A French place?"

"The official name is Le Restaurant du Pavillion. We should honor your father's taste in fine dining."

"And pay homage to Paris." Eva blinks. "Honestly, doesn't it sometimes feel as if we're living during two wars?"

"It does, yes, but if I had a choice, I wouldn't live during war at all." I reach to open the door, but a doorman gets to it first. When we walk in, I say, "Right now, let's enjoy a good meal."

I admit the Pavillion is a splurge. The restaurant has the reputation of being the most lavish eating place at the New York World's Fair a few years ago, and the view of the Lagoon of Nations is a treat for us both.

The maitre d' greets us in French. "Bonjour, mesdames." He asks if we desire a table for two and checks a paper on his podium.

"Oui," Eva says.

He mutters to himself then says, "Bon chance—une seule table pour deux."

Eva whispers to me, "I believe he'd like us to be grateful he's giving us the last table."

I whisper back, "It's the French manner." When Chess and I ate at restaurants in Paris, diners always looked bored if not slightly annoyed. *Malheureux* the French call it, as if it's impolite to laugh or appear to be enjoying a meal even though French dishes are the best in the world.

When we're seated, the waiter speaks English with a thick French accent and announces that the restaurant's wines and tins of food have been brought from France—before the occupation. Chateaubriand with sauce Béarnaise is a specialty. With rations what they are, I wonder what chefs do with the inferior steaks they tie around the tender meat to give it more flavor. Rosa would toss butter in the frying pan to make those fatty cuts of meat a delicacy.

In France, restaurants frown on women drinking wine in the afternoon, so I order coffee and Eva asks for hot tea. Besides, the wines here are *très cher*, and I can enjoy spending more on the food.

Eva blows into her teacup before she sips. "The girls at school said when their mothers had their debuts there were big bands, French champagne, and flowers brought in from the south."

"I'm afraid those days are past," I say. "The champagne most likely will be American this year, flowers if we can find them, music of some kind, and a hundred young ladies. The more damsels we include, the larger the contributions for our soldiers."

"If it's December, will I need a wrap?"

"I have a fur stole I'll lend you." I don't tell her it was my mother's lest she think it's outdated. She can wear it going into the Grand Ballroom of the Waldorf-Astoria and then lay it aside.

"And you'll have to practice a proper curtsy." I tap the table with my index finger. "I do hope Will can get back to New York before December 20th."

"We'll see." She'll probably write his superior officer herself to request he get leave.

I sense there's something else on her mind, so I take a sip of my coffee and wait.

"The girls at school said it's tradition for their fathers to escort them in," she says.

I expected the father escort would come up, but not so soon. Taking a breath, I say, "Would you like your Uncle Tax to escort you, or should we fly Oliver back from Guatemala?"

She tilts her head and looks sadly at her teacup. "Uncle Tax will do very well."

When the waiter comes to take our order, Eva chooses Foie gras parfait, a popular dish at Le Pavillon, and Crudos, a lime-cured striped bass. I have French Veloutés with mussels, potatoes, watercress, and caviar, thinking it's prudent to get the best France has to offer before everything is shipped to Hamburg or Cologne.

"Danny," Eva says, "some of the girls at the soda shop are quitting to train as nurses' aides. I'd like to try that."

"That's a sensible idea." Working in a hospital sounds more noble—and safer—than cleaning counters and being cordial to servicemen at a soda shop. Not that I don't trust Eva. It's the servicemen hypnotized by her loveliness I don't trust.

26

Pride and Glory

When we return from lunch, Eva declares she wants to spend the rest of the day with her father's letters. She's reading one dated in early September where he writes about being at the second battle of the Marne.

She tilts her head. "He doesn't say much about the fighting. What do you know about it, Danny?"

I tell her what I've read. The Marne River is east of the city of Reims, and Jack's division joined with French fighters. For weeks there was heavy firing on both sides with enemy troops dropping dead or wounded to the trampled ground. Still more came in what seemed inexhaustible throngs. The French commander had the idea of running three lines of trenches parallel to each other, one behind the other. It must have taken days to dig trenches some five feet into the ground. Jack was in a trench three rows from the front, manning the telephone with a direct line to the Colonel who passed the communique to Major General Edwards. Jack's job was to keep information going between pilot observers and headquarters and to pass orders from the superiors to sergeants commanding the troops. When German soldiers attacked the first and second lines, they found the trenches empty. By the time they reached the third trench, they were surrounded, trapped by Allied forces. Hundreds of the maneuverable French Renault tanks moved in, two-man vehicles with one driving and the other operating a machine gun. So effective were the tanks in killing and wounding the enemy, those German soldiers left standing retreated.

Once again, Jack's letters protected me from the details, but the newspapers didn't. More than a hundred thousand Germans were killed in the weeks of fighting as well as thirteen thousand British, twelve thousand American soldiers, and nearly a hundred thousand French. What was Jack feeling during the battle, I wonder. Fright? Anxiety? Responsibility for the men under his supervision? His letters leave me only to imagine.

"Danny, the President of France, French generals, and General Pershing showered my father's division with citations after the battle," Eva says. "He writes, 'Nobody need ever tell me there is a better body of troops in the AEF.' American Expeditionary Forces, I think he means. Weren't they called the Yankee Division?"

"I believe they were, yes."

"The troops were victorious because of my father's training and leadership." Eva pulls back her shoulders. "I'm so proud of him."

"I am as well," I say, "but he didn't return to the States for another year. I'll tell you all about it later so you can picture his homecoming."

"I'd like that."

She's looking through the box when I ask, "Have you had word from Will? I haven't found any letters in my mailbox." I've seen a few letters from her mother. She says the family is settled in Guatemala City where everything is lush and green. Joanie likes it there and is already speaking some Spanish. Oliver is orienting himself and meeting dignitaries. Eva says her mother sounds a little disoriented by the language, the food, the services—especially where to have her hair done and where to shop—even the humidity of the climate.

"As for Will," she says, "Before he left he said he'd be on a ship in the Pacific checking on American naval stations and I shouldn't expect a letter for a while, but since Pearl Harbor, the Japanese aren't much of a threat."

I don't tell her that according to the *Times*, the Japanese haven't given up. Their troops are guarding dozens of islands in the Pacific ready to take aim at American ships in range. But I'd rather not disillusion her.

"He told me he'll probably be stationed on Maui. I imagine he'll go to the beach every chance he gets."

"He should have plenty of time to write you, then."

She glances toward the door, and I know she's thinking of the mailbox. "In the meantime, I have these from my father."

The sun is setting and she reaches to turn on a lamp. "Listen to this one. 'My dear, brave Muz. It is awful to be so far away in times like these with you suffering and my not being there to comfort you at this time.' How sweet he is to think of what you must be going through—what you went through after Wells died."

I clasp my hands and squeeze my fingers together. "I want you always to think of your father as kind and considerate. He was a loving son and I know he was a loving father to you and your brother and sister." Talking of my dead sons invites that familiar lump to my throat.

"Oh," Eva says, "he mentions his birthday. 'My twenty-first birthday passed uneventfully except for continuous thoughts of home.' We always celebrated his birthday by having friends over for drinks and cake. I guess he didn't have cake that year. Such a pity."

"When he was a boy he liked ice cream on his birthday. I wish we could go back to those happier times." Eva is doing her best to take me there, and I love her for it.

"Danny, he writes he may be promoted to captain. That's the good news," she says. "The sad news is he hasn't heard from Sue in months and thinks she has forgotten him. He says, 'It breaks me up.' So she was his sweetheart, as I suspected. He says he had dinner with a diplomat and his beautiful Persian wife. 'She is twenty-two and very pretty and they are staying with an aunt who lives here. She is the prettiest girl I have seen here and is very much like Sue. Tell Sue she had better beware and write me!' Goodness," Eva says, "Sue might have been my mother."

"I doubt that," I say. "Margaret won his heart in a way Sue never did."

"And listen to this," she says. "He's in Paris for a few days and went to the opera. And today he's going to Versailles to play golf and see the chateau with Frank. But he can't get Sue out of his mind. He says, 'I saw Charlie King and he had all sorts of news of Sue. He also intimated that she was engaged. Still, it may not be true.' Oh, poor Daddy. He so wanted Sue to love him. I wonder if I should name my first daughter Sue — or Susan — in honor of his lost love."

"I wouldn't mention that to your mother." I squint one eye, thinking. "But I believe your grandfather mentioned there was a Susan long ago in the Cumings family. Susan Wells, her name was. Your grandfather's family liked to keep the ancestors' names alive."

"Well, then, if I happen to have a girl one day, Susan she shall be."

Eva goes back to Jack's letter. "One of the things I love most is the way he ends the letters. In this one, he says, 'The moon is bright tonight and I am thinking of and praying for you and Thayer as I always do. Heaps of love and all the kisses in the world.'" She looks up with a far-away expression. "I wish I had some of his kisses right now."

I Will Not Leave You

I have much on my mind tonight, too much to fall asleep. The dress, the winter ball, Eva's birthday, the war. Wars, I mean, those past and the one present. In the Great War it was Germany and Kaiser Wilhelm. Now it's Japan and Hirohito, Italy and Mussolini, Germany and Hitler, the North Africa Campaign. When will fighting end?

When I reach to turn off the light, I see the journal. Wasn't there another paper tucked inside?

I open the back cover and pull out the second letter. The postmark is June 1918. The penciled writing is fading from so many years ago. It begins, "Dear Mrs. Cumings." I get a chill whenever I'm referred to that way. Three years later I would be Mrs. Swain, a name I'll keep for the rest of my days.

My name is Dick Dilworth, a Marine in the 6th Division with your son Wells. Private Cumings and I fought side by side at Belleau Wood near Les Mare Farm. There were 200 in our Division against more than a thousand German forces, but we are Marines, and Marines run toward conflict, even if we face overwhelming odds. Throughout the days of shelling, Private Cumings never faltered in his courage and conviction that we would prevail against the enemy. He was an inspiration to me as well as to our entire Division.

At the moment I am in a field hospital with a wound to my left arm. Private Cumings was on a cot near mine with a severe stomach wound. Before he was wounded he was in such excellent physical condition that even afterward he was able speak and asked me to put down his words to send to you. I have done my best to write what I could hear him utter.

On his deathbed, my son thinks of me. I brought him into this world and, at least in his thoughts, I ushered him out.

"Dear Mother, do not worry. The pain is not so bad. When I was brought in, on the cot next to me was the pale corpse of a man who did not survive. A medic crouched over my body and felt my neck for a pulse. I felt I was hanging in midair watching him cut off my bloody uniform and tend to me. If I leave this world, I will not leave you. You will hear me in the music of Mozart and Chopin, see me in red poppies blooming in the spring, feel me next to you at the piano. I am not afraid. I am like my father who faced his end bravely. I will love you through all eternity, my dear, dear Muz."

Mrs. Cumings, Private Cumings died after enduring for four days. He was given morphia for the pain, but morphia was no cure for the demon death that worked its way into him and into so many of our soldiers. Of the 200 in our Division who went into battle, 19 came out. I was a lucky one. Your son spilled his blood to turn back the enemy. He helped save Paris, save France, and save the Allied hope of victory.

With my condolences,

Private Richard Dilworth, 6th Division, U.S. Marines

I fold the letter and return it to the journal, then reach to turn out the light. In the darkness I whisper, "Bradley, why were you not with him, protecting him? Why were you not his angel?"

As Somnus, the god of sleep, approaches me, I hear a quiet voice. "I was there." It's the voice of my first husband, the father of my sons. Again the voice. "I can no more stop a bullet than I could move an iceberg, my love, but I was at Belleau Wood taking his pain into myself. I was his guide into the afterlife. He is with me now, resting, peaceful."

Then I am on a ship sailing down the River Lethe in that interval between wakefulness and slumber. I struggle to hold onto those last words — resting, peaceful — but memory is elusive and I drift into the dream world.

I don't know how long I've slept before, still half asleep, I sense someone in the room.

"Rosa?" Has she come early, even before dawn to start her workday?

"It's Eva, Danny."

"Eva? What are you doing up?"

"I heard voices." She's by the bed. In the moonlight I can tell she's looking at me with an expression of concern.

"Voices? In your room?"

"No," she says. "In your room. A man's voice."

"There's no one here, darling. Just me." I pull back the cover. "See?" Patting the mattress, I invite her to climb in. "You can sleep with me tonight."

She snuggles in and pulls up the cover.

"I thought it might be Bert Marckwald," she murmurs. Then she giggles. I giggle, too.

The window is open, and a breeze tickles the sheer curtain. It's cool tonight and quiet except for an occasional car rumbling down Park Avenue. She turns on her side and takes my left hand in her right. We fall asleep that way and when daylight filters into the room, my granddaughter is still there next to me, our hands touching.

28

Bally

On her birthday Eva spends the morning working at New York Hospital as an aide to nurses. Thayer got us two tickets for the Ziegfeld Follies at Winter Garden Theatre this evening. He and Ginny are too busy with the baby to join us.

When Eva returns from the hospital in the afternoon, she is carrying a bag.

"Look what the nurses did." She shows me cards, candies, and holds up a writing pen. "A soldier gave one of the nurses this pen. It's ink, and you don't have to carry around an inkwell. She wanted me to have it. Eventually everyone will own one of these, she said." She hands me the pen, the first one I've seen.

"There's a tiny ball that lets the ink flow out slowly." She points to the tip with the ball.

"How convenient," I say. Often new inventions are first tested by military personnel.

I put on the kettle for tea while Eva tells me about soldiers in the hospital, some with minor wounds and others missing arms or legs. At first she was horrified, but the nurses trained her to stay calm. She is to smile, to ask about where they're from, their parents, what they enjoyed doing before they went to war. A few don't make it, and she learned not to be distressed that they were beyond help but to move on to the living men, those who could be healed. When I think about the young teenager who arrived in Maine early last month and the young woman with me now, I'm astonished at what she has learned, her growing confidence, her maturity. Not that I can take credit. It's the war, the city of

New York, and her father's eloquent letters that have seeped into her.

I serve tea in the kitchen because we have a busy evening ahead of us. "We ought to dress up a little tonight because we'll be in Midtown." I lift my teacup to her.

"Midtown?"

"As you requested for your birthday, we're off to the theatre."

"The theatre? Marvelous!" she says. "What's the show?"

"Let's let it be a surprise." With comedian Milton Berle as the host, the Follies should lift us both out of the blues. I read in the *Times* English actor Arthur Treacher will be singing and dancing, and the Rhythmaires will sing songs like "Come Up and Have a Cup of Coffee." With Eva's time in New York running short, I look forward to a bit of fun tonight.

"Did you pick up the mail?" she asks.

"Not yet, but we can get it on the way out."

Eva finishes her tea and dashes to get ready. Within an hour, we're heading for the lobby and right on time, she finds a letter in the box from Private First Class Will Robbins. She holds the letter to her chest for a few seconds.

"I'll read it later." She is trembling, and I doubt she'll enjoy the show with the anticipation of reading his words. And rereading them, I can bet.

"Are you sure?" I ask.

"Of course," she says. "I'll tell Will I took him to the theatre."

"He'll enjoy that—a vicarious experience."

On the Park Avenue sidewalk, Eva raises her arm to hail a taxi as she no doubt has seen New Yorkers do. Now that she's seventeen, I suppose I can loosen my reins on her although as her grandmother, I'm still protective.

A taxi stops, and we slide into the back. I tell the driver to take us to the theatre, and as we drive away, Eva takes Will's letter from her purse and looks at it again. I don't want to pry, but I see some writing on the back of the envelope. A secret message they share, something endearing, no doubt. Falling in love through mail can't be easy. And yet one can learn a lot about a person by his handwriting, his grammar, his phrasing. Will had a year at Harvard before he joined the Marines but in these times, defending our allies takes priority over schooling.

She holds the letter until we get to the theater, then slips it back into her purse.

After the show, I expect Eva will want to hurry home to read her letter but instead, she says she's hungry. We find a diner and she orders a sandwich and a cola. I have a glass of wine, grateful that one of President Roosevelt's first orders of business was to end Prohibition. While he's still in the White House, I'm hoping he'll put an end to the war and bring Eva's young man home.

"The theater was remarkable," Eva says. "The painted ceiling, the chandeliers."

"Winter Garden is the largest theater and one of the oldest in New York." I add, "I hope you enjoyed the show."

She picks up a potato chip and crunches it. "This is a birthday I'll never ever forget."

"You have one more year of school, darling. Is it time to think about what happens next?"

Eva washes down the chips with her cola. "I have some options," she says. "I'd like to spend some time in Guatemala with my family. I'm sure I can find some way to be helpful there."

"In diplomacy?" I ask.

"Perhaps. Or nursing." She turns her head toward the window by our booth as if she's just thought of something. "Oh, I've forgotten about Will. How odd. I guess the show distracted me. Could we go back to Park Avenue now so I can read his letter?"

Outside the window, light from the streetlamps shines on the pavement. Even after nine at night people scurry along the sidewalk and cars rush by. I haven't the stamina of this teenager, and the wine has made me sleepy.

"We ought to look for a taxi, then." I hold up my wine glass before taking one last sip. "Here's to you. Happy birthday, Eva."

Born in 1899, Wells would be turning forty-four on his birthday, just before Eva's. It seems impossible. His plans, his talents, all buried in a French battlefield. But Eva and her beau are alive and well, and she comes to the kitchen the following morning, beaming.

"Did you get good news from the Pacific?" I ask.

"He misses me," she says. "He's positively dismal being away from me."

"Dis-mal?" Rosa says.

"Gloomy," I say. "Very sad." Rosa came to America from Cuba where the U.S. has air bases. The Cuban Navy protects Allied ships coming through hostile waters. We're grateful to the Cubans, and I'm very grateful to have Rosa helping me. Her English is good, and she's studying to become an American citizen.

"It's odd how he knows my brother and went to the same schools as my father." Eva accepts a cup of tea from Rosa. "It's — it's as if Will was made for me."

I felt the same way about Bradley, a Unitarian and a Harvard man. Will seems like a gentleman. I just hope he's strong enough for Eva.

"He may well be made for you, but we'll have to have your birthday party without him."

"Party?" Eva says.

"Your Uncle Tax, Ginny, and the baby are coming for dinner tonight. Maybe a few others. War or no war, turning seventeen deserves a celebration."

I can't tell from Eva's expression whether she's pleasantly surprised or dismayed. She looks at Rosa. "I'll try to get home a little early to help."

I ask Henry to direct our guests to the courtyard where I've set cut vegetables on a small table and a bowl of pimento cheese with saltines. Bert Marckwald brought a bottle of good whiskey, and Thayer has supplied Pepsi Colas. Rosa provided a bucket of ice. We'll save the wine for dinner. Ginny sits on a garden bench holding baby Gay. At four months old, she's wiggly but smiling—and drooling.

We're waiting for Eva to change from work and join us when Rosa appears.

"Mr. Henry rang," she says. "One more guest is here."

"Another guest?" I hold my breath, hoping it's Will. "Did he say who?"

"He name Bally."

"Tell Henry yes, let Bally in." I thought Eva's brother had deployed overseas. She must be in touch with him, or else he's surprising her because he knows it's her birthday.

Eva emerges, her hair still damp from washing, cheeks glowing. She's in a sort of costume, a white blouse with short sleeves puffed at the shoulders, embroidery at the neck, and a three-tiered skirt in ocean blue with more embroidery at the hem.

"Here I am," she says, "dressed in my mother's birthday gifts all the way from Guatemala."

Earlier, I retrieved the box from the mailroom and put it on her bed.

"What a delight you are," Bert says. "If I had marimbas, I'd ask you to dance."

"It's like your mother is here and brought Guatemala with her," Thayer says.

Eva goes to Ginny and little Gay. "May I hold her?" she asks.

The baby lifts her arms to Eva who looks natural with a child on her hip. At that second Bally walks into the courtyard wearing his dress uniform. Ginny stands up, probably afraid Eva might drop the baby when she sees her brother, but Eva takes Gay with her to wrap one arm around Bally's neck.

"I hoped you'd come," she says.

"Happy birthday, Eva." He kisses her cheek. "Fortunately, I was given leave before I head out for Europe. I hate to miss a party." He looks at the whiskey bottle on the garden table. "Now, how about a drink?"

Bert pops open a Pepsi, pours half a glass, adds a generous jigger of whiskey, and tops it off with ice cubes. Then he hands the glass to Bally who holds up the drink toward Eva. "To your health, Sister," he says.

Bert puts an arm around Eva. "A birthday cocktail?" he asks.

"Just cola, thanks."

Eva is using good judgment. A birthday is no excuse for silliness.

Rosa has planned dinner for six-thirty, and we make our way upstairs, three at a time in the tiny elevator with the uniformed lift man. The six of us, Thayer with Gay on his lap, gather at the table. Before he sits, Bert opens two bottles of wine and pours a small portion for each of us, including Eva. In the last two years, we've grown used to small portions, grateful for domestic wine and food made from cans or local gardens. A piece of meat is cause for thanksgiving. Rosa serves a hearty pistou, a French soup made with canned beans and noodles to which she added shreds of chicken she acquired somewhere, maybe from her own chicken coop. We use her home-baked bread to sop up the rich juices.

Talk shifts to war.

"Did you join up or get drafted?" Bert asks Bally.

"Draftees serve twelve months in the Army and afterward have a ten-year commitment with the reserves." Bally jerks his head side to side. "That's not for me. I enlisted. Already served six months, counting Officers Candidate School, so I should be up for discharge in a year or so—that is, if I make it through combat in Europe."

"I wish you wouldn't talk like that, Bally," I admonish.

Bally straightens his back. "I'm sorry, but that's the reality, Danny."

As if I don't know the reality of young men going to war. I study my grandson, memorizing his exquisitely handsome face. If I had a camera, I'd take a snapshot of him so I never forget what he looked like before the horrors of war carve crevices into his flawless skin.

He raises his eyes to Thayer. "What about you, Uncle Tax?"

"I did my service with the U.S. Navy. You're looking at Lieutenant Cumings." He puffs out his chest. "The draft wasn't started until 1940, so even if I'd had to register, I'd likely have been given a family exemption, thanks to this baby." He grins at his daughter.

Bally swivels his eyes toward Bert.

"Don't look at me," Bert says. "I'm way beyond fighting age."

"Damn shame women don't have to be drafted," Bally says.

He's sitting next to Eva who gives him a light punch on the arm. "Someone has to run things while our men are away," she says.

"Speaking of running things," Bally says, "Harvard is giving Winston Churchill an honorary degree in September—cap, gown and all."

"Will you be there?" Eva asks.

"I'll be on the other side of the world, but attendance is mandatory for current Harvard students."

"It would be quite an honor to meet the Prime Minister," Bert says.

"Well," Bally says, "Churchill's not perfect. India, part of the British empire, is suffering from famine, and he advocates using chemical weapons in war."

"Mustard gas was a chemical weapon in the first war," Thayer says.

"I think we've come to realize gas is an inhumane way to wage war." Bert this time. "It burns the lungs and blinds men. Lots of men in combat died from the gas."

Eva breaks in. "It's war that's inhumane."

"Sometimes," I break in, "war is necessary."

A few seconds' pause follows. Thank goodness Rosa comes in.

"I take the dishes?" She begins to clear.

"Let's bring Eva's gifts to the table," Ginny says, graciously changing the subject. She and Bert get up to carry a few boxes and place them in front of Eva. Meantime, Rosa brings out plates and the magically concocted War Cake I saw her making earlier. Sugar is hard to come by, so she used molasses and syrup for sweetening, and lard, raisins, cinnamon, and cloves to give the cake flavor. The cake is passable, but not like the gateau we enjoyed before the war.

As Eva opens her gifts—a Harvard crew shirt from Bally, scented soaps from Thayer and Ginny, a luxury even I appreciate. From Bert, Jean Genet's book *Notre Dame des Fleurs*. Paper is in short supply, but Bert must have found an old copy of Genet's book in a store. Or perhaps it had sat unread on his own shelf. I've never heard him speak a word of French.

"You'll have to bone up on your *français*, Eva," he says. "Your father was fluent."

My gift is last and the smallest box, a gold bracelet Chess gave me when we were first married. Eva's eyes well up when she opens the top. It's a bangle, fourteen karats.

"Chess had it engraved FCS for Florence Cumings Swain," I tell her. "You'll want to have the initials changed."

"For some reason I was never given a middle name. EC seems inadequate."

"Then wait until you're married," Bally says, "and use Cumings as your middle name."

Bert speaks up. "ECR has a nice ring to it."

"Bert," I caution, "you're jumping the gun. They've had only two dates."

"And how many letters has he sent her?"

Eva blushes. Will has professed his love. What comes next feels almost inevitable.

"What's the R for?" Bally asks.

"I think you know him," Eva says. "Will Robbins. He went to school with you."

Bally raises his brows. "Will? Sure I know him. He was a year behind me at boarding school. Quiet fellow but a sterling athlete. He excelled at ice hockey. Everyone seemed to like him." He gives Eva the side-eye. "You're seeing him?"

"He's in active service," Eva says. "The Marines. His regiment is somewhere in the Pacific."

"The Marines are lucky, then." Bally raises his glass up. "Let's have a toast to Will Robbins and my sister, and to the U.S. Marines."

"Here, here," Bert says.

Thayer echoes, "Here, here."

Eva slips the gold bracelet over her hand and stares at it. "I'm going to keep the FCS," she says, "so my grandmother is always with me."

A knock on the door startles me. Who would be coming at the dinner hour? I haven't invited anyone else. Eva is on her feet before Rosa can get to the door. She probably imagines Will has miraculously flown across an ocean and a continent to get to her birthday party.

When she opens, Henry is standing with a bouquet of roses in his arms. Two dozen, it looks like. Red roses peeking above tissue paper. Far too costly for Henry's salary.

He hands the roses to Eva. "Someone's having a birthday," he says and dips his head before he goes back to his post.

"Goodness," Eva says.

Bally approaches and examines the roses for a note. When he finds a small envelope, he opens it and reads aloud. "Happy birthday, Eva. Eternally, Will."

"How would he have ordered flowers from a ship?" Ginny asks.

"I doubt the florist knows Morse code," Thayer says. "He probably made the arrangement with a florist before he boarded ship and asked to have the flowers delivered today."

"He knows when your birthday is?" Bally says.

Eva's cheeks pink. "He asked me how old I am, and I guess I told him how soon I'd be seventeen."

"Good man," Bert says. "Takes notes on what's important."

Rosa takes the flowers and puts them in a vase for the table.

It's too late to wind back the clock to Eva the golden-haired child, her brother holding her hand as they walked with their father. And then little Joanie joined the clan. But I have to embrace the joy of having Eva with me and the great promise her future holds.

29

Paris

For two nights Bally slept on the sofa in the den. Eva took time from her hospital work to wander around Manhattan with him. In the evenings laughter shook the chandelier over the dining table. For days after her brother took the train back to the base in Virginia, Eva floated on air. To be seventeen, in love, and so much to look forward to. She is a full moon rising on a clear night, and the stars flush at her radiance.

This morning she comes from her bedroom carrying several of her father's letters.

"Danny," she says, sitting at the table, "listen to this: 'I am not with the troop anymore but am in the Intelligence Section of the General Staff as Divisional Observation Officer.' He has twenty men with him on the front line where he can see what he calls the Boches walking around."

Rosa brings her a cup of tea, and Eva frowns at the page in front of her. "They're not fighting, but he says it's just a matter of time. And he's in a 'very comfortable dugout about thirty feet below the ground.'" She looks up at me. "How can that be at all comfortable?"

"Good question." I sit across from her with my coffee.

"It's like living the life of a mole," she says.

"At least he was safe, darling."

"He has to walk from trench to trench to check on his observers, and on this particular day in mid-September he walked seven miles, once within five hundred yards of the German troops. And the trenches were ankle-deep in mud and water. He says the going was rather difficult." She looks up again. "Rather difficult? Gosh. How awful."

"Your father was prone to sarcasm, I think."

"You really have to read his letter of September 19."

"Would you read it to me?"

"All right." She takes a deep breath and starts.

We have made the attack so long expected, and I got through so far with nothing but my cold. We went over the top at 8:00 a.m. on September 12th in pouring rain after an all-morning artillery bombardment. Everything went smoothly until we got into some woods and machine guns.

Eva runs a finger under the lines of writing. Machine guns in the trees—like the Belleau Wood attack. If Jack was an intelligence officer, why was he dodging machine-gun bullets with the infantry?

"Go on," I say.

She starts again.

Two of my men got separated, but in so doing they captured one German officer and thirty-nine prisoners. Another man and I were near the edge of the woods when seven men appeared and began signaling. It then occurred to me they were Boches wanting to surrender.

When I first read the letter, I recall thinking: *He's still alive. He's still alive. He's still alive.* Now I can't help but wonder how two men captured forty. But the surrendering had begun. Thank heaven.

Eva sips her tea. "The war must be almost over, Danny. He'll be coming home soon." She says it as if the war is happening now. It is, of course, but a different war. I wonder if her beau has as much courage as her father had.

"Maybe President Roosevelt will work some magic for our men in this war," I say. "Two years is such a long time to make sacrifices."

"I don't know how long the first war went on."

"Four years, I think. American soldiers were involved for two."

She goes back to the letter. "Goodness—Jack says he hasn't had time to eat and no sleep at all, but he took another six prisoners."

"I worried about him, of course. It's easy to make mistakes under those circumstances—fatal mistakes." Worry was my primary preoccupation then.

Rosa brings us bowls of oatmeal for our breakfast with brown sugar and raisins. She places big spoons beside the bowls and nods.

"Is good for you," she says, as if oatmeal will disappoint us. I don't recall ever being disappointed by anything Rosa has served.

"Do you have the next letter?" I ask. "The one to his grandmother?" I was relieved when Bardie gave me that one to read. He wrote only pleasantries to her.

"Yes," Eva says. "Apparently she had asked him about Paris, and he seems delighted to talk about it. He says everything is expensive and the cafes and theatres are crowded with American officers passing through. 'I never hope to see a more beautiful city than Paris,' he says." She frowns. "I wonder what Paris is like today, in 1943."

I don't want to talk about what the newspapers say, but Eva asks, and I owe her an answer.

"This past winter Parisians had no heat and no way to get a supply of coal. No electricity either, and food is scarce. The German army feeds itself first and rations what's left for the French. They're lucky to get bones and gristle. And the Nazis are arresting Jewish people and taking them to camps in Germany and Poland." I pray she doesn't ask me about the camps. The news hints of mass genocide, but it's hard to fathom. And I don't want to burden a teenage girl with the ugly details.

For Eva's sake, I need to be optimistic. "The good news is the French, English, and Russians are marching toward Paris with the Americans. The city is sure to be liberated before long."

"I hope it will be what it once was," she says. "Jack writes he went to the Opera Comique twice, once to see *Carmen* and the other *Manon*. I've never been to an opera. He says they were not as good as at the Metropolitan."

"Then we should put the opera on your wish list," I say.

She gives me a quizzical look and dips her spoon into the oatmeal. "What's *Carmen* about?"

"I've read reviews but haven't seen the opera myself. I believe an exotic gypsy seduces a soldier. He leaves the service to be with her and forsakes his sweetheart back home."

"Oh dear," Eva says. "Let's not let Will see that one."

I give a soft laugh. "I doubt Will is meeting many gypsies aboard ship."

"Well," she says, "there's Maui—and hula girls."

I can tell Eva is drifting away from the past and looking toward the future.

"Anyway," I say, "*Carmen* played at the Met this past winter. I'm sorry we missed it."

Rosa has put the *Times* on the table and I slide it toward me. The headline reads "FIFTY PARIS HOSTAGES SHOT AS REPRISAL FOR DEATH OF A NAZI." I turn the paper over before Eva sees the gruesome news. I'd rather she not know hostages are being killed for revenge or the most minor of fabricated offenses. As if shooting innocents is sport.

"What's in the paper?" she asks.

"Oh, something about an oil shortage because of oil being shipped to Europe for the troops. And there aren't as many automobile accidents because gasoline is so expensive—

shortages again. Nothing surprising. I'll read the rest of the stories later." I have to change the subject. "Are you going to the hospital today?"

"Yes. Some of the badly wounded men are in despair and I like to cheer them up."

"No doubt opening their eyes and seeing you will be just the cheer they need." Even as the words leave my mouth, I think of Wells lying in the field hospital, a canvas shelter his sole protection from the fighting. So far from home and helpless in his damaged body. Did anyone cheer him? Was he able to open his eyes and see beauty anywhere? My darling boy, what I wouldn't give to gaze at your angelic face again, to hear you at the keyboard one more time.

While Eva is at the hospital, I wander to the piano. Rosa has kept the black surface dusted and polished. The baby grand has been with me since Bradley and I lived in the brownstone before we sailed on the *Titanic*. I played every day then, mostly classical pieces, never the popular ragtime music. It's been months— maybe more than a year since I touched the keys. Whether it's having Eva with me or feeling a connection with Wells, it seems like time to open the fallboard. The panel makes a creaking sound at first and then a soft thud as it settles open.

When I started playing at age nine or ten, the keys reminded me of big teeth with gaps between them. The white keys were the good people and the black keys the devil's notes. Now I realize the black keys make beautiful sounds, too. At first my fingers found the keys as a robot might play, and I struggled to read the music. I wanted to control the piano, to discipline it to my wishes. Always there was the sense of weight, the resistance of each key to strike the string. My mother scolded me for holding the pedal down too long, but I loved to hear the notes fade slowly away. Eventually the music began to vibrate through my body and it didn't matter whether I always hit the correct note or added my own variations to the composition.

Now the white keys have yellowed over nearly five decades. I suppose I've faded—or tarnished—over as many years. The piano and I are growing old together.

I let my fingers rest on the keys. They're surprisingly warm, as if someone else has recently had hands on them, and I wait for music to come to me. Debussy answers with a suite that begins adagio, and I lean into the rhythm of the sounds. Even with my eyes closed, my fingers find the right keys. Wells didn't favor Debussy—too slow, he used to say. I don't recall him playing ragtime either, even though Thayer asked for it. But Debussy's music is velvety, ethereal, as if it comes from another realm. A better realm than this war-torn one. An antidote to Wagner. If Debussy's music were paintings, it would be Monet or Renoir—but not even those. Debussy was in a group of his own making. He wrote that he could not live in the world of people and objects. He preferred solitude, and his music was like a gathering of wraithlike beings. Living ghosts.

I finish with Clare de Lune, the French word for moonlight. Debussy wrote the composition for a pastoral poem. The melody is like a landscape, the type of landscape I see on clear nights in Maine with waves rising and falling, frothing and lapping the shore. Under the moon's cast, the water shines like a wavy mirror reflecting a moment of pure pleasure.

When I reach the end, I sit in silence until Rosa comes in.

"Very nice, Mrs. Swain," she says, "but don't you have a hair appointment this afternoon?"

"Oh, right—I suppose I should get ready." I'd like to linger with Debussy's ghostly wraiths, but I am still in the world of the living, in the world of conflict and hardship. At least I know there is another world waiting for my escape.

30

A Hard Edge

Now that wounded men are returning, Eva works at the hospital most every day. In this war, far more suffer injuries than are killed. In the evening when I ask her about the work, she's reluctant to talk about it, and she drops into a chair almost too tired to eat.

"You don't have to tell me," I say, "unless it helps to air what you've seen."

Rosa has made a nice dinner of lamb chops — because lamb is more available than beef — with mashed potatoes and peas. Eva picks at her food.

"Burns are the most painful," she says. "But they heal eventually. Some have had legs or arms blown off — or both, but there are artificial limbs and the pain is tolerable." She tries to smile to soften the impact on me. "A few have spinal cord injuries and will never walk again." When she looks up, tears rim her eyes. "Imagine having to use a wheelchair for the rest of your life — and you're barely twenty years old."

I think about my boys, how if Wells had lived, he would be scarred and traumatized. He would have so many problems to overcome.

"If it's too hard to talk — " I start.

"No — you're right. It does help." She puts down her fork. "The worst are brain injuries. One man has seizures several times a day. There's shaking, difficulty speaking, blindness or deafness — all of which I hope are curable." She shakes her head as if in disbelief. "Nearly all of them have battle fatigue. They stare straight ahead and don't answer even when I know they can hear me. Some are extremely depressed. Others yell out with angry curses. When they sleep, they scream from nightmares." She pushes her plate away, crosses her arms on the table and stares at the grain in the wood. "Danny, everyone talks about how terrible the war is, but no one's talking about what happens after the soldiers come back." She takes a deep breath.

I know she's right. But *after they come back* relates to only one of my sons. The long-term effects linger. Jack was hard of hearing. Margaret says he sometimes hid behind a newspaper and looked at a single page for half an hour at a time—not reading, just lost in his thoughts. And yet he was jovial with his children. And he was always kind. I shudder to think what the effects would have been with Wells—if somehow he had survived.

I reach across the table and lay my hand on Eva's arm. "It might be better if you stop reading your father's letters for a while."

"No. I want to read them." Her eyes meet mine. "He made it through."

She gets up and goes to the den while Rosa clears the table. When she returns, she has several letters in her hand.

"When did the war end?" She sits at the table again.

At first I think she's asking about World War II. But we're still fighting this one for however long it takes.

"You mean the Great War, what was then called 'the war to end all wars.'"

"Yes."

"At precisely 11:11 a.m. on November 11, 1918, Germany signed an armistice with the Allies."

"This letter is dated October 2, 1918," Eva says. "There must still have been battles."

"Most likely."

"Jack says, 'Please don't worry about me facing life and death. I have done it many more times than once without the least hesitation. It is just like being in a storm.'" Eva blows a puff of air. "A storm—a storm of deadly metal."

Working at the hospital is changing her. I see a hard edge to her now. An armor has formed around her since she came to Maine two months ago.

She reads again. "He says, 'Since February, this division has seen continuous front-line service, so it is nothing more than getting used to it.'" She puts her hands on her hips. "Danny, I've seen the effects of what he calls front-line service. I don't see how anyone could possibly get used to it."

"That was a different war, Eva. We could have avoided this war if the Treaty of Versailles hadn't forced punishments on Germany. They spent the next fifteen years planning how to regain their territory and their dignity."

"What were the demands of the treaty?" she asks.

I think for a second. "Let's see—Germany had to pay reparations, lose part of their territory, and give up all their overseas colonies. And Kaiser Wilhelm had to stand trial for causing the conflict."

"Germany had colonies? Where?"

"In China and islands in the Pacific, I believe."

"At least in October Jack was safe in what sounds like an underground city. Near Verdun, he says." She raises her face from the letter. "Where is Verdun, Danny?"

"Close to the German border, I think."

"He says there are barracks, stores, recreation halls, all hundreds of feet underground. He eats out of a mess kit but says the food is good and everyone is friendly. His men call him 'Sir.'"

I ask Rosa to bring us tea. To be honest, I have a slight case of claustrophobia, and thinking about living underground makes me uncomfortable. I like the open spaces of Maine and my apartment high up in Manhattan. Maybe that night in the lifeboat still haunts me, the closeness of fifty people crowded into one tight space, the darkness pressing in on us, thoughts of Bradley in his underwater grave.

Eva thanks Rosa for the tea then goes back to the letter.

"Jack is sad to learn that General Edwards' daughter Bessie died of pneumonia at Camp Meade in Maryland. She was his only child. And he mentions Sue again. He received six letters from her at one time." She reads from Jack's letter. "'They're the kind of letters I had been looking for these past months, and it sort of set me up again. Of course, if all this love and devotion she sends me is just camouflage for friendship, I am being quietly misled.' Gosh—even then he's still hoping they'll end up together." She presses her lips together. "I wonder what happened to separate them."

"I honestly don't know." Even if I did know I wouldn't share it with Eva. She needs to believe—as I do—that her mother was his lasting love.

"He ends the letter by saying, 'Why worry about it? I have a real girl in a world where there is no doubt about mutual love, my own mother.'" Eva drops the paper onto the table and flops her palms over it. "How absolutely sweet is that?"

"I'm lucky," I say. "My sons were my three pillars after their father—"

"The *Titanic*." Eva draws her mouth to the side. "That awful ship."

I don't want to speak of 1912. "That was so long ago, darling. So let's hear more about Jack."

Eva sips from her teacup before she begins the next letter. "Late October was rainy and 'we are all dirty and muddy,' he says. Two of his signal men were killed in battle. He had twenty men under his supervision, so losing even one greatly affected him. Talk of a truce seems to have fallen through, he says, because the machine guns are still firing at them. Even so, the artillery and gas were terrific." Eva pauses to drink the last of her tea then continues. "I think he means the mustard gas. He must have had to put on one of those buggy-eyed masks. I don't know how he can call artillery and mustard gas terrific."

"I think he means horrible," I say. "Or maybe the literal meaning of terrific — terrifying."

Eva gives an ironic giggle at the next line. "Then he writes he has a painful wisdom tooth. What irony that a toothache is his sole complaint."

"After he got home, I had a dentist pull his wisdom teeth. Imagine Jack on the front lines with gunfire coming at him and he didn't have a scratch. Then he had to undergo the ordeal of having teeth pulled."

"By the way," she says, "he was passed over for the promotion to captain."

I knew that, of course. He was very disappointed, but as the youngest lieutenant in his division, he should have anticipated the promotion would be go to someone in service longer.

"Does he mention Major General Edwards in that letter?" I ask. "The general would have recommended him for the higher office."

Rosa brings tea cookies, and Eva eats two while she reads down the page.

"Yes. He calls General Edwards 'our dear old man.' He says General Pershing didn't like General Edwards very much and had him transferred using the excuse that two of his men befriended German soldiers who offered to stop shooting because a truce was about to be signed. Before General Edwards left, he told Jack to say goodbye to his boys at the front and thanked Jack for all he had done. Jack says the general 'shook hands with every officer and man at headquarters. There were many wet eyes, from which I was not excluded. He certainly has meant the world to the Yankee Division.' Jack says *Je suis completement degoute.* Can you translate it?"

"My French is rusty, but I believe it means 'I am completely disgusted.'"

I recall Jack telling me the general's dismissal was a misunderstanding with General Pershing about consorting with the enemy. Jack had great respect for Edwards. The general had organized Jack's division, the first Americans to go into combat. The battle of Chemin-des-Dames, I think it was. And he commanded Jack's troops in the second battle of the Marne that led to Germany's surrender. After he returned to the States, Jack visited General Edwards in Boston where he was headquartered with the Northeast Division.

"General Edwards sent me a letter thanking me for Jack's service," I tell Eva. "He wrote that Lieutenant Cumings was one of the finest soldiers in the American Army. I was touched by that. After forty years of service, Edwards retired and Massachusetts named a bridge after him."

"He and Jack must have had a close relationship," Eva says. "Daddy was that way. He had so many friends."

"Maybe we should stop for tonight," I say. "I'm worn out from all this time travel."

"As am I," Eva says. "But I have one more letter to read tonight, one from an island in the Pacific." Her face has an impish expression. "But I think I'll read this one in my room."

I'm restless tonight and think opening the window might help me get to sleep. Below on Park Avenue, taxis pause to pick up a customer or let one out, people coming home or leaving a gathering. On past nights when sleep eluded me, I poured myself a whiskey, and this is one of those evenings. Eva will be going off to school soon. I've given up my volunteer work and rarely see Thayer now that he has a family. In a few weeks it will be just Rosa and I again, Henry outside guarding the door, and the daily *Times*. Bert every now and then. And hundreds of strangers on the streets and in the parks.

Rattling in the freezer for ice feels like too much effort, and I don't want to risk another injury or wake Eva with the clatter. Whiskey without ice tastes like medicine, and sleeping medicine is what I need tonight. I pour a shot into a glass and toss it into my mouth the way I've seen it in Western movies like *The Carson City Kid* with men sidling up to a saloon bar. It must have been young whiskey—moonshine they used to call it. They drank it fast not for the taste but for the effect. That's the point, isn't it?

I find my way through the darkness back to bed and wait for sleep to bear down on me. When finally it comes, it brings a battlefield, my feet stuck in half a foot of mud so I can't lift my legs, much less walk. The enemy approaches, their eyes blazing with hatred, rifles against their shoulders, pointed at me. I'm not alone, though. The first to take a bullet is Bradley. The lead enters his chest at his heart and he falls, disappearing into the muck as if it's quicksand pulling him under. Wells steps forward to protect me. Machine-gun fire hits his belly, a spray of metal meant for me. When I try to scream, no sound escapes. Next to me, Jack holds a telephone to his ear. He's talking to someone but I can't hear what he's saying and he fades away like the final scene of a movie before the words *The End* appear, white letters on a black background. Then I'm alone facing the firing squad. Chess suddenly stands in front of me, a smile on his face, a golf club in his hand. When I try to tell him about the rifles, the war, a bullet enters his back, comes through his chest, and hits me in the neck. He dissolves and my hand goes to my throat trying to stop the blood that gushes from me, choking me, and I fall to the mud, soft and warm. Then the dream is gone and I'm afloat in a sea of black silk.

When I wake in the morning, I wonder how it is the dream world seems as real as daylight on the sidewalks of Manhattan. The letters from my sons, too, bring them so alive I feel I can reach out and touch them. Or maybe that's wishful thinking. If the past is gone and the future exists only in the imagination, what is the present, then? A mirage? Or a creation of my own making?

I drag my legs from under the covers and work my feet into my slippers. If I am the creator of my own reality, then I intend to create coffee with Rosa in my kitchen and my beautiful granddaughter greeting me with "Good morning, Danny. Did you sleep well?"

31

Muy Hermosa

"As late as November 8, Jack's division was still involved in fighting the German forces." Eva has taken her morning cup of tea to the den and is sitting on the sofa with the box. "You'd think the fighting would start to wind down. Didn't they know about the negotiations?"

I'm in a chair opposite her. "In war, nothing winds down until it's over." According to today's *Times*, even now in early August, Russia is attacking German armies invading Russian territory, the U.S. is dropping bombs over Germany, and although Mussolini has been arrested, British forces are still a presence in Italy. What I don't tell Eva is U.S. Navy ships have sunk Japanese destroyers. There may be retaliation, and Will could well have been part of that action.

Eva doesn't look up from the letter on her lap.

"Jack marched his men toward the German border on November 11, and at nine o'clock in the morning the commanding officers gave an order to attack," she says. "He must have been on his telephone because he received a call that the armistice would be signed at eleven o'clock that morning." She looks at the window where sun filters through the sheer draperies. "So they must have fought right until the bitter end."

"I guess neither side was willing to give up."

"What's so significant about the number eleven?" she asks.

"I've heard eleven represents transformation and an awakening."

"I guess that's appropriate," she says then goes back to the letter.

"'On the dot of eleven,' he says, 'there was suddenly a terrible, unbelievable silence. We did not cheer but tried to believe the Boche was really finished. The boys had been through so much and their minds were deadened to the realization that on the eleventh month, eleventh day, eleventh hour, the war was over.'"

Eva takes a breath. "I'm so relieved," she says as if she has been part of that war. In a way, I suppose she has.

She continues studying the letter. "He was told his division may come home in six weeks, but he doesn't know where they might be headed then. He hopes 'Heaven, Hell, or Hoboken by Christmas.'" She snorts a little laugh. "Did he make it back for Christmas in 1918?"

"That was twenty-five Christmases ago, but I don't think he got leave, no." I nod toward the box. "His letters should say. I do recall him coming home in the heat of summer."

"That must have been a hard time."

"At least the war was over by Christmas. Thayer was home from boarding school and wanted to spend the holiday in New York. We may have gone to a show, and it's likely he saw some friends. I was content to take walks, listen to music, enjoy a glass of wine."

Truth be told, I'm still angry with the U.S. military for keeping Jack away from his grieving mother. He should have been given special consideration after his brother's death. But I don't want to put my anger on Eva. My duty was to accept the decisions of the powers that be, even if I didn't agree with them. I certainly don't need to tell Eva the last five holiday seasons have been hard without Chess or her father. They must have been hard for her, too. When Thayer was on active duty with the

U.S. Navy, my sister Elaina invited me to spend Christmas with her family in Boston, but I preferred a week of solitude. I didn't want sympathy, and I felt closer to my dearly departed when I could play the piano and have a nice meal alone.

"What did you and Thayer do when the war ended?" Eva asks.

I appreciate a question I can happily answer. "In November New York came more alive than I had ever seen it. Horns blared, people cheered and waved flags on the streets. Strangers clasped hands, men wept. The Salvation Army band played music on Fifth Avenue for tens of thousands of people crowding the streets." I smile to think of that day. "By mid-December, things had quieted down and shop windows glowed with red and green displays. The best Christmas gift for me was knowing Jack was safe."

Eva is studying one of the last letters in the box. "He has been in a small town southeast of Paris for the last month." She runs her finger under a line in the letter. "He writes that Germans are wandering the town, but he says, 'Fraternizing with the German soldiers, even here, is forbidden, so I don't have a chance to try out my pitiful attempts at the German language. The attitude of these Germans is very polite, very obliging and, with a few exceptions, not antagonistic. But I can't learn to like them or sympathize with them in the least.'" Eva shifts her eyes to me. "It must have been hard for Daddy not to befriend the enemy. I never met anyone who didn't absolutely love him."

"Growing up, he had dozens of friends." I laugh to think about it. "I had trouble keeping food in the house when he had his buddies over. Boys are always hungry."

Eva holds the paper up to the light. "You'll be glad to know he had a big meal on Christmas day and his division decorated a tree for the children of the town. They gave little toys and chocolates to each of them and dolls to two little girls who lived in the chateau where he was being housed."

"If Jack couldn't be where he wanted to be, he made the best of wherever he was. And he reached out to people around him."

"Yes, that's my dad."

I slap my palms on my knees. "Now, how about some good news, darling?"

"I would love good news."

"You had the final fitting for your dress last week, and it was delivered yesterday afternoon before you returned from the hospital."

"Oh, Danny! May I see it?"

The dress arrived in a long garment bag, but I haven't looked at it yet, wanting Eva to do the unveiling. She does more than that—she takes the dress from the bag, slips out of her clothes, and carefully steps into the pretty gown.

"Fasten me up, will you please?" she says.

She raises her left arm so I can get to the zipper. The dress is a perfect fit.

"Now the shoes." She paws through pairs of shoes on the floor of her closet.

"I put them on the top shelf," I tell her. "In the box."

"Oh, I'm practically breathless." She kicks off her shoes and slides each foot like Cinderella into the bone-colored slippers.

"You have four months to wait before you present yourself, but I know you'll be the belle of the debutante ball, darling."

She whisks by me and twirls around the front room, pausing to catch glimpses of herself in the mirror over the liquor cabinet.

"I shall not ever sit in this dress," she says. "I don't want it to have a single wrinkle."

"You will have to curtsy," I remind her. "The rest of the evening you'll most likely be dancing."

She gasps. "I haven't danced in so long!"

Rosa comes from the kitchen and stands in the doorway. "*Muy hermosa*," she says.

I feel my lips curl upward, the apples of my cheeks lifting. "Yes, Rosa. *Muy hermosa* indeed."

32

Fraunces

With a week before she leaves for school, Eva is spending more time with her father's letters. While she's working at the hospital, I search through the few unread letters to find one particular envelope. I know its contents, and I don't want the message to deflate her jubilant mood. She's looking forward to her last year of secondary school, to being with her friends, and to seeing her mother. I'll wait until a better time to let her read the one dated April 16, 1919.

Margaret has written a few times, most recently to thank me for having Eva in New York which, of course, has been my delight, but also to say she'll fly from Guatemala to meet her daughter in Richmond, near the boarding school. They'll spend a few days together before she escorts Eva to her dormitory room. I'm trying not to be envious. After all, I'll see her in December. I've offered to help with the ball preparations, which will keep me occupied while she's away.

I have an idea and ring Thayer at his office.

"Do you have a few minutes to talk?" I ask him.

"Talk to you, Muz? Of course. In fact, are you free for lunch?"

"Am I free to have lunch with you, darling? Of course."

"Then meet me at Fraunces Tavern in an hour and a half."

Fraunces is the oldest tavern in New York, dating to Queen Charlotte's reign before the Revolutionary War. General Washington and his staff dined there. It's one of Thayer's favorite eateries.

I get ready and, still not savvy enough to take the subway alone, I hail a taxi. The driver knows the way to Fraunces.

I'm a little early, so the host seats me at a booth with red leather seats and I ask for a glass of white wine while I wait for Thayer. Everything is dark polished wood, including the coffered ceiling supported by fluted posts. I feel as if I'm two hundred years into the past.

By the time my wine arrives and I've spooned ice from my water glass into it, Thayer rushes in and finds me. Before he sits, he motions to the waiter, says "Draught," and points to his side of the table. Businessmen are always in a hurry, and if he wants a second beer, he'd better have the first one right away. He leans in and kisses me on the cheek before finally sitting, a bit out of breath.

"What's so urgent?" he asks.

"It looks like the urgency is yours, darling."

"I have a client meeting this afternoon."

The waiter brings Thayer's beer and two menus.

"I haven't been to Fraunces in years," I tell Thayer. "Your father took me here several times."

"The old man had good taste."

"Thayer, don't call him old. Your father didn't live long enough to be old."

"It's an expression, Muz. Fellows call each other old man all the time."

"He was a year younger than you are now."

Thayer stops his glass halfway to his mouth. "A year younger?"

"Your father was thirty-eight when he perished on the *Titanic*."

He puts down the glass without taking a drink. "I didn't realize."

"When your brother Jack died, he was exactly your age."

"Good Lord, that's right," he says. "In that case, I'd better be careful crossing Manhattan streets."

"I have no doubt you'll live to a ripe old age, darling. You have a youthful spirit." I lift my wine glass to him.

"Let's toast to our youthful spirits." He touches his glass to mine.

Service at Fraunces is excellent. Our waiter watches from the bar to see if we're ready to order.

"Do you want to share a plate of raw oysters?" Thayer asks, eyeing the menu.

"Your father adored oysters on the half shell, but I never developed a taste for them. I'll just have the turkey pot pie."

"It's a classic here." He decides on clam chowder and the scotch egg.

I bring up Eva's debutante ball. "Traditionally fathers escort their daughters."

"And you want me to do it?"

"Yes. If you're willing."

"Absolutely willing—if I can fit into my old tuxedo." He pats his generous belly. "If not, I'll have it altered."

I give him the December date. He guesses correctly that the ball will be held at the Waldorf-Astoria. I describe Eva's dress and tell him about her excitement.

The waiter brings his soup and my turkey pie. Thayer plants an elbow on the table next to the bowl, a bad habit I tried to break for the first ten years of his life.

"Anything else?" he asks.

The pie is too hot to eat, so I add more ice to my wine and sip while I wait for the pie to cool.

"There is something else, yes."

"Let's have it." He glances at his watch.

"It's about Eva's beau, Will."

"The Marine."

"Yes. Eva is hoping he'll be her date for the ball."

Thayer nods. "Where is he stationed?"

"I believe he's in Hawaii."

"Maui?"

"I think so."

Thayer's face transforms. He's serious now. "I flew in there when I was in the Navy. It's a training ground for both the Navy and the Marines. He's probably practicing jungle warfare exercises. Maybe amphibious operations, too. There are bivouac camps all over the island. It would be hard to find him unless you know what division he's in."

"I think Eva said the Fourth Division, but I'll have to check with her."

He finishes his soup and the waiter brings his egg. I start on my pie.

"If you can find out, I'll look up the commander and write him a letter," he says.

"You'd do that?"

"I can't make any promises. Last I heard there was talk of the Marines advancing on Japanese bases on the island of Tarawa. It's in the Marshall Islands. That may not be Fourth Division. They may still be in training."

Thinking Will might be in danger, I push my plate away. I've finished my wine and would like another, but Thayer has inhaled his Scotch egg in three bites and now has to get to his meeting.

"Before you go, tell me how Ginny and Gay are doing," I say.

"Superlative, both of them." He doesn't want to talk about family. His mind is elsewhere.

"Tell you what," he says. "Write down what you know about the—" He searches for the right word. "Eva's coming-out party and about Will's location and bring it to dinner Friday night." He signals to the waiter for the bill. "And make sure my dazzling niece comes with you."

33

Jack's Return

The next week, Eva resigns from working at the hospital and is getting her wardrobe ready for the fall session at school. I suggest she leave summer clothes with me, and I give her a smaller piece of luggage from my closet, more manageable for traveling. In the morning I find her rifling through her things, the bed covered with clothes either to take, pack away, or discard.

"My tastes have changed since I've been in New York," she says. "How will I ever get by with my old clothes? Everything is either too little girlish or too grownup. Some don't even fit anymore."

"Sounds like you need a shopping trip," I say.

"I don't want to look matronly, Danny."

I'm tempted to be offended, but I am matronly, I suppose. "You'll have to tell me what seventeen-year-old girls are wearing now. We can shop at Macy's. They'll have anything you need."

"Will Macy's have pleated skirts and button-up sweaters?"

"I believe so." Not that I've shopped for those things. When I was her age we wore skirts that fell to the floor.

"All right," she says. "But I want to finish my father's letters before I leave. Can we take an hour with them and then go downtown?"

"Of course." I perform a bob of a curtsy. "It's a grandmother's privilege to grant all wishes."

The piles of clothing in Eva's room can wait. We settle in the den with the box. I had placed the first letter sticking up to mark the beginning. We're down to half a dozen unread letters, and Eva puts them all on her lap. She reads one before she gives me the summary.

"Jack says he's with the First Battalion as an animal transport officer," she says. "He has eighty men and eighty-four horses to supervise. He must like working with horses. I wonder what kind of work he does with them."

"They're mostly transportation, I'd think. Pulling wagons or riding them." When he returned from Europe, Jack bemoaned living in New York where he had to take taxis. He would rather have ridden a horse.

Eva skips the salutations and closings and gives me the highlights.

"He's in the Moselle Valley and says it's a beautiful place with mountains and hills along the river."

"I believe that's just south of Luxembourg. He's probably on guard for fighting outbreaks."

"Even though the war is over?" Eva asks.

"As one war ends, another begins."

"Oh, gosh," she says. "He's been to the city of Koblenz. That sounds like it must be in Germany."

"Yes. There was an American military base in Koblenz."

"The Marines motored boats on the river with the American flag flying overhead. It must have been such a sight. I'd like to see the city someday."

"You won't be visiting Germany anytime soon," I say.

She opens another letter. "He has two-weeks leave and is going to Cannes." Turning her face toward me, she says, "Isn't that the French Riviera?"

"It is." Chess took me to Cannes on a business trip. It's one of the most expensive cities in the world but absolutely beautiful with sandy beaches curving along the Mediterranean coast. My Jack lived well.

The next letter is to Bardie. I steel myself for what I know the contents to be.

"He writes to his grandmother that there was a memorial service for Wells in New York." She reaches out her hand to cover mine. "You and your mother must have been there. Was it awfully hard?"

I take a breath. "It was." I don't want to say more. That day I tried to envision Wells out of harm's way, relieved of pain and fear.

"Jack is taking classes at the Sorbonne now." Eva shakes her head. "He certainly gets around, doesn't he? And he's staying with Bert Marckwald. Uncle Bert didn't mention that when he was here."

"He didn't know you were reading your father's letters. Besides, your brother drew most of the attention at our party."

"Oh," Eva says, "this is the last letter. Funny — I thought there was at least one other."

"Do you want to save it for later? I think he wrote it just before he shipped back to New York."

"No," she says. "It's very short. You can tell me about his homecoming after we read this one."

Darling Muz. After a month in Paris, I have learned that I cannot live the life of the Permissionaire. I can hardly do the few things I want to like Opera Comique, Comedie Francaise, or a trip to Montmarte with friends. Things are terribly expensive here and I am trying to live as simply as possible. I walk a lot and am well acquainted with the Metro.

Eva raises her brows at me. "*Permissionaire?*"

"French for a soldier on leave," I say.

She nods. "The rest is about Easter, taking communion at Holy Trinity, meeting someone from boarding school which put him in mind of you. He had tea with a girl who had several attractive friends with her." She pauses. "I wonder if one of them was my mother. She might have gone to Europe when the war ended."

"I don't know the answer to that. Jack married your mother barely three years after he returned from the war. Then, just as now, things move quickly during wartime."

She sighs and says, "I suppose they do."

I'm wondering how quickly things will move along with Eva and Will. She must have read my mind.

"You haven't asked about Will's letters," she says.

Of course I haven't asked. If she wanted me to know what's in his letters, she would have told me.

"All I know about Will's situation is what your Uncle Tax discovered. Will is in the 4th Division in Maui and not likely to be part of the charge on Tarawa. Tax wasn't able to find out when he might return to the States. Although Italy's Mussolini surrendered, the Germans are very much engaged in combat, and the Japanese are still a threat. The Second World War is far from over."

Eva looks as if she might cry. "Will's letters are very—affectionate."

"He must be lonely. And he seems smitten with you." Of course he's smitten. It's Eva who's cautious. Will might be gone another year or even two, and so much can happen during that time. On the other hand, her mother married Jack at nineteen, and I was barely twenty when my pastor father performed the ceremony for Bradley and me at Boston's College Club. But seventeen is too young to be thinking that far ahead.

I clap my hands together. "That's enough moping. Let's get on with shopping now and have lunch somewhere."

When we've captured two skirts, two sweaters, and a blouse at Macy's, Eva says she wants to have lunch at Mama Leone's.

"The nurses at the hospital raved about it," she says. "We might see someone famous there."

"It's a bit of a walk." We tramped around Macy's for an hour and I'm dog tired. "And we have the bags. Let's get a taxi."

I can tell Eva wants to protest. She enjoys walking in New York, taking it in before she leaves, but she takes pity on her old grandmother.

"Oh, all right," she says.

In all my years living in New York, I've never been to Mama Leone's. I'm hoping I can find something light on the menu even though the restaurant next to the Majestic Theatre is known for its quantities of Italian food—bread and pasta especially. At my age a lunch of soup and salad suits me better. But Eva wants Mama Leone's, and to Mama Leone's we will go.

Except for the fake clusters of purple grapes hanging from the rafters, the atmosphere is authentic—checkered tablecloths, chianti bottles wrapped in straw, basket of bread on each table, and the thick aroma of garlic and tomato sauce. In spite of the war with Italy, the waiters are Italian as is the accordion player roaming around the tables and playing songs of Italy, currently "O Sole Mio." Before we order, our waiter brings a fresh bread basket and a brick of yellow cheese. If I'm going to enjoy the meal, I must have a glass of wine and the waiter practically runs to get it for me before I can ask for ice on the side. He brings the wine and the cola Eva has asked for. Her glass has ice, and she scoops some out with her spoon and drops it into my wine.

Eva orders first, asking for spaghetti a la carbonara. The waiter nods at her and smiles, indicating her order pleases him. When I order prosciutto with melon and a cup of minestrone soup, he waits a heartbeat as if he expects me to order an entrée. When I say, "That's all," he presses his lips together in disappointment and does an about-face for the kitchen.

"Aren't you hungry, Danny?" Eva asks, raising her voice over the accordion music now playing "Funiculi Funicula." To answer, I take a piece of bread from the basket and slice into the cheese. I want to tell her in fifty years she will understand, but for now I'll linger in this fleeting moment with my ravishing and ravenous granddaughter.

The farewell day has arrived. Eva hails a taxi and the driver puts her suitcase in the trunk. She and I slide onto the back seat together. Of course I'm going to see my granddaughter off, even though she tells me there's no need.

As the driver pulls away from the curb, I pat Eva's hand. "I said I'd tell you about Jack coming home."

"All right," she says, but I'm not sure she can focus with New York whizzing by outside the taxi window and her thoughts fixed on what lies ahead.

"I hadn't had much contact with Jack after his last letter," I begin, "and I waited for a telegram to tell me when his ship would arrive. The first unit to return was the hundred-and-first French Mortar Battery. That was April 30th. The second ship was a German liner docking in Boston with nearly six thousand soldiers aboard. They were mostly men of the 26th Division as well as military police and headquarters engineers. Still no Jack."

"That must have driven you mad," Eva says.

"I had no choice but to learn patience. Other units followed, including one of the outfits Jack served with." I hesitate, trying to clear the lump in my throat.

Eva squeezes my hand. "Go on."

"A few weeks later, the *USS New Jersey* streamed into Boston Harbor with most of the remaining units of the Division."

"Was he on that ship?"

"I'm afraid not. I was beginning to worry."

"Oh, Danny, I'm sure you were."

"Finally, on July 22nd, the SS Rotterdam put in at Hoboken, New Jersey, with the last of the 26th Division. I recall it was a blisteringly hot day. Hoboken was drab with no bands or flags and very little excitement on the dock. The men looked weary, but they were smiling. And the broadest, whitest smile in the lot was on Jack's face as he came ashore with his gear."

Eva emits a low giggle.

"Thayer was fifteen then. He and I stood on the dock laughing and crying and hugging Jack in front of his men, entirely against military regulations. I'm sure he was embarrassed, but we didn't care. My boy, Thayer's brother, was home."

"What did he look like?" she asks. "Was he exhausted?"

"He was so handsome in his uniform, and so fit. He looked rested and relieved as well."

Eva is quiet for half a minute. Then she turns her face from me and speaks to the taxi window. "It's odd. I want to stay in New York until my father arrives. I feel as if he's taking a taxi or the subway from New Jersey at this very minute. I don't want to miss him."

I sandwich her hand between mine and lean toward her. She turns to me, our foreheads almost touching.

"Darling," I say, "whenever you talk about Jack or even think about him, he's with you. You must feel how very proud he is of his daughter."

She tries to respond but manages only a faint nod.

When the taxi stops in front of Penn Station, the driver gets out to retrieve Eva's bag as I struggle out of the back.

"You don't have to come in," she says.

I know she wants to do this on her own, a seventeen-year-old carrying her suitcase to her train, finding a seat, settling in, reading again the letters from the boy who loves her. And, if I'm lucky, she'll think about her old grandmother who loves her as well.

34

Maine

Since Eva left, I've leaned on Rosa for conversation and company.

"Where can I find flower seeds?" I ask her.

She is stripping beds to launder the sheets as she does once a week, the towels every few days.

"Goldfarb's Seed Store," she says, not looking up.

"Is that the one down Park Avenue a way?"

"Yes. You need flower bulbs, Mrs. Swain?"

"No—poppy seeds. Do you think Goldfarb's has them?"

"It is a store for seeds. Should I get you poppy seeds?"

"No, I'll get them. It's not far, is it? I should be able to walk."

"I walk with you."

It's not unusual for a woman to walk alone on the Upper East Side, but I welcome Rosa's company. With servicemen on every street, the city feels safe. Two people having good conversation can walk miles and not realize it.

Goldfarb's is a gardener's paradise, although I can't think where anyone would plant daffodil and iris bulbs in Manhattan. In pots, most likely. Rosa finds the poppy seeds for me, several varieties, and she helps me choose. We settle on ornamental poppies, and I buy a small bag of wild poppy seeds, too.

When we get back to the apartment, I ring Thayer.

"Are you going to Maine this fall to close up the York house?" I ask.

"Next month," he says. "Why?"

"I'd like to go along."

"Do you want to take the letters up there?"

"No, Eva may want to look at them again when she's here in December." For some reason, I'm not willing to let the letters go. Bert says the closing on the new apartment is soon and the box would be one less thing to move, but the voices on the paper have come alive for me in the past months. Eva brought them to life.

"We'll be heading up in about three weeks. It will be good to have a babysitter along."

"That's fine—I'd love to take care of little Gay."

Eva writes that she misses me and misses New York, too. She says when she returns she wants to join the Junior League to volunteer with disadvantaged women. I got my start with Junior League shortly after moving to New York City, offering to teach literature to women living in the settlement houses on the Lower East Side. Some needed help learning English and all of them wanted to improve their reading skills. During the Depression, we provided food, shelter, and sanitation, and we raised money to set up a hotel for working women who paid a few dollars a month for rent. Now I'm a sustaining member and attend meetings at the league's brownstone farther down Park Avenue. With her desire to help people, Eva would be an ideal member of the New York Junior League.

In September Thayer picks me up for the trip to Maine. Ginny sits in back with Gay and I ride up front with my son.

Once we're on the road, I ask Thayer, "Did you write Will's commanding officer?"

"I did," he says.

"And—?"

"I got a rather boilerplate letter back."

"What does that mean?"

"Thank you for your letter. Your request will be taken under consideration."

"Well," I say, "at least it's not impossible Will could just appear at the debutante ball."

Thayer shrugs. "Usually a deployment is at least a year. But if there's not much action, it's possible the men will get leave for Christmas." He glances at me then turns back to the road. "But I wouldn't get Eva's hopes up."

Gay falls asleep, so we dare not stop and risk waking her.

"We can stretch our legs and have lunch when we reach Worcester," Thayer says. He leans his head side to side to loosen his muscles. Because it's such a long drive, our family used to spend the entire summer in York Harbor. Bradley took the train to Manhattan, coming back on weekends. The boys kept me so busy that the week sailed by, but it was cause for celebration when the trolley dropped off their father every Friday evening. Thayer doesn't want to leave Ginny alone with the baby, so he's taken the week off to shut down the house for winter.

We fall quiet and as I listen to the hum of the car motor, I pat my purse thinking of the seeds inside.

It's autumn in York Harbor and leaves are changing from green to red and orange. The salty smell of the sea mixes with pine and loam, aromas I miss when I'm in New York. I need a sweater during the day and at night we cozy up to the fireplace and sleep under two blankets.

Thayer and Ginny take the big bedroom with a crib that has been there since my boys were little. Gay is not yet sleeping through the night, and Ginny wants her close for nursing.

The walls of the old house are thin, and I'm in the next room. With rustling, cooing, and talking coming through the wall, it takes me a while to fall asleep the first night. Then I dream I am in a field hospital near the front line of a battle. Men are wounded, some of them severely, but I don't know how to ease their pain. I walk from bed to bed trying to calm the men, some of whom are crying. Then I find Wells lying wrapped in bandages. Blood has seeped through at his forehead, his chest, his stomach. He is weeping, calling for his mother. I try to say I'm here, but I can't get the words to form. I try again. I'm here, I'm here. But he doesn't see me. Then I hear "Shhhhh" and I'm awake. It takes a minute to shift from the hospital to New York and then to York Harbor, to the house on the ocean, and Ginny in the next room with her daughter, comforting her, nursing her, putting her back to sleep.

When daylight comes, I'm disoriented thinking about the move to the new apartment, about Eva in Virginia, about the end of the York Harbor season. The house is cold and I don't want to leave the bed I've warmed with my body. Finally, I hear Thayer poking at the fire's embers, crumpling paper, dropping a log onto the andirons. Ginny must be tending to Gay, and I get up, wrap my robe around me and pad to the kitchen to make coffee.

We've brought breakfast food—eggs and bread—but nothing for lunch or supper as we don't want to leave anything to spoil over the winter. We eat early dinners at the Reading Room, Ginny and I taking turns staying with Gay. Mostly I'm with her in the evenings, and they bring me a meal the chef has bagged up. Gay is a healthy little girl and no trouble.

On the third day I take the spade outside to the garden behind the house. The front is too close to the road for planting, so the gardens are at the back. I'm wearing trousers today and have tucked the bag of seeds into a pocket. The clerk at Goldfarb's told me poppy seeds need to be planted in the fall so they'll freeze over the winter. The spring thaw activates them. With luck, the poppies will propagate, and there will be orange and red blossoms forever.

On my knees, I use the spade to loosen the soil around the peonies and sprinkle in the ornamental seeds. I'm not sure how

     SHELTERING ANGEL OF BELLEAU WOOD

far apart to plant them, but I'll check on them in the spring if I have the energy to venture up again.

Rising to my feet, I brush my gloved hands together. Now to wait. Waiting is what I do best.

Bert tells me the closing on the new apartment is in October and I can move in immediately after that. If I want to have redecorating done, moving will have to wait another month. From what I saw when he first took me through, the space looks pristine—wainscoting, polished wood floors, walls recently painted. I'll have another walk-through after the closing and can decide about redecorating then, he says. When I'm ready, he'll have a realtor put my apartment on the market. I call it mine, but the apartment has never felt like home to me. In fact, it reminds me of the *Titanic*, everything overly ornate. When I first moved in, I had nightmares of being in the lifeboat again. Bert says the war will end soon and then the real estate market will boom. I should be able to get a good price for it.

When I'm not working with the committee on details for the December ball, I spend time going through my closet, picking out dresses, hats, shoes, and handbags to give to charity. No sense in moving things I'll never wear again. Chess collected artwork and carvings from his business trips around the world, objects that don't mean much to me, and Rosa helps me box those up to give away. I want the new place to be airy and spare in case Eva chooses to add some of her touches. Margaret and Oliver are transferred around so much—from Guatemala to Ecuador, and in January they'll be in Bordeaux, France—and Eva says she prefers having a solid home base with me.

I help Rosa pack up the kitchen, and we lay aside utensils she doesn't use. The new place is a short distance down Park Avenue, so Rosa agrees to keep working for me, although she says she may need to make adjustments to the new kitchen. She can concoct a gourmet meal out of a sow's ear, so I'll agree to whatever she wants.

Before Eva returns to New York in mid-December, I need to have the new apartment ready and the final preparations for the ball, too. Now, if only I can make Will Robbins materialize.

35

The Ball

December in New York is a festive time. It's not unusual to have snow near the holidays, but I'm praying bad weather will hold off until after Eva's train arrives. In the meantime, I order a tree for my entry, which the realtor called the gallery—a small tree to adorn the round welcome table. Rosa helps me string little lights and add a silver garland. When we plug in the lights, the colors reflect in the white marble floor, freshly polished.

Eva insisted I not meet her train. I could never be sure if the train is on time, she said, and she doesn't want me to wait at Penn Station. On December 18, at ten p.m., she bursts in the door. Before I can get to the gallery, she shouts, "Danny?"

A brown scarf around her neck, her face is flushed with color. She has brought with her scents of fresh air, cold and, oddly, lilacs.

"I'm sorry to be so late," she says. "I had to change trains at Union Station in Washington and the second train was late."

"I'm just glad you're here," I say, hugging her. She drops her suitcase and hugs me back.

"I want to see your new apartment," she says.

I carry her suitcase to the guest suite while she wanders from room to room, oh-ing and wow-ing.

"It's beautiful," she concludes. "Much better than the other apartment. More feminine, and I adore the entry."

"I'm glad. Are you hungry?"

"I ate something in Washington. But a glass of sherry would be nice."

"Sherry?" Has she acquired a taste for sherry at school or is it New York's influence? In any event, I'm willing to have a nip with her. I like the nutty flavor of the fortified wine.

"If you don't mind. I'm rather keyed up and don't think I'd ever fall asleep without it."

While I pour sherry into two cordial glasses, Eva prattles from the sofa. "The lights downtown are all aglitter. People are bundled up on the sidewalks, and everyone seems so jovial. Oh, I do love being back in New York."

"Tomorrow we're due at the Waldorf Astoria for a run-through before the ball on Tuesday."

"After church?"

"Yes, let's do go to church. I have some things to thank the Lord for."

"And—" she starts. "Have you had any word from Will's commanding officer?"

"Thayer told me he hasn't heard anything, but as they say—"

She breaks in. "No news is good news."

The sherry is warming me on such a cold evening. "How was your semester at school?" I ask.

"The girls are all talking about what they'll do after graduation. Some are planning for college and others are determined to find rich husbands. Travel is out until the war's over."

"Is there a chance you might go to Bordeaux to be with your mother and stepfather?"

Eva finishes her sherry and holds out her glass for another. It feels strange to drink with my granddaughter, so I take the glass and fill it halfway.

"Hardly," she says. "Mum would rather not be there herself, but President Roosevelt gave Oliver the order. He says the Germans have occupied the city and refugees are pouring in from northern France. The German army has requisitioned homes and controls the port, and rationing is strict." She gives her head a shake. "Imagine being able to buy just a quarter pound of meat a month. I really can't think why the President is sending them there. Certainly Oliver won't be throwing many gay parties."

I have to agree with Eva. It seems foolhardy to station any American in occupied France. Even the refugees are rabbits hiding from swooping raptors. But I say, "I suppose Oliver has to try and keep spirits up for the French people and any U.S. citizens living there."

"Hopefully he and Mum won't be there long," she says. "Anyway, I'd prefer to stay in New York with you, if you'll have me. There's so much I want to do here."

I know I can't hold onto Eva forever—and forever may not be long at my age. But watching her blossom is my delight.

I finish my glass of sherry as Eva sips the last of hers.

"Yes, of course I'll have you. You can be helpful to me and to the war effort as well." I take the glasses and start for the kitchen. "Now, my darling, would you like some help unpacking?"

"No, Danny—you scoot off to bed. I won't be far behind you. I may try on my dress one more time and hope I haven't filled out since August. The food at boarding school is very rich."

I am rich, too, in having Eva with me.

December 20 arrives with frigid temperatures but a warming sun. Dickens famously said it's "summer in the light and winter in the shade." By sunset it will be below freezing. The sidewalks are clear, and thank goodness Eva won't have to trudge through snow and slush in her gown and shoes, and she'll have my fur stole around her shoulders. Not that young people feel the cold, especially when they're looking forward to one of the biggest experiences of their lives—and they're in love.

Late in the morning I take her to my hairdresser to have her hair styled, although I like its natural waves. After a light lunch, we go home so she can rest. I doubt resting is what she does, however. She's unusually quiet around me.

"Anything the matter?" I ask.

"Not really." She's looking at the little Christmas tree in the gallery, touching the green velvet skirt around the trunk. "It's just—" She takes a deep breath and begins again. "I hope there will be someone besides Uncle Tax for me to dance with."

Seventeen is a difficult age. She must feel everything is changing at the speed of light. Just a few months left of schooling, no specific plans for the immediate future, her family so far away, and without an idea what the boy she loves is going through, when he might return, and when he does, whether his feelings for her have changed. She's wandering in a mist without a clue about which direction to head. I was just that lost when I left Bradley on a sinking ship so many years ago, not knowing when I'd see him again or whether he'd survive. Then lost in the darkness, searching for anyone around our little boat still alive, still drawing breath. A night of waiting for rescue and, later, waiting for Bradley to come home. Part of me waits still—waiting to join him wherever he is.

Right now I am Eva's fulcrum, her assurance, and here we are, both of us trying to get used to a new living situation.

"Dozens of young men will want to dance with you, darling, some in tuxedoes and some in uniform. You won't be at a loss for dance partners, I guarantee you."

"Thank you, Danny," she says although she doesn't sound convinced. "Now I think I'll lie down for a little bit."

I climb into my blue cocktail dress, fix my hair, apply a touch of rouge, and leave for the hotel well in advance of the debutantes' arrival. As one of the organizers, I have to see all details are attended to—flowers, dinner settings, table for selling war bonds. The band should have arrived to set up their instruments, and I need to make sure they have refreshments and anything else they need. Rosa has agreed to help Eva with her dress, long white gloves, shoes, and the old stole, and Thayer will pick her up and escort her to the event.

When I arrive at the hotel ballroom, the other committee members are bustling, and everything looks in order. We have been saving ration tickets for months and have pooled them to offer a formal dinner for the debutantes and their guests. But first, the girls gather outside the ballroom with their fathers, all in black-tie tuxedoes. The men are distinguished looking—successful men—and each stands tall with the pleasure of having an attractive young woman on his arm and the affluence that allows him to pay for her debut.

As each name is called, the debutante appears escorted by her father, stops to perform a curtsy, then gathers to one side with the other girls, a chorus of white. When Thayer leads Eva forward, I'm shocked by how much he looks like Jack. Hair the same color, parted on the same side, both of them tall and lanky. The difference is Jack's smile was friendly and earnest, whereas Thayer carries a faint smirk of irony that suits his impish nature. Eva looks timid, almost shy. She hasn't spent enough time in New York to make good friends, and I doubt she knows any of the other girls. She does her curtsy perfectly and as she stands, her eyes dart about. I know she's searching for a familiar face.

If only—

After all the girls have been presented, photographs must be taken, standing, sitting, the photographer posing them, spreading their skirts, instructing them about their facial expressions. Eva forces a smile and I know she must be having second thoughts about participating. It's probably a tribulation for her, and I hope she doesn't hate me for foisting the ball on her.

Fathers, mothers, and guests sip champagne during the photo hour and then gather for the dinner. The starter is lobster bisque followed by a salad. For the entrée, roast beef with mashed potatoes and watercress garnish. The finish is an assortment of pastries, all excessively opulent in light of war shortages.

During the dinner the band plays soft music—"Moonlight Serenade," "Embraceable You," "You Go to My Head," and other slow songs. Oh how I wish Bradley were here to slip his arm around my waist and dance me across the floor. My time has come and gone, of course. This is Eva's night but from the look on her face, she must wish the evening were over.

After dinner, the committee chairwoman takes the stage to thank everyone for coming and encourage the purchase of war bonds. Other members of the Junior League speak about the importance of supporting our troops and helping the less advantaged during this difficult time. Eva looks bored until the speeches end. The band leader snaps his fingers for a faster beat and invites couples onto the dance floor.

Thayer is the first to hold his hand out to Eva for a dance, but "Baby Won't you Please Come Home" is not the song she wants to hear. I see her dab at her nose with her left gloved hand. This is not a night for tears, even though she has good reason. But I haven't given up hope for a fairytale ending.

When the song finishes, the band takes off on "Tangerine" and a soldier in a Navy dress uniform asks Eva to dance. My good-natured granddaughter agrees. She dances again to "Taking a Chance on Love" and then makes an excuse to sit down. A young fellow asks her to the floor, and another, but she declines.

As the music flows into the evening, Eva's pretty face dims. She watches her gloved hands, clasping and unclasping the white fingers. The band leader announces the last two songs, glancing at my granddaughter as if he, too, wants to raise her spirits.

I'm about ready to dance with her myself when I see a Marine standing at the ballroom entrance. He's a good-looking lad, his eyes searching the room. It takes him a minute to spot Eva and when he does, a light sparks in his face. My breath catches as he works his way around the dance floor to where she sits looking down, oblivious to what's around her. Then a hand reaches out and slowly lifts her chin so her eyes meet his.

The song changes to "Comin' In on a Wing and a Prayer," and I have no doubt that prayer and some winged chariot got

Will to New York in the nick of time. He and Eva dance at first like Cinderella and Prince Charming, in complete enchantment with each other. When the music quickens, they are Fred Astaire and Ginger Rogers, sometimes Will leading and sometimes Eva, both of them laughing as if there's no one else in the room.

The song ends, and I find myself fading when Thayer rescues me.

"I asked Will if he'll see that Eva gets back to the apartment, so let's get you home, Muz. You must be bushed."

"I suppose we can trust a gentleman in uniform," I say with relief.

As Thayer and I leave, the band plays the final song "I'm Dreaming of a White Christmas," and I catch a glimpse of Eva, her head on Will's shoulder, a look of perfect bliss on her face.

"You knew, didn't you?" I say to Thayer.

"I might have," is all he says.

Much later, in the wee hours of the morning when I hear the front door open and softly close, I fall finally into a heavenly sleep.

36

Christmas Eve

"Danny," Eva says in the morning, "what a superb evening last night was." She is wearing her robe and sipping tea in the kitchen with Rosa.

"Coffee, Mrs. Swain?" Rosa hands me a cup and saucer then looks at Eva. "Your beau, he arrive?"

Eva grins. "He did arrive, Rosa, yes." She pivots in a slow twirl. "And we danced until the band stopped playing. I lost track of time."

"He saw you home in a taxi, I hope?" I say.

"Oh, we walked, Danny."

"But it was so cold last night."

"I had your stole and he had his arm around me. It's a mile, but I didn't feel at all cold."

I raise my brows. "You walked in your white gown?"

"I hope it's not ruined." She sets down her cup. "We stopped at a café open all night and had coffee and a pastry." Holding up two fingers, she says, "Two people asked if we were just married. I laughed, but Will didn't."

"He didn't think it was funny?"

"No—he just said, 'Good idea.'"

"Goodness." In my prehistoric opinion, it's too soon to talk about a wedding. When Will gets out of the Marines, they'll have time to plan out their whole lives.

"Don't worry, Danny. We didn't elope."

"Elope?" Rosa asks.

"Run off and get married, Rosa," Eva says.

"Ah—*fugarse con un amante*. Like my *esposo* and I did."

I break in with as calm a voice as I can manage. "Perhaps it's a little premature to talk of elopement—or marriage, for that matter."

"Danny, I have to tell you and I hope you won't be upset, but Will invited me to spend Christmas with his family in Boston." She puts her hand on my arm. "Would you mind terribly?"

"Boston? For how long?"

She turns to Rosa. "I might need another cup of tea," she says then looks at me. "He has a week before he'll have to fly back the day after Christmas. We'll take the train up on Christmas Eve morning and spend two nights. Then he'll see me to the station before he leaves for the airport."

"So you and I have three days together before you go to Boston."

"Will says you're welcome to join us. His mother would enjoy meeting you."

How nice of Will to think of me, but it's not my place to intrude on the Robbins' holiday—or Eva's romance.

"No," I say. "I don't want to miss little Gay's first Christmas."

"Of course." Rosa hands Eva the fresh cup of tea and she speaks to the cup. "Also—"

I sense what comes next.

"Will would like to see me today and tomorrow. And the next day, too." She raises her face as if an idea has just occurred to her. "Danny, you could come along. We'll be going to art galleries mostly."

I pull my lips between my teeth before I speak. "It's important for you two to spend time together without your grandmother tagging along." My chest rises in a deep, aching breath. "As for Christmas, of course you should go to Boston. I'm sure Will's family will love you."

She sets down her teacup and hugs me. "Oh, Danny, thank you!" Pulling at the collar of her robe, she says, "Now I really must get dressed."

For the next few days I see Eva only at breakfast. The bulk of the days I work with the ball committee to evaluate the event and take notes for next year. That, along with buying Christmas gifts, keeps me occupied. A scarf for Ginny, two cute outfits for Gay, and a copy of the novel *The Fountainhead* by Ayn Rand, which I found nearly new at a used bookshop, thinking Rand may give Thayer some fresh ideas about consumerism.

Eva isn't expecting a present, but I want her to have something of mine. I've spent so much money on her that she wouldn't want me to expend another dime after outfitting her for the debutante ball. But there has to be a gift.

In the bedroom I go through my jewelry box. I have a string of pearls, but they seem too matronly for a teenager. I find two rings I rarely wear, but the granddaughters can decide about those after I'm gone. The jewel box has a lower drawer and I pull it out. I'd forgotten about my grandmother's diamond brooch, the one I grabbed at the last minute from our cabin on the *Titanic*. Bradley was rushing me, urging me to get into my floatation vest and join our steward and the others on the boat deck. The ship was sinking and he had to get me to a lifeboat—a lifeboat without him. A funny word, lifeboat. I didn't think it was possible to have a life without Bradley. I recall Isidor Straus standing against a wall of the captain's office with his wife Ida at his side. She gave her coat to her maid and told her she wouldn't be needing it. I'll never forget her words. "As we have lived, so will we die together." Mr. Straus was sixty-seven, the age I'll soon be, and Ida was four years younger. If I hadn't had three young sons waiting for me at home, if I had been her age and married for more than forty years, if I had been so courageous, I'd have made the same decision.

     SHELTERING ANGEL OF BELLEAU WOOD

I pick up the brooch and hold it in my palm. It's cold to the touch. Larger than a Walking Liberty silver dollar, the gold setting is an oval shape with three diamonds across the center, smaller diamonds circling them. It must be worth hundreds of dollars, but what difference does its value make? The diamonds remind me of the iceberg, and I haven't worn the brooch since 1912. While Eva is in Boston, I'll have a jeweler clean it and set it in a nice box. A keepsake bequeathed by generations of her grandmothers.

Late morning on Christmas Eve, Eva and Will leave for the train station. While she was getting ready, I tucked the brooch, boxed and beautifully wrapped by the jeweler, into her bag so she can open it Christmas Day.

I gather the things I've bought for Thayer and his family. Because of a paper shortage, gifts under the tree will not be wrapped this year, but I bag them in pillowcases and tie on a tag, "From Danny." While I change for dinner, I turn on the radio, hoping for some holiday music. Unfortunately, the news is on. German submarines torpedoed and scuttled two allied destroyers, one American and the other British. Another American destroyer sank one of the German subs northeast of the Azores. Winston Churchill met with Joseph Stalin in Tehran, and Stalin agrees to support international security. The war seems to have reached a turning point with victories in Stalingrad, North Africa, and Sicily, and there are plans to liberate Paris.

I'm ready for this promising news.

Rosa asks about dinner. I forgot to tell her Thayer invited me for a late supper.

"Before you leave, Rosa, please have a glass of sherry with me."

"All right, Mrs. Swain," she says. "But whiskey is better."

I can't help but chuckle. Apparently I don't know Rosa as well as I'd thought.

"Whiskey, then."

She goes to the kitchen and returns with a bowl of ice.

"I do it." She steps by me and puts two cubes of ice in each tumbler, pours the whiskey, and hands a glass to me.

"Please sit with me." I point to the sofa and take the chair across from her. "Rosa, you have been such a good friend to me over the years. Thank you."

"It is my pleasure." She scans the room. "This place is a second home to me."

"What is your plan for Christmas?" I've given her tomorrow off.

"*This* is my plan."

It's odd that I've never inquired about her husband and children, and she has never offered.

"Tell me about yourself," I say.

She shrugs. "Nothing much. My *esposo* died. Influenza, like Mr. Swain."

"I didn't know. I'm sorry, Rosa."

She nods. "No children."

"Then you'll be alone on Christmas?"

"Being alone is good. I connect with myself." She touches her temple. "Good for understanding oneself." She pulls back her shoulders. "Especially now that I am an American citizen."

"Rosa, why didn't you tell me? I would have gone to the ceremony."

"You were busy, Mrs. Swain. Not to worry."

I have been busy. The trip to Maine, plans for the ball, and Eva.

The entry table has a drawer where I've placed an envelope of money for her, and I retrieve it as she puts on her coat.

"Tomorrow is Sunday," I say. "You always have Sunday off. Please take Monday as well." I hand her the envelope. "Merry

Christmas, Rosa. Rest tomorrow and do something nice for yourself."

"Thank you," she says, "but I be here Monday morning. Eva will return, and she will be hungry."

That makes me gleeful—Eva returning, Rosa cooking for us, an odd little family.

Thayer's apartment is a short walk from my new place, and I wrap a scarf around my neck, pull on gloves, and take to the sidewalk. The cold reminds me of the winter storm in Boston before Thayer was born when the housekeeper complained the cupboard was nearly bare and the boys—Jack and Wells—were hungry. I've never been so cold as when I trudged out into the snow in search of groceries and ended up with Bert Marckwald at the Saint Botolph Club. Bert had the cook fill a bag with food from the club's larder and saw me home. We had such plenty then, at least compared to the sacrifices we have to make now.

"It smells glorious in here," I say when I walk in.

Thayer takes my coat and scarf. "Thank heavens there's no ration on turkey, but I had to go damn well to New Jersey to find this one. I was beginning to think I'd have to shoot a wild one."

Even in the hardest of times, my youngest son is in a high mood.

"Now let's get you a drink."

Ginny is in the living room, sitting near the radio with Gay. I deposit my bag of gifts under the small tree they've decorated and give Ginny a hug, a kiss to little Gay.

"It's Roosevelt's Christmas Eve address." Ginny tosses her thumb at the radio. "There's likely to be a railroad strike right after Christmas."

"Oh dear. I hope the strike holds off until Eva gets back to New York."

Thayer brings me a Campari and soda with ice. "This might do you," he says.

I'm delighted with the red color. "I haven't had one of these in years," I say.

He sits down and listens to Roosevelt's talk. "Tensions are high between business and labor," Thayer says. "Unions pledged not to strike, but wartime shortages and frozen wages have them unraveling. The advertising business has been hit hard, too." He shakes his head. "This damn war had better end soon or we'll all go to the poorhouse."

"I'm afraid poorhouses are full," I offer.

The President announces that General Dwight Eisenhower will lead the Allied invasion of Europe early next year.

"I've heard Eisenhower is a capable military leader," Thayer says. "He served in the Great War and led the troops to victory in North Africa."

"I don't know," I say. "It sounds like the Germans are more determined to succeed this time. I can't think of a war that went on forever, but the fighting in Europe is going on five years."

"The Trojan War lasted ten years," Ginny says.

"Bite your tongue, woman," Thayer says.

"I'm going to nurse Gay as long as I can." Ginny again. "But I'll need nutrition to keep up my strength."

"I can get as much Kraft macaroni and cheese as you can eat," Thayer says. "They're one of our best clients. Campbell's Soup, too—'Cooked to order in the USA.'"

"I miss home cooking," Ginny says.

"If the soup's good enough for our troops, it's good enough for the Cumings household," Thayer says.

"We all miss home cooking." I try to mollify Thayer's tone. I know how having a baby can be exhausting, especially during the holidays—and in wartime.

Ginny gets up with Gay and says, "I'm going put the baby to bed. Then we'll have a nice, quiet dinner."

I turn to Thayer. "I can help get things on the table."

"Nonsense," he says. "You're our guest. All you're going to get is another Campari."

My son is the embodiment of hail-fellow-well-met. It's a delight to be around him.

After the President's talk finishes, Bing Crosby's voice rolls out of the radio singing "I'll Be Home for Christmas." I think of 1918 when Jack didn't make it home for the holiday. At least this year Eva's beau has returned, and I can't begrudge him taking my granddaughter to Boston. Who am I to stand in the way of romance?

Ginny looks more relaxed when she returns from the nursery. Thayer has opened a bottle of champagne and hands a glass to his wife. I've had two drinks and certainly don't need champagne but I'm walking home, so what's the harm? He takes my tumbler and replaces it with a champagne glass.

Dinner is as delicious as can be under the circumstances of tightened belts. When I'm ready to leave, Thayer hands me a bag of Christmas goodies—foodstuffs from his clients, I suspect— and he walks me home. I'm grateful he's with me, grateful to lean on him, grateful for so much on this brisk New York night.

37

Christmas Supper

On Christmas morning I make myself coffee and find that Rosa has left a tin of muffins for me. Four golden prizes with raisins. I put one on a plate and sit by the window with coffee and the muffin. I'll save the others to have with Eva when she returns.

Very few cars pass down the avenue, a rushing taxi and a slow-moving limousine. Usually Unitarians celebrate Christmas with singing and candle-lighting on Christmas Eve but since it's Sunday, All Souls might have a service. The *Times* is outside my door, as usual, and I check the local page for worship services. Chess had no interest in Unitarianism, so we began attending the Episcopal church. Since he died, I've gone back to my Unitarian roots. There's a service at ten, and I have just enough time to finish my muffin and get ready.

It's a crisp morning, and I decide I'll walk the half mile to the church. Directly across Park Avenue from my building is number 740, an Art Deco structure built in 1929. According to Bert, some of the richest and most powerful people in New York live there. The daughter of the builder and her Bouvier family are residents, as is John D. Rockefeller, Jr. Some of the apartments are over ten thousand square feet on two levels, Bert says. My building is fifteen years older and my apartment is miniscule by comparison, but it suits me fine.

I cross Park to where the morning sun warms the sidewalk and amble up to 79th Street, cross again, and turn up Lexington. I'm early and settle myself near the front of the sanctuary where I always sat with Mother and Elaina at my father's church in

Cambridge. Above, in the balcony, I hear the trumpet players getting their instruments ready.

When the minister enters in his robe, he sits and signals with a look toward the balcony. "Oh Come All Ye Faithful" begins, the horns—half a dozen of them—blare in harmony. The minister stands and raises his arms for the congregation to join him in song. I've always liked this carol, especially the words joyful, triumphant, and exultation. Our troops were triumphant in the Great War. Let's hope we can return to joy and exultation at the end of this one.

Some people think Unitarians aren't really Christians, but we do celebrate Christmas although not really as a miracle. Unitarians aren't given to the idea of miracles. The minister's homily is about beauty, generosity, kindness, family—the extended family that includes all of humanity. He invites merrymaking on this holiday and, finally, he puts out a call for peace. I wish it were that easy, to call for peace and have it materialize.

After the service, I walk west on 79th Street and cross over Fifth Avenue to the park. A trail leads to The Lake where people have gathered to watch skaters on the frozen surface. I never feel alone in New York City. Here strangers bundled in hats and overcoats greet me with "Good morning" and "Merry Christmas." I want to tell someone my boys learned to skate on this lake. But that was a very long time ago.

On the walk home, I stuff my hands in my coat pockets and feel a small bundle. At first I think—mouse. When I pull it out, I see it's the bag of wild poppies. I've forgotten to plant them, and I scatter some along the trail back to Fifth Avenue. When I get to my apartment house, I go directly to the courtyard behind the building. A small garden has been cleared, only stubs of plants remaining. Without a spade, I sprinkle the rest of the seeds over the ground and hope in spring the wet soil will nurture poppies into bloom.

Then I step back and as if casting a blessing on the little garden, I whisper, "Merry Christmas, Wells."

Thayer calls to encourage me to come for lunch, but I beg off. The church service and walk have tired me and I want a nap. Many Jewish New Yorkers who immigrated as refugees when the war began don't celebrate Christmas, and British and American troops are observing the holiday far from home, surrounded by fellow soldiers instead of families. The day doesn't feel festive for me. Maybe if Eva were here—

A nap feels luxurious, but the ring of the phone awakens me. It's Bert Marckwald calling to see if I'm having a pleasant Christmas. I am, actually. There is bittersweet delight in doing whatever I want to do without having to consider anyone else. December is the darkest month, and after I hang up with Bert, it's nearly dusk. How long have I slept?

I don't feel the least bit hungry and, anyway, I have no idea what's in the cupboards to eat. It's ridiculous to think of going out to a restaurant by myself even if just to the deli, but I'm sure there are other widows having similar thoughts. And anyway, I've forgotten to give the doorman his Christmas gift. So I fix my hair, take the envelope I've marked for him, and head to the elevator.

The doorman is handsome in his blue uniform. The double-breasted overcoat has eight gold buttons, and he wears a military-style cap.

"Working on Christmas day, Mr. Burgess?" I say?

He wishes me a happy Christmas and says, "Someone has to get the door for you, madam, even on a holiday."

"In that case, that someone ought to be rewarded." I hand him the envelope and he slips it discreetly into an inner pocket of his coat.

"That someone is very grateful." He gives a slight bow. "May I call you a taxi?"

"No, thank you. I'm just going a block."

"I'll be here when you return, then, Mrs. Swain," he says.

I realize I haven't spoken to anyone in person today—other than Bert and a few greetings in the park. If I think about it, I'm not at all sad. There has been enough sadness in my life. I suppose I've found acceptance, even relief that the grieving is over. In fact, with my new living space I have a newfound appreciation for life. I suppose Eva has something to do with my feeling younger than I did a year ago.

At the deli I'm still not sure what I want to eat—certainly nothing I have to cook. And a sandwich doesn't suit for a Christmas supper. So I settle for a hunk of bleu cheese. While the clerk is wrapping it, I pick up a small bouquet of delphinium, chrysanthemums, and anemone to take home.

I start arranging the flowers in a vase and realize Eva hasn't called. Will must be keeping her busy, and she's trying to be a good guest. Besides, I'll see her tomorrow if all goes according to plan.

But now it's 7:30, and as I'm unwrapping the cheese for my dinner nibble, the door opens. Eva rushes in, breathless.

"Danny, I ran from the station—all the way!"

"Eva—what in the world are you doing here? Why aren't you in Boston?"

"It's a long story, but don't worry. Everything's fine. Even more than fine, in fact." She puts down her overnight bag. "How about I tell you all the news over dinner?"

I look at the cheesecloth on the counter. "I'm afraid you'll have to settle for cheese."

"Not on your life. Get your coat. There must be something open. And we have lots to talk about."

38

Old South Church

I suggest we walk down Madison to the Perrine Hotel where the restaurant will be open for hotel patrons treating themselves to a New York winter holiday. As we make our way, Eva fairly gushes.

"Boston is sleepy compared to New York," she says. "And Will's house is in the countryside. Not a shop or restaurant in sight."

"I'm sure it's lovely there," I say.

"Yes, of course. Not what I'm used to, but quietly tasteful."

I'm grateful for the nap I had but even so, I can hardly keep up with Eva and am relieved the Perinne is less than a mile away. In the dining room, we have no trouble being seated. Diners must either have eaten earlier or found another place open for late dinner.

For the first time, I notice the brooch on the collar of her coat. She hasn't mentioned the gift, nor do I need thanks. Eventually the brooch would have come to her, and it looks natural on her coat, as if she's always had it, the perfect accessory for my beautiful granddaughter.

We shed our wraps and scan the menu. Turkey dishes mostly, no doubt left over from Christmas Eve dinners. When the waiter comes to the table, I ask for Turkey a la King, and Eva, always hungry, chooses Turkey Tetrazzini. At her age, she can eat noodles without expanding her waistline. After the war ends, I may never eat turkey again.

Because Eva looks as if she could use something to help her wind down, I order two glasses of white wine. The waiter doesn't ask her age, probably because she's with an elder.

"Were the Robbinses pleased to meet you?" I ask.

"Mrs. Robbins and Will's sister Maryanne were very gracious. His father is stationed in North Africa. Tunisia, I think. The Axis troops have surrendered there, and Will thinks his father is on a peace-keeping mission. So Christmas Eve it was just the four of us. We went to church — the candlelight service — and afterward Maryanne and I made a late supper."

"You cooked?"

"Not very well. But Maryanne knows what she's doing in the kitchen. It was light — just vichyssoise and some greens. Mrs. Robbins doesn't eat much. She seems rather fragile."

"It must be difficult being married to a military man during wartime. She's probably alone much of the time."

"It seems so, yes. But Will says his father's work is essential to the war effort."

When the wine appears, I've forgotten to ask for extra ice.

Eva catches the waiter's eye. "Sir," she says, "please bring my grandmother a glass of ice."

The waiter looks confused for a moment then nods and disappears.

"That doesn't explain why you came back on Christmas day."

"I missed you, Danny, and I didn't want you to be alone. Not on Christmas."

I'm unconvinced. She mooned over Will's letters and he, apparently, couldn't wait to get home to her.

"You know I'm used to being alone. Is there something else?"

"Well — perhaps."

The waiter comes back with the ice and I scoop some with my spoon and drop it into my wineglass. From the corner of my eye, I see the young man watching with a perplexed expression. Of course, I ignore him.

"Why are you being so mysterious, darling?"

Then she blurts her secret. "Will and I are going to be married!"

I breathe a sigh of relief. Actually, I half expected as much. Two people in love, a war on, the future uncertain.

"Have you told your mother?" I ask.

She shakes her head. "I wanted you to be the first to know."

"I'm glad you thought of me, but that doesn't explain why you left Boston early."

She sips her wine and leans back in her chair. "Well, we felt a little —" She thinks for a second.

"Confined?"

"Yes. Exactly."

Our food comes, but I'm too intrigued to eat and have so many questions that want answers.

Eva dives into her tetrazzini, talking around the noodles.

"I mean, I like his little family, but we were with his mother and sister every minute. Will and I wanted some privacy. So we left after having a small Christmas celebration and spent some time at the train station waiting for the three-o'clock."

I raise my eyebrows. "That's not exactly a private place."

"Oh, but no one knew us, and he was in uniform. And other couples were smooching, too."

I want to ask how much smooching went on but thought better of it.

"Are you sure about getting married, Eva?" I ask. "You're only seventeen."

"Danny," she says, "I have not one iota of doubt. I feel safe with him. It's as if our love is ordained. Will used that word, too — ordained."

"You haven't had much experience in romance, have you?"

"I've lost a father and in many ways I've lost a mother, too. I'm living in wartime, and I've served soldiers who are rather boldly fresh and nursed badly wounded ones as well."

Eva sounds like she has taken offense at my question, and I can't blame her. Although she may not be experienced in love, she certainly has seen a great deal in her short life, more than I had seen when I first met Bradley that Sunday in church eons ago. Papa invited him to dinner, and after that I was certain destiny meant for us to be together, as certain as Eva is about Will.

"I think your father would approve," I say.

"Thank you for saying that," she says. "I think he would, too."

"Did Will give you a ring?" I notice her fingers are bare.

"When we told his mother, she went to her room and came back with a necklace clasp, gold with a diamond embedded in it. She said we could have the diamond set in a ring."

I have rings from Bradley and from Chess. I gave one to Jack to have the diamond set for Margaret. I would have offered Will the other if I had been asked.

"And where is this necklace clasp now?"

"Will took it to have the diamond set in a ring while he's in Hawaii." She pauses eating to take a sip of wine. "But it doesn't matter. I don't even care about a ring. I just want to be with Will."

"I understand." When Bradley proposed, the pressure of war wasn't bearing down on us and since he didn't feel the need to rush, we put off the wedding until I was twenty. But for me, the wait was agony. My sister had left home for college, and I was eager to break away from the parsonage.

"How soon do you and Will want to marry—and where?" I ask.

"I want the wedding right here in New York. I wouldn't allow the ceremony anywhere else on earth. Will should return to the states next summer, he thinks. Maybe the war will be over by then."

"Maybe," I say. "In the meantime, I suppose there's planning to be done."

"And I can't think of anyone I'd rather plan with than my fabulous grandmother."

"With help from my fabulous granddaughter." I lift my glass to her. "And speaking of fabulous, we raised ninety thousand dollars in war bonds at your debutante ball."

"Here, here!" She stops eating and raises her glass to meet mine. "But I've almost forgotten. I brought you a Christmas gift." She rummages in her purse. A slender package wrapped in purple velvet appears, and she hands it across the table to me.

"I hope you like it," she says. "Mrs. Robbins let me pick it out of her collection." She points to the bundle in my fingers. "Open it, Danny. It's Christmas."

The velvet reveals a silver souvenir spoon with Old South Church engraved above an etching of the church. In the eighteenth century Samuel Adams organized the Boston Tea Party there to protest Britain's domination of the colonies. Like the Unitarians, the Old South Church accepts everyone, no matter their denomination.

"We had your father christened at that church." I can hardly speak. It's such a thoughtful gift. "Thank you, Eva. It's very special."

"Will was christened there, too. I think it's a sign. Don't you, Danny?"

She is glowing, and I'm so delighted to have her with me that I can only answer, "Yes, it's definitely a sign.

39

Happy Birthday Muz

Eva spends the next week reading, taking long walks around the city and Central Park — often but not always with me — and writing letters to Will. Earlier, she wrote to her mother who sent back her best wishes and asked Eva to postpone the wedding until Oliver retires and they return to the States. I offered to buy the dress and pay for flowers, and Margaret agreed to take care of the reception and other expenses. A wartime wedding will be a scaled back affair but as elegant as we three women can make it. Rosa keeps us fed except when we go out to lunch or join Thayer's family for supper. Every spare minute, we scour magazines for ideas and talk of wedding plans.

And suddenly it's New Year's Eve.

Neither Eva nor I have any interest in going to Times Square to watch the ball drop. Mostly the crowd will be visitors, tourists who want to grab New York bragging rights. Thayer is having a small party and asked us to come. Eva says she would like to go and see little Gay, and I'll tag along.

In years past, New York parties were bright and festive affairs, but during war it's cocktails and light hors d'oeuvres. Nothing as extravagant as gatherings before 1942. Has the U.S. been in the war since Pearl Harbor? That was December 1941. The last two years have seemed an eternity.

I suggest we get dressed up for the party. What I don't say is today I'm turning sixty-seven. When I was young, I used to think all the hubbub of parties and fireworks on New Year's Eve was for me. I suppose my mother wasn't able to celebrate the year I was born. It's just like me to get in on the tail end of everything. Even though our *Titanic* lifeboat was the first to load that night in April, it was the last to launch into the water after getting hung up on a spar. I hoped Bradley would jump in with me while he had a chance but, sadly, he followed protocol of women and children first. My honorable and self-sacrificing Bradley.

I put on the cocktail dress I wore to the ball, but Eva says she didn't bring anything that fancy. We go through my closet and she pulls out a black dress several years old. In 1937 it served me for two funerals and although I swore I'd never wear it again, I can't part with it. With a few safety pins and a belt, I adjust it to fit her. When she checks herself in the mirror, she looks satisfied.

It's already ten o'clock when we arrive at Thayer's, the time I normally go to bed, but I rally for Eva's sake. Bert is there, and he gets to us before Thayer does and takes our coats.

"Let's see," he says, "a white wine for Florrie and a Shirley Temple for Eva?"

"It's New Year's Eve," I tell him. "A Campari and soda is more in order." I figure I can sip a single cocktail all evening and not do myself harm.

"Is there anything besides a Shirley Temple?" Eva asks. "I'm not a child."

"And she knows Shirley Temple personally," I add.

"Aha," Bert says. "I know just the thing." I expect he'll mix a little wine with club soda. Maybe add a maraschino cherry for color.

Thayer comes to greet us, and Eva thanks him for negotiating Will's return in time for the ball.

"It was a small effort to make my niece happy," he says.

"More than happy," I suggest.

"What do you mean?"

Eva tells him about their engagement.

"Oh, the poor sap," Thayer says. "Does he have any idea what he's in for?"

"Thayer, really." I fake being appalled. My youngest son can make light of anything. "Marriage has been good for you, darling." I swing my arm around his living room. Friends have gathered, the tree is decorated with baubles, the New York Philharmonic plays Christmas music on the radio, a baby is asleep in the nursery, and a loving wife is at his side.

"You're right, Muz. I'm a lucky man." He nudges Eva with his elbow. "This fellow Will is damn lucky, too."

There must be a dozen people in Thayer's home, mostly associates from work, a few old friends, some of whom I've met before. Bert is introducing Eva around. Guests chat about prices, the end of the war, business. The mood is festive and genial, everyone younger than I am. What I've discovered as I've aged is where men used to look at me as an attractive woman—sometimes even with desire in their eyes—now I'm regarded with deference. Talk grows serious around me as Thayer's friends and associates try to think of topics that might interest me. How an elderly widow gets along, plans for the future—which I assume means death and burial. When I hear, "We're all going to be in your shoes one day," I smile and say, "Not anytime soon, I hope."

Around eleven, Thayer stands in the middle of the room striking his glass with a spoon.

"May I have your attention." He looks at me. "Muz, come over here."

I think, oh no. But I make my way to his side. "Thayer, don't," I whisper, but he ignores me.

"Ladies and gentlemen," he starts. "I want you to recognize the best mother a boy could wish for. This woman holds steady in the strongest ill wind, always setting her sails for a sure tack to move her family forward. Through adversity and heartache, she has kept her head above the fray and soldiered on. Even the *Titanic* couldn't sink her. Florence Cumings Swain is the most true and loving woman I know, and I've known her since before I was born."

I hear tittering at this last comment. Thayer continues, "And today is her birthday. So let's everyone give my mother a cheer."

As the group does three hip, hip, hurrahs, I feel myself blush. Then someone starts the Happy Birthday song and the rest join in, ending with applause. I don't think I've ever been so moved. Still working on that first drink, I raise my glass in thanks.

Eva appears at my side. "Danny," she says, "why didn't you tell me?" She puts an arm around my shoulder. "No—I should have known. I've been too wrapped up in myself. I'm sorry."

"You deserve to be wrapped up in yourself, darling," I say. "This is the most important time in your life."

People crowd around us, offering to get me another drink, giving me cheek kisses. Bert bends to my ear and says, "We'll celebrate your birthday in the New Year." I'm not sure what he has in mind, but with a few cocktails in him, tomorrow he may not remember making the offer.

As we approach midnight, couples pair off. Ginny holds Thayer's hand. I find Eva and put my arm around her waist as the radio counts down the seconds until midnight. I see Bert standing alone and motion for him to join us, which he does. On the stroke of midnight, Thayer pops open a bottle of champagne, then another, and pours glasses that are passed around. I kiss Eva on the cheek and when I turn around, Bert is there, leaning in to kiss me square on the lips.

"Been wanting to do that for a long time," he says. I suspect drink has given him courage and, oddly, I find myself kissing him back. After all, 1944 is a new year, and anything can happen.

40

Marine Recruit

A few days after Thayer's party, Eva packs her bag for her last semester of high school. January is frigid in New York, and she must be eager to go where the weather is more agreeable.

"Danny, you'll come to my graduation in May, won't you?" she asks.

"In Virginia? How in the world would I get to Virginia? I haven't been south of the District of Columbia."

"Joanie is in Bordeaux with Mum, and Bally is being shipped out." Her eyes are pleading. "Richmond is an easy train ride from New York. If you don't come, I won't have anyone there."

I can't tell her I'd rather have teeth pulled than take a seven-hour train ride. But as I've promised, a grandmother fulfills wishes.

"I suppose—"

She interrupts. "If you catch the early train, you won't have to change anywhere. You can take a book or sleep. And watching the countryside roll by will help the time pass."

In my younger years, when we took the train to Maine, I had Bradley and the boys with me so there were plenty of distractions.

"I can have someone meet you at the Richmond station," she says. "And I'll come back to New York with you after the ceremony."

Once again, Eva has overpowered me.

I sigh in surrender. "Of course I'll come." I have four months to prepare myself, four months in which I'll be that much older.

And with any luck, kind strangers will help an aging lady in distress.

"Oh, Danny, you are an angel," she says. And those words give me the determination to undertake the trip.

I spend most of the winter helping Ginny with Gay, watching her so Ginny can run errands and have a semblance of social life, often in the evening with Thayer. Gay is an easy child, petite but strong and very smart. When I'm not tending to Gay, I sit in on Junior League meetings, volunteer at church events, write Eva letters and read her replies again and again. Bert visits occasionally and takes me to his club for the birthday dinner he promised—but we get no further than that. A few times I've walked through bridal shops looking for gowns that Eva might fancy. They haven't set the date, so browsing is all I do without Eva along. Somehow I always make time to play the piano, read, and nap.

Weeks melt into months that creep by, and days warm as I tear another page off the calendar. Thayer calls in early May to say he's going to Maine to open the house and would I like to come with him, but I tell him I'd rather go in June when I have Eva with me and the poppies will be in bloom. Besides, I need to buy a train ticket for Richmond.

The day before my scheduled trip, I phone Thayer about helping me with the train. He tells me he has a busy day tomorrow and can't get me to Penn Station. Ginny takes the telephone and offers to help me find the right train. Gay is now walking and rather than risk losing her in a crowd, Ginny says her sister is visiting and will watch Gay. She'll pick me up in a taxi in the morning.

"It's an early train," I tell her. "Are you sure?"

"Absolutely," she says. "In fact, I wish I were going with you." She sighs. "It's been so long since I've been anywhere."

"Besides Maine?" I ask.

"Yes. I mean, I like Maine, but I'd give about anything to go to Europe." Ginny is a slender woman, very pretty. I want to ask what happened in her first marriage, but it would be in bad taste to pry. In time, she may tell me how the divorce came about. If there are any issues in her marriage with Thayer, they hide it well.

She's in a taxi waiting outside my building at six-thirty the next morning. It's a short ride to Penn Station, and Ginny takes me through the main entrance at 32nd Street and Seventh Avenue. The station is grand with its vaulted glass ceiling, the largest indoor space in New York City.

"Someone called this building a Doric temple to transportation," Ginny says.

I peer upward. "I can see why."

The concourse bustles with men and women in uniform, duffels slung over shoulders, and tourists tramping through with suitcases like a scurry of chipmunks rushing hither and thither.

Ginny finds the ticket office and I'm able to get a seat on the next train to Richmond. She halts in front of a tall board announcing which trains are leaving on which tracks and studies it for a minute.

"Your train departs in ten minutes." She points to a door leading to a stairway. "This way."

The station smells of metal and oil, masculine smells. There's a confusion of voices and the screech of locomotive brakes on the tracks. The trains are electric now, but in the last century the engines were steam powered. Men got wealthy investing in railroads, and a hundred years later the engines are more modern, but not much else has changed.

Ginny leads me right to my train. A steward waits by the door and takes my bag.

"Have a lovely trip." Ginny is almost in tears. I tell her I'll be gone just a few days, but I believe her sadness is less about missing me and more about her confinement.

I put my hand on her arm. "Ginny, hold onto your baby. Cherish every moment. The worst feeling in the world is having a child die before you. No—the very worst is having two children die ahead of you. Take good care of Gay."

She nods in understanding. Her mouth moves, but she can't get words out.

"We'll get together when I return with Eva." I lean into her for a quick embrace then turn and climb the few steps ahead of the steward.

He finds my seat and puts my bag on an overhead shelf. I'm lucky to get a place by the window, although there's nothing to see just yet as the train sits below ground level.

When we jerk forward, I'm transported back more than sixty years to Bradley and the excitement of three little boys on the train to Maine. But now I'm alone, surrounded by strangers and heading south. Some say we should let go of the past, that holding onto memories keeps us from being contented with the present. Negative past experiences make us sad or resentful, but what purpose do sadness and resentment serve other than fear of the future? I have no fear of what's to come, even if hard times are ahead. Nothing—absolutely nothing can be as distressing as what I've already experienced. The challenge for me is not to define myself by my past. If I look backward, I am a *Titanic* survivor, the essential word being "survive," even though my husband and most of the others aboard fell prey to the ill-fated ship. Second, I am twice widowed. Both my husbands will remain young men for all eternity. Third, I am twice a bereaved mother, middle son killed by war, eldest son by illness as a result of war. Three grievous titles.

At this point in my life, I'd rather be known as loving mother, loving grandmother, or the French term, *femme âgée*. I can even accept the title family matriarch, though there's little left of my family. With luck, Jack's children and Thayer's will fill out the Cumings family tree.

The seat beside me is vacant but when we stop in Newark, a crowd of passengers sidle in. Not wanting to invite anyone to take the empty seat, I don't make eye contact, but a man in a suit swings himself down without so much as a word. He puts a briefcase on his lap, opens it, and takes out some papers, then uses the briefcase as a portable desk. I'm not looking for conversation, so I let my head fall back and close my eyes.

When I wake up, we're in Delaware and the seat beside me is empty again. The gentleman must have gotten off in Philadelphia. Out the window the wide Delaware River extends across to New Jersey. We still have a long way to go.

By the time we reach Baltimore, the train is four hours from Richmond. I get up and walk the aisle, finding my way to the dining car. One table is available, and I take it. When the waiter comes, I order the pea soup and a cup of coffee. While I wait, I enjoy the scenery out the large windows, the light brighter here than in the passenger cars.

The soup is fine, and I've finished half of it when a young man approaches and asks if he may sit with me.

"Of course." I point to the empty seat across from me.

He orders a muffin. That's all. He's quiet, head down, not even glancing at me.

"Where are you heading?" I ask.

Finally, he looks up. "Washington," he says.

"Family?"

"No." He hesitates. "Marine recruiting office."

"You're joining the military?" I can't keep myself from making the next statement. "You seem very young."

"I'm eighteen," he says. The number quickens my heart.

"Why the Marines?"

"I—" He starts again. "I want to be the biggest help. The French wouldn't have won the last war if it hadn't been for the Marines."

How does one so young know about the Great War?

"Aren't you planning to go to college?" I ask.

He nods twice. A pensive fellow. "I've been accepted at Princeton, but I want to get my military duty behind me first."

"Princeton?" I regard him more closely. So fair and such a kind and handsome face.

"They have a good music program." He sits up straighter. "I want to be a composer."

I feel a prickle on the back of my neck. Is it coincidence this fellow has chosen to sit with me?

"My name is Florence Cumings." How odd that I didn't say Swain. I haven't been Cumings for two decades.

He extends his hand across the table. "William Corkins. My friends call me Wills."

I take his hand. "Good to know you—" I almost say Wells but correct myself. "Wills. You must be just out of high school."

"Yes. I just graduated from boarding school."

I'm afraid to ask which one. I glance around the dining car to see if I'm dreaming or if this Wills Corkins is real.

"I play piano mostly," he says.

"Chopin?"

"Sure—the etudes. Some Mozart, too."

"Sonata in A?"

"You must know the Turkish March." He stops and looks at me with a quizzical expression. "Mrs. Cumings, you look strangely familiar. Have we met before?"

I feel as if I've known this man for a long time. But how?

"Perhaps we have. I live in New York City."

"I'm originally from Baltimore, but my family moved to Manhattan some time ago," he says. "I prefer Boston, actually. It's where I was born."

Wells was born in Boston. I suddenly feel hot and wish I could open a window. Am I still asleep and is this a dream?

"Do your parents know your plan to join the Marines?" I ask.

"I've been at boarding school since I was twelve. They don't know much about me." He has finished his muffin and now talks openly. "The Marines might not even take me. Since my eighteenth birthday I've been having awful stomach aches." He puts a hand on his midsection. "It comes and goes, but the pain is sometimes intolerable."

"Have you seen a doctor?"

"The nurse at school said it's probably nerves is all."

"What if I get you a cup of tea? They must have mint tea. It will settle your stomach." The waiter is attending to someone else and doesn't see me signal to him.

"Wait here," I say. I slide out of the booth and go to the counter. When I glance back at my table, Wills is gone. Looking up and down the dining car, I don't see any sign of him.

My seat is two cars ahead, and as I work my way forward, I check on the right and left for the young man, but he's not there. The train hasn't stopped, and he couldn't have gotten off. I stagger ahead through the rocking train. Two more cars and still I don't find him.

When I sit back down, I go through the conversation again. So many similarities. And then to have him vanish in a moment. Is there such a thing as a supernatural visitation? But that's absurd. There are hundreds of eighteen-year-olds accepted to Princeton who want to study music and who have stomach aches—aren't there?

When the conductor comes down the aisle, I stop him.

"Excuse me, sir. Do you know where the passenger William Corkins is sitting?"

"Let me check." He looks at a flipchart, scrolling his finger down the page. "I don't see a Mr. Corkins listed. Are you sure you have the correct name?"

"Eighteen-year-old male, blond hair, not quite six feet tall? His destination is Washington."

"Sorry, Miss," he says. "Someone you know?"

I thought so, hoped beyond hope so. But I say, "No. I guess not. Thank you."

I turn and look out the window. Maybe Wills used a false name to board the train in case his parents try to stop him from joining the military. Or maybe — no, that's absurd. He was as real as I am, not a ghost and not a figment of my imagination.

The train slows down going through a town. By the tracks I see a church. Atop the spire, an angel carved of stone, robe reaching to her feet, wings raised toward the heavens. Wherever you are, Wills Corkins, I think, may an angel shelter and protect you.

When the train rolls into the Richmond station, I pull my bag from the shelf and line up with several others at the exit door. Without a clue which way to go, I follow the crowd to the terminal. There, waving her arms and yelling "Danny!" is the prettiest girl in the world — Eva, my granddaughter.

41

Omaha Beach

The weekend is filled with lunches, tea and cocktail parties, awards ceremonies and, finally, graduation. In what feels like no time, Eva and I are back in Manhattan. She doesn't want to go to Maine this June, she says. There's too much planning to do for the wedding.

She thumbs through a magazine in the living room.

"Will expects to be home by next spring," she says. "We'd like the ceremony to be in the fall of next year."

"You mean 1945? You'll be nineteen. Shouldn't you wait another year?"

"These are uncertain times, Danny. She who hesitates is lost, after all."

I don't tell her some women get lost in their marriages. But from the magazines on the coffee table open to photographs of bridal gowns and bridesmaid dresses, it looks like the wheels of the wedding bus have started rolling—and there is no stopping it.

"I have lots to show you," she says.

The phone rings and when I answer, Thayer says, "Muz, turn on the radio. You have to listen to the news."

He doesn't say whether the news is good or bad, but I know immediately it's about the war.

When I hang up, I ask Rosa what today is.

"June 6," she says.

I dial the radio to a news station and catch the announcer in mid-sentence.

". . . known as D-Day, stormed the beaches of Normandy, France, the largest seaborne invasion in history. Twelve Allied nations sent more than one-hundred-fifty thousand troops by air and sea, some parachuting in and others wading or swimming ashore onto Omaha Beach in northern France."

"What's happening?" Eva is on her feet and standing with me in front of the radio, Rosa behind us.

There are times when an event is too large to be believed, an event over which most of us have no control, like an earthquake or a meteor plummeting straight for the planet. The bombing of Pearl Harbor was one such event. This time, though, a ray of hope comes through the radio with pride in our boys who are risking their lives to free the world of evil. We three women stand together, silent, each launching prayers aloft for success, victory, and an end to this miserable war.

"Overlord, as the mission is named, began in the late hours last night when supreme commander General Eisenhower ordered flat-bottomed boats loaded with troops to cross the English Channel," the announcer says. "From southern England, the distance to the French coast is ten miles of turbulent water. The crossing was treacherous with high winds that sent cold water rushing over the gunwales."

"Oh dear," Eva gasps.

I know about cold water. Even in a *Titanic* lifeboat, cold reached up from the frigid sea and grabbed me by the ankles, shooting sharp needles of pain up my legs and into my chest so I thought I might be having a heart attack. In the quiet of the night, I didn't know—any more than those soldiers in boats on the English Channel knew—whether I would survive the night.

"The largest amphibious landing force ever assembled approached Omaha Beach while German forces perching on cliffs above the beach opened fire with machine guns." The announcer's voice sounds like a megaphone of urgency. "As the first wave of men fell or came ashore, more followed. While troops fought to reach the bottom of the cliffs, Allied airmen parachuted behind enemy lines, blowing up bridges and damaging rail lines to prevent German reinforcements from advancing. By midday French time, Americans had surmounted the cliffs and claimed victory of Omaha Beach. Sadly, of the thirty-four thousand who came ashore that day, an estimated twenty-four hundred were killed, wounded, or are unaccounted for."

"Miss Eva," Rosa says, her hand covering her chest, "your boyfriend is there?"

"No, Rosa. At least, I hope not." Eva puts a hand on Rosa's shoulder. "Last I heard, he's still stationed in the Pacific."

The radio announcer continues. "The effort of pushing back and defeating the German army will continue for our courageous military personnel. Have no fear, boys. A million more are on the way to aid and support you." He ends the report with "God bless America."

"Is this the turning point, Danny?" Eva asks. "Are we near the end of the war?"

I don't want to disappoint her, not while her hopes for the future are so high. "I'm afraid it's not over until Kaiser Wilhelm surrenders." I realize too late my mistake.

Rosa speaks. "Kaiser Wilhelm?"

I'm back in the Great War, back worrying about my sons risking their lives for our European allies.

"She means Adolf Hitler." Eva understands. Through the letters, she has been with me on those poppy-laden fields where

the red blood of American Marines — the blood of my own son —
splattered on the red blossoms of the flowers.

I pull back my shoulders. "It's not time for celebration. Not yet." To calm our rattled minds, normalcy is called for. "But, Rosa, it may be time for supper."

"Yes, Mrs. Swain. I serve a little supper now."

In spite of war and death and deprivation — in spite of everything — life must go on.

42

A Simple Cross

Eva has decided her marriage will take place in the Church of the Holy Trinity on 87th Street. Founded in the Anglican faith, the church was established in 1899, the year Wells was born. According to their program, the church's mission is to "do justice, love kindness, and walk humbly with God," a charge I can embrace.

We've just left the church after Sunday service and I suggest we walk east. I want to show her Gracie Mansion.

"The problem with Holy Trinity Church," Eva says, "is Will and I have to agree to pre-marriage counseling with the parish clergy."

"Why is that a problem?"

"Counseling goes on for six months. If he doesn't return to the States until this time next year, we'll have to delay the wedding."

"That puts the date—when?"

"November at least. Probably December." She has a note of desperation in her voice.

"And you'll be closer to twenty."

"Yes, but I don't see how that matters, Danny. We love each other, and we want to be married."

I'm rather glad they'll have to wait. After six months of being close to each other, they should know for sure whether they're ready for a lifelong commitment.

Eva points toward the Gracie Mansion. "What is that building up ahead?"

"It's the home named for Archibald Gracie, a shipping magnate. It was built in 1799 and is one of the oldest historic homes in New York City."

"Goodness," Eva says. "Do they host receptions?"

"Maybe at one time when the building was the Museum of the City of New York, but now it's the mayor's residence."

"What a pity," she huffs.

"I was with Mr. Gracie's great-grandson on the *Titanic*, Colonel Archibald Gracie. He was fascinated with Civil War history and also invested in real estate. It was Colonel Gracie who helped me into a lifeboat."

"Did he survive?" Eva's interest is piqued now.

"Yes. He stood on the bottom of an upturned lifeboat until another lifeboat picked him up. There were dozens of men standing up to their ankles in water. All were rescued."

I don't want to relate details of that night, not even of the rescue. I doubt she will ever read the book the colonel wrote about the tragedy. He died in December 1912 without finishing it. I suppose he never recovered from the trauma of that night. I know that feeling. In fact, two other times I've felt ready to die myself. But now I live for my son Thayer and my grandchildren. And I've got to see that Eva has the wedding of her dreams.

I suggest we amble through Schurz Park next to Gracie Mansion.

"What is this body of water?" Eva squints her eyes toward a nearby river.

"That's Hell Gate, a channel in the East River."

"What a pretty spot."

I suspect for her every large area holds the possibility for a formal reception, but an outdoor venue is not a pleasant place for a December party.

"I wonder," Eva starts.

"Wonder what, darling?"

"I wonder if we could get something to eat now, Danny."

I chuckle. My dear Eva, always ready for love and lunch.

"It's such a nice day," she says. "Could we take lunch in the courtyard of your building?"

"Of course," I say.

When we get home, I ask Rosa to wrap sandwiches and we take them down to the courtyard.

"Oh, look!" Eva says.

I'm stunned to see a host of red poppies blooming among the perennials in the garden.

"I'd forgotten I planted them."

"They're brilliant." She thinks a minute. "Didn't my father and Uncle Wells mention poppies in the fields around the battles?"

"They did, yes."

We munch our sandwiches, each of us lost in our own thoughts. When we finish, I say, "I'd like you to read one more letter."

She looks at me quizzically. "I thought I'd read them all."

"Not quite."

When we go back upstairs, I retrieve the letter from my bedroom, the one from her father I had removed from the box.

"It's the appropriate time to read this one," I say.

"All right." She sits on the sofa with the onionskin paper and reads it aloud.

April 16, 1919

Darling Mother,

I am thinking of you very much today, as I always do, and wish I were with you. I am still staying with Uncle Bert here. Saturday we started on our trip in Mr. Prosser's car, Uncle Bert, Mr. Olds (Mr. Prosser's secretary), and myself. We drove to Chateau-Thierry, where we spent the night in a lodge. The next morning we went to Belleau Wood and found Wells' grave. There are hundreds of other American boys buried there, mostly the 6th Marines and the 26th Division. The American section is at one end of a beautiful French Cemetery overlooking the river and the hills beyond. All the graves are simple, one not decorated any more than the other. Each has a humble white cross engraved with the man's name and his date of death. French girls take care of the plots and plantings. I've enclosed pressed flowers from near Wells' grave.

It is impossible to tell my feelings there, but amidst the sorrow of being so near Wells, there is that pride I always have to think he gave up all in the most critical battle of the war and lies with his comrades as a monument to America's part.

Uncle Bert should be home in two weeks, probably quicker than this letter, and he will tell you better than I can how I am. I shall be thinking of you when I take early communion Easter as we used to.

Heaps of love to my own darling Muz.

Jack

When Eva finishes, she looks up at me with tears in her eyes.

"The poppies hadn't bloomed yet." She wipes a tear from her smooth cheek with her fingers.

"Eva—" I sit beside her, our knees touching. "I want to take you to France. To the grave. We'll stay in Paris as your father did. I want you to see where his letters came from."

"Danny, we can't—there's a war."

"Not anytime soon. But from the sound of what happened in Normandy, the war may be nearing an end." I sit up straighter. "First, a wedding. Then a honeymoon, of course. And when the war is over and you can tear yourself away from your handsome husband, we'll go."

Eva nods. A tear falls onto her lap.

"Danny, you are so good to me."

I put my arm around her. "You're the good one, darling. I couldn't make the trip alone."

A half smile brightens her face. "All right," she says.

42

Harm's Way

The Church of the Holy Trinity has set the date for the marriage on December 15, more than a year away. For Eva that seems an eternity, but she'll be so busy the time will feel like three breaths. I sponsored her to join the Junior League, and she is volunteering at the hospital again. On her own, she enrolled in secretarial school.

"You want to be a secretary now?" I ask. "I thought you were interested in nursing."

"I can make more money doing secretarial work," she says, "And I want to help with the wedding expenses."

"What does your mother say about your being a secretary?"

Eva sighs. "When my father died, my mother drew into herself. If I tried to talk to her, it was as if she didn't hear me. Joanie couldn't reach her either and started coming to me for whatever she needed." She gives a little shake of her head. "I love my mother — truly I do — but I have to make my own choices now."

I let the air settle between us. After a few seconds, I say, "And live with them."

That very day I receive a letter from Margaret, postmarked Bordeaux. What few letters get through from France have been for Eva, and I'm surprised to find one addressed to me. Bordeaux has been Oliver's most challenging consulate assignment, she writes. German soldiers control every aspect of the town and dissenters are arrested. In spite of Oliver's efforts, a pall of gloom hangs over the city. She asks that I not mention to Eva what a difficult time they're having of it. Oliver plans to retire next spring, and they're eager to get back to the calm and safety of Bedford Hills. She ends by thanking me for stepping in as surrogate mother for Eva, especially when Eva needs mature guidance for what lies ahead.

I'm sitting by the window overlooking the courtyard, a cup of tea next to me. At least Margaret and Oliver will be in New York before the wedding. In the meantime, I'll walk the tightrope between mothering Eva and letting her make her own decisions, as she wishes.

The poppies have dropped their blossoms, summer heat sits heavy on New York, and Eva is about to turn eighteen. She's out most evenings with new friends she met at secretarial school or Junior League. I don't recall ever being so busy at her age. Margaret's letter said Joanie is at summer camp this year but would like to stay with me in New York next year. From what I know of Joanie, her request is more of a demand. At thirteen, Eva's younger sister is old enough to be of some help with wedding details, and she'll return to school in the fall. I hope I can handle another responsibility while Joanie's with me.

I sip my tea and ask myself if my cup is half full or half empty. Another sip brings the level close to halfway up the cup. Or is it down the cup? I suppose it's for to me to decide. At one point in my life, the cup was full to overflowing. Then suddenly, with the sinking of a great ship, it seemed empty. Eva's life is nearly full and in a few years hers, too, will overflow with more than she can now imagine. I suppose it's up to us to fill our own cups.

In late afternoon Eva comes in breathless. "Danny, I just got the most horrible letter from Will!" She waves an envelope in front of me.

I think his division must be under attack or he's injured, in the hospital. Or else he's calling off the engagement, met someone else. Nothing I can help with.

"What is it, darling?"

She takes a deep breath. "He was standing in the chow line and heard machine-gun fire."

I'm losing patience. "Is he all right?"

"Yes, thankfully. But the bullet hit the man in line in front of him. In the head. He died immediately." She hugs me, her face against my shoulder. "Oh, Danny, the man was a foot away from him. The bullet could easily have hit Will."

I think about Wells' journal, about the soldier who was shot beside him, how close Wells came to the bullet hitting him. All wars are ugly and unpredictable. But I have to comfort Eva, and I put my hand on her back.

"I'm sure he got out of harm's way. And he's fine, isn't he?"

She drops into the chair next to me. "He's shaken, as you can imagine. And he'll be on that island months longer." Holding the envelope against her chest, she says, "The war in the Pacific is not over, I'm afraid."

"Will has good reason to stay alive." I think for a minute and then recall part of a poem I read in school—"Paradise Lost," I think it was. "'Long is the way and hard that out of hell leads up to light.' You are Will's light, Eva. Keep writing him, and be as positive as you can. Then trust with all your heart that he'll come back to you safe and sound." What I don't tell her is that trust is not always enough.

A reception venue has to be booked a year in advance. I consider the Harold Pratt Mansion at 68th and Park. It would be an easy walk from the Church of the Holy Trinity. Harold Pratt's father was in the Standard Oil business, and when I mention my late husband's name, I'm able to book the evening of the wedding. In 1928 when Chess was a vice president of Standard Oil, the company named a freighter for him and even though the old tanker is about to be sold as scrap metal, Chess carried weight in the business.

I say a silent thanks to my late oilman husband. When I tell Eva about Pratt mansion, she couldn't be happier. Another essential ticked off the to-do list.

It's nearly Christmas and we're having breakfast before Eva heads out for her busy day. Rosa's French toast is delicious.

"Danny," Eva says, "I've made so many new friends here in New York."

"Of course you have. People are drawn to you."

"Two of them took me to look at wedding dresses yesterday."

"But—" I stop myself. I'm paying for the dress, so shouldn't it be up to me to take my granddaughter shopping for one? On the other hand, I want her to be satisfied with her gown, and if girls her own age have a better idea of current wedding fashions, so be it.

Her smile is so broad her eyes crinkle. "And I think we found just the one."

I don't want Eva to have the same conflict I had with my own mother about what to wear on my most special day. She insisted on a dress with frills and ruffles. I wanted simplicity. I was lucky to help Eva choose her debutante dress, but the choice of her wedding gown should be up to her—and her friends, I suppose. A strange emotion falls around me, though. Never having had a daughter, I want to cling to this offspring of my offspring, to hold onto her as a replacement for the eighteen-year-old son I lost. Now I feel her slipping away from me, and there's nothing I can do except concede.

"Did you try on the dress?"

She has finished her French toast and pushes the plate away.

"Yes." She hesitates. "But of course it will need alterations."

"Of course." I try to hide my disappointment.

"Danny," she says, "I want you to see it. It's important that you like it."

Is she humoring me? Or patronizing me? I've lost my appetite and lay my fork over what's left of my breakfast.

"Can you meet me at noon today at the bridal shop on Madison?" she says.

     SHELTERING ANGEL OF BELLEAU WOOD

My hurt feelings are less important than my granddaughter's joy.

"Of course I can meet you," I say. "Will you have time for lunch afterward?"

"I'm afraid not. I have to be at the hospital at one." She reaches over and squeezes my hand. "But absolutely another day."

How silly of me to feel scorned, even betrayed. A grandmother is not a best friend, and at the ceremony I will be among the guests, not maid of honor or even a bridesmaid. Grandmothers perform duties, and we perform them cheerfully, without reward. The words "after all I've done for you" will never pass my lips.

"Yes," I say, "another day."

43

Happy New Year

On Christmas Day Eva and I are with Thayer and his family. Little Gay, now one and a half, runs around the apartment. She's more interested in the lights on the tree and gift boxes than the outfits inside. She hugs the big teddy bear Eva gave her, then climbs inside the box as if it's her own tiny house. Christmas lunch is simple but adequate and afterward, Eva says she wants to go back to our apartment. She has letters from Will she wants to reread. He sent photographs of the island where he's stationed and she wants to start a scrapbook.

Before we leave, Thayer puts his arms around me and whispers, "You're a marvelous grandmother, but you'll have to let the little chick go when it's time for her to fledge."

Tears are too close for me to answer, so I hug him and flash back to my father saying, "Be nice to your sister. Your mother and I will be gone one of these days, and you'll be left with each other." I know I have Eva only another year. Then most likely she will move to Boston with her new husband. Again, it will be just Thayer and I, all that each other has.

On New Year's Eve, Eva tells me she has plans to go out somewhere with friends. A party, I think she says.

Before she leaves, she kisses me on the cheek and says, "Don't wait up."

I may not wait up, but I doubt I'll sleep until she returns.

Rosa joins me in a whiskey. Then she says, "I must go home now." We have this argument every holiday — take tomorrow off, no I'll be here in the morning, but it's New Year's Day, that's all right I have nowhere else to be.

Good friend Rosa.

After she leaves, I turn on the radio and think about another whiskey. I'd rather open a bottle of wine, but that might be dangerous because I'd want to find the bottom of the bottle. I can hear revelers on the street and doubt I'll sleep without help, so I pour myself a bitter Campari and rummage in the freezer for ice. The radio announcer ticks off first the hours, then the minutes until midnight. A quarter of an hour to go and I'm thinking I may fall asleep right here on the sofa. Then a knock comes at the door.

When I open, there stands Bert Marckwald with a silly grin on his face. He's wobbling a bit like a sapling in a breeze.

"Don't think I can make it home tonight," he says. "One helluva party at my office."

"You've retired, Bert," I say.

"They like to invite the alumni for old time's sake."

"And get them soused?"

"The sousing I did myself. May I come in?"

I realize we're still standing at the door.

"Of course." I step aside and let him enter.

He sheds his coat and looks around for the closet. "I have yet to learn my way around this place. What happened to the closet? It was here just the other day."

"That was the other apartment, Bert." I take his coat, which I believe he is about to drop on the floor, and drape it over a chair. Certainly he won't stay long.

"And by the way—" He takes himself to the sofa and falls onto it. "I'm not soused. I'm fermented. Fermentation is more natural."

I can smell the alcohol on him. I suppose we both reek of it. Like a sailboat, it takes me a couple tacks to get myself to the kitchen and fill a glass with water. When I take the water to Bert,

I slosh some on the floor. I give him the glass and go back to the kitchen to get a dishtowel but when I get there, I've forgotten why I came.

"Come back here, Florrie," Bert calls to me. I remember the dishtowel and the spill and get the cleanup done.

"I can't afford to leave a mark on the floor," I say.

"That's my Florrie," he says. "Ever practical."

"I should call a taxi to get you home, Bert."

"Nonsense. I'll just sleep right here." He pats the white linen of the sofa.

What to do with this fellow? "You can't sleep on the sofa. Eva will be coming back later, and you'll frighten the daylights out of her. I'll get you a blanket and pillow and you can take a nap in the den. Then you'll have to scoot home."

"Was it Twain who said bed is the most dangerous place to be?" Bert slurs. "More men die in bed than anywhere else."

"The den has a sofa. It's not a bed. I'm sure you'll live through the next few hours."

"Florrie, you've always been such a good friend," he says.

By the time I get the bedding, the radio announces ten minutes until midnight. Bert has fallen asleep and I half drag him to the den. I help him off with his shoes and tuck him in as the ten-second countdown begins.

"We're going into 1945 together," he mumbles. "I like that."

"Good night, Bert," I say, but he reaches up and pulls me down for a sloppy kiss on the lips.

"Happy New Year, sweetheart." Bert has never called me that. He's probably thinking of his late wife Isabelle.

When I climb into my own bed, I'm glad not to be alone in the apartment, and I glide off to sleep.

Sometime in the night I feel a presence near me.

"Eva?" No answer. I haven't heard her come in.

"Is it you, darling?" I whisper, hoping Bradley is visiting me again.

No answer.

Light touches on my skin. Feathery touches. Everywhere. I'm tingling, then lifted, weightless. There is tension between desire and restraint. I have loved two men—still love. At first there was restraint before surrender. Now, if I'm dreaming, why not submit to desire? My reward for having lived.

A surge of yearning presses me against the ceiling until I can hardly breathe and I break through into black sky and blazing stars of euphoria, of rapture. Then slowly I float back into the softness of my bed, into a deep and dreamless sleep.

When we meet in the kitchen on New Year's Day, Eva looks none the worse for wear.

"Did you have a grand time last night?" I ask.

"We played games until one. It was fun. But honestly, I'd rather have spent the evening with you. It was your birthday, after all."

"Pshaw," I hiss. "I've had enough birthday acknowledgments."

Rosa has coffee ready, much to my delight. Strong and black, the best remedy for my headache. A woman my age should know better than to overindulge in liquor, even on New Year's Eve.

"By the way, Danny, who was here last night, if I may ask? There was a man's overcoat on the chair when I came in."

Oh dear. Was Bert a good boy and stayed in the den all night—or did he roam the apartment and end up in my bed? I could swear someone was with me. Or was alcohol playing its shenanigans?

It suddenly occurs to me Bert might still be in the den.

"Is the coat there now?"

"No," Eva says. "Whoever it belonged to apparently left in the wee hours of the morning."

I breathe a sigh of relief. "Uncle Bert was at a party and needed a place to rest before going home."

"Uh-huh," she says.

"Uh-huh," Rosa repeats.

We chortle, the three of us. Keeping secrets is a good way to start the year.

44

Forebear and Persevere

My granddaughter is in the gallery fixing her hair in the mirror. These days she is a fawn springing off in bursts of speed to explore the city's forest of concrete.

"Darling," I say, "you are about to step onto a stony path where your journey begins."

"Why stony?" She's speaking to the mirror.

"At different times, everyone stumbles over stones. Some fall into pits and have to climb out."

"Oh, Danny, you are so—so figurative." When she's satisfied with her hair, she turns to me. "Anyway, I expect after this dreadful war my path will be clear of rocks and pits."

"Watch out for cobblestones, my darling, for twisted ankles and broken hearts."

"My dear grandmother, I'll watch for the cobblestones, but the road in front of me is full of sunshine and lined with orchids. "

"Orchids require careful tending, you know."

"My, but you're acting strange this evening." She kisses my cheek. "I'll be having dinner with friends tonight, but I won't be late. We can continue this fascinating conversation when I return."

"As you like," I say.

After she leaves, Rosa asks, "What was that about?" She's a terrible eavesdropper.

"I don't know. I've been reading poetry. It must have seeped into me."

"Do you feel well?"

"Yes. I suppose so." Actually, I'm not sure. I've turned sixty-eight and have trouble remembering things. Has Eva mentioned attendants for her wedding? Her maid of honor? The color for their dresses? Whether the event will be black tie? Where they'll go for their honeymoon?

Chess took me to Prince Edward Island after our wedding. Not my idea of a romantic spot, at least not in April when snow was still on the ground. Dalvay By the Sea, I think it was called, a Tudor-style manor that was the summer home of a Standard Oil president in the nineteenth century. All wood with wide stone fireplaces ablaze. Outside, there was still ice on the lake but in places the water was so clear I could see the sandy bottom. Wind whistled and bent the treetops. Hawks screeched overhead and I wished to grab the tail of one and fly to someplace warm. Even in the sun the air was cool. I had wanted to go to Jamaica and let ourselves melt slovenly into the sand. But then he was behind me, his big arms around my shivering shoulders, and I smelled his sweet aftershave, sweeter than sandalwood, and my shaking stopped. I was warm — so warm that even the night in the lifeboat faded from my memory.

Chess was a good husband. An excellent husband.

Do all women in their sixties dwell in the past because there is so little future to think about?

When Eva has gone, I find an envelope on the entry table. It looks to be from Will and has been opened. I guess Eva read the letter on the elevator on her way up to the apartment. I shouldn't read it, but curiosity gets the best of me and I slide the paper out of the envelope. It's dated a week ago, February 12, 1945.

My Sweet Eva,

You probably don't want to hear about war activities, but I must tell you that by the middle of this month my Marine division will be attacking an island off the coast of [location sliced out by censors] held by the enemy. One of our destroyers was hit by heavy artillery and sank, killing dozens of sailors. This attack will be a difficult task as the [sliced out by censors] are well fortified on the island of [sliced out by censors] hiding in caves with machine-gun nests, so we've been informed.

Please do not worry about me. Thirty thousand troops will be first on the island followed by my division along with another several thousand. As a sergeant, I will be directing the troops, and we expect to make short work of the enemy. I know we will be victorious.

With any luck, I will return to you in May, just a few months hence, and then will be in officer's training somewhere in Virginia.

Give Danny a kiss from me and save a thousand kisses for you.

Your own, Will

I find this morning's copy of the *Times* and read the news from the Pacific. The attack is on an island named Iwo Jima off the coast of Japan, the article says. The Japanese army is fortified in bunkers, caves, and tunnels but U.S. Navy and Marine Corps aviators have bombed the island. Surrender is expected within days.

I pray Will was not harmed. His family would be notified, and they would contact Eva through me. So far, no bad news, thank goodness.

When Eva returns that night, I don't tell her I read the letter, but I let her know about the battle of Iwo Jima.

"Goodness," she says, but her face contorts in alarm. She plops into a living room chair.

"It sounds as if the Navy and Marines have the situation under control," I tell her. "Try not to worry." I pour two glasses of wine and hand one to her. "This might help."

"Thank you." She takes the goblet. "But I doubt anything will keep me from worrying."

I lean on my diverting tactics. "By the way, it's not too early to think about getting an engagement announcement in the *Times*. The usual timeframe is a few months in advance of the event."

"So, August?"

"I'll take care of it, but you may have to sit for a photo."

"All right." She seems tired tonight—or worried about Will, so I press for more diversions.

"Have you decided on attendants?"

"I think so. Four good friends. And I'd like my sister to be my maid of honor. Mum has put Joanie in the boarding school I went to, so she'll be able to get to New York even if Mum and Oliver are still in France."

"How old is she now?"

"Fourteen—going on eighteen. She's always been precocious."

"What about dress colors for the bridesmaids?"

"Oh, there's so much to think about. What do you suggest, Danny?"

I'm delighted to be consulted about colors. "For ten days before Christmas, I'd go with navy blue or burgundy. Maybe royal blue or pink for Joanie."

"I'll take the girls to look at dresses." She sips her wine.

More activities with friends, less with grandmother. It is well and appropriate, I tell myself. Besides, the young go at a faster pace than grandmothers—and without backaches.

"That's enough wedding talk for tonight," Eva says. "Weddings and wars are both so stressful. And now I have Junior League meetings, hospital work, and the secretarial school demands nothing short of excellence. We must stand above the crowd, the teachers say, not just in class but as a way of life."

Of course she'll stand above the crowd. She looks so grown up now and after she marries, she will be a woman in every sense of the word.

She cups her cheeks with her palms. "How am I supposed to juggle everything required of me?"

I take a breath. "With grace, my dear. Patience, perseverance, and grace."

"No more poetic words for me?"

"Hmmm. I recall a line by Robert Louis Stevenson, I think it was. I'll try to paraphrase it. 'Give us grace and strength to forbear and persevere. Give us gaiety and a quiet mind.' Something like that."

"A good prayer," she says. Then, "Danny, what should I expect?" She bites her bottom lip. "I mean on the marriage night? I'm a little — naïve. I haven't even had a boyfriend. Not a serious one, anyway."

I've been expecting her question. Now that it's here, I have to tread carefully and draw from my own first night with Bradley.

"Don't you think Will might have questions, too? He went to an all-boys boarding school and an all-men's college, so he may not have any more experience with the opposite sex than you do."

"I was wondering about that."

"What I suggest is that you relax on your wedding night. Being tense and nervous won't help. Think about your own body and what gives you pleasure. You'll both probably be shy at first, so touching is a good way to begin. If you enjoy being touched lightly, tell him that."

"Should I be taking notes?"

I hum a soft laugh. "No, darling. Just follow your heart." My apprehension is that Will is taking instruction from his Marine buddies and they may advise him to be rough with her — man talk. "If he does something you don't like, tell him. A man who loves a woman the way Will loves you wants to please her, and in order to give you pleasure, you may have to tell him where your most sensitive areas are. Every woman is different, and how is Will to know unless you direct him?"

Her cheeks redden and she clasps her hands together. "Danny, direct him where? My private parts?" Her hand goes to her chest and she breathes out, "Goodness."

I don't laugh this time. This is a serious conversation. "Any area that makes you feel — aroused. For some women — " I pause to take a breath before revealing my deepest intimacy to my granddaughter. "It's the nipples. Soft pinches are nice." Eva is asking me to be honest, to be open. I take another breath. "And a point between the legs."

"Oh" is all she says.

I have to finish what I've started — what she has demanded of me.

"Eva, there is nothing wrong with exploring yourself, especially that spot. When you do, you'll have more confidence to show Will the way."

"I see." She holds out her wine glass to me. "Danny, if you don't mind, I think I'd better have a bit more wine."

"One glass is plenty for tonight, dear, and also for your wedding night with your husband. That night will be the first of many. Just try to enjoy it, even if you feel clumsy, even if you're embarrassed. Each time will be better."

Bradley and I both were nervous and awkward the first time but so in love it didn't matter. My heart felt as if it would fly out of my chest. So many years later with Chess, we were relaxed, slow, confident. Bradley and I grew with each other over the years whereas Chess and I had grown within ourselves. Did I prefer one over the other? No. Eva, too, will find what is weak and what is strong within herself, and I have no doubt she will help her husband find similar qualities in himself. He'll be a fortunate man to have her by his side.

45

Little Boy

It's a blistering August 6th in New York City. I'm sitting at an open window hoping to catch any cool breeze before the noon sun sets us all afire. Across Park Avenue a woman pulls on a leash to constrain her little dog. The entire city is taut, fraught with anticipation of news about the war. The radio is on in every apartment, and we tap our toes waiting for delivery of the morning *Times*. Six years is far too long for the world to be at war.

While I wait for Eva to deliver her sister from the train station, my mind turns to what President Truman plans to do. The Vice President took charge in April when Roosevelt died of a cerebral hemorrhage. April saw Mussolini executed, and Hitler committed suicide before Germany surrendered, but Japan still refuses to yield.

American airplanes have dropped flyers over Japanese cities threatening that if the country doesn't surrender, it will experience a rain of ruin like the earth has never seen. Last month when a test of the atom bomb was conducted in a remote New Mexico desert, the paper reported the explosion was equal to fifteen thousand tons of TNT and could devastate an entire city. Because oil rigs at sea have potential for exploding, Chess had to know about volatile power. He said half a ton of TNT would shatter windows and cause damage to buildings, and intense heat would combust any burnable material in the area. Any living thing within a thousand feet of the blast would be killed instantly. A fifteen-thousand-ton explosion is beyond my comprehension.

Years ago, I read about a Catholic priest in Belgium who developed the theory that our universe was created from the explosion of a single atom so dense it contained all matter, space, and energy. I wonder if detonating an atom bomb will create new universes with worlds beyond our imagining. If Japan ignores the threat, most of Asia — and the life of Will Robbins — may lie in the hands of Mr. Truman. My hope tonight is that Emperor Hirohito will make the decision to circumvent more death and destruction by conceding to Allied victory.

Rosa goes to the door and picks up the *Times*. She drops the paper on the gallery table and brings me the society section.

"Look, Mrs. Swain." She points to Eva's engagement announcement. *Miss Eva Cumings to wed U.S. Marine Warrant Officer William Robbins of Boston.*

"Finally some good news," I tell her. "The announcement should be in the August issue of *Vogue* magazine, too." I paid a hefty fee to have Eva pose for a photo in her debutante gown and gave *Vogue* exclusive rights to use it.

Just then my granddaughter Joanie bursts through the door, Eva right behind her.

"Danny!" Joanie says. "At last!"

She speaks in exclamations as if everything she says is extraordinary and exciting. She is vivacious and, if possible, more beautiful than Eva.

After I am captured in an inescapable embrace, Joanie announces, "I want to see every show in Manhattan. And go dancing. We really must all go dancing."

Rosa surveys us from the kitchen doorway. "*Hola, niña,*" she says.

Joanie chatters back to Rosa in fluent Spanish, and they both laugh at some joke to which I am not privy. Rosa's face lights up at this adolescent who speaks her language, and with such enthusiasm. The time in Guatemala and Ecuador with her mother and stepfather obviously sharpened my younger granddaughter's skill with Spanish.

Joanie turns to me.

"I've skipped the last week of summer camp to help plan the wedding. What do we need to do next?"

"The wedding is still four months away," I say, "but we've ordered flowers. Eva's gown and the bridesmaids' dresses have been altered, and Eva has decided on the menu for two hundred."

Eva takes the reins. "We must have Joanie try on her maiden of honor dress."

"I'm going to marry a doctor," Joanie says. "A rich doctor." She looks at her sister. "What's Will going to do?"

"He hasn't decided yet," Eva says. "He's still in training to be a Marine officer."

"That sounds awfully dull."

"I'm very proud of Will for his military service, Joanie."

Rosa relieves the tension by asking, "*¿Quieres algo para comer?*"

"Oh, no thank you, Rosa. How could I possibly eat when there's too much to see?" Joanie says. "And we're going to have dinner someplace fabulous." She looks at me. "Could we go to the Colony Club?"

"Well—" How in the world does this child know about the exclusive—and very expensive—Upper East Side women's club? I am a member, but people make reservations for dinner weeks in advance.

Eva intervenes. "Don't bother, Danny," she says. "I'll take Joanie downtown for her fitting and then we'll have a walk around the city." She gives Rosa an apologetic look. "We'll worry about dinner later."

I thank heavens for that. Joanie is quite a handful.

That afternoon Rosa comes from the den where she has been making up a bed for Joanie. Her face is blanched, her mouth moving, but no words come from her.

"What's the matter, Rosa? Are you ill?"

"Something," she starts. "Something happening—listen."

Complete silence. All of New York has come to a stop as if every building, every vehicle, every person is holding an intake of breath.

"Dear Lord—what is it?"

I point to the radio, unable to move. Rosa turns it on and raises the volume. The announcer speaks fast, his voice in near panic.

This morning the U.S. dropped an atom bomb on Hiroshima. Called Little Boy, the bomb's explosion killed one hundred thousand instantly. Another hundred thousand are expected to die of wounds and burns. President Truman has declared that if Japan's Emperor Hirohito does not surrender within twenty-four hours, a second bomb, the one they've named Big Boy, will be dropped on Nagasaki.

A bolt of lightning runs through me. "My granddaughters are out in Manhattan somewhere. Eva wanted to show Joanie Times Square. The news must be up on billboards." I look toward the door, hoping they'll rush back.

Rosa presses her palms to her cheeks but doesn't speak.

"Heavens," I say. "Does the Emperor really believe he's ordained by God and God will protect him and his people?"

"Foolish man," Rosa says, staring at the radio.

It's terrifying to think how many thousand more will die before Hirohito admits he's not divine.

Rosa's hand presses her chest as if to slow her pounding heart, and she shakes her head. She and I stand, both helpless as we experience horror and relief. The war has to be over soon and everyone can begin getting back to normal life. But there will be no normal life for the Japanese. Maybe not for the French, either. And after so many years of devastation and sacrifice, how can life resume any semblance of normality for anyone—at the cost of millions of lives, most of them civilians. Millions killed in German concentration camps, two thousand American sailors killed in the bombing of Pearl Harbor, entire cities destroyed, and disgusting acts of inhumanity perpetrated in Italy, North Africa, and all over the world. How can I forgive the number of souls lost to war when the deaths of two sons devastated me?

I don't have to look at Rosa. I know she can hear me. "I have survived the greatest maritime disaster in history and now two world wars. I swear to you now, Rosa, I will live to see my granddaughter married. No matter the outcome of this war, I will watch Eva Cumings walk down the aisle of the Church of the Holy Trinity and marry the man she loves."

Rosa steps closer and puts a warm hand on my arm. When she speaks, it's not Rosa I hear and they are not Rosa's words—they're Bradley's.

"I know you will, my darling."

46

The Wedding

After atom bombs have obliterated the cities of Hiroshima and Nagasaki, Emperor Hirohito yields, and in September President Truman declares an end to World War Two. Crowds gather in Times Square to celebrate, strangers hugging strangers, huzzahs of victory rising to the neon billboards attached high on skyscrapers. Even on Park Avenue, people are on the sidewalks, car horns blare, cheers rise into the air. The weight of dread has been lifted, and the very air of the city feels fresher. Once again mothers will welcome their boys home with relief and joy. My own heart is with the mothers and fathers who will never see a triumphant look on the face of a loved one who gave his life for his country.

In early September Joanie tearfully and reluctantly returns to boarding school after declaring she is smarter than her teachers and would serve better being my assistant in Manhattan. Fortunately, Eva convinces her of the importance of finishing her education. She pouts but declares she will take her exams early and be back in New York a week before the wedding.

Later in September, Oliver Smithson retires from his job as consul, and he and Margaret return from Bordeaux. They expect Eva to live with them in Bedford Hills, but she chooses to stay in the city with me to prepare for her nuptials. At least Margaret will be nearby to give her motherly advice, taking some of the responsibility from me.

In November, after Will Robbins has completed his military duty and received his discharge from the Marines, he comes to scoop up Eva in his newly purchased car. Before he sweeps her up to Bedford Hills for Thanksgiving with her family, he tells me he has rented a cottage on his uncle's property, a gentleman's farm on Boston's North Shore. He and Eva will be surrounded by rolling meadows where guernsey cows graze, chickens peck in the barnyard, and dogs scamper freely. I know my New York granddaughter will acclimate to country living. As is said, love conquers all. Anyway, Eva knows I'll always reserve a bed in Manhattan for her—at least as long as I inhabit this urban island.

Margaret invited me to the family Thanksgiving, but I declined. I don't venture far from Manhattan these days. I prefer to walk to Thayer's house for supper with his family. Thayer and Ginny are expecting their second child. When rationing was discontinued, Thayer swore to prepare anything except turkey for the Thanksgiving feast. We have pork roast.

The Sunday before the wedding, I suggest to Eva we attend Holy Trinity Church to give the Almighty thanks for getting us through these last years of struggle. She agrees.

The red brick church is grand with arches and turrets, one tall chimney reaching toward the heavens. The double front doors are imposing with scrolling ironwork and a triple arch embedded with carvings of saints and priests.

Inside, tall stained-glass windows grace the high ceiling of the sanctuary. Eva and I slip into a middle pew and follow the program a deacon handed us when we came in. The order is more elaborate than at the Unitarian church. Here priests wearing robes carry tall crosses down the aisle, and the service is marked by pomp and circumstance.

When the first hymn is called, I stand with my granddaughter who lowers her eyes to the hymnal. There is no need for me to look at the written words of the song I know only too well. "Eternal Father, Strong to Save" was the final hymn at the last Sunday service aboard *Titanic*. That cold April morning I stood beside my beloved Bradley with no way of knowing it would be only hours before he disappeared from my life.

I get through the first two verses, but it is the third verse that clutches at my heart:

> *Most Holy Spirit,*
> *Who didst brood*
> *Upon the chaos dark and rude,*
> *And bid its angry tumult cease,*
> *And give, for wild confusion peace;*
> *O hear us when we cry to Thee,*
> *For those in peril on the sea!*

On the night of April 14 and early hours of April 15, 1912, there was such chaos, such wild confusion, and so much peril.

It is not until I see a drop of water on the page of the hymnal that I realize Eva is crying. She probably shed dozens of tears as she prayed for Will's safety when he was in the Pacific, and hers must be tears of relief that a war has ended and her love has returned.

When I feel a tickle on my face, I reach up a gloved hand to touch my cheek and find the fingers of the cotton are wet. The angry tumult has ended for our soldiers and for our country. For my first husband whom the wounded ship dragged to the bottom of the sea, there is rest and, I hope with all my heart, tranquility.

The night before the ceremony, Joanie is staying in the spare room next to Eva's. After a siren startles me, I have trouble falling asleep—police or ambulance, I suppose. Someone has had a heart attack or has fallen down a flight of stairs. I listen as the squealing grows fainter. Poor soul, whoever it is. I've known squeals. Screams, wails, and moans, too. For weeks, even months after that frigid spring night, I wondered if I'd slept at all. Now I watch shadows in the room cast by streetlights or lamplight from windows of other night dwellers, insomniacs who worry their worst fears will materialize.

My attention wanders to a dark figure outlined in the bedroom doorway. Hadn't I closed the door last night? No matter—ghosts walk through the thickest of wood. And who is with me tonight? He's wearing a tuxedo, I think. Bradley? No—he wouldn't hesitate at the threshold. Jack, you always wore a tuxedo well, your slim frame, straight posture. You were born for formalwear, even for a uniform, my love. He stays but a few seconds then dips his head toward me and backs out of the room.

A few moments later, I hear my bedroom door open. A smaller figure stands there—an angel wrapped in silk.

"Danny," Eva whispers, "I've had the most wonderful dream."

The siren must have awakened her, too.

"Come tell me about it." I pat the mattress next to me.

She steps closer. "My father was in my room."

"Yes?" I wait for her to say more.

"He was wearing a formal suit, the kind with long tails. Swallow-tail, I think they're called. He looked so handsome."

"A morning suit. He married your mother in a morning suit. Probably your groom will be wearing one, swallow-tails and all."

Her hands hang loose at her sides. "He smiled and held out his right elbow as if inviting me to slip my hand through, as if he wanted to escort me somewhere."

"Down the aisle, maybe." I know Jack was here. He wouldn't like to miss his daughter's special day. But I don't want Eva upset before her wedding.

I pull back the comforter. "Do you want to stay with me tonight?"

"Oh, no," she says. "He may be back and I don't want him to find my bed empty."

"What's going on?" Joanie pushes past her. "I heard voices. It's the middle of the night."

"Eva had a dream. That's all."

"Oh—about Daddy?"

"How did you know that?" Eva says.

Joanie's brows arch. "I dreamed about him, too. It was like he was really there, watching me."

Eva checks me for an explanation.

"Shadows," 'I say. "Just shadows and wedding jitters. We all would like your father to be there tomorrow. And he will be." I doubt either of them is satisfied with my dismissal.

"I'll sleep with Eva tonight." Joanie looks at her sister. "If you don't mind."

"Of course." Eva takes Joanie's hand. "Come on, little darling."

The following afternoon an usher, one of Will's friends, seats me in the front pew of the Church of the Holy Trinity. Next to me, Margaret could be a fashion model in an embroidered jacket of royal blue over a matching dress, a column of velvet with complementing hat. Her husband sits to her right, stiff and straight in a tuxedo that looks as if it has been worn dozens of times, most likely at consulate parties. Oliver offered to walk the bride down the aisle, but Eva told him her Uncle Tax was like a father to her. I doubt Oliver was hurt by her comment. His daughter is seated on his other side, and he'll give her away in marriage one day. Oliver Junior, released from the Army, is beside her. I say a brief prayer of thanks that Oliver's son made it through the war unscathed.

We wait for the priest to enter with Will and his best man, a friend from childhood. The groom takes his place next to the priest and locks his hands in front of him. The best man appears to be holding him up, their shoulders almost touching. Will's mouth twitches, his gaze on the doors at the back of the sanctuary as he watches the aisle for his bride's appearance.

When the organ music begins, I twist my neck to see the four bridesmaids come one by one up the aisle, each on the arm of an usher, Will's classmates or soldier buddies. My grandson Bally, now twenty-two, escorts his sister Joanie, Maiden of Honor.

Bally got his discharge from the Army and now works at a publishing house in New York. He's handsome in a black tuxedo. Joanie is smiling and petite in a pale blue dress that falls to her ankles. She looks older than her fifteen years.

The music changes and Wagner's Wedding March begins in its splendor and dignity, true fitting for the Marine and his bride. I stand with the others and turn to see Eva entering the aisle in a creamy satin gown that shimmers in the afternoon light coming through stained-glass windows. She is a heavenly vision. Her hand rests inside the elbow of her uncle, my youngest son. My eyes narrow and my stomach lifts as if I am in an elevator suddenly dropping downward. I hold back tears that threaten, but in my periphery I catch Margaret dabbing her cheeks with a handkerchief. She must feel as if she's losing a daughter — or lost her when she went off to boarding school and New York. I've known losses, but not today. On this day, I have a sense of triumph with my small part in getting Eva ready for the life ahead of her.

The priest speaks about the sanctity of marriage, leads a prayer, a hymn, offers communion to the two who have come to be united, then calls the congregation to come forward and receive communion. When we return to our seats, Eva and Will recite their vows to each other and Will slides a ring on Eva's finger. They kiss, a quick, shy touch of the lips for the public, saving passion for the wedding night. Finally, Eva Cumings and Will Robbins are pronounced man and wife.

A sigh escapes me, one I've been holding in for what feels like years. A different breath from the one I released when Jack married Margaret, my eldest son having survived a horrific war. I'd like to think my letters sustained him during his time in France through his loneliness, his hard work, his constant danger. Then I release another breath, one to honor my middle son whose heart stopped on the battlefield twenty-seven years ago and almost stopped my own. My chest expands again, and I feel a buoyancy I haven't sensed in a very long time.

Just before Mendelssohn's recessional music begins, I hear a soft whisper.

"Florrie, my darling, how elated we were on our own wedding day. Life held such promise for us, and so much love."

Bradley.

To my hands folded in my lap I murmur, "I knew you'd come."

Margaret looks at me strangely and leans against my shoulder.

"What is it, Mrs. Swain?"

I glance at her with a quick smile that means she shouldn't worry about me. No—everything is as it is meant to be.

I recall Mendelssohn wrote his Wedding March score as part of a suite for the wedding of fairy queen Titania and Duke Theseus in Shakespeare's *A Midsummer Night's Dream*. Titania was named for the Titans, as was the ship *Titanic*. But today is not a time to think about sinking ships. Today is a time to celebrate the marriage of my fairy-queen granddaughter to the man she loves.

In January I ask Thayer to take the box of letters and have them typed, as he offered. When I go to the den where Eva left the box, I can see the old cardboard is worn out from opening and closing, pressing and reaching into it. Now the ends barely hold together. I lift it to carry the tattered thing to the gallery, and am surprised by its lightness. The box contains the same number of letters and envelopes as it did three years ago in Maine, but something has changed. I've read that at the moment of death, a body weighs slightly less than before the heart stops. A fraction of ounces less, but a discernable amount. If the soul is in pain or aggrieved, then it must carry some sort of weight—emotional weight, perhaps. That must also be true of material objects. When I first picked up the box in Maine and found it heavy, it wasn't the weight of the contents I was feeling but the heaviness of my own heart. In the last few years, Eva has lifted the burden of grief from me by reading the letters that opened my own wounds in order for them to mend. If only she knew how grateful I am for the gift she has given me.

47

Belleau Wood, June 1946

Eva is supposed to take the train from Boston to New York next week. It's been months since I've seen her, and I've booked us tickets for France. But since early spring, railroads—steel laborers and coal miners, too—have been on strike. Ten percent of the country's entire workforce walked off the job. I was probably foolish to book travel before the strike. Fortunately, President Truman threatened to have the National Guard take control of the railroads, and the workers have ended their strike just in time for my granddaughter's arrival.

I meet her at the door with open arms. The doorman brings in her suitcase, the small one I gave her a year ago. It's spring in Paris, and she has learned to travel light.

"You look well, Eva," I say.

"I'm very well, yes, thank you." She's nearly twenty now and stands taller, as if she has even more confidence than before the wedding. I hope when we get to Paris she'll exude some of her old vivaciousness.

I ask Rosa to heat water for tea.

"Hello, Rosa," Eva calls.

"Hola, Miss Eva," Rosa says. "We have been missing you."

Eva hugs Rosa and says, "I'm glad to be back on Park Avenue."

I wait for her to offer details about her marriage and when she doesn't, I ask, "How do you like Boston?"

"We rented an apartment on Beacon Hill for the first few months. Boston has more of a small-town feel than New York. Then last month we moved into the cottage on the North Shore."

"Are you pleased with the cottage?"

"Oh, it's charming, really." Her head dips to the side. "Chic in a rustic way."

There is rustic and there is chic and ne'er the twain shall meet, in my opinion.

When Rosa brings cups and a plate of cookies, we sit at the dining table. Eva looks pensive, as if her eyes have not yet refocused on the New York cityscape, and I wait for her to speak.

"Will and I are out a lot," she says. "Dinners mostly, with Will's friends. Some with his family. And cocktail parties." She hesitates. "We're on the go much of the time."

"I'm glad you're keeping busy." I have a pang of jealousy. For most of the past three years, Eva was on the go with me.

Her face brightens when she says, "Will is starting a business partnership with some friends. They're calling it Robbins Associates."

"That sounds promising. What's their business?"

"I'm not sure." She contemplates for a second then shoos away the thought with a toss of her hand and says, "Oh, never mind."

She seems calmer, even a little remote. A husband and new surroundings must be a big adjustment for her, and I move to another subject.

"Well, you'll be going again tomorrow. We have to be at the airport by late afternoon. We'll be flying TWA on a plane known as The Star of Paris."

"That sounds enchanting." She blows into her cup before she sips.

"Have one of Rosa's cookies," I offer.

"No, thank you. With all the dinners and parties, I have to watch my figure."

I've never known Eva to turn down a sweet, but things change.

"I've made a reservation at the Colony Club and asked your mother and Oliver to join us for dinner tonight."

"That's fine," she says, the new princess of understatement. Just after the turn of the century, J. P. Morgan's daughter raised money to establish the club exclusively for women, and ladies with names like Astor, Roosevelt, Rockefeller, and Vanderbilt have been members. I consider it better than fine—at least a good enough dining spot for Oliver and Margaret.

That night a maître d' leads the four of us to a table sparkling with china and crystal goblets under a cut-glass chandelier. Tall mirrored arches make the room feel larger than it is.

"I haven't dined here in a few years." I sit and take in the tasteful furnishings.

"Well," Oliver says, "there was the war." He's wearing a jacket and tie, de rigueur for men at the club.

"An awful time," Margaret agrees. "We're well done with it."

"Let's not bring up the war, please." Eva worried herself sick when Will was away, and no doubt she has heard stories from Margaret and Oliver about the German occupation. I've had enough of war talk myself.

Oliver orders a bottle of wine—red. Margaret scans the menu and when our waiter mentions a special of sea bass with artichokes a la barigoule, she says, "I'll have that."

Eva echoes, "I will as well."

I order the chicken schnitzel, a Colony Club standard that reminds me of the chicken a la Maryland I had aboard the *Titanic* when we lunched with the Astors. At least Mr. Astor's body was recovered. I waited years in vain for Bradley to show up.

Oliver changes course and orders the steak. The waiter brings the wine and when he starts to pour, I put my hand over my goblet.

"None for me, thank you."

"Oh, come now, Mrs. Swain," Oliver says. "Join us."

Eva says, "She usually has white."

"Well then." He holds up a finger to the waiter. "Bring a bottle of Chablis—chilled."

Eva adds, "A glass of ice as well."

Oliver's bushy eyebrows arch.

"That's kind of you, Oliver," I say, even though the dinner bill will be delivered to me.

"Chablis comes from the Burgundy region." He's adept at pleasantries. "It's a relief to get French wines in the States again."

The waiter brings the bottle of white, and I must admit the Chablis is delightful. Our food comes and while we eat, Margaret brings up France's gratitude for American involvement in the war. Eva says she wonders what Paris will be like now that the Germans have relinquished it. Oliver speaks of his son and his heroism in the Second World War. Eva is quiet and although we must all want to ask about her marriage, it's Oliver who poses a question.

"What's your husband up to?" He leans forward as if he's earnestly interested.

Eva presses her lips together then says, "He's thinking of buying a boat."

"A boat," Oliver says. "Jolly good—a boat. Always wanted one myself."

A consul's job is to keep even the most challenging situations pleasant, and Oliver is good at that. I wouldn't blame him for being a little ill at ease—dinner with his wife's former mother-in-law whom he hardly knows and the stepdaughter who left home shortly after he married Margaret. But he is a man who steps up to the occasion and invites everyone to feel engaged in the moment.

After dinner, we give each other warm farewells and Oliver wishes us bon voyage.

In the morning Rosa makes us a breakfast of eggs, stewed tomatoes, and freshly baked cinnamon scones. I've given her the next week off, but she insists on coming to dust and bring in the mail. When she holds out a small bag of scones for us to take on the plane, I tell her we will be well fed on the long flight.

"Of course we'll take the scones, Rosa," Eva says. "They're irresistible." And she accepts the bag. When we're in the taxi to the airport, I have no doubt Eva will leave the scones with the driver, safeguarding her slender figure—and mine.

We board the plane and settle in for the flight. When we're airborne, the stewardess brings us dinner, a choice of meat or fish, wine, and some kind of sweet. It's six hours later in France, and we head swiftly into darkness. After the meal, the lights are dimmed for passengers who want to sleep. I hope to have a talk with Eva, maybe get her to tell me why she doesn't seem quite herself. But when I look over at her, she's sound asleep.

In Paris a car is waiting to transport us to the Hotel du Louvre, a five-star accommodation with ancient elegance. Our room has double windows reaching floor to high ceiling and looks out to nearby Renaissance-style edifices.

"Your father stayed here," I tell Eva.

"We rented an apartment when we lived in Paris before. I was nine and don't remember much, really."

"During the war, Jack stayed wherever the majors were housed so he could assist them." I look around the posh room. "Apparently the majors liked comfort." I don't tell her both my husbands liked comfort too, although we never checked into this hotel. Chess preferred the sixth arrondissement. Our hotel is in the first arrondissement, much too busy with tourists for his tastes. Funny that I don't recall where Bradley and I stayed.

We unpack our things and Eva asks for a walk. It's spring in Paris, the most lovely time of year. Pink magnolia and cherry trees put on their show, and purple wisteria dangle from arbors. Parks and gardens are abloom with color, and it's impossible to be gloomy in a Parisian spring.

"The city doesn't feel as it did when I was last here," Eva says. Soldiers in uniform are everywhere—French, English, American, even Scandinavian. I read relief on the faces of Parisians but also tension. After two attempts to overthrow France within two dozen years, would a third attempt be the charm for the Axis Powers? Jack wrote about the tension even in 1919 after Germany's surrender. But the Eiffel Tower, l'Arc de Triomphe, and Notre-Dame Cathedral still stand. The Seine still flows through Paris to the Normandy coast, emptying into the English Channel. And I can feel Jack's presence here.

As we amble down Boulevard de Sebastopol to the river, the beauty of La Ville Luminère gives me courage to ask Eva what's troubling her. She's silent for half a block then says, "Danny, both your husbands died, and my father, too. You and my mother were left widows. How did you bear it?"

Why would she ask me such a question, and why now when she's just beginning her life with her young husband?

"Is Will all right, Eva?"

"Oh, yes. He's fine. But he means the world to me. Now he wants a boat and there might be accidents and I don't know if I could stand anything happening to him the way you lost my grandfather and my mother lost my father."

When she starts to cry, I want to tell her she's being silly, but I don't want her to think I'm belittling her feelings. Being in Paris and staying at her father's hotel must bring the memory of loss closer.

"Eva," I start, "why not dwell on today instead of the past or a future no one can predict? Look around you. These buildings are testament to our mortality. Every single person who built this city has passed from the earth, yet they're still here in what they left behind—these monuments, these buildings. You said your father's letters made you feel he was alive again, as if he might return from France any day." I take her hand. "He's here, darling. Can you sense him in these streets, the scents of the blossoms, the river, the glimmer of light everywhere?"

Just then a man in uniform walks toward us, a U.S. Army beret slanted over his dark hair. He's young—twenties, I'd guess. When he gets closer, he slows down.

"Good afternoon, ladies," he says with an American accent. "Or is it good eva?"

Eva stops. "Excuse me—what did you say?

"You speak English." His lips curl into a smile. "I said good eva. I can't recall the French word for afternoon."

I notice the lieutenant bar on his sleeve. The nameplate on his uniform says "Comyn." My heart nearly stops. Comyn was the original Scottish name for Bradley's family before it was Americanized to Cumings. I'm still holding Eva's hand, and I feel her tremble.

"Have we met before?" the lieutenant asks, his head cocked, questioning.

"Perhaps somewhere," I hear myself say.

Eva blinks at him. "Some other place, some other time."

"Certainly," he says.

"And by the way," Eva adds, "good afternoon is *bon apres midi*."

"Then *bon apres midi, mademoiselle et madame*," he says in clumsy French.

"*Et vous aussi*," Eva responds.

He nods and continues on his way.

Eva lets go my hand and wipes a tear from her cheek.

"Danny," she says, "I see what you mean. He looked so much like my father."

And then everything changes.

We spend the next few days exploring the city—Jack's city. Museums, galleries, shops, gardens where children sail toy boats across ponds, and restaurants where we adventure into Indian and African cuisine. I buy tickets to see an opera at the Palais Garnier, the Paris Opera House, and that evening we mount the grand staircase, more splendid than the one on the *Titanic*.

"My father walked up this staircase," Eva says. "It must have made him feel he was climbing to heaven."

If there is a heaven, Jack is surely there, but tonight I won't bring up his death. Tonight Eva's father is alive and watching an opera through the eyes of his daughter.

An usher leads us to our seats in the ornate auditorium, and we face the deep stage.

"I feel—" Eva pivots her head as she regards the enormous room. "I feel small and insignificant here," she says.

"My dear," I say, "you are anything but insignificant."

The orchestra begins the overture for *Samson et Delilah*. The program tells the story of Hebrews enslaved by the Philistines, an appropriate production after the French came so close to losing their freedom. As the lights dim, I look at Eva, at how enthralled she is, the intensity I recognized in her father's face.

At intermission we mingle with others in the Grand Foyer that looks like it could be in the Palace at Versailles with gold trimming and the ceiling painted with images of the muses, music, and comedy.

"It's magnificent," Eva says. "I wonder what my father thought when he stood in this very place."

"I hope he thought how lucky he was," I say.

The following day we eat at boulangeries, forgetting to watch our figures, and drink our fill of good French wine.

On the fourth day, I hire a car and driver to take us sixty miles east to the community of Château-Thierry. It's nearly a two-hour trip past rolling meadows of green, some dotted with wild poppies. The fields, once scarred by trenches and muddy ruts, are lush and grassy under a bright spring sun. Château-Thierry is now a quiet land, a peaceful land.

The driver stops at a monument to American forces who fought here during the Great War. The massive structure stands on a rise above the Marne River valley. Attached to the monument, two giant sculptures representing the United States and France clasp hands in solidarity. Eva and I leave the car and climb the steps to the colonnade where we look out over the valley, shielding our eyes against the sun.

"What happened here?" Eva asks.

The covered colonnade leads to an engraved sign in English. Together we read the inscription explaining this area is where the allied forces kept the German army from crossing the Marne River on their way to attacking Paris. Sixty-one thousand American soldiers lost their lives defending the Allies here.

"Your father fought in this area." I can't bring myself to say that was barely weeks after Wells was killed.

"Brave souls," Eva says. Then she adds, "I'd like to visit the place my uncle died."

Back in the car, the driver takes us a few miles northeast to Belleau Wood. My heart begins to pound.

We enter through an iron gate supported on each side by tall blocks of granite.

As we go straight down the long driveway, Eva says, "Look, Danny — poppies."

The brilliant red flowers sway in neat beds lining the drive. Wells said they would be here, didn't he?

Suddenly the road opens to a field of white crosses. Hundreds — no, thousands of them. The headstones stand in rows on what must be forty acres.

The driver stops at the edge of a wooded hill where a stone chapel rises above the grave markers. Eva and I go in, and she runs her fingers over names of the dead carved into the stone walls. Against the back wall a marble altar invites reverence. Benches have been placed for prayer and meditation, but otherwise the building is austere.

"I thought there were more men than listed here," she says.

I look above the entry door to a sign engraved in the stone.

"These are names of soldiers whose bodies weren't identified."

She gives a slow shake of her head. "How sad for the families."

More than sad, I feel the tragic weight of losing a son and not knowing where he lies buried. At least the soldiers are together in this place. Once scarred by violence, the cemetery is now covered with green grass, the air perfumed with spring flowers. Wells and his fellows gave their lives for these fields. I wouldn't want my boy anyplace else.

"How will we find Wells' grave?" Eva asks.

"I think the graves are organized by the date they died. Wells should be toward the east. Look for June 30." I squint in the direction. So many graves.

My legs are unsteady. "It looks to be a long walk."

Eva grasps my arm. "We'd better take the car."

When we go back to the car, the driver is outside, leaning against the automobile. For the first time, I notice he looks familiar.

"I wonder if you would—" I start.

"Yes," he says and opens the back door for us.

"Before I get in I ask, "Have we met somewhere?"

"I was thinking the same thing," he says.

"You're American."

"Yes. From Baltimore." He offers me his hand. "Private William Corkins of the U.S. Marines. I'm not in uniform when I'm off duty."

"Where—"

"I believe we met on a train," he says. "I was about to join up."

"We spoke about music. You wanted to be a composer."

"Still do." He waves a hand to the back seat. "Plot A, you said?"

I didn't say. Weeks ago I called to ask the location of the grave and memorized it—Plot A, Row 6, Grave 43. But how did Private Corkins know? Such a strange man and so much like Wells.

He drives slowly and pulls to a stop six rows in front of grave number 43 as if he knows the exact location.

"I come here whenever I have a chance," he says. "There's a music station on the radio and I play it for them. These men—they feel like my brothers."

I remember now he goes by the name Wills—Wills and Wells, brothers.

He gets out and opens the door for us then says, "Take as much time as you'd like."

Eva and I weave through the cross markers until we find his name—Wells Bradley Cumings. We've brought nothing to lay on the grave because the cemetery forbids it. A small American flag is planted in the ground by the cross as a simple decoration.

"Hello, my darling boy." I drop to my knees, my hand on the white cross. Words come to me from somewhere. Was it John Milton? As a schoolgirl, I found him heavy reading but now I understand. *Some blood more precious must be paid for Man.* Oh, Wells, your blood was so precious.

A warm breeze comes from somewhere and wraps itself around us. Then I hear music.

"Listen," Eva says. "It's Mozart. My father played this on the Victrola. He said Wells loved it, too."

Eva takes my hand and helps me to my feet. "The Turkish March. Yes, I believe they did love it."

Wills has the car doors and windows open, his fingers on the radio. He looks at me with a sad smile.

A shadow comes over us and Eva says, "Danny" and points to the sky. Two white clouds have formed like giant wings hovering over us.

I put my arm around Eva's tiny waist. "Never doubt," I say, "angels are all around us. You have one, too, Eva."

"I know." She leans her head against mine. "She's standing right next to me."

Epilogue
1949

In late August, Bert Marckwald sits at Florence's bedside. A nurse dressed in white presses a cloth to her forehead.

"Is there anyone you feel you should call?" the nurse asks. "There isn't much time."

Rosa stands in the doorway. "You must call Eva," she says.

Bert goes to the phone and dials her number. When she answers, he says, "Eva, you'd better come to New York. Right away."

When Eva arrives that evening, Rosa lets her in.

"Mrs. Swain not well," Rosa says, her palm pressed to her cheek. Her eyes are swollen as if she hasn't slept—or has been crying.

Eva finds her grandmother in bed, pale and drawn.

"Danny, I'm here," she says.

Florence presses her lips together, but her eyes smile.

"How is the baby?" Her voice is weak, almost a whisper.

"Susie is two years old now and talking a bit. She says to give Danny a kiss for her." Eva leans in and kisses her grandmother on the forehead. "A new little one is coming soon."

Florence nods without strength to speak.

"If it's another girl, I want to name her Florence—after you."

Lifting her left hand, Florence wags a finger. "No," she says. "After your mother."

"But—" Eva's throat clutches and she holds back tears.

"Your—mother," Florence says again, her voice more forceful this time.

"Oh, Danny," Eva says. "I love you so much."

Florence nods again. Then her head falls to the side.

"She'll sleep now," the nurse says.

Eva goes to the kitchen.

"Tea, Miss Eva?" Rosa asks. She has aged, her face lined with worry.

"You haven't left her side, have you, Rosa?"

Rosa's silence answers Eva's question.

In the dining room Bert is sitting in front of papers fanned out on the table.

"We're all getting on." His hand rests on one of the sheets. "Eva, I want you to know your grandmother's will leaves an inheritance to you, Joanie and Bally. Thayer, too, of course. She's also leaving a good deal to charities—and something to Rosa."

"Yes—she'd want all that."

Bert clears his throat. An emotional clearing.

"What about the box?" Eva asks.

"What box?"

"The box of letters. And the journal."

Bert gives a slow nod. "They've all been typed. Tax has the binder. He can make you a copy if you'd like. He has the journal, too."

"I'm glad." She hesitates then asks, "What does the doctor say? I mean—how long?"

Bert looks down at the papers. "Not long. She's been ill for months, apparently." He glances up at Eva. "Never complained, of course."

"Of course."

"You're welcome to stay as long as you like." He eyes Eva's rounded belly. "But in your condition, you might want to be close to home. Thayer and I will see to things."

"The baby's not due until November, and Susie's with my mother. This is where I need to be, Uncle Bert. I'll stay as long as necessary."

On September 2, Florence Cumings Swain slipped away serenely, without a fuss, the way she lived her life. Eva, Thayer, Bert, and her faithful Rosa were around her. As she wished, she was buried in Boston's Auburn Cemetery near the cenotaph she had erected to her beloved Bradley. Eva asked to have a statue of an angel placed at the gravesite, but Bert said her will directed nothing but a simple marker with name and date.

After the funeral, Eva took Susie to the cemetery. The two-year-old pointed above the marker.

"Mummy, look—a angel." Although Eva saw nothing through her tears, she knew her grandmother was there, and she knew Danny would always be there.

Afterword

A few years ago my husband handed me a red spiralbound notebook. In it were nearly two hundred letters his grandfather Jack Cumings sent to "Muz" and to "Bardie" from France where he served in the U.S. Army between 1918 and 1919. In 1943 Jack's brother Thayer Cumings (who was called Tax) had the letters typed from handwritten originals. The letters from Jack included in this book come directly from those in the typed notebook.

As far as I know, no journal or letters from Wells Cumings have been found. The letters from Wells and his journal entries are from my imagination and from research about trench warfare at Belleau Wood during the Great War. The Library of Congress has an extensive file detailing the role Saint George's School played in the war and biographies of SGS students who served in the military during that time. Included in that file are a photograph and biography of Wells Cumings who died in the battle of Belleau Wood and is buried in the American cemetery there.

Thayer Cumings served as a lieutenant in the U.S. Navy and was released from service before the beginning of WWII. He was a New York advertising executive married to Virginia Richardson with whom he had two daughters, Gay and Julie, and a summer house in York Harbor, Maine, where he died in 1989 at age 84.

In the novel, I have kept as close as possible to real events and details, including where Florence Swain lived, the debutante ball held on December 20, 1945, *New York Times* reports during WWII, and people and places of the time.

Many of the characters in this novel are based on real members of the Cumings and Reynolds families. To honor and protect them, I have changed most of the names. Florence and Bradley Cumings, passengers aboard *Titanic*, Chester Swain,

Jack, Wells, and Thayer Cumings, and Bert Marckwald are original, used with permission of the families.

Although Florence had three servants while living on Park Avenue, I have depicted the fictional Rosa as her only hired help.

Acknowledgments

Writing a novel reminds me of trick candles on a birthday cake that burn until you blow them out, then light themselves again. So it was with my novel *Sheltering Angel, Based on a True Story of the Titanic.* When the book was published, I knew the tale wasn't completely told, and the candles lighted themselves again.

It takes commitment to write a novel but a universe to produce one. Alan Axelrod's book *Miracle at Belleau Wood: The Birth of the Modern U.S. Marine Corps* laid out the strategic actions of the battle that killed Wells Cumings. *All Quiet on the Western Front* by Erich Maria Remarque presented the viewpoint of a German soldier engaged in fighting against French armies during WWI. Ed Tick's books about the souls of soldiers, especially *Warrior's Return*, gave me insights into the psychology of war. Dozens of websites were of great help, especially the extensive Library of Congress file on St. George's School and students involved in the Great War. Angélique Girard, Interpretive Guide at the WWI Monument in Chateau-Thierry, France, gave me documents about Wells' death and burial at the Aisne-Marne American Cemetery at Belleau Wood. Standing in front of Sabin Howard's enormous detailed sculpture at the Washington, D.C., National WWI Memorial brought alive the struggles and emotions of soldiers in battle.

My husband's cousin Susan Cumings helped with genealogy about family names and offered editing advice. Julie Cumings Kennedy provided information about the York Harbor house her father Thayer Cumings owned. Hunter Marckwald allowed me to include his great-grandfather Bert Marckwald in the story and also offered editing suggestions. Much of Eva's background came from the November 2020 obituary of Lea Cumings Reynolds Parson, on whom the character of Eva is based. My sister-in-law Kathy Chandler provided details about many events in Lea's life. Thanks go to Lea's second husband, centenarian Steve Parson, for sharing his experiences as a U.S. Marine stationed in the Pacific during WWII. Steve was a good friend of Lea's husband Philip Reynolds, called Willie, and was an usher in their wedding. I owe so much gratitude to the Cumings and Reynolds clans for their blessings in writing this novel.

Author Geronimo Johnson astutely advised me on the novel's structure. A special thanks to Connie May Fowler who organized the InkBlossom Writers workshop in Rome where parts of this book were discussed while the breathtaking art of the city surrounded us.

Bushels of gratitude to my dear friend Allison Golinkin for teaching me about New York's Junior League, about debutante balls she attended, and for always being on the other end of the phone.

My writing critique group are the smartest, most encouraging people I know. Thank you to Sally Baldwin, Ann Moreau Kensek, Liza Myers, Tory Riley, Carol Talmidge, Jacquelyn Lenox Tuxill, and Tom Verner, who helped give my words wings.

I'm ever grateful for my community of Lincoln, Vermont, for holding me up. The Lincoln Library and Lincoln General Store always open their doors and hearts to present my work. Without my tai chi classes, I couldn't maintain my focus, so thank you to my instructors Madeline Piat-Landolt and Andreas Landolt-Hoene.

I appreciate Black Rose Writing publisher Reagan Rothe and the Black Rose staff for believing in my writing. The support of my fellow BRW authors is a special gift.

I am most grateful to my husband Harrison Reynolds, my rock and advocate, for allowing me to use his grandfather's letters in this book and for being my biggest fan.

Finally, dear readers, you give me reason to put sentences together, so thank you for purchasing this book, reading my pages, and writing a review. I curtsy to you all.

About the Author

Louella Bryant is author of ten books of fiction, memoir, and biography. Her award-winning writing has appeared in magazines and anthologies. A former professor of creative writing, currently Louella blogs, directs a writing group, and works as an independent editor from her home in Vermont. In her spare time, she practices tai chi and dreams up new recipes in which Vermont maple syrup is always an ingredient. Visit her website at www.louellabryant.com.

Other Titles by Louella Bryant

Sheltering Angel, A Novel Based on a True Story of the Titanic

Cowboy Code, A Novel of Three Women of Appalachia

Beside the Long River

Hot Springs and Moonshine Liquor

Willie, Rum Running Queen

While In Darkness There Is Light

Father By Blood

The Black Bonnet

Note from Louella Bryant

Word-of-mouth is crucial for any author to succeed. If you enjoyed *Sheltering Angel of Belleau Wood*, please leave a review online—anywhere you are able. Even if it's just a sentence or two. It would make all the difference and would be very much appreciated.

Thanks!
Louella Bryant

We hope you enjoyed reading this title from:

www.blackrosewriting.com

Subscribe to our mailing list – *The Rosevine* – and receive **FREE** books, daily deals, and stay current with news about upcoming releases and our hottest authors.
Scan the QR code below to sign up.

Already a subscriber? Please accept a sincere thank you for being a fan of Black Rose Writing authors.

View other Black Rose Writing titles at
www.blackrosewriting.com/books and use promo code
PRINT to receive a **20% discount** when purchasing.